Stephen Leigh

A Rising Moon

Book Two of *The Sunpath Cycle*

DAW BOOKS, INC.

DONALD A. WOLLHEIM, FOUNDER

375 Hudson Street, New York, NY 10014

ELIZABETH R. WOLLHEIM
SHEILA E. GILBERT
PUBLISHERS

www.dawbooks.com

First Printing, November 2018
1 2 3 4 5 6 7 8 9

This book is dedicated to my youngest sister, Pam Leigh Griffis, who sadly lost her own final and valiant battle before this book could see print, though she knew it would be dedicated to her. Pam, we love you, and we miss you!

And, as always and ever, to Denise, whose support and love makes all of my books possible.

Table of Contents

Year 22 of Pashtuk's Reign

"**O**RLA! HURRY, GIRL! YOU MUST COME WITH US!"

Orla glanced up from cleaning the miserable shriveled potatoes she'd scavenged from the little plot in back of the hut; she saw a rain-soaked and dripping Sorcha at the crude wooden door. Behind Sorcha—who was not much older than Orla herself—was a Mundoan woman with hair turning gray at the temples: Azru, First Wife of the Mundoan officer Bakir, to whom Orla was Second Wife.

Outside the clouds were weeping and the encampment's grounds were a morass of sloppy mud, but despite the weather, Orla could see other camp wives running through the lanes between the warren of huts. Orla's eyebrows lifted at the sight.

"Sorcha? Azru? What's happening?"

Sorcha only shook her head, beads of water flying from the strands under her hood. Her brown hair looked nearly black with the moisture. She rubbed water away from eyes the color of ripe sweetnuts. Azru answered instead, her voice tinted with the nasal accent of the Mundoa as she spoke in halting Cateni. She glanced out toward the camp, then her gaze moved quickly back to Orla. "No time to explain. Just grab whatever you can carry—anything you absolutely don't want left behind—and come with me. Here, let us help you . . ."

Sorcha ducked under the low lintel and entered the room with

1

Azru following. Orla could see that Sorcha was carrying a linen sack stuffed with clothing and household odds and ends, though Azru held only an empty sack that she thrust in Orla's direction. Sorcha went to the battered chest at the foot of the bed; Azru busied herself elsewhere, grabbing Orla's best teapot and skillet and wrapping them in a tablecloth along with a tinderbox.

Orla watched, wide-eyed and openmouthed, not moving. "Wake up, girl," Sorcha said. "Tell me what clothing you want to keep." Sorcha was tossing the chest's contents onto the bed. "Do you have any jewelry or keepsakes you must have?"

Orla touched the silver oak leaf that hung around her neck on a leather string: a gift from her mother and the only thing she'd managed to keep when she'd been taken forcibly from Pencraig, her old home. "Only what I'm wearing," she said, going to the bed and starting to shove her least worn clothing into the sack. "Sorcha, Azru, what's happened?" she asked again.

"No time," Azru told Orla. "Just . . . trust me."

"Is it Bakir?" Orla asked. "Is he . . . ?" *Dead?* Orla couldn't bring herself to say the word, not knowing if she might laugh in joy at the thought and not certain how Azru would respond. She glanced at Azru, who was still tying up good kitchenware in the tablecloth. Bakir had treated Orla like a despised slave to be used in any way he desired; Azru, however, had treated Orla gently and if she couldn't stop Bakir's abuse, she had at least sheltered Orla from the worst of it. For that Orla was grateful. Azru's treatment of Orla was unlike that of many of the other Mundoan wives, who thought of the Cateni wives as simply chattel. "The other wives . . ." Orla managed to husk out. "They're not going to let us leave. They're always watching, and they'll stop us if we try to run."

Azru gave a short bark of a laugh. "Most of the camp wives have gone to the southern gate." She took a long, airy breath. "Orla, our Bakir's dead, and so is Sorcha's Alim. That's part of why you must go. But not all. Please, Orla, no talk. You need to *go*. You *especially* need to go. With Bakir dead and what your mother has done, you *must* go. Now, before they realize . . ."

Bakir dead . . . She'd often wished that, even imagined this glorious moment since he'd beaten her mother nearly to death, sent her brother to the copper mines, and taken Orla as his Second Wife. She had no love for the man, only a smoldering and futile hatred. She'd attempted to escape from him a dozen times. Azru had always pretended not to see her leave, but someone else had always seen her and raised a cry. She'd been dragged back each time and punished harshly. *That one, she's the Mad Draoi's daughter. Voada's child. You can't let her escape. When we get the chance, we'll kill her for everything her mother's done. We'll make her pay. . . .*

Strangely, the news that Bakir was gone didn't give Orla the joy she'd always thought it would. She only felt . . . empty, and sad for Azru and her children, who were blameless.

Azru had gone to the open doorway as Sorcha and Orla continued to stuff clothing into the sack. "That's enough," Orla heard Azru say. "Tie it off. Give it to Orla." The woman tossed Orla her rough woolen cloak, hanging on its hook at the doorway. "Here. Follow me."

Azru was already outside, and Sorcha moved into the downpour again after her. Pulling up her hood and putting the sack under her arm, Orla followed the two women. The encampment, built on the southern side of the River Meadham halfway between Muras and the Storm Sea, was alive with movement, as if someone had rammed a stick into a beehive and stirred it. There were people rushing toward the southern gate—mostly women and children, since nearly all the men but for the severely injured had gone south with Commander Savas to confront the Cateni army more than a week ago. For the moment, no one seemed to pay much attention to the trio as Azru led them against the flow to the northern end of the encampment and the meadow leading down to the river's shore.

"My mother?" Orla asked as they hurried between the last few huts and onto open ground along the river. "Has something happened to her?"

"They're saying there was a great battle near Siran," Sorcha said breathlessly. "A messenger came not a turn of the glass ago with the news that the Cateni fled the field in defeat."

"My mother?" Orla asked again. "Ceanndraoi Voada?"

Sorcha only shook her head. "She was mortally wounded, according to the messenger, and Ceannàrd Maol Iosa was taken dead from the field," she answered between breaths. "But Commander Savas' army suffered great numbers of casualties, too many for them to pursue what's left of the Cateni forces. The remnants of the army are returning here, and everyone's gone to hear if her husband is one of the dead or wounded. Far too many of them will be."

Azru had stopped as Sorcha was talking. She took a long breath and stared at Orla. "The women—and the men—are going to blame *you* for the deaths and injuries your mother's inflicted, Orla," she finished, "and you won't have Bakir's presence to hold them back. I know how disgracefully he's treated you, and I don't blame you for hating him, but whether you know it or not, he *did* protect you when other soldiers or their wives would have killed you for the death and destruction your mother brought. You have to leave here, Orla. Sorcha does too, because without Alim . . ." She shrugged, leaving the rest unsaid. Orla knew what she meant: the Cateni wives were the underclass, looked down upon and reviled. A widowed Cateni wouldn't live long.

Orla turned to Sorcha. "Your children—Erdem? Esra?"

A look of deep pain crossed Sorcha's face. "Azru has promised to look after them for me. The boys will be better off here than with us," she said. "They're half Mundoan, and Commander Savas will make sure they're looked after. With your mother dying and Ceannàrd Maol already dead, I have to believe their prospects are better here than with me in the north."

"Sorcha . . ." Orla touched the woman's arm in sympathy; Sorcha sniffed and wiped at her eyes with the rain-soaked sleeve of her cloak. "You should go back and get them. I'll wait here, or I'll go with you—"

"No!" Sorcha's denial was both a wail of grief and a cry of desperation, and she looked at Azru helplessly. "Azru will take them in. It's done. Just be glad that you miscarried the child Bakir put in you so you'll never have to make a decision like this."

"Enough," Azru interjected. "Hurry now. Come on—I know where there's a boat tied up on this side of the river. We don't have much time before they notice you're gone, and I have to get back for my children and Sorcha's."

Azru moved toward the river at a quick walk. Sorcha took Orla's hand, pulling her along. Orla followed, glancing back once at the encampment where she'd lived for the last several moons. She could see people gathering in the central court and the gleam of armor on the soldiers marching in. From the camp she heard the long wail of a woman: a cry of grief and pain. The sound put speed into their feet, and the trio raced to the rush-choked bank of the river.

"There!" Azru pointed to a small *currach* sitting upside down on the bank, rain dripping from her forefinger. She handed Orla the wrapped kitchenware she carried. "I have to go now. Good luck to you both." She embraced Orla quickly, then Sorcha, and turned without another word to run back toward the camp.

Sorcha and Orla went to the small boat, turned it over, and put their bundles in. Sorcha held the currach steady for Orla as she climbed in and took the single oar. She could feel the pull of the river's current wanting to take the boat. Then Sorcha stepped in, holding the rope that had been tied around a rock at the river's edge, and the tide-driven water took them quickly out as Orla paddled desperately.

The Meadham's swift current carried them westward toward its mouth at the Storm Sea even as Orla and Sorcha steered the little craft slowly north toward the opposite bank, away from the life Orla had known ever since Bakir stole her from her mother and her home.

They rowed toward Albann Bràghad. Toward the clans of the north. Toward an uncertain and frightening future.

PART ONE

YEAR 23 OF
PASHTUK'S REIGN

1

The Acolyte

OFTEN ENOUGH, ORLA WONDERED why she'd ever bothered to come to Onglse.

The opportunity to go to the island home of the draoi was the
culmination of an impossible dream, a path she'd been destined
to take from the moment back in Pencraig when she'd realized
that—like her mother Voada—she could see the ghosts of the
dead. The soldiers' wives in the Mundoan army encampments
had spoken of how Voada was an awful monster, how she'd been
trained on Onglse before she'd taken on (or stolen, depending on
who was telling the story) the title of ceanndraoi, joining with
Ceannàrd Maol Iosa to lead the rebellion against the Mundoa.
Together, Voada and Maol had laid waste to the Mundoan settle-
ments south of the River Meadham.

The camp wives had hated Voada—even those, like Azru, who
had some sympathy for the Cateni. They hated that she had killed so
many of their husbands and sons. In turn, most of them also hated
Orla simply for being Voada's daughter. Still, like all the Cateni attempts to throw off the yoke of Mundoan rule south of the River
Meadham, Voada's war was ultimately a blood-drenched failure.

It had been close to a year since Orla and Sorcha had crossed the
River Meadham into Albann Bràghad. Orla's eighteenth birthday

had passed unremarked. Orla had heard the tales of Ceanndraoi Voada whispered everywhere: in stories, in poems, in songs. She'd listened to the wondrous, contradictory, and still-growing legend of her mother hands upon hands of times, from hand upon hands of mouths, in every clan house she'd visited. Orla was hardly able to reconcile the fierce, vengeful, and merciless Voada they described with the woman she'd once called Mother.

Her mother was now famous, if not universally beloved, while Orla was a burnished copper mirror reflecting a warped image of that maternal fame. The northern Cateni passed her carefully from clan àrd to clan àrd, pretending to be pleased to meet the famous Voada's daughter but heaving a sigh of relief when they sent her on her way again, as if they'd somehow escaped contagion or attack.

For nearly half a year, Orla and Sorcha passed from village to village, always hearing the words, "Oh, you *must* go on to Onglse. You need to speak with Ceanndraoi Greum. He'll be able to help you. We wish we could, but we can't." What exactly Ceanndraoi Greum could help her with was never quite voiced.

When she and Sorcha finally reached Onglse, the Isle of the Draoi, Ceanndraoi Greum made little effort to mask his feelings toward Orla. The Red-Hand, as Greum was also known, remembered Orla's mother all too well, and that was the problem. Yes, he had helped train Voada, and he had commanded the forces defending Onglse when Commander Savas of the Mundoa had attacked the island.

But Voada had stolen away Greum's military chief, Ceannàrd Maol Iosa, when she abandoned Onglse to organize the rebellion in the south. And it was Greum's title of ceanndraoi that Voada had claimed as well.

Greum was obviously less than happy to find that Voada's daughter had arrived on the island asking for training. His voice was a deep, rich baritone that lent authority to his words, and he leaned on a wooden staff he always carried for support, as his leg had never quite healed from a wound he'd taken in the battle for Onglse.

"You say you can see the *taibhsean*, the ghosts of the dead, and I'll accept that," Ceanndraoi Greum declared when she was presented to him at Bàn Cill, the sacred temple set at the center of Onglse. Greum Red-Hand had the build of a warrior, with dark hair now well-laced with gray, a long braid down his back, and a thick, oiled beard. His eyebrows, like fat caterpillars perched on the ledge of his brow, were already more white than dark, though the eyes beneath them were the black of a moonless night. As ceanndraoi, he wore an outer cloak of deep red, sewn at the hems with silver threads in a knotted pattern. Orla immediately saw why he was called "Red-Hand"—not for the blood he'd shed in battle, but because the hands emerging from the sleeves of his léine were mottled with orange-red splotches, as if the Goddess Elia had splashed pigment on them as he was born. An older woman draoi, whom he introduced as Ceiteag, stood alongside him. The woman stared at Orla with an intensity that unnerved her.

"Given your lineage," Greum continued, glaring at Orla, "I've no reason to doubt your word. But seeing taibhse doesn't make you a draoi, only a potential *menach*—a cleric of Elia." Greum bowed his head slightly as he spoke the goddess' name.

"She sees the *anamacha* as well," Ceiteag broke in. "Go on, girl—point to the Ceanndraoi's anamacha or to mine. I know you see them, even if your friend is entirely blind to them."

Greum scowled as Orla pointed to Greum's right side, where a ghostly figure stood, its head flickering as several visages came and vanished, the faces of dozens of the former draoi caught within it. "Draoi Ceiteag is correct; I can see the anamacha too, not just the taibhse," Orla told Greum. "I know now that back in my old home of Pencraig, both my mother and I saw Leagsaidh Moonshadow's anamacha, and we all know what my mother became when she bonded with the Moonshadow."

Greum's scowl deepened at the mention, irritation knitting together bushy eyebrows. "And where is the Moonshadow's anamacha now?" he scoffed. "Lost again, as it was for so long before it found your mam. I don't see the Moonshadow's anamacha or any other standing alongside *you*, girl. Do you think I *need* another menach or another servant to clean the temple? What use are you and your unsighted friend to me or to Onglse?"

Sorcha, who had been Orla's constant companion since they'd fled the Mundoan army encampment, took a sudden step back at the ceanndraoi's evident rage, as if afraid the man might strike them or cast a spell. Since their arrival on Onglse, Sorcha had become increasingly reluctant to speak out and more reserved, despite being the older of the two. Orla forced herself to stand erect, lifting her chin and staring silently at Greum, her lips pressed together tightly.

"Here's what I will do," Greum spat at last. "It's two moons until the next solstice. You and your friend may stay until then. I'll have Menach Moire see if you've any potential at all, and if you don't, you'll both be asked to leave."

Ceiteag touched the arm of his robe. "Ceanndraoi, perhaps I should—"

"No," Greum said loudly before Ceiteag could finish. "Not you, Ceiteag. Menach Moire will be in charge of the girl's training."

And with that he stalked away with a swirl of his red cloak. With a final glance back toward Orla, Ceiteag followed him.

Orla had little contact with Ceanndraoi Greum after that first day, though his red-clad presence was often in the periphery of her vision and the sound of his brass-tipped staff on the temple's tiled floors in her ears. Menach Moire undertook teaching Orla the duties and responsibilities of a menach. Sorcha, unable to see the taibhse at all, was taken on as a lowly temple servant—mostly, Orla suspected, because Orla had insisted that if Sorcha were sent away, Orla would go with her.

That was what little power she had from being Voada's daughter. No one wanted her, but no one wanted to cast her away either.

Menach Moire was one of the staff members always hovering around Greum—nearly all of them women, Orla noted. She had a thin face and body that reminded Orla of a human-sized weasel, and her darker complexion along with the shape of her cheeks and nose made Orla wonder if she wasn't part Mundoan. The woman treated Orla and especially Sorcha with a cold disdain that Orla suspected was simply a reflection of Greum's attitude. Menach Moire was both menach and draoi, though the acolytes whispered that her anamacha was extremely weak and that she could barely control it. She was never referred to as "Draoi Moire," and she refused to give any draoi training to Orla.

"If an anamacha comes to you, then Ceanndraoi Greum may change his mind," she told Orla when questioned. "Until then, young woman, be content with your lot in life. You should be grateful that you're suffered to be here at Bàn Cill at all, after what your mother did to us."

She waved a gaunt, wrinkled hand that was meant to encompass all of the temple grounds and Onglse itself. She'd kept Orla at her side the entire day, something that Orla was certain made the woman as irritable as it made Orla. "Most of the draoi here would tell you that your mother couldn't handle the Moonshadow's power and that it eventually drove her mad. She wasted Elia's gift. It's my task to see that you don't do the same. Now tell me again the three ways to direct a taibhse to the sun-path that will lead them on to Tirnanog."

With a barely suppressed sigh, Orla recited back to Moire the lesson she'd been given—one she knew from experience— stroking between her fingertips the silver oak leaf pendant that was her only legacy from her mother. She saw Moire's gaze following her fingers' movements, though the woman said nothing.

There had been taibhse enough in the army encampments Orla had endured after Bakir had taken her forcibly from her parents to be his wife. The Mundoa permitted no worship of the Goddess Elia in their camps, but there were Cateni wives among the men who still clung to the old beliefs and who celebrated on the solstices cautiously, silently, and in private. When it became apparent that Orla could not only see the ghosts of the Cateni dead but could direct them toward the afterlife that was Tirnanog, Orla became their unspoken and untrained menach.

Moire sniffed when Orla was done. "Adequate," she said. "But only that. Go on and eat your supper, if Cook has anything left at this point. You have the night watch. And this time make certain the watchers don't find you asleep."

Bowing with relief, Orla left Menach Moire and returned to the acolytes' dormitory on the periphery of the temple grounds, where both she and Sorcha slept when they weren't expected to be at the temple. Sorcha was there already on the straw-stuffed bedding next to Orla's. She was holding a crudely carved wooden soldier painted in the colors of the Mundoan army and no longer than her little finger, staring at it cupped in her hands.

"Difficult day?" Orla asked her, and the woman started at the sound of her voice, then tentatively smiled up at her, closing her fingers around the carving.

"It's that obvious?" Sorcha's smile vanished like thin frost under a spring sun, and she looked up at Orla with eyes shimmering with moisture. When she blinked, twin tracks slid down the slopes of her cheeks. "This is all I have left of Erdem and Esra: a silly, stupid toy they used to play with, and one I *hated* seeing them with. They wanted to be just like their father and go into battle. Now I can't bear to throw it away because it's all I have left of them." Her fingers tightened around the carving, her knuckles turning white with the pressure. "I miss my children, Orla. It hurts. I thought . . . I thought that because Azru promised to watch over them for me, I wouldn't grieve about losing them. I thought the pain would go away in time, but it hasn't. It still hurts just as much as it did the day I left them."

"Sorcha . . ." Orla felt her own tears emerge in sympathy. She sank down next to Sorcha and pulled the woman to her; as she did, Sorcha began to sob, clutching at Orla's shoulders. Orla simply held her without speaking, feeling the woman's deep sorrow as she stroked Sorcha's hair and rocked the woman as she might a child. After several breaths, Sorcha sniffed loudly and lifted her head. She wiped at her eyes and nose with the back of her sleeve.

"Sorry," she said. "Sometimes . . . sometimes I just start thinking about it, and . . ." Her voice wavered and broke.

"You don't have to apologize. I understand."

Sorcha gave a short laugh freighted with self-deprecation. "I know you think that, but you don't really understand. It's not your fault—you never had a child, so . . ." Her voice trailed off, and one shoulder lifted in a shrug. "But I love you for the lie," Sorcha added.

"Then I'll keep lying to you," Orla told her. "And you can keep telling me how Onglse is where I'm supposed to be."

Sorcha placed a hand over Orla's. "Menach Moire acting the bear again?"

"The bear, the wolf, the ogre. All of them at once. She hates me, and so does Ceanndraoi Greum. They'll be sending me away soon enough." She grinned at Sorcha. "And when they do, maybe you and I will just go back across the Meadham, find Azru, and check up on your children."

Sorcha's smile returned for a moment before fading. "If Elia wills it."

"Even if She doesn't," Orla answered. "I don't care if She wills it or not."

"Hush," Sorcha told her. "You shouldn't be saying such things, especially here. Sometimes I think that Menach Moire can use the walls for ears."

They both laughed at that. Orla gave Sorcha another hug and stood up. "I have to be at the temple for night watch in three stripes of the candle. I'm going to try to get some sleep so Menach Moire doesn't catch me dozing again. I didn't hear the end of that for days. I *still* haven't heard the end of it."

"Have you eaten?" Sorcha asked her, and Orla shook her head.

"Then get to your bed and try to sleep," Sorcha told her. "I'll go to the kitchens and see what I can find and bring it back to you. Go on now."

Orla smiled, sighed, and did as Sorcha requested. She fell asleep quickly, and when the evening watch's acolyte came to wake her, she found that Sorcha had left a tray of bread, cheese, and an apple on the floor between their beds.

2

The Imperial Arrival

COMMANDER ALTAN SAVAS had met Emperor Pashtuk once before in Mundoci, the capital city of Rumeli, when Pashtuk had given him command of the imperial army on the conquered island of Albann. The emperor had been a beardless young man of fifteen then. He had ascended to the throne of the Mundoan Empire as a boy of eleven, though he wore a false beard of woven human hair whenever he appeared in public, as custom demanded of young kings (and even of the rare queens who had sat on the same throne).

Now a man of thirty-four, Pashtuk had no need of a false beard. His own—oiled, perfumed, dyed midnight black with kohl, wrapped in golden threads, and immaculately groomed—fell halfway down his chest atop a bright green tunic. His face and uncovered arms were the color of weathered bronze. Over his tunic was draped a long open cloak called an *entari*, this one of a rich blue that shimmered in the afternoon sunlight. The emperor's head was wrapped in a *sarik*, a bulbous turban the same iridescent blue with the golden seal of the emperor set on its front. Pashtuk had the body of a former warrior who had, for the last several years, largely given up exercise and significant exertion. His hips were padded, and a paunch was beginning to show underneath his tunic and wide trousers. Still, he looked regal standing on the boarding plank of the warship that had brought him to Savur, banners bearing the imperial sigil of a stooping hawk fluttering in the breeze off the great harbor of Iska Bay.

Savur had once again become the capital of Albann Deas after Voada's razing of Trusa the previous year. Trusa, up the River Iska from Savur, was being rebuilt, but Great-Voice Utka, sent by Pashtuk to replace the murdered Great-Voice Vadim III, had decided to remain in Savur from which, admittedly, it would be easier to escape should another uprising of the native Cateni people occur.

Altan thought Utka's choice cowardly, but he also knew enough to keep that opinion entirely to himself.

Great-Voice Utka stood alongside Altan, dressed similarly to Emperor Pashtuk in Mundoan finery—that was unlike Great-Voice Vadim, who before his death had largely adopted the more comfortable and relaxed Cateni clothing, albeit adorned with jewelry and gold brocade. Great-Voice Utka's chariot, a gilded, too-wide, cushioned, and linen-canopied affair that Altan found ostentatious and generally useless as an actual vehicle, was placed alongside Altan's own war chariot. Altan's driver, Tolga, was seated in the harness of the war chariot just in front of Altan, looking uncomfortable in the fine entari that Altan had ordered him to wear over his polished armor. Tolga's hand steadied the nervous horses as a quarter of long brass horns blared a fanfare at the emperor's appearance. Double-headed drums called *davul* thrashed out a loud cadence that matched the emperor's slow, deliberate procession down the ramp toward the quay where the Great-Voice and Altan awaited him.

"This is a worse noise than battle," Tolga said quietly over his shoulder to Altan, rolling his eyes. Altan shook his head slightly in admonishment, maintaining a serious, half-smiling expression as the emperor came closer. Tolga turned again to pat the horses' rumps as the horns blared a new tribute and the drummers continued to flail at their instruments.

Altan, the Great-Voice, Tolga, and the driver of Utka's chariot all stepped down as the emperor reached the end of the ramp and prepared to step onto the quay—it wasn't proper for them to be standing higher than the emperor. They dropped to one knee as Pashtuk stepped onto dry land, as did the other minor dignitaries of the Great-Voice's court.

Pashtuk stood in front of them, his expression serious. He nodded curtly to Altan, then more courteously and carefully to Great-Voice Utka. "Utka, my loyal friend," he said, "it's good to see you again and to finally be here in Albann." Pashtuk held out a many-ringed hand toward the Great-Voice, helping him to his feet; he offered no hand to Altan. Utka accompanied Pashtuk to his chariot, the emperor ascending first to cheers from the crowd on the quay. Only after both Pashtuk and Utka were seated in their chariot did Altan rise, grimacing at the cracking of his knee as he did so. He went to his own chariot, stepping into its familiar confines. The Great-Voice gestured for him to precede them on the way to the Great-Voice's keep. "Let's go, Tolga," Altan said, and the driver gathered the reins to turn the horses.

They moved up the wide Avenue of the Emperor between a double row of cheering inhabitants of the city, crowded behind two lines of Mundoan soldiers in full dress armor, clashing spears to shields as Altan passed and holding the salute until the Emperor and Great-Voice also went by. Many of the buildings they passed were adorned with banners of the imperial hawk.

The openmouthed, praise-shouting faces they passed were nearly all Mundoan. The Great-Voice had made it clear to Altan that any Cateni who came within a stone's throw of the emperor must be thoroughly vetted and cleared.

It wouldn't do for the emperor to notice that there were still seeping, bloody cracks in the facade of his rule over Albann.

Later that afternoon Altan received a summons to come to the emperor's rooms, delivered by a haughty page with a thick Rumeli accent. He followed the page through the palace to the east wing of the Great-Voice's estate, where the page paused before closed double doors and gave a quick knock. Another attendant opened the doors, first bowing to Altan, then gesturing for him to follow. They passed through the room beyond and another set of doors where a crowd of milling highborns appeared to be waiting for an audience. Their eyes tracked Altan as he was escorted past them to yet another door where an attendant with the sigil of the emperor on his entari waited. That person knocked twice on the door with the head of his staff of office; when a muffled "Come!" was heard from the other side a few breaths later, he opened the door and motioned Altan through.

"Commander Savas," Pashtuk said. The emperor was seated on a dais flanked by twin imperial banners, the embroidered hawks glaring down as Altan approached. The high-backed chair on which Pashtuk sat was cushioned and draped with sumptuous, gold-brocaded cloth dyed the expensive and rare Tyrian purple. Large open windows permitted sunlight to dance across the tiles, the curtains pulled back. A simple, plain wooden chair was set on the floor below the dais in front of the emperor; to either side, clerks at desks stacked with rolls of parchment books were writing or reading, seemingly paying no attention to Altan. Pots of burning incense on either side of the dais filled the air with an overly sweet fragrance. Soldiers of the Emperor's Guard in full dress armor were stationed in the corners of the room and on either side of the dais.

"Sit," Pashtuk told Altan, gesturing to the empty chair. Altan took the chair, trying to gauge the emperor's mood from his face. There was no warmth there, only a cold, stern regard. Altan remained silent, waiting. The sound of the nearest clerk's quill on paper seemed loud in the room. Just as Altan thought he'd better speak, even if just some empty platitude, Pashtuk finally stirred.

"Commander Savas, you disobeyed the express orders of former Great-Voice Vadim, who was *my* Voice here in Albann. He told you to send only a few cohorts of the army back to Albann Deas to confront the rebels of Ceanndraoi Voada, under the direction of one of your sub-commanders. You were to remain on

Onglse and press the attack on Bàn Cill, yet you instead abandoned your invasion of Onglse and brought the entire army south." Aside from the distinct emphasis on "*my* Voice," the words were delivered in a clipped, emotionless manner, a simple recitation of irrefutable facts.

Altan tried to reply in kind. *Be careful here. You don't know what he intends or how he truly feels. Your life could very well be at stake.* "I deny none of that, my Emperor," he answered. "Great-Voice Vadim underestimated the ability of the Cateni to organize and fight, and worse, he had no idea of the power Ceanndraoi Voada wielded. I had directly experienced that power as well as the military abilities of Ceannàrd Maol Iosa during our initial attacks on Onglse. When I learned that both of them had departed Onglse to invade Albann Deas, I felt that for the safety of our people, the full army was needed to put down the rebellion or we risked losing everything."

Pashtuk's nose wrinkled as he sniffed. "So you disobeyed direct orders from Great-Voice Vadim, who was your superior and who spoke with my authority here in Albann." Under the emperor's sarik, his dark eyes glittered.

If he wants me dead, I'm dead. If he wants me removed, I'll be removed. So be it. "Yes," Altan said simply. "And I was right in doing so. To be blunt, you wouldn't be sitting here now if I hadn't, my Emperor."

Altan wondered if he'd gone too far. Pashtuk's fingers prowled the long, oiled strands of his beard, his mouth tightened, and his eyes narrowed. "Do you always speak so impudently?" Pashtuk asked.

"I'm a poor diplomat, my Emperor, just a simple soldier and a loyal one. I feel I owe it to those above me to speak the truth as I see it, unvarnished and plain, so they can make the best decisions. I don't intend to give offense."

"And if they give you orders you think misguided after your plain advice, you will ignore those orders?"

"I've done so exactly once, my Emperor, and you know the results: Ceanndraoi Voada and Ceannàrd Maol Iosa were both eliminated." *And it was close enough even then*, he wanted to add. *If*

*Ilkur's cohorts hadn't arrived when they did, I would have been dead on
the field of battle at Siran, and only the fates know what Voada might
have done then. As it was, we lost so many troops that we couldn't even
pursue the remnants of the Cateni army over the River Meadham.
There was no final and complete victory.* But he said none of that,
only stared placidly forward as the hawks glared ominously on
either side of the dais, his hands folded calmly in his lap as if this
were just a conversation with his officers.

Another sniff. "Great-Voice Utka questions whether you can be
trusted, Commander."

There it is—the reason for this audience. "And do you wonder
that also, my Emperor? If so, I freely offer you my sword, my resignation, and my life if you wish to take it."

Pashtuk gave a barking laugh that lifted his beard. "By all the
old gods, you *are* blunt to a fault," he spat, his volume causing all
the clerks to look back toward him. The guards stationed around
the room stiffened, as if ready to move. "Tell me, Commandant
Savas, did you agree with the Great-Voice's decision to invite me
to come here?"

"I did not," Altan answered. "I told him that we should wait
perhaps another year or even two. I feel the level of unrest among
the Cateni is still too high. Voada's death has only enflamed them
further. Our army is continually quashing small uprisings, especially in the northern towns of Albann Deas, and all of our incur-
sions over the River Meadham meet severe resistance from the
clans there. Too many of our soldiers are Cateni conscripts rather
than Mundoan regulars, and I don't entirely trust *them.* I asked
Great-Voice Utka to request replacement troops from Rumeli:
loyal and well-trained Mundoan soldiers, not Cateni."

"He's made that request, and I've granted it; the first cohorts
should be arriving within a moon." Pashtuk paused, sinking back
against the cushions of his chair. "The question is whether you'll
be their commander or some other. I know which Great-Voice
Utka would prefer."

"And is that Emperor Pashtuk's preference as well?" Altan
asked.

"No, it's not," Pashtuk replied, and for the first time, Altan let himself relax. The tension drained away in one swift breath. *You live to fight again, to live in this world another day. At least as long as he doesn't find out what else you've done without the Great-Voice's knowledge* . . . "But don't misunderstand me," Pashtuk continued. "You are still alive *only* because Great-Voice Vadim and Ceann-draoi Voada are both dead. Utka will continue to be my Voice here once I leave, and I expect you to obey him as you would obey me whether you agree with his orders or not. Follow your instincts again rather than the orders you're given, and I *will* have your head presented to me on a platter. Do I make myself clear, Commander?"

"Completely so, my Emperor."

"Then you may leave, Commander, with your head still on your shoulders for the moment."

Altan rose, saluted, then bowed deeply to the emperor. "Thank you, my Emperor," he said. As was customary, he walked backward toward the door, continuing to face Pashtuk, his head inclined to the floor. The guards at the door opened it for him as he approached and turned.

He tried not to look relieved as the faces of the highborn outside all stared at him.

3

A Visitor in the Night

TEMPLE NIGHT WATCH.

To Orla, it was the most boring duty possible for an acolyte. She was stationed there on the remote chance that a taibhse—the soul of a dead Cateni—became lost on the way to its final resting place in Tirnanog and wandered into the temple, where Orla could show the ghost the sun-path that would lead it to the otherworld. But Onglse was populated largely by draoi and menach, none of whom were likely to become lost should they happen to die during Orla's watch, and Onglse was too far from the shore of Albann Bràghad for any Cateni souls on the mainland to find their way across the water to the Temple of Bàn Cill.

No, this was drudge work that was far more punishment than reward for the acolyte. At least on day watch there were people moving in and out of the temple and other duties that kept one alert. That was rarely the case during night watch. The most difficult task was keeping your eyes open so that if Menach Moire happened to look in, as she inevitably did, you weren't found asleep.

Orla sat on a cushionless wooden stool to one side of the central altar. The polished marble of the temple's sun-paths gleamed in the guttering, shuddering light of the torches set in the sconces around the temple, which Orla would be expected to replace at least once during the night. The sun-paths formed an X whose center was the altar and the lines of which led to the temple's four large windows framing the sunsets and sunrises of the two solstices. Above the altar, the roof of the temple was open to the sky, and tonight wan moonlight trickled down erratically from between streaking, pale clouds. Orla pulled her cloak closer around her for warmth and tried to find a comfortable position on the unyielding seat of the stool.

She expected this to be a long and boring night.

True to form, Menach Moire appeared at the temple's main door a few stripes after Orla's watch began. Orla saw the movement and a glimpse of the red cloak that looked black in the dimness. "Menach," she said, rising from the stool and bowing her head as custom required. She heard the menach's sniff echoing along the stone walls.

"Acolyte Orla," the woman answered. "Anything to report?"

"Nothing, Menach," Orla told her. "No one's come by other than yourself, and I've seen no taibhsean to send along. It's been a quiet night." *Just like every other night you've made me spend here.* She didn't add that, but she suspected Menach Moire could see the complaint on her face.

Another sniff echoed. Orla caught a glimpse of Menach Moire's pale nose emerging from under the shadow of the hood of her cloak. "See that you stay awake, acolyte," she said. "And I expect you to be at the temple tomorrow for lessons no later than Fourth Stripe."

"*Tha*, Menach," Orla told her. *Yes.* She suppressed the sigh she wanted to heave. Having to return by the fourth stripe after sunrise meant she'd have very little sleep.

With a final sniff, Menach Moire left the doorway and continued on, and Orla furtively gave the gesture of the Horned Spirit to her back. She resumed her seat on the stool, shivering in the cold as overhead the moon slid behind clouds once more.

She wasn't sure how late it was when she first noticed movement near the door. Orla saw a glimmer of pale light—a form that appeared to be a person's, though blurred and indistinct. At first, she thought that against all the odds, someone had died and their taibhse had become lost and needed help finding the sun-path. But as she rose from her stool, she saw the specter more clearly. The apparition's face was especially difficult to distinguish, as its features seemed to change from moment to moment. Orla knew it then for what it was: not a lost soul taibhse but an anamacha, the merged ghosts of dead draoi who served as the conduit of power for a living draoi. An anamacha allowed its draoi to gather and harness the power of Magh da Chèo, where the spirits of the draoi dwelled eternally, never permitted to go on to Tirnanog to join their relatives, their spouses, or their friends in the Otherworld of the Cateni.

Orla had seen the anamacha who accompanied the draoi here on Onglse—that of Greum Red-Hand, of Ceiteag, of Menach Moire, and of all the others. The anamacha were presences unseen by any but other draoi. This anamacha, though, was alone, without a draoi. Its elusive face seemed to stare at her, and it lifted a hand as if beckoning her. Orla remained still, shivering not just from the night's chill but from seeing the anamacha. Finally, as the anamacha gestured again, she started to take a step toward them.

"No!" The imperious command came from beyond the anamacha. Ceanndraoi Greum Red-Hand stood there with Draoi Ceiteag, the torcs around their necks gleaming in torchlight, both of them flanked by their own anamacha. The night air seemed bright with all their presences. "Stand away from them," he said as the anamacha continued to glide into the room as if riding on the air itself, moving toward Orla and the altar.

"Ceanndraoi?" Orla queried, confused and uncertain what to do.

"Don't let that anamacha touch you," Greum told her. "Come here, now. Toward me."

Orla started to obey, but the anamacha moved quickly to interpose themselves between her and Ceanndraoi Greum. The misty, multiple faces stared at her, the arm lifting again—pointing, Orla noticed, to the silver oak leaf pendant that she wore. Then the features suddenly settled, and Orla let out a gasp.

"Mother," she whispered. "Mam, I see you . . ."

"Orla!" Greum and Ceiteag barked warningly in concert, but she only distantly noted their voices. She could feel the chill of the anamacha, their hand hovering near her arm. She stared into her mother's face as the anamacha's mouth moved silently, and Orla read her own name on those ghostly lips.

<Orla . . .>

Orla nearly sobbed, a hand flying to her mouth to hold back the mingled grief and joy. "Mam, it's truly you?"

The anamacha nodded wordlessly, and Orla reached for the specter's hand. The anamacha walked *into* her as if they were entering a room. The shock of contact was immediate. *<She who was called Voada is part of us, but we are not her alone . . .>* she heard the anamacha say, their voice that of a chorus speaking in stuttered unison. Suddenly the temple and Greum's shout of outrage faded around her, and she was standing somewhere else, the world she'd known all knotted and tangled and overlaid with another. In that second world, a storm raged over a bitter, broken landscape, lightning splitting the sky and a frigid wind howling. Orla blinked, trying to combine the two worlds into a single reality, but she could not. They remained stubbornly intermingled. She could smell the sharp acrid scent of the storm, and the wind was loud with voices, and ghosts walked around her: female, male, young, old, handsome, scarred, smiling, angry, frightened.

One voice dominated. It was not her mother's, even though the ghost nearest Orla had Voada's face and it was that ghost who spoke. *<We will help you, Orla. We've come to be with you. This is what we wanted, even back in Pencraig . . .>* The anamacha's voice was not a single one; it was a dozen voices or more. *<We are one with you now, and you will be with us forever.>*

And with that statement, the anamacha stepped away from her, gliding to her side, and the real world snapped back into place around her. Greum Red-Hand was glaring at her. "I told you to stay away from that anamacha, girl!" he railed, speaking the words so angrily that she thought he might spit.

"Ceanndraoi, you saw . . . I couldn't . . ."

"Nor did you make much of an effort," he answered, then released a long, bitter sigh. "That is your mother's anamacha? This is the Moonshadow?"

"You know it is, Ceanndraoi," Ceiteag answered before Orla could respond. In the flicker of the torches, Orla could see moving shadows in the deep wrinkles that carved the old woman's face. "I can feel it. I remember it from when Voada had it."

Orla nodded her assent. "Draoi Ceiteag is correct," she said to Greum.

Greum uttered another sigh as bitter-sounding as the previous one. "It's too late now. The best we can hope for is avoiding the madness that overcame your mother. The Cateni can't afford another catastrophe like that, not now."

He gestured to someone unseen behind him, and Orla noticed Menach Moire lurking in the deep shadows of the corridor with another of the acolytes—a young man—standing alongside her, yawning. "You'll return to the dormitory for the rest of the night, Orla. Menach Moire has brought another acolyte to finish this night watch for you. You'll come to me tomorrow, and we'll determine whether you're even capable of being a draoi. You're no longer an acolyte destined to be a menach, and if you think that means a better and easier life for you, you're mistaken. It remains to be seen whether you have the strength to handle your anamacha, *especially* this anamacha. It may be that they will simply consume you when you try." The ghost of a smile drifted across the ceanndraoi's lips with that statement, as if the thought gave him momentary pleasure. "Still, you've given us no choice but to try. For now, you're not to let the anamacha enter you again until I'm with you to guide you. Do you understand me?"

"*Tha*, Ceanndraoi," she told him, though she wondered how she could stop the anamacha if they decided that was what they wanted to do.

"Ceanndraoi," Ceiteag said, "perhaps I should take on the task of training her. You have other and more important duties before you. After all, I was the first to teach Voada."

Greum was already shaking his head before Ceiteag finished. "I will do it," he said, and there seemed to be some unspoken communication between the two. Orla found herself staring at Ceiteag. *She knew my mam? She taught her?*

But she had no chance to ask about that. Greum Red-Hand gathered up his cloak, gestured for Orla to accompany him, and with Ceiteag following behind, they left the temple. Orla inclined her head to Menach Moire as they passed her and the acolyte in the hall outside, but there was nothing but anger in the glare Menach Moire gave her. To Orla, the Moonshadow's anamacha was painfully visible in the night, a glowing apparition that shadowed her footsteps, a cold presence at her side that gave her little comfort.

Sorcha was awake when Orla returned to the dormitory, sitting in the hallway outside the bedroom with a steaming cup of mint infusion. She stood up and silently handed the cup to Orla. "Ceanndraoi Greum came into the dormitory half a stripe ago with that old woman draoi," Sorcha said as Orla sipped at the mint-laden brew, relishing the sweetness of the honey Sorcha had put in it. "They were staring at the empty air like they were following someone I couldn't see. They walked over to your bed, then turned to leave again a few breaths later. The Red-Hand saw me watching them and asked me where you were. I told him you were on night watch. 'That's where the anamacha must be going, then,' he said to the other draoi. They left the room still staring at the empty air."

Orla glanced at the Moonshadow's anamacha. "You don't see them?" she asked Sorcha.

"See what?"

"My mother's anamacha. The Moonshadow's anamacha. They came to me in the temple. They're here now, next to me, at my right side."

Orla saw Sorcha's eyes moving as she searched the hallway, then the woman shook her head. "I'm sorry. I don't see anything." Her lips tightened in a forlorn half scowl. "But then, I don't see the ghosts of the dead that you and Menach Moire and the other acolytes can see, either. And you . . . you see *both* taibhsean and anamacha. I don't have the gift of either sight."

"You have other gifts, Sorcha," Orla told her. "Better ones. You and Azru saved me when no one else would. You were my one true friend in the soldiers' encampments. You kept me alive and hopeful when I would have despaired after I miscarried Bakir's child, and you helped me escape from the Mundoa when the time came. I owe you nothing less than my life."

She reached out her hand to stroke Sorcha's cheek, but the woman stepped back from her before she could touch her, her eyes widening. "Menach Moire came in after Greum Red-Hand left and told me that you're no longer an acolyte," she said, her eyes downcast.

"The Ceanndraoi said he's going to teach me to be a draoi," Orla told her. "I'm to start in the morning."

Sorcha nodded. "I thought the mint infusion might help you sleep. You should go to your bed now. The sun will be up in less than a hand of stripes."

"Sorcha . . ." Orla began, but she was thinking that Ceanndraoi Greum must have known that the anamacha would claim her. He had to have surmised that nothing he could say or do would stop that from happening, since he'd already told Menach Moire to bring a new acolyte to the temple to replace her before Orla ever saw the anamacha. She looked down at the mug in her hand as if she could find answers in the tan ripples there. "Sorcha, there's no glory and no privilege in being able to see taibhsean or anamacha. My mother could also see both, and those abilities brought her nothing but pain, loss, and death." She remembered seeing the Moonshadow's anamacha as a child in the temple at Pencraig and how everything had changed for them horribly afterward. "And having those gifts has done nothing but bring me the same so far," she finished.

Sorcha lifted her chin and attempted a smile that faltered quickly. "Go on and sleep," she said.

"I don't know that I can. I have so much to think about . . ." Orla stopped. "But I'll try. Will you stay close enough that, if I need you, you could hold my hand?" Orla held out her left hand, the side away from the anamacha. Sorcha looked at it, then silently lifted her own hand and took Orla's. Together they walked to the dormitory's door.

4

Meeting Dead Draoi

DESPITE HER WORDS, she must have slept, for it was Sorcha's hand on her shoulder that shook Orla gently awake in the morning. She opened her eyes to find the dormitory's windows alight with burgeoning dawn. Sorcha was already dressed, crouched at Orla's bedside. "Menach Moire wants me to attend to her," Sorcha said, "or I'd have let you sleep a little longer. Good luck today. Promise you'll find me later and tell me all about your lesson with Ceanndraoi Greum?"

Orla nodded, finding Sorcha's hand and squeezing it once. Sorcha gave her a fleeting smile as she rose to her feet to leave, her gaze drifting past Orla as if searching for the anamacha she was unable to see. Orla looked herself, though she found she didn't need to; she could feel their presence like a cold stone wall alongside her. Orla could see the anamacha as well, standing on the other side of the bed, a pale wisp in the dawn light. In full daylight, she knew, it would be entirely invisible even to her, though she was certain she would still feel their proximity. *A creature of shadow and darkness, always . . .*

The dormitory was empty except for those few who had been on night shifts, now sleeping in their beds. Orla dressed quickly and used the midden down the hall, an experience made uncomfortable by the fact that the anamacha remained with her as she relieved herself. Orla realized that this was something to which she would have to resign herself; in many ways she would never again be alone in this life, though she didn't know if those within the anamacha knew or cared what she was doing. She hurried down the corridors of Bàn Cill to the temple itself, coming to a halt at the side door when she saw Ceanndraoi Greum, Draoi Ceiteag, and Menach Moire speaking together near the altar. Sorcha was standing well away from them and pointedly not looking at Orla.

Orla cleared her throat. Greum Red-Hand looked over at her as Menach Moire scowled, bowed to the ceanndraoi, gestured for Sorcha to follow her, and hurried off into one of the rear rooms. Ceiteag remained behind.

Greum was staring more at Orla's side and the Moonshadow than at her face. He tapped his staff on the tiles. "So I see the anamacha remains with you. You've not gone inside them again?"

"No, Ceanndraoi," she told him. He nodded.

"Then come walk with me," he told her. "Ceiteag, we'll talk more later." With that, he turned and limped toward the main door of the temple, leaning on his staff. Orla nodded to Draoi Ceiteag as she followed Greum outside and into the gardens that covered the steep, verdant walls of the valley in which Bàn Cill stood. It was a slow walk with Greum's bad leg. At the summit of the hills around them an undulating stone wall followed the ridgeline, studded at intervals with large towers: the last defense against armies that might invade Onglse, a third and final wall never breached in the long history of the island. Barely two years before, Commander Altan Savas had managed to break through the two outer rings of the island's fortifications, but he had abandoned his siege of the island before reaching Bàn Cill.

Orla knew why Savas had retreated. Every Cateni knew why. She wondered, seeing Greum's gaze flickering over the wall, whether the ceanndraoi ever thought that Savas might have taken Bàn Cill itself, the center of the draoi universe, had he not been compelled to return south to confront Voada on her rampage through the cities of Albann Deas. *Is that something I could ask her inside the anamacha? She stood here once, and she fought Savas here for a time. . . .*

It was a question that would have to wait. Greum moved slowly through the gardens, his staff prodding the soft ground, until he came to a low wall where the gardens ended and the forested lower slopes of the hills began. There he finally stopped, his breath labored as he planted his staff in front of him. "This place will do," he said. "Here, if you lose control of the anamacha, at least I can stop you from doing terrible damage." The words made Orla shiver, both at the thought that using the anamacha might be so dangerous and as she tried to imagine how Greum would "stop" her.

"When I taught your mother how to use this anamacha," he continued—Orla saw his lips press together tightly beneath his graying beard as he paused after the words— "she at least had some previous, if inadequate, knowledge from Draoi Ceiteag of how a draoi works with her anamacha. You've had no such training, I understand."

Orla shook her head. "No, Ceanndraoi. I never had the opportunity, and Menach Moire told me it was nothing I needed to know."

"Menach Moire was entirely right, at least until the Moonshadow's anamacha came here."

"You didn't want the anamacha to come to me."

"No." His answer was short and curt. He shook his head. "But when you came here, I suspected the anamacha might follow. However, better to have it find you here than somewhere else, where there'd be no one to guide you at all. Elia only knows what might have happened then."

"You think I would have gone mad like . . ." Orla couldn't complete the sentence. She glanced guiltily at the anamacha next to her, invisible in the sunlight but the coldness of their presence palpable at her side.

"I know that trying to contain the Moonshadow's power can send even a strong will into madness; I've seen it happen." That last was spoken with a significant glance at Orla. "But if your mother's anamacha had come to you without training, no, you wouldn't have gone mad. The experience of trying to become one with the anamacha would likely have killed you outright, and your spirit would already be in there screaming with the rest of them who weren't prepared for their task. Your mother was fierce, strong-willed, and well trained, both by Ceiteag and by myself here in Bàn Cill. I saw her wield the power of your anamacha, perhaps better than any other draoi could have—perhaps even better than myself, had the Moonshadow come to me instead." His lips tightened again as he made that admission, and Orla wondered if there was jealousy and envy within the words. "Yet when she tried to use the Moonshadow's spirit over the other draoi inside, even she succumbed."

Orla shivered as the cold of her unseen anamacha pressed against her side. "It's already too late for your anamacha to be given to some other draoi," Greum continued. "The Moonshadow has claimed you, and you will either learn to use those inside or they will take you into their world entirely and go seek another draoi. Are you ready to start?" Greum asked her, as if sensing her fear. Orla could only nod silently. Her fingers involuntarily sought the silver oak leaf at her breast, her mother's gift. Greum's gaze followed the motion.

"Good," he said. "Then pay attention. I'll be with you as you enter Magh da Chèo, the Otherworld of the anamacha, and I can— and I will—pull you back if I see the need." Greum Red-Hand didn't appear happy with the prospect. "Listen to me carefully. You will *not* call either your mother or Leagsaidh Moonshadow from your anamacha. The Moonshadow would destroy you in a moment, and your mother . . . well, she might be capable of doing the same. You have to remember that while it is Voada's spirit that dwells there, being in Magh da Chèo changes the dead draoi; they become fey and dangerous, and your mam will be no exception. You'll be able to hear me. If you wish to live, you will listen to me and do exactly as I tell you. Do you understand?"

Orla nodded again, swallowing heavily. Greum took in a long

breath as he lifted his staff from the ground and cradled it in the crook of his elbow. "Take my hands," he said. "Then call the anamacha to you, and I will do the same with mine and follow you into Magh da Chèo. Bring the anamacha to yourself. . . ."

His hands were dry and warm, and he clasped her almost too tightly. At the same time, as if she'd spoken a summons she hadn't heard, she felt the cold embrace of the anamacha sliding into her body. At their touch, the world around her dimmed and became transparent, and the stormy chaos she remembered from her first bonding with the anamacha returned. Snarling branches of lightning flickered in a black, roiling sky as thunder grumbled. The ground underneath her feet was cracked and broken rock, and there were figures moving restlessly around her. Their massed voices whispered and shouted and called to her. She couldn't see Greum, couldn't feel his hands on hers, but she heard his gruff voice: "A draoi has to be a perfect vessel, without cracks or flaws. If you aren't able to contain your anamacha, they will consume you. Be that perfect vessel. Let them become you."

She could hear their multiple voices, hands upon hands of throats speaking the same words: male, female, young, old . . . <Orla. We have waited to be with you, and you have come. We can lend you our strength. Take it. Use it . . .>

"Mother?" Orla called. "Are you here?"

"No!" she heard Greum snap angrily. "Don't call her. Don't bring her out!"

The anamacha only repeated what they had told her the night before. <We are her. Yet we are not her alone. We are many. We are draoi going back and back in time to the First. . . .> With the statement, the figures spun dizzily around her; she saw her mother's face replaced by another and another until finally she felt something impossibly strong approaching her, the power radiating from it as if it contained the very essence of the ferocious storm around her.

"Mother?" Orla felt a growing fright as the presence came closer. She pleaded for her mam as if somehow if she were there, Orla would be protected despite what Greum had told her.

"Orla!" Greum's voice shouted, and the sense of that wild, uncontrollable presence receded, the figures now still and silent around her again. "This isn't the time. I warned you—don't call for Voada. Don't call for the Moonshadow. Call instead for Iomhar of the Marsh. He was your mother's first channel to the power; if she could handle him, so might you. Call for him."

"How?" Orla asked. "How do I call him?"

"Think his name. Tell him he must come to you. You need to be the one in control of your anamacha, Orla, or they will destroy you. Don't ask him to come. *Order* him to be there for you."

Orla shut her eyes, if only to block out the sight of the ghosts around her and the storm-wracked landscape. <*Iomhar, I call you. Come to me. Come . . .*>

<*We are here . . .*> A chorus of voices hammered at the inside of her head. She opened her eyes to see a single ghost standing before her, its features blurred and mutable, but the same man's face came and went over and over.

"Ceanndraoi?" Orla said aloud. "I think he's here. What do I do now?"

Even as she spoke, the anamacha was talking to her. <*Let go of the mortal's hands, Orla. We will lead you. We will help you. We will teach you. Let go, let go. Trust us . . . Let go of him.*> Orla shivered at the anamacha's words.

"I will give you the form you must make and the release words you must say," Greum's voice answered her. She thought she could feel his fingers press her hands, holding her tightly so that even if she wanted to release his hands, she couldn't. "Tell Iomhar you want fire to cast. That will do."

<*Give me fire to cast,*> she thought. She imagined it in her mind, holding that energy inside her and letting it burst from her hands. With the thought, she saw the shade in front of her begin to glow as if the figure had been formed from a brilliant sun. Orla's hands were moving—or rather, Greum was moving her hands for her, forming a complicated knot in the air. She could see the shape in her mind, a sphere formed of intricate curves and knots: a vessel. At the same time, she heard Greum's voice whispering words to

her. She repeated them, syllables that sounded like Cateni but were older, the forms archaic and foreign-sounding on her tongue. The shape of the spell, the vessel, seemed to harden between her now-motionless hands. "Now speak the word," Greum said. "*Teine!*"

"*Teine!*" Orla shouted after him: *Fire!* Iomhar—or the ghost that she thought of as him—gestured too, and flames burst into existence inside the cage she and Greum had formed, leaping and snarling. The heat and energy battered at Orla, painful to view and to hold.

"Now," she heard Greum say, "look past the Otherworld. Can you see this world? Our world?"

Orla blinked, trying to see beyond the caged inferno. Like a mist laid before her, she glimpsed the garden and the forest beyond it. "Yes," Orla breathed. "I see it."

"Then find one of the trees in front of you. Keep it in your sight. Imagine the fire striking it and say this: *I release you.* Say it!"

"I release you!" Orla shouted. In that moment, the spell cage she and Greum had made shattered, and the world of the anamacha fell away from her. Orla staggered and nearly fell as she saw the gout of fire streak away from her to strike the oak that she'd chosen. The flames encased the tree, crackling and fuming: as gray smoke rolled upward toward the sky; as the green oak leaves shriveled, went black, and dropped as burning ash. The smell of woodsmoke came to them. Greum gestured, and a quartet of acolytes from the temple rushed forward with buckets of water to douse the flames. Orla realized that Greum must have forewarned them.

Orla was panting heavily, as if she'd been running for a full stripe of the candle. The exhaustion made it difficult for her to keep her head up. She wanted to sink to the ground; she wanted to sleep.

"Not bad for a first effort," Greum said. His dark gaze held her, and she forced herself to stare back. "But you'll need to do far better," he finished. He waved a hand toward the temple. "Go back to the temple and give thanks to Elia for having spared you.

I've arranged with Menach Moire for Sorcha to serve you; she'll show you to your new room. Go on. You'll be useless for the rest of the day."

Her chamber was more plush and comfortable than any she could remember since her days as a child in Pencraig, and certainly far more luxurious than the army encampments she'd endured after her forced marriage to Bakir. She'd been given a suite of two rooms in the hallway outside the rear of the temple with a view of the gardens and a small sleeping alcove just off her bedchamber that was Sorcha's room. Greum Red-Hand's even more lavish chambers were close by, a few doors down the same hall.

Sorcha was there, as Greum had promised, with mulled wine, bread, cheese, and fruit arrayed on the small dining table in the outer room. "The ceanndraoi said you would be tired and probably want to sleep but that you should eat first," Sorcha told her. "So I went to the kitchens and found what I could."

"Thank you," Orla said. The exhaustion from using the anamacha threatened to close her eyes, but the sight of the food made her stomach rumble, and she realized that she was also famished. She sat at the table, Sorcha sitting opposite her but not eating. She had finished half the bread and most of the cheese when someone knocked on the door to the rooms. Without asking, Sorcha rose from her chair and went to the door. "Draoi Ceiteag," she said, glancing back at Orla, who nodded to her. "Please come in."

The elderly draoi shuffled into the room. Her gaze found Orla as Sorcha gestured for the draoi to take her chair at the table; Ceiteag ignored her. "The ceanndraoi told me you survived," she said to Orla.

"Was that in question?" Orla asked, and Ceiteag shrugged, the folds of her cloak shifting with the motion of her thin shoulders.

"Not everyone survives their first time," she answered. "Menach Moire barely did, and she still avoids entering Magh da Chèo.

But for you . . . No, your survival was never in question. I knew because I knew Voada, and you're her child."

She paused, and for a long breath neither of them spoke. "So you taught my mother," Orla said finally, when the silence threatened to linger.

"I was the first draoi to find her after the Moonshadow came to her," the woman said. "Even though I didn't realize at first which anamacha had claimed her, I did what any draoi would have done in those circumstances: I taught her the basics so that the anamacha wouldn't simply consume her. Your mam . . . she was stronger than any of us knew. With that anamacha, she had to be." Ceiteag licked dry and cracked lips. "Have you met her yet? Inside?"

Orla shook her head. "I've glimpsed her and felt her presence," she admitted, "but the ceanndraoi told me not to call her yet."

"Good," Ceiteag said. "Listen to Ceanndraoi Greum. His advice may keep you alive and sane."

Orla thought the woman was about to turn and leave. She hurried to speak. "Draoi Ceiteag, you knew my mother. How . . . how was she?"

Ceiteag looked past Orla, toward her anamacha. "When I first met her, she was lost and frightened and wounded from everything that had happened to her in the south. She was like a boat adrift after barely surviving a storm. She wept, she raged, and I comforted her as best I could. She mourned for you, for all her lost family, and she was angry at what the Mundoa had done. She was so *angry* . . ." Ceiteag's gaze came back to Orla. "If you want me to tell you what a wonderful person your mother was, I can't. I saw anger and bitterness consume her. I saw the Moonshadow's grasp on her tighten the more power she drew from her anamacha. I saw her become brittle iron, unbending and strong but driven by rage. She was unwilling to listen to anyone who tried to advise her or who contradicted her. I tried to help her. Ceanndraoi Greum tried, but she wouldn't listen. No—to Voada, her way was the *only* way, and in the end, she abandoned us. She claimed the title of ceanndraoi that wasn't hers, and she led far too many Cateni to their deaths." Ceiteag's face seemed to furrow even more. "For what? What did she accomplish? The Mundoa have only tightened the chains they place on us. Their soldiers destroy more Cateni villages; they imprison and execute and enslave more of us. Voada failed us. And I . . . I share some of the blame for that, for not being able to help her see the awful path she had chosen."

Ceiteag's lips pursed as if she were tasting sour fruit, and Orla thought she might spit. But the woman lifted her chin, the loose skin underneath swaying. "I know that isn't what you wanted to hear," Ceiteag finished. "But it's the truth, and I tell it to you as a warning so you don't try to follow that same path. Don't listen to her voice, not if you want to live."

In the days after Ceiteag's visit, Orla kept mostly to herself.

Other draoi lived at the temple in chambers much like Orla's, though she seemed to be the only one actively in training. Some of the draoi were visitors, come to Onglse to see Bàn Cill, to consult with the ceanndraoi, or to bring news to the island. Others were stationed here on a permanent basis, several of them draoi who had fought with Ceanndraoi Greum against Commander Savas' army during his siege of the island. Those draoi, she realized, had known her mother and would have seen Voada with the anamacha that now shadowed Orla.

The other draoi nodded to Orla silently if they happened to pass her; she could feel their stares on her back afterward, appraising and curious, and she could hear their whispers, if not the actual words they spoke about her. When they did speak to her, they carefully avoided mentioning Voada. It was as if her name was forbidden to be spoken here, especially with the title of ceanndraoi she'd usurped once she'd left Onglse.

Orla wondered if they all felt the same as Ceiteag and Greum Red-Hand.

If Ceanndraoi Greum had transferred his anger with Voada to

Orla, that wasn't immediately evident. He trained her hard and diligently. A few weeks after her first lesson with him, he gave her a bronze torc to wear around her neck, an oak leaf sigil stamped in the smooth, cool metal: the same torc that all Onglse-trained draoi wore. Those in Bàn Cill now called her "Draoi Orla."

For more than two moon cycles, Greum Red-Hand tutored her, guiding her hands through the various spell shapes that allowed a draoi to handle the power an anamacha could lend her, as well as the words required to summon and release the spells. The overwhelming exhaustion that came from using those spells slowly started to recede with continued practice, though Greum never allowed her to enter the chaos of Magh da Chèo alone; he was always with Orla when she called the anamacha to her.

Until one day . . .

"Call your anamacha," Greum told her. The morning was cold with the sky spitting rain, dark enough that both of their anamacha were visible. Both Orla and Greum wore oil-soaked hooded cloaks against the wet. They were standing at the edge of the south garden of Bàn Cill, looking out to where an ancient and massive standing stone adorned with carved spirals and glyphs had fallen in the meadow beyond. "I want you to pick up that *menhir* and place it upright again. We've allowed it to be down too long, and it's disrespectful to the old gods."

Orla waited for Greum to extend his hands to her as he always had before, but they remained at his sides. Under the shade of his hood, his face was unreadable. Orla blinked back a spray of wind-driven rain. "Ceanndraoi?"

"Do it," he said. "You know the shape of the spell and the words needed. Do it. I will only watch this time."

Orla felt her stomach churn. "As you wish, Ceanndraoi," she told him. Even as she thought to summon the anamacha to her, she felt their cold presence at her side, and the stormy landscape they inhabited quickly overlaid the meadow and the standing stone. The voices came to her: <*You're alone. And you're afraid. You should be. You'll be with us soon . . .*> The voices were sinister this time, their words laden with mocking laughter that lashed at her like the freezing rain. Fear sent spasms down her spine, and she had to force herself to stand still, not to back away from the anamacha and return to her own world.

<Be quiet!> she shouted to them in her mind. <Bring Iomhar to me.>

<Alone. Afraid. You'll be with your mother, with us . . .>

<No,> she told them. <Iomhar, come to me.> She thought that the anamacha would ignore her, that her mother—or worse, the Moonshadow herself—would come instead, but the shades of the dead draoi faded until only one was left and its many-throated voice was dominated by one she knew.

<You've called, and we've come,> it said. <And you are alone . . .>

<Yes,> she told it. <I am alone because I no longer need Ceanndraoi Greum guiding me.> She lifted her hand to the torc around her neck, then let it drift to the pendant of the oak leaf below. <I am Voada's child, and I am not afraid of you.>

<You lie, then,> the anamacha answered, hand upon hand of voices mocking her. <We can taste your fear, sweet and rich. You will be with us—if not now, then soon enough. Like Voada. Like all of us. Your voice will become part of us.>

<In time, that will be,> she answered. <But now isn't that time.> Forcing the fear into the back of her mind, she began to shape the spell cage with her hands, the shape she knew she would need, and she chanted the words that would cause Iomhar to draw the necessary power from their world. The anamacha seemed to sigh as one, and lightning flared around them, the thunder shaking the ground. The ghost of Iomhar began to chant with her, drawing strands of energy from Magh da Chèo and passing them to her.

The anamacha mocked her as she worked, and Orla wasn't sure if it was only one of the draoi inside or all of them. <Are you certain the shape will hold? It looks so fragile, and if the power bursts out, it will consume you. You'll come to us, screaming . . .>

<I am Voada's daughter,> she repeated. <And I am strong.>

They laughed as she completed the shape and spoke the final word. "Neart!" Strength! With the command, a wild blue energy formed in the center of the knotted spell cage she had made before her, and she could feel it pulsing and pushing against the bars she'd woven in the air. She brought her consciousness back to the real world, focusing on the stone lying in the grass. Greum had taught her that she didn't need to say a release word any longer, that she could control the spell with her mind alone. She allowed the power to snake out toward the great stone, wrapping the energy about the menhir with her mind and lifting it. Slowly the massive block rose and turned, floating in the air. When it was properly aligned, she pushed hard at it with the remaining power, slamming the menhir into the soft ground.

She felt the concussion of the impact through her feet; the standing stone, the height of two men, was upright once more, the spiral carvings on its face visible. Orla sighed. She looked at Greum Red-Hand; grudgingly, he nodded. He said nothing to her but only turned and began walking back to the temple.

Orla could feel the cold presence of the anamacha at her side as she looked out at what she'd just done. Satisfaction banished any exhaustion she might have felt. *<You see? I've nothing to fear from you.>*

In her head, she thought she heard faint answering laughter.

5

Killing a God

COMMANDER SAVAS: THE EMPEROR will address the populace at the Great Temple tomorrow. You are to ensure that there will be no trouble.

The order had come from Great-Voice Utka by messenger. Altan had immediately requested an audience with the Great-Voice or with Emperor Pashtuk himself, hoping to convince them that having the emperor appear in such a public and difficult-to-secure venue was a mistake. Both requests had been denied: the Great-Voice's secretary had responded that the Great-Voice felt his orders were sufficiently clear; the emperor's secretary had simply sent a message that the emperor was too busy with imperial affairs and that if the commander had concerns, he should take them up with the Great-Voice.

Altan slammed down the parchment roll on his traveling desk. "Idiots!"

"Commander?" he heard Tolga ask from a chair across the room. The two were in Altan's chambers in the Great-Voice's palace. Tolga smelled of horse, just back from the stables after checking on the geldings for Altan's war chariot.

Altan shook his head. He yearned to be back at one of the army encampments or back in the field. "I wasn't born for this," he said. "The incessant bowing and scraping . . . Give me my army and my cohorts, not this infernal political dance."

"You mean you hate not being the one who *gives* the orders—like those you've already issued without the Great-Voice's knowledge."

For a breath, Altan felt a surge of irritation, then he saw Tolga's raised eyebrow and satisfied himself with simply scowling at the driver. He had become a friend over the last few years, if not the lover that Tolga's predecessor had been. *What would Lucian tell me if he could? I swear I sometimes hear him at night, saying, "Altan, you've grieved for me enough. It's time for you to move on, and Tolga is there with you. Go to him; he's a good man, and he's waiting for you. . . ." But is that truly Lucian speaking or just my own selfishness and loneliness?*

"Are you going to tell me how wrong I am?" Tolga asked Altan, breaking the reverie. A smile lurked on the man's lips.

Altan's scowl collapsed. "No," he said. "You know me too well. But when I'm ordered to do the impossible . . ." Altan gave a sigh. "How can I protect the emperor if he won't listen to me?"

"Perhaps in the same way you protected the emperor's holdings here when Great-Voice Vadim wouldn't listen to you, or with what you're already doing without Great-Voice Utka's approval. You'll do what's necessary because if you fail, your head is lost anyway. Better to do what's right than to simply obey."

"Perhaps I should let you give the orders, since it all seems so simple to you."

Tolga managed to look abashed at the rebuke, ducking his head. Altan sighed. "I'm sorry, Tolga. That's my irritation with the Great-Voice and the emperor talking, nothing more. You should never be afraid to talk honestly with me—in private, at least. I trust you. Forgive me."

Tolga shrugged. "There's nothing to forgive, Commander. I should be the last one to question you or pretend to give you advice."

"Altan, not Commander," he told the driver. "Here, when we're in private, you should call me Altan."

That caused Tolga to smile. "Altan, then." Altan took a long breath. "I should go," Tolga continued. "I want to make sure the stable master has properly oiled the livery for tomorrow. Have a good evening, Comm— Altan."

The decision came to Altan suddenly, fierce and quick. "Tolga," he growled. "Let the stable master wait for a turn of the glass. Stay. And perhaps you should take off that lovely entari of yours. It's very attractive, but . . ."

Altan watched the younger man's eyes widen, then relax again. Tolga undid the bronze clasp at his throat and let the heavy brocade cloak slip from his shoulders to pool at his feet, standing before Altan only in his white léine and loose salvar trousers. "Better?" he asked. Then, with a raise of his eyebrows: "Altan?"

"For the moment," Altan told him. He sat up straighter in his chair, leaning forward. "Now, come here . . ."

Unlike what Altan had seen in most of the towns and villages in Albann, the edifice in which they stood wasn't a repurposed Cateni temple with four windows aligned to the sun-paths of the equinoxes and a central altar on which the statue of the Cateni mother-goddess, Elia, had been replaced by a bust of Pashtuk.

No, the Great Temple at Savur had been constructed from the ground up as a proper Mundoan structure: a tall and massive dome set over a three-story facade studded with balconies, surrounded by taller minarets that seemed to pierce the lowest clouds. The entire structure gleamed in the sunlight: polished white marble facings and decorative gold leaf that covered the dome and sparkled on the friezes and architectural supports. An expansive, intricately tiled plaza spread out in front of the building, now filled with the poorest residents of Savur who had been unable to gain entry to the temple itself. The imperial banners hung on either side of the Great Temple's main doors, three men tall and just as wide.

Well above the crowd, the dome was painted with murals depicting the emperor as the representative of the One-God, the

First Maker who had created the world. Altan knew that the mural had been repainted several times over the long decades of Mundoan rule in Albann Deas. First it had borne the face of Emperor Beris, whose armies had originally subjugated the Cateni tribes south of the River Meadham. Later his figure had been replaced by that of his son, Hayat, then briefly by the image of his granddaughter, Empress Damla—wearing her required false beard—before she was deposed and executed and the young Pashtuk was placed on the throne. Altan could see the faint outlines of the previous rulers in the murals, surrounding Pashtuk's likeness. A bust of the emperor also adorned the niche behind the dais on which Great-Voice Utka now stood. Altan also stood on the dais, well to one side and staring out into the space before him. The area beneath the dome was huge and filled to overflowing with those who had come to view the emperor, considered to be the mortal avatar of the First Maker.

Altan had set a line of soldiers three paces out from the entire perimeter of the dais with strict orders to keep the crowd back. The only people permitted closer were the cluster of black-robed *sihirki* to the Great-Voice's right, the Mundoan magic-users who— as Altan knew all too well—were far less impressive and powerful than the Cateni draoi.

Great-Voice Utka had nearly finished his introduction of the emperor, his voice echoing from the dome overhead. As he waved his hand and spoke Pashtuk's name, the curtains to the rear of the stage lifted, and Emperor Pashtuk strode out onto the dais to a roar of praise and adulation from the onlookers. Even a few of the soldiers tasked with controlling the crowd craned their heads back to look at the emperor; Altan glared at them, and they quickly looked outward once more. Pashtuk was dressed as befitted the earthly manifestation of the One-God: his entari was floor-length with deep, flowing folds, sewn from the deepest blue cloth and brocaded with golden thread and studded with sparkling jewels. Beneath it was a shimmering under-robe of yellow satin. His head was crowned with gold, rays like a sunrise lifting behind his oiled hair. Expensive rings adorned every finger. He spread his arms as if to embrace the crowd, his bearded chin lifted, and his eyes closed as he basked in their praise.

The cheers and chants continued for several breaths before finally fading. Emperor Pashtuk brought his arms back down as his head lowered. He looked out upon the throng. "The One-God's blessings be upon you," he proclaimed loudly, and with the words, the sihirki stepped forward to the edge of the dais, tossing handfuls of silver coins minted with Pashtuk's likeness into the crowd as more coins were released from the rear balconies onto the throngs underneath. Altan was pleased to see that none of his soldiers moved, but the crowd responded, dropping to their knees to snatch up the money.

But not all of them. Altan saw a group of two hands or so who remained standing near Altan's side of the dais, only a few strides from the line of soldiers stationed there. His eyes narrowed, noticing their more angular and paler faces: Cateni. Even as he gestured to Musa and Ilkur—his sub-commanders stationed on the temple floor—and started to call out to his troops, the cluster of Cateni rushed forward. None of them had true weapons; a few had walking sticks they wielded as cudgels, others had small knives they'd manage to conceal from the temple guards tasked with making sure no one was armed, while some had only their fists. Altan saw a guard go down from a blow to the head, but the other soldiers surged toward the disturbance quickly, even as Pashtuk himself noticed it and backed away. Great-Voice Utka gaped in distress.

One of the Cateni stayed back, not attacking with the others. He was standing alone, and Altan saw his hands moving and his lips mouthing silent words. His cloak was collared, rising high on his neck, but Altan thought he glimpsed a glint of metal underneath it: a torc. A surge of fear stabbed at Altan, knowing that he was seeing a draoi. None of the soldiers or officers appeared to have noticed the greater danger.

Altan didn't allow himself to think. He muttered an obscenity even as he started to run toward the front of the dais, gauging distances and hoping he had enough speed and sufficient strength in his legs. He leaped outward over the crowd, reaching for the draoi but fearing that he would see the man finish the spell and release it even as he was in midair.

He came down on the person in front of the draoi, the impact nearly taking the breath from his body. But the force of the blow sent the man stumbling backward and into the draoi, who also went down, his torc glinting under the cloak as he fell. Altan forced himself up from the floor and onto the draoi, reaching for the Cateni's hands to stop the motion of the spell. A few breaths later, his soldiers arrived. "Take him!" Altan ordered as they helped him up. "Tie his hands and gag him—he's draoi. Bring him to the palace and hold him there."

Altan shook off the soldiers' hands and nearly fell, his right knee collapsing under him as pain shot through his leg. His right shoulder ached as well. On the dais, the Great-Voice and the emperor were huddled together. All the other Cateni were down, most of them evidently dead given the amount of blood spilled on the tiles. Two soldiers were sitting up, cudgeled but recovering. Altan nodded to Pashtuk, and the emperor stepped forward to the edge of the dais. "Bring that man to me, Commander!" he said, gesturing at the draoi, his stentorian voice hushing the calls of distress from the audience in the temple, still confused as to exactly what had happened. Altan nodded to the soldiers holding the draoi.

"Do as the emperor wishes," Altan said. "Just keep a good hold on his hands. He can't do anything unless he can make the spell shapes."

The soldiers dragged the draoi roughly over to the dais. Two soldiers had already vaulted up to take him, the Cateni grimacing but silent as they pulled him up by the arms. Altan's officers were reforming the line to keep back the crowd while other soldiers started to haul away the bodies of the dead Cateni, trailing bright red smears across the tiles.

Altan limped over to the dais; it was nearly the height of his head and he wondered how he was going to get back up, but Tolga and another one of his men were already moving toward him. They lifted him onto the platform as Altan struggled not to cry out at the agony radiating from his knee and shoulder. He forced away the pain, locking his knee so he could walk stiff-legged as the emperor gestured for him to approach. "This is one time I don't mind that you didn't wait for orders, Commander," Pashtuk said softly. "This man, the torc he's wearing—he's a Cateni draoi, then?"

"Yes, my Emperor. A draoi, and he was preparing a spell against you."

Pashtuk nodded slowly, the golden crown dipping and rising again. His dark stare moved to the Cateni, sagging between the two men holding him. Altan could see blood flowing down the side of the man's head from a deep cut on his forehead; Altan wondered when that had happened, or if he had somehow done it himself.

Pashtuk took two steps toward the draoi. Carefully, deliberately, he spat in the man's face. "Did you think you could kill a *god*?" he asked the man, his voice raised again so most of those in the temple could hear him.

"I almost did," the man answered in heavily accented Mundoan—from the northern clans, Altan decided. *This shouldn't have happened . . .* "Release me, and I will show you how easy it is. Or is the god Pashtuk afraid?"

With that last challenge, Altan saw Pashtuk step forward, taking the draoi's bearded chin in his left hand and lifting it. His right hand slid a thin dagger from a sheath on his belt. More a ceremonial weapon than a practical one, Altan saw, the hilt studded with jewels, the blade thin and narrow enough that it would likely snap or shatter if struck hard. But the point was sharp and its edge keen: without hesitation, Pashtuk plunged the blade into the draoi's throat and yanked it hard sideways. The draoi's eyes went wide, and he gave a gasp that was liquid with blood. His body shuddered in the grasp of the soldiers as Pashtuk thrust the knife deeper. Blood drooled from his mouth, the desperate gasping for air turned to a gurgling sigh, and the man went limp.

Pashtuk pulled the dagger from the dead man as the soldiers

struggled to keep the body upright. He casually wiped the blade on the draoi's cloak, though he didn't sheath it. "Take the body away," he told the soldiers. "Impale it on the city gates and leave it there for the crows."

As they dragged away the corpse, Pashtuk faced the now-silent crowd. "I am the One-God's visible body in this life," he said. "The One-God blesses those who love Him." He paused and lifted the dagger toward the apex of the dome. "Those who would oppose Him are given what they deserve. So tell me, do you love Him or not?"

The crowd answered with a roar that beat against Altan's chest like a physical blow, a cheer that sent the pigeons perched along the balconies of the dome flying. Pashtuk stood still and silent, as if absorbing their adulation, then sheathed the dagger with a sudden motion.

"You've seen the One-God's will here today," he said. "Let that be a warning to any who oppose us."

Altan was hardly surprised when Emperor Pashtuk requested his presence in the wake of the assassination attempt at the Great Temple. Tolga fussed over him, changing his torn and bloodied clothing, cleaning the worst of the cuts and scrapes, and wrapping his knee before letting him go to the emperor's chambers. Altan could feel his body growing increasingly stiff and sore in the wake of the activity, and he was limping heavily by the time he reached the emperor's wing of the palace and was escorted in. *Two hands of years ago, you'd have shrugged it off. The years and the battle scars are taking what's due them.*

The attendant opened the door to the emperor's reception chamber—the usual throng waiting their turn in the outer chamber—and as Altan started to make his obeisance toward the dais, Pashtuk waved a hand. "No," he said, then gestured to one of the attendants in the room. "You—bring the commander a chair, and you two"—with a wave at two of the guards—"help him to his seat." A chair was quickly brought forward and placed at the foot of the dais, directly in front of Pashtuk, still attired as he had been in the Great Temple, as the guards half carried Altan forward.

"Thank you, my Emperor," Altan said as he sat, unable to stop the grimace that twisted his face or the accompanying groan as his right knee bent. "I apologize for what happened. Evidently one or more of the temple guards were negligent."

Again Pashtuk waved his hand. "The security of the Great Temple and the city weren't your direct concern but that of Great-Voice Utka. He tells me that interrogations of the guards whose duty it was to check those entering the temple are already underway. Your personal cohort prevented anything from happening as a result of the temple guards' obvious failures."

A pause. Pashtuk's gaze held him. "And you, Commander," he added, "did more than anyone. Great-Voice Utka seems to feel that since Ceanndraoi Voada's death, the Cateni are little more than a nuisance. Today they appeared to me to be rather *more* than a simple nuisance. I'd like your opinion as the commander of my forces here in Albann. Please speak freely; I don't need someone else who's only willing to tell me what they think I want to hear."

Pashtuk leaned back in his cushioned chair. *You can't tell him the truth, as much as you'd like to. . . . You've already overstepped your bounds.* The banners flanking the dais fluttered in the breeze from the open windows, making the hawks embroidered there seem as if they were flexing their primary feathers to catch an updraft. Altan could see the palace guards at their posts in the room, carefully not looking at him or the emperor, but he knew they were listening and that whatever he said here would eventually find its way to Great-Voice Utka's ears—and when Pashtuk finished his tour of his Albann province and returned to Rumeli, it would be Great-Voice Utka that Altan would have to deal with as his immediate superior. He chose his words carefully and slowly, trying to blend truth with diplomacy and lies of omission knowing that this wasn't his strength.

"We've largely restored order to Albann Deas since Voada's re-bellion," he said. "Great-Voice Utka isn't wrong there. But above the River Meadham, as was the case before Voada, we control very little. No, let me be blunt: above the Meadham, we control *nothing at all*. The clan àrds still rule the north, and the island of Onglse still harbors Ceanndraoi Greum Red-Hand and his draoi. And . . ." Altan shifted in his chair, and his knee and shoulder both protested the movement; he muffled the resulting groan as much as possible. "We know that the Mad Draoi Voada had a daughter: Orla. She'd been forcibly married to one of my lower officers who died at the Battle of Siran, which unfortunately wasn't reported to me until well after the battle. Orla fled the army encampment near Siran the day after the battle. I've learned that she crossed the Meadham into Albann Bràghad. Since then, there are only rumors of her."

"Rumors?" Pashtuk said. His head tilted slightly as if inviting Altan to elaborate.

"We have spies in a few of the clans she stayed with initially, and the tale is that she moved west and north toward Onglse. The ru-mors also say that she has the gift of seeing ghosts that her mother had—as all draoi supposedly do—but that she didn't appear to have an anamacha with her when she passed through. But those are only rumors and tales. I've had no hard evidence as yet."

"But you believe these *rumors*?" Pashtuk put decided emphasis on the word.

"'Believe' is too strong a word. I *worry* about the rumors, my Emperor. I worry that the daughter of the Mad Draoi is someone around whom the northern Cateni might rally. I worry that she might become a draoi, as her mother was." *I worry that she could potentially replace Greum Red-Hand, which would ruin everything I've tried to set up.*

"Do you think what happened today had anything to do with this woman?"

Altan shook his head quickly. "No, I don't believe so. Today . . . well, that merely showed that there are still embers in the ashes of the rebellion Voada started and that we must be careful to stamp those out when we find them."

"And how can we be sure those embers are finally made cold, Commander?"

Pashtuk's eyes narrowed with the question, his gaze intent on Altan. *Ah, that's what he really wants me to answer. Do I give him the truth or not?*

"As I've told you before, my Emperor, I'm a poor diplomat. A good one would give you either a clever evasion or—as you said—tell you what you wish to hear."

A smile seemed to lurk in Pashtuk's oiled and coiffed beard. "And what is it that I want to hear, Commander?"

"That the embers of the rebellion are nearly cold now, that today was an unfortunate and entirely unusual flare that will never occur again, and that all we need do is continue what we're doing."

"And the reality, as you see it?"

"That fire in the Cateni might *never* die, my Emperor, unless and until we have brought all their clans under our control and their draoi, especially, are destroyed forever." *Or . . .* But he couldn't tell Pashtuk the other option. Not yet.

"Spoken like a soldier," Pashtuk commented. His finger stroked his beard. "And can you accomplish that?"

Altan shook his head. "Not with the troops I have. Give me at least another two full armies, and perhaps." *And with that, I might even change my current plans.*

"You ask for much."

"You've asked me to speak frankly, my Emperor, and the truth is that you've never seen their warriors in battle nor experienced what their draoi can do. Nor has Great-Voice Utka, as yet. I have, many times. It *will* take that much to quell the Cateni. It might even take more."

Pashtuk nodded as if taking in what Altan had said. "I'll consider your words, Commander." He started to rise, and Altan hurriedly began to push himself from the chair, but Pashtuk gestured for him to remain. "I can see that you've injured yourself protecting me, Commander. Please remain sitting, and I'll have my personal archiater sent in to see what she can do to ease your pain. She's very skilled with potions and salves, as I can testify. I'm grateful to you, Altan Savas, for having been there today, for not hesitating to act, and for your honest appraisal of the situation. I'm starting to suspect that the judgments regarding you that were related to me are in error. We'll talk again, I promise."

With that, the emperor nodded to Altan and stepped down from the dais, already handing one of his attendants his gilded crown. Even before he'd left the room, Altan saw a woman whose spine was bowed with age enter the chamber, a younger woman behind her carrying a leather satchel. The old woman was Cateni, as most archiaters were. She approached Altan, regarding him with clear, dark eyes that carefully concealed whatever she might be thinking.

"Let me see that knee, Commander Savas," she said.

6

A Mother's Touch

ALL THE TALK WAS about Draoi Frangan MacCraig and his attempted assassination of Emperor Pashtuk, the news taking over a moon to reach Onglse. Most of the gossip was conducted in whispers among the draoi, the menach, and the staff of Bàn Cill—conversations that would abruptly end if Greum Red-Hand entered the room or if someone was heard walking in the corridor outside.

The other draoi were largely quiet and wary around Orla as well. It was Sorcha who told her what she'd heard about the events in Savur. "I overheard Menach Moire telling one of her acolytes that Draoi Frangan left Onglse not long before your mother was killed," Sorcha told her as they took their evening meal in an alcove off the common dining hall of the temple. "Ceanndraoi Greum was furious when Draoi Frangan told him he was leaving Onglse and ordered him to stay, but Frangan left anyway, intending to join your mother. He wasn't the only draoi who left the Red-Hand to join Voada around that time. But the Battle of Siran took place before Frangan could reach her."

Orla shivered at that statement, remembering Sorcha's and her flight from the Mundoan encampment just after Siran. "Frangan stayed in the south afterward?" she asked, and Sorcha nodded, mopping up remnants of the lamb and potato stew with the crust of her bread. Orla's own serving sat mostly untouched on the small table in front of her, though she'd sipped at the wine and plucked a few pieces of tender lamb from the broth steaming in its bowl. The news from the south, though, was less the reason for her lack of appetite than the fact that it was her moon-time, and her stomach ached from the bleeding. She would have to change the blood cloths soon.

"Evidently. He never came back here. I suppose when he learned that Emperor Pashtuk was coming, he decided to try to assassinate the man. They say . . ." Orla saw Sorcha shudder as she swallowed her bread. "They say that it was Commander Savas himself who stopped Frangan, killing a hand of those who were with him, and that the emperor had Frangan impaled alive on the city gates for the crows to eat. His skeleton still hangs there."

Orla could see Frangan in her imagination, dangling above the city gates with black crows flapping around him like flies on rotten meat, swaying and screaming as the crows pecked at his face and eyes. She felt her stomach churn with the vision, and she quickly set down her spoon. "I'm sorry," she heard Sorcha whisper. "I shouldn't have told you. The story may even be a lie, just gossip and rumor. If it did happen, it was several hands of days ago now. There's nothing Ceanndraoi Greum or anyone here can do."

Orla felt a chill along her side: her anamacha touching her. She heard their voices in the same moment. <It is the truth. We heard Frangan's voice wail here in Magh da Chèo. He has since joined with his anamacha—as you will with us one day . . .> Ethereal laughter followed that statement, and Orla felt the cold withdraw from her, the anamacha gleaming in the dimness of the alcove.

"That's certainly true," Orla said—an answer not only to Sorcha's comment but to her anamacha. "But it's more important to know what Frangan's attempt means to us."

"That's indeed the issue, Draoi Orla," a much deeper male voice intruded, and both Sorcha and Orla started at the sound. They rose quickly to their feet, Sorcha curtsying deeply.

"Ceanndraoi Greum, a good day to you," she said, grabbing her own bowl as well as Orla's mostly full one. "I'll just take these to the kitchens. Excuse me."

She left with a glance at Orla and a shrug. Greum stood silently, watching, until Sorcha was gone. Orla waved a hand toward Sorcha's chair. "Would you like to sit, Ceanndraoi?"

An inarticulate grunt was her answer, but Greum set his staff against the table and pulled out the chair. He sat, folding his hands together on the wood. She could see the large red-orange blotches that patterned the man's hands to the wrists. She thought they looked like the scars of old burns. His anamacha—which the other draoi had told her was named *Dòrn*, or Fist—hovered near him in the hallway outside the alcove.

"After Voada left Onglse with Ceannàrd Maol," he began, "I was afraid that the island and Bàn Cill would fall. Your mam was the strongest of the draoi except perhaps for myself, and even then it was mostly her inexperience that held her back. The potential your mother held with the Moonshadow . . ." Greum shook his head even as he glanced at Orla's anamacha, his fingers tightening against each other on the table. "When she left, I didn't know if we could hold back Commander Savas without her and Maol. And the truth is that I don't believe we *would* have if Savas hadn't taken his army south in order to deal with your mother."

"Why are you telling me this, Ceanndraoi?"

Greum pursed his lips as if tasting something sour. "I've received communications from the south. From Savur. Draoi Frangan's actions against Emperor Pashtuk have reminded the Mundoa that the Cateni are still an active threat, even below the Meadham. My fear is that Savas will be sent to finish what he began when your mother came here. And we can't afford to make the same mistake again."

"You're telling me not to do what my mother did and abandon Onglse? Ceanndraoi, I'm hardly as experienced at handling the Moonshadow's anamacha as my mother was, and I've never been in battle, so—"

His hands lifted, then slammed back down on the table. "You

misunderstand me," he said. "Back then . . ." He stopped, the red-tinged fingers of his right hand prowling his gray-specked dark beard. "Back then," he continued more quietly, "your mother insisted that it was a mistake for us to think only of Onglse. She wanted us to take our strongest and best draoi, go to the clans and their àrds, and gather up an army of the north to take south. She said that if we did that, the south would rise up with us and we could drive the Mundoa back over the sea from whence they came. I didn't listen to her then. I thought her ideas foolish. But she left and did exactly as she'd told us we should do, and she nearly defeated them. Now . . ."

He gave a long sigh, his shoulders sagging, and Orla realized again just how old Greum was, the years sitting heavily on his shoulders. The Moonshadow's anamacha had drifted close to her again, and she felt their cold and the whisper of their many-throated voice.

<*He has few years left. He knows it. We can feel it . . .*>

Orla tried to ignore the interior voices. "And now?" she prompted Greum.

She thought he might not answer. Then his head lifted, and his dark stare impaled her. "Voada very nearly succeeded all on her own, and I've come to realize I made a mistake with her. Had I listened, had I followed her suggestion, I believe her vision might have been fulfilled—with *all* the draoi behind her and all the clan warriors. But I stayed here even after Savas abandoned the siege. I, along with the draoi and warriors I commanded, did nothing while she battled Savas and his army in Albann Deas, while your mother and Ceannàrd Maol were taking the old Mundoan capital and removing the Great-Voice there. I have to wonder: had I not done that, had I listened to Voada, perhaps your mother would still be alive, and perhaps all of Albann would belong to the Cateni again."

<*Listen to his fear. Listen to his doubt. . . .*>

Orla's eyes narrowed against his stare. "You're saying that you want to attack the Mundoa *now*?"

"I'm saying that I think that's what Voada would be telling me if she were here. Last time I listened to my own pride. This time . . . I wonder what your mam would be telling *you.*"

<*He only wants to use you, and through you, us. If you die, he won't care. . . .*>

"Ceanndraoi, you told me that I shouldn't call on my mam, just as I shouldn't call on the Moonshadow. Ceiteag warned me against that too. I've heard Mam's voice, but it's lost among all the others."

"I know," Greum said. "But you *can* separate her voice from the others as you've separated Iomhar's. It's difficult and even dangerous, but she's there, and perhaps you and I should know her thoughts."

"Then show me," Orla said impulsively, and she heard her anamacha burst into conflicting voices, none of which she could easily distinguish. There was mocking laughter, and amidst their amusement, voices. . . .

<*Fool!*>

<*Yes! You must try!*>

<*You don't have the strength or the will to survive us. . . .*>

<*Voada only fell to the Moonshadow. . . .*>

<*You can barely control us now, and you expect to control one of the strongest of us?*>

Then, another voice: <*Orla! Our daughter, our love . . .*> it began, and the familiar tones brought a shimmer of tears to her eyes, but then it was gone again, lost against the shouting of the others.

Greum was watching her; he could see the anamacha next to her and knew she was hearing their voices. "Tomorrow, I will help you make the attempt," he said. "If you wish to try."

Orla was afraid to blink, not wanting him to see her tears. She only nodded.

The landscape of Magh da Chèo seemed more furious and stormy than usual, but perhaps that was only a reflection of her own fear and uncertainty. The thought of meeting her mother within the anamacha was at once compelling and terrifying, and Orla couldn't decide which of the emotions was the stronger.

Brilliant slashes of lightning clawed at a black sky through which sullen gray shreds of clouds scurried, propelled by a gale that shrieked in Orla's ears and pressed her cloak tight against her skin. The ghosts of the draoi within her anamacha surrounded her, their faces shifting and fleeting. Their voices were the howling of the wind and the booming of the thunder.

<You shouldn't have listened to the Red-Hand. He's old, and his anamacha will consume him all too soon.>

<You can't trust him. He's devious. He wants you to fail . . .>

<You'll be here with your mother and with us if you do this . . .>

<Our storm has come for you . . .>

"It's simple enough—you only have to think of her," was all Greum Red-Hand had told her in preparation, when the two of them met in Greum's chambers. "Call her to you as you've called Iomhar before. She'll come to you; she won't be able to deny your summons. She won't *want* to."

Orla saw the ghost that was Iomhar already gliding toward her, and she gestured with her hand. <No!> she thought into the roaring chaos that tore the word from her mind and hurled it away. <Mother, I want you to come to me. I need you now—come to me!>

At first there was no response from the crowd of dead draoi around her, then those in front of her slid aside as if pushed, and one shade glided toward her. Its arms were outstretched in invitation, and Orla could see her mother's face shimmering above it. <Orla . . .> the ghost, the taibhse, called, and its voice was Voada's, reverberating with the tones of all snared within the anamacha.

<As I will be one day?> Orla thought, and the taibhse of Voada gave a laugh adorned with a bitter, cutting edge.

<Yes,> it said, <but not until your task is done and you need to rest. And you see, daughter, here we can talk without speaking aloud . . . I'm your mam. We don't need words—we are already linked . . . Don't be afraid. We . . . I . . . am no danger to you.>

With that statement, the other draoi within the anamacha all began to shout and laugh and taunt her as one.

<That's a lie . . .>

<The power in her will burn you to ash, girl . . .>

<She went mad and is mad still . . .>

<That's what Greum wants for you . . .>

Their mockery sparked in Orla like flint striking steel. She shouted at them aloud, her fury mirroring the storm around them: <Be silent, all of you! You are my anamacha, and you'll do as I say!>

There was more jeering laughter at that, and underneath Orla heard a single woman's deep amusement that seemed to shiver the air around her, but the voices faded. Her mother's taibhse remained in front of her, waiting. <Why did you call us?> the shade began, then shook its head. <Why did you call me?>

The answer poured from Orla's mind unbidden. <Because I miss you, Mam. Because I loved you and Da and Hakan, and I wanted you to know that. Because you were stolen from me long before I was ready, and when I heard that you were the famous Ceanndraoi Voada, I wanted to go to you, but those around me wouldn't let me do that.>

The anamacha loosed a many-voiced wail in response, and lightning flared from cloud to ground around them, flinging dirt and rocks from the blackened earth, though none came toward Orla and the ghosts of the anamacha seemed entirely untroubled. Yet the face of her mother's taibhse remained oddly stoic, and Orla found herself wondering whether this was truly her mother before her. The anamacha heard the thought as well.

<We are her, we are not her . . .> it answered. <We . . . I . . . Sometimes it is difficult to remember our other lives, to know what we thought and felt. Often we are simply one of many. But I remember loving you, Orla. I remember Meir and Hakan, and I've grieved for them.>

Hearing that, Orla gasped. <Then Hakan . . .>

<Hakan is dead too. Yes. Like his father. Like me . . .>

Orla could feel a hot wetness tracking down her face. She wiped at her eyes with the back of her hand, angrily. <How? How did he die?>

<Bakir, your husband, put him in the copper mines. He died there.> Voada's face was impassive, but with that statement, the chorus began again:

<The Mundoa . . . It's their fault . . . We nearly defeated them . . . They deserved the death and blood we brought them and more . . .> Their anger shook the world of Magh da Chèo, broke the clouds and sent rain lashing down on them, made the land quiver under Orla's feet with the mad thunder. Orla wanted to roar with them, to shout her grief and pain to the Otherworld. Only the taibhse of Voada remained still and quiet as the uproar slowly faded.

<There's more you haven't said, my daughter. We can feel it,> Voada said to Orla. <Why else did you call for me?>

<Ceanndraoi Greum asked me to,> Orla answered. <He said I should.>

<Why?> The question echoed throughout Magh da Chèo: <Why? Why? Why?>

Orla started to answer, then stopped. <If I think of all he said to me, if I could give you the memory, would you see it as I did?>

Her mother's ghost simply nodded. She came up to Orla, placed its hands in hers. <Now,> it said. <Remember for us . . .>

Orla closed her eyes, remembering the conversation with Ceanndraoi Greum and trying to visualize that moment as clearly as she could. It was harder than she had thought possible; even such a recent memory was slippery, as difficult to grasp and hold as a salmon swimming past in a stream.

<It's the old memories that are strongest, the ones that burned themselves into us like brands,> Voada's presence whispered. <We remember those even when we wish we could forget. We remember Pencraig and the night our children were taken from us. . . .>

Other voices from the anamacha joined in then—<We remember . . .> <We remember . . .>—all of them reciting their own histories: muttering, shrieking, wailing, weeping. Orla wanted to clap her hands over her ears, to shout at them to be silent, to let her think.

But the taibhse's hands tightened on hers, and the anamacha—all of them—sighed as one a few breaths later as the specter of Voada released Orla's hands.

<So Greum Red-Hand claims he made a mistake, and now he wants

to use us again . . .> The anamacha gave a curt breath of a laugh. *<And you, Orla? How do you feel about that? Do you trust the man?>*

<I don't know,> Orla answered. *<This is all so new to me, so strange. I don't know. I can't answer.>*

Orla felt a shift in the anamacha at that. Voada's specter slid away, fading into the crowd of the others within the anamacha, and there was a sense of a greater presence moving toward her like a gathering storm. A new voice dominated the chatter of the others, rendering them silent.

<The Red-Hand will force you to answer,> it said: a woman's voice—no, perhaps it was a man's, or both—a deep and solemn bass but also another alto one. The sound of it made Orla shiver. She suspected who this presence was, and it frightened her. *<After all, an anamacha can do nothing on their own. We are in the thrall of a living draoi, the weapon clasped in her hand. At least until she falters and we take her into ourselves. Are you faltering already, Orla? Are you unworthy of us?>*

With the question, the presence rushed toward her as the other ghosts wailed and shouted in alarm. A new wild storm broke around Orla—a gale howled, hard rain tore at her, lightning crashed to the ground nearly at her feet as thunder deafened her. The lightning's heat burned her, the concussion tossing her violently to the ground as if some giant had plucked her up and hurled her down again. She could feel the storm gathering energy again, and she desperately tried to force her mind away from Magh da Chèo and the anamacha.

She fell into her own world with a scream.

"Orla!" she heard Greum Red-Hand call to her, and she opened her eyes to find him crouched over her. The expression on his face struck her as odd; he appeared more disappointed than concerned. "What happened? Did your mother come when you called? Did she attack you?"

Orla barely heard the barrage of questions. Part of her was still back in Magh da Chèo, still listening to the fading echo of the anamacha's voices. She realized that she had collapsed and was lying crumpled on the rug spread over the wooden floor of Greum's chamber. She forced herself to sit up, closing her eyes as the room tilted and spun around her. She saw Ceiteag enter from an adjoining room and hand Greum a mug that he then passed to Orla. She gulped eagerly at the cool water it held. Ceiteag remained in the room, watching and listening.

"I spoke to her," she said. Her voice sounded weak and cracked compared to the roar of the Moonshadow.

"What did she say?"

"She asked how I felt about what you were asking of me, Ceanndraoi. Then . . ." Orla swallowed hard. "Then the Moonshadow tried to come forward."

Ceiteag sucked in a breath, and Greum cocked his head toward her. "The Moonshadow? You're certain?"

Orla nodded. "Yes. I could feel it. The power . . ." Orla took a long shuddering breath, putting down the mug. "But I sent it away. I did what you told me to do. I didn't let it touch me."

Greum was staring at her, almost scowling, and Orla realized then why he'd suggested she seek out her mother in the anamacha. It wasn't so that Orla could tell her that Greum realized he should have helped Voada, that he wanted Orla to join him to succeed where Voada had failed. The Moonshadow itself had said it: *An anamacha can do nothing on their own. We are in the thrall of a living draoi, the weapon clasped in her hand.* There had been no need to ask permission of Voada or the Moonshadow or any of the shades within. They were all bound to Orla, dangerous but powerful prisoners that she could force to do her bidding.

No, Greum had expected Orla to fail, to be unable to control Voada's presence. He'd expected her to die in the attempt and set the Moonshadow's anamacha free once more.

Which would leave some other draoi available to bond with the Moonshadow and use the anamacha. She was certain of it. She wondered who it was to have been: Ceiteag? Greum himself?

Some potential draoi without an anamacha? She didn't know if a draoi *could* abandon his or her anamacha once they were bonded.

Orla forced herself to stand, shunning the hand that Greum extended to help her up. She could see all three of their anamachas, dim in the sunlit room: his hovering near him, Ceiteag's near the door of the other room, her own at the outer door as if waiting for her. "I'm tired," she told Greum. "Where's Sorcha? I'd like to go to my chambers and rest."

"Of course. I'll have one of the servants call for her." Before he moved to the door, though, he stared at her once more. "The Moonshadow . . . you met it? Truly?"

"Aye, I did," she told him. She brought her shoulders back, matching his glare. "And my mother also. And I'm not afraid to meet either of them again, Ceanndraoi. I'm not afraid of them at all."

She wondered whether he could hear the lie in her voice.

7

The Great-Voice Speaks

ALTAN'S KNEE THROBBED UNDERNEATH the desk be-hind which he sat.

He leaned forward in his chair to hand the messenger the sealed parchment roll in its oiled wrapper along with a heavy leather pouch of coins, but held onto the pouch as the man reached out to take it. He stared hard at him: a middle-aged Cateni from the town of Muras on the River Meadham, dressed in the plain clothing of a merchant. "You understand whom this must reach? No one else can be permitted to read this—no matter what you need to do to prevent that."

The man nodded. "Of course."

"And you understand that if you fail to deliver it and if you don't bring me his reply, your life and those of your entire family are forfeit?"

"Have I ever failed you in the past, Commander?" the man asked. "I've done this nearly a hand of times already, after all. You can trust me."

"Good. I'll look forward to seeing you again within a moon. Don't spare the horses—I've given you enough to buy what you need."

Another nod. Altan released the pouch, and it and the

parchment quickly vanished under the Cateni's cloak. "I'll see you soon with the reply, Commander," the man said.

"See that you do," Altan told him and waved his hand in dismissal. The man bowed and walked backward from the room.

Tolga entered as the man left, closing the door behind the Cateni. He was holding a parchment roll similar to the one Altan had given the messenger, though Altan could see that the wax seal had been marked with the Great-Voice's insignia. "You'd have his entire family killed?" Tolga commented. "Truly?"

"No," Altan admitted, "but I want *him* to think that. Money isn't enough to buy trust, so I leaven it with threats. And what is that you have?"

Tolga looked at the rolled parchment in his hand as if suddenly remembering it. "Oh! One of the Great-Voice's overdressed and abrasive messengers just delivered this." Tolga handed the parchment to Altan. Altan broke the seal and unrolled it, scanning the words there.

Commander Savas is to meet with Emperor Pashtuk and myself tomorrow midday to discuss the Cateni problem and our options to deal with it.

Options. For a soldier there was only one option to discuss.

Altan sighed heavily, laying the parchment on the desk. He rubbed at his aching knee.

"Bad news?" Tolga asked.

"Is there ever any other kind?" Altan replied. He handed the roll to Tolga. "Here. Burn this, then make sure that you get the new whites ready for tomorrow. We have to make a show of them."

Altan rode toward the Great-Voice's palace with Tolga standing in the traces, holding the reins of two magnificent white geldings that Emperor Pashtuk had sent to Altan a few days before, a gift for his quick action at the Great Temple. Altan had to smile, watching Tolga's muscular back as he deftly handled the powerful but skittish steeds, but he also shook his head. The geldings might one day be worth what the emperor had undoubtedly paid for them, but not now. They were barely able to tolerate the crowds along Savur's wide boulevard, their eyes wide, with Tolga reining them back at every sudden loud noise. The pair would be utterly crazed and useless on a crowded, chaotic, and noisy battlefield. No, the gray-and-black pair back in the stable that he'd had since he'd lost Lucian and their last two warhorses on Onglse were far superior. The emperor's gifts were showy but—at least for the moment—useless in any real situation.

But it wouldn't do for the emperor to see Altan without his present; Altan understood that was simply part of the strategy and tactics of politics. Altan watched the muscles on Tolga's arms bunching as he kept tight control over the pair and heard the man cursing them under his breath.

"Tolga, it really won't do to let the emperor or any of his minions hear you calling his lovely gifts 'twin stinking white turds' and 'ball-less boar spawn,' though I appreciate the sentiments," Altan chided gently.

"Sorry, Commander," Tolga answered without looking back. "These two might be from fine stock, but whoever trained them should be put in the harness so I could whip them instead. It's going take a year or more to undo what's been done with them."

Altan chuckled at that. A movement above them caught his eye: a goshawk gliding across the sky with two much smaller thrushes chasing it, climbing above the hawk and diving toward it to peck at the raptor's wings and body. As Altan watched, the goshawk continued to flee as its attackers harried it until all three vanished behind the palace walls.

"Look how the thrushes protect their nest and young even when the predator is larger and stronger . . . and how they're able to force it to retreat," Altan mused aloud.

This time Tolga did glance back quickly. "Commander?"

"Sorry," Altan told him. "I was talking mostly to myself. Do you believe in omens, Tolga?"

Tolga yanked hard on the reins to turn the geldings toward the palace gates and the guards waiting there. "I suppose," he said. "My mother always said that our plow horse gave a loud whinny just as I was born and that it was an omen that I was destined to deal with horses. And here I am."

Altan smiled. The guards scurried to push open the gate as they approached, and they passed between the imperial banners placed there because the emperor was in residence. Altan glanced up again at the sky—the goshawk and thrushes were gone. "And here I am as well," he added as the chariot moved past the banners into the courtyard beyond and Tolga pulled the horses to a stop near the steps leading up to the palace's main door. Already servants had rushed over to take the reins from Tolga, and well-dressed attendants were hurrying down the stairs to escort Altan. Tolga leaped down from the traces and stood alongside the chariot. "Let me help you, Commander." Normally Altan would have ignored that, but his knee still ached and throbbed, and so he allowed Tolga to take his arm and support him as he descended.

Another omen: the commander needing help to attend a meeting to discuss war. But he dismissed the thought, nodded to Tolga, and limped toward the stairs.

"We must end the Cateni threat forever, and that means taking the north. And *that* means starting with Onglse."

Altan listened to Great-Voice Utka deliver his ultimatum, the words echoing in the reception chamber, now largely empty of courtiers, scribes, and servants. A quartet each of Pashtuk's and Utka's personal guards (who were very carefully pretending to neither listen to nor look at the three men) and a few servants stood at the walls to respond to any needs. Altan resisted the temptation to sigh. Utka was nothing if not predictable; he'd expected the Great-Voice to bring up this point sometime during Pashtuk's visit.

Pashtuk, seated as usual on the dais, didn't reply, the fingers of his right hand continuing to stroke his oiled beard as if he were petting a cat. His gaze seemed directed somewhere between Utka and Altan, both of whom were sitting on chairs placed before the dais. The silence evidently bothered the Great-Voice, for Utka began speaking again. "Once we take Onglse, my Emperor, we'll have plunged a sword into the very heart of the northern clans. It's what we should have done before. It's what Great-Voice Vadim wanted and what we might have accomplished if Commander Savas hadn't decided he was the one who should make decisions and not the Great-Voice."

And there it is, Altan thought, *the center of the matter.* His spine crawled as it did sometimes during a battle, as if he were anticipating a killing stroke from behind. He wondered, even after having saved the emperor's life, whether he was going to walk out of this room today. *If not, you've had a long and mostly good life for a warrior.* The thought seemed a false and cold solace.

Utka kept his face toward Pashtuk, not even glancing at Altan. It was Pashtuk's regard that swiveled then, as he looked directly at Altan. "Commander?" he grunted, his face impassive and unreadable, his fingers still stroking his beard as if he could conjure the answer from the glossy strands.

Does Pashtuk want the truth, or does he want platitudes that he can take back to Mundoci with him when he returns to the emperor's throne? Altan felt like he was playing a game of verbal zar atmak with a weighted and untrue die, but without knowing how the die was weighted and what number it would bring up. He knew Great-Voice Utka had been one of Pashtuk's favorite sycophants back at the capital of Mundoci, that after Great-Voice Vadim's death at the hand of Ceanndraoi Voada, Utka had petitioned the emperor to be named as Vadim's successor. He considered the province of Albann to be an easy plum, the next rung in his political ladder. . . as long as he could quell those pesky clans with their annoying tendency to rebel. Utka had never served in the Mundoan army, had never commanded soldiers, had never had to consider battle strategies and tactics. His battles had been with scrolls and laws, and the often deadly combat of those who scrabble for position and favor at the emperor's court.

But Altan's disdain for the man didn't alter the irrefutable fact that the Great-Voice could order Altan's head to be hewn from his body, imprison him for his failure to carry out orders, or simply strip him of his command and send him back to Rumeli in shame.

This wasn't Altan's form of battle, but it *was* that of both Great-Voice Utka and Emperor Pashtuk. They'd been long immersed in that world and knew its maze of pathways.

Altan realized he'd hesitated too long, that Pashtuk was still staring at him, waiting. Impatience was beginning to crawl over the man's face. It would have to be the truth, then, since Altan had neither the time nor the skill to craft a believable lie—though this wasn't the time to tell either of them the whole truth. Not yet, and perhaps never.

"As I've said to you before, my Emperor," Altan began, speaking slowly and carefully and not daring to glance over at Utka, "we need more soldiers—trained Mundoan cohorts—before we can consider invading the north again and taking Onglse. We lost at least a double hand of excellent Mundoan cohorts between trying to take Onglse and our battle with the ceanndraoi and ceannàrd at Siran. The replacements we have now are almost entirely Cateni conscripts, and though they're commanded by good Mundoan sub-commanders, I would hesitate to trust their skill and especially their loyalty in such a war as Great-Voice Utka is advocating."

Utka started to protest, but Pashtuk's right hand left his beard, and he raised his index finger in the Great-Voice's direction. Altan saw Pashtuk's dark gaze move to stare blandly at Utka. "I will hear the commander," he said, and Utka subsided with an audible huff of irritation.

Altan inclined his head to the emperor. *More truth, then* . . . "It's not enough to simply attack Onglse, my Emperor. To prevail there, we have to do so with massive forces against trained draoi whose spells and abilities, like it or not, are far superior to those of our sihirki. The Cateni warriors are no small problem on their own, though they're just soldiers like any others and just as easy to kill. However, we've no easy answer for the draoi, and that means we have to have a much larger and disciplined force to compensate. But we could manage that with an army sent from Rumeli as reinforcement. The other problem that has to be addressed is the safety of the south while the bulk of our army is in the north. Taking Onglse, as I know from experience, will take time. We have to have sufficient and well-trained troops stationed here in Albann Deas to protect our towns and cities should the northern clans send a secondary force south over the Meadham, such as the army Ceanndraoi Voada and Ceannàrd Iosa led, and to quell any popular uprisings by the Cateni."

Altan took a long breath, studying Pashtuk's face, which remained stolid and silent. "Past that, though, I agree with Great-Voice Utka that ending the Cateni threat requires controlling the north," he continued. "But at the moment, it's my opinion that we don't have the necessary resources."

"Is Commander Savas simply afraid that he'll fail as he did before?" Utka interjected, glaring at Altan. "Perhaps one of your sub-commanders should take command, then. Musa, perhaps, or Ilkur."

Altan looked with feigned calm at the Great-Voice. "I serve entirely at the pleasure of the emperor," he said, "and I'll do as my emperor orders. Should he want my resignation, he may send for a scribe, and I'll dictate and sign it now. If he wants me to take the army I have and attack Onglse again, I'll also do that. But if he asks me what I believe is the best strategy to accomplish Mundoa's goals, then I'll give him my best advice without worrying about what others might think."

"You've hardly shown a propensity to obey orders in the past," Utka grumbled, but Pashtuk cleared his throat, and Utka's protest trailed off.

"This bickering does us no good," Pashtuk said. "I've listened to you both. Great-Voice Utka's determination to put down the Cateni rabble once and for all is a desire I share, especially after what happened in the Great Temple." Utka gave a satisfied sniff at that and sat back in his chair; Altan felt the knot in his stomach tighten. "But," Pashtuk continued, "Commander Savas saved my life with his actions, and I have no reason to doubt his ability to lead our soldiers into action. It's clear to me that had he *not* disobeyed Great-Voice Vadim's orders, then Voada's rebellion would have spread, and her army would have laid waste to more cities and murdered more of our people. If the commander says that our current army isn't sufficient, I'm inclined to believe him. That's a situation I can remedy. I've already sent word by ship to Mundoci that I wish three full troop ships with Mundoan soldiers sent here to join Commander Savas' army: a full double hand of cohorts."

"Thank you, my Emperor," Altan said.

"Don't thank me," Pashtuk answered with a scowl. "I expect you to prove to me that I've not just wasted time and money sending you the reinforcements you asked for. I expect you to begin making the necessary plans to execute the Great-Voice's orders. That will be all for now." Pashtuk rose from his throne; Great-Voice Utka rose quickly after him, but Altan was slower to get to his feet, grimacing as twinges ran through his swollen knee. The guards stationed around the room stiffened to attention. Pashtuk gathered his entari around himself and vanished through the curtains at the rear of the dais, held open by liveried servants then released as soon as Pashtuk stepped through. The heavy azure folds swayed.

"Don't think that you've won here, Commander, or that I'll forget what you've said," Altan heard Great-Voice Utka say before he could move to leave. "I'll have Onglse and the north, or I'll have your head. Preferably I'll have both."

Great-Voice Utka sniffed. He gestured to his guards and left the room. Altan watched him depart. He could feel the others in the room staring at him, and he forced a wry smile onto his face as if he were amused by what the Great-Voice had said. He then gestured to one of the waiting servants: a Cateni. "Tell my driver that we'll be leaving," he told the man, who bowed and hurried away.

Altan waited a few breaths before slowly following after him, not trying to disguise his limp at all. *Let them be reminded of what*

I did in the Great Temple. He wondered if he fooled any of those watching and how quickly they'd report what they'd seen and heard to the emperor.

"It went well?" Tolga asked as one of the palace servants placed a small set of stairs next to Altan's chariot and another held out his hand to help him up. Tolga was holding the reins of the two whites firmly, glancing once at them with a scowl. Altan shook his head at the servant's offer of aid, stared at the stairs for a moment, then reluctantly used them to enter the chariot's car. Tolga leaped up into the traces, slapping the reins onto the whites' backs.

"I still have my head," Altan told Tolga as he turned the horses away from the palace toward the gates and the city streets. "And the emperor is sending additional troops to us."

"That sounds good," Tolga said over his shoulder as they passed through the palace gates. The chariot's wheels chattered over the rutted cobbles of the street. "Though you may not need them if your own plans go well."

Altan didn't answer directly. "We're to return to Onglse," he added. "So no, I'd say the meeting didn't go particularly well."

Altan looked up at the sky as Tolga turned toward the barracks where Altan was staying. The goshawk and the thrushes hadn't reappeared, but now thunderheads were rising and spreading in the west, the hidden sun painting the edges of the clouds a brilliant, fiery white.

Altan sighed. Addressing the clouds, he raised his voice. "Do you really have to be so obvious?"

"Commander?" Tolga answered.

"It's nothing," Altan told him, still staring at the storm clouds and the blue-gray darkness underneath them. "Nothing at all."

8

A Mother's Companion

ORLA AND SORCHA WERE SITTING on a stone bench in the south garden of Bàn Cill, the air perfumed by bog myrtle shrubs while blackcaps, garden warblers, and blue tits sang to one another in the surrounding trees. A quartet of red-billed crows prowled among the tall purple-headed thistles and gorse nearby. Orla's anamacha wasn't visible in the strong sunlight that washed over them as they ate the lunch Sorcha had prepared, though Orla could feel its presence close to her side, a chill against the sun's warmth. The incident of two days before still dominated Orla's thoughts; she had avoided calling the anamacha to her since, something she was certain Ceanndraoi Greum had noticed though he hadn't yet resumed their "lessons" together.

Part of that was because two people had arrived on Onglse the day following Orla's attempt to reach her mother's shade— Ceannàrd Comhnall Mac Tsagairt and his wife, Magaidh—and they seemed to have taken up much of the ceanndraoi's time. As Orla learned from Sorcha, who seemingly knew all the good sources of gossip around Bàn Cill, Comhnall Mac Tsagairt was àrd of the Mac Tsagairt clan. After Ceannàrd Maol Iosa's death on the battlefield of Siran, he had taken the title of ceannàrd as he guided the remnants of the Cateni army back across the River Meadham. It was a title he still held.

To Orla, the title mattered less than the fact that Mac Tsagairt kept the Red-Hand occupied and away from her. For now, it was better to take the slice of nut cake that Sorcha offered her and drizzle honey over it.

"That looks delicious."

The voice—a woman's—came from the garden's entrance. Orla looked over her shoulder to see someone standing there: a woman no more than three double hands of age, perhaps a double hand of years older than Orla. Her hair was the color of new corn, long and braided; the bog dress she wore was well made and fine with filigrees of gold and silver at the hem and collar. The brass torc of a draoi adorned her neck. Her eyes were fixed on Orla; the woman's irises were so pale a blue that they looked like winter ice. Orla could sense the presence of an anamacha alongside the woman.

"You're Orla Paorach?" the draoi asked, and when Orla nodded, she added, "I'm Magaidh Mac Tsagairt. I knew your mother very well. May I join the two of you?"

Orla slid closer to Sorcha on the bench, gesturing at the space next to her. Magaidh walked toward them, Orla searching the woman for some clue, some sense of why she was there. She wondered whether Greum had sent for her, if perhaps she was the one he'd hoped would take the Moonshadow's anamacha from Orla. Magaidh smiled gently at her as she approached; Orla couldn't help giving her a tentative half smile in return.

"I'm so pleased to finally meet you," Magaidh said, still standing. "You should know that Voada loved you dearly. She said that often to me. I'd like to tell you about my time with her, if you'd like to hear that." Orla saw her glance toward Sorcha.

"This is Sorcha," Orla told her. "She helped me escape from the Mundoa, was my companion in finding my way to Onglse, and is my good friend. You may speak as freely in front of her as you would to me. And yes, I very much want to hear what you have to say."

Magaidh nodded and sat with another glance at Sorcha. Orla could see fine wrinkles around the woman's eyes, and there was pain hidden there that Magaidh's smile couldn't touch, as if she'd seen things she would rather forget. Orla saw her glance at the silver oak leaf on its leather string around Orla's neck. "You look so much like your mam," she said. "I'd have known you for her daughter without being told."

"You knew my mother that well, then?"

"Voada taught me to be a draoi. She was with me when I first merged with my anamacha." Her fingers lifted to touch the polished knobs of her torc. "My husband and I were the very first to follow her and Ceannàrd Iosa after they left Onglse. My husband served as Maol Iosa's First Àrd, and I . . ." One shoulder lifted and fell. "I was First Draoi to the ceanndraoi and as much of a friend to her as anyone could be. We were with your mother when she first crossed over the River Meadham into the south; we were there when she took Trusa from the Great-Voice of the Mundoa." A look of pain crossed her face, and her eyes glistened. She released a breath. "And we were there with her at Siran, the last battle," she finished.

"And why are you here now?" Orla asked her.

"I came because I heard you were here."

"Was it Ceanndraoi Greum who told you to come?"

Magaidh gave a small shake of her head. "He asked my husband to come. Not me. He . . . well, I don't think the Red-Hand ever forgave your mother for allowing the people who flocked to her to give her the title of ceanndraoi. *His* title. He probably told you she stole the title, but I'll tell you that's not true; the title was given to her freely by those around her. And because I was one who followed her, because I was close to her . . ." Her voice trailed off, and she glanced away toward the white dome of the temple of Bàn Cill, just visible through the trees nearest the garden. "I don't think Ceanndraoi Greum cares much for me as a result. The Red-Hand isn't a bad man, Orla, but he's a proud and stubborn one. Those are qualities he shared with Voada, though I don't think either one could have admitted it."

"He didn't request that you come here? He didn't say anything about the Moonshadow's anamacha?" *Are you the one Greum wants to take the Moonshadow?*

If Magaidh could hear the unspoken accusation in Orla's voice, she gave no indication, only another shake of her head. "I know that the Moonshadow is yours now; I can feel them next to you—the same raw power that surrounded Voada." At Orla's side, Sorcha shivered at that and moved away a little, as if to give the anamacha room to sit. "I have something to give you," Magaidh continued. "Here." She untied a small leather pouch from the belt of her dress and handed it to Orla.

Orla pulled at the drawstring of the pouch and turned it over. A silver chain poured out of the pouch; on the chain was a silver oak leaf, the twin of the ornament she wore around her own neck. Orla gasped, her eyes suddenly full of unbidden tears.

"Your mother died in my arms," Magaidh said to Orla. "Before the Moonshadow's anamacha took her soul, she asked me to find you and to give you this. I'm glad I'm finally able to fulfill her last wish."

Orla closed her fingers around the pendant so tightly that she felt the points of the oak leaf pressing into her palm. "Thank you, Draoi Magaidh," she managed to say through the threatening tears. "And I would love to talk with you more about my mother."

"That would be my pleasure," Magaidh told her. "This evening after supper I'll come to your chambers, and we can talk then for as long as you like." With that Magaidh rose. Her hand lingered on Orla's shoulder for a breath, then she bowed to the two of them and walked back toward the temple.

"What can I tell you, Orla?"

Orla managed to smile at the question. "Everything," she answered. "Tell me everything."

Orla and Magaidh had retired to Orla's chambers immediately after supper. Sorcha had brought in pastries for them, poured wine, then made her excuses and left them alone. Ceannàrd Mac Tsagairt was in counsel with Ceanndraoi Greum. Sorcha had found tapestries of Elia and Her minor deities in the temple and had hung them to adorn the whitewashed walls of Orla's rooms. The gods stared with fabric eyes at Orla and Magaidh as they talked while their anamacha gleamed in the dimness of the corners.

Magaidh laughed softly at Orla's request, though her gaze remained serious. "Everything would make for a long, long tale, and if I'm to be honest, some of it I'd rather were left forgotten. Your mother was as good a friend to me as she could be, and I loved her for that. I'll be grateful to have known her for as long as I live."

"'As good a friend as she could be . . .'" Orla repeated the phrase, her head cocked to one side in question. She reached for the mug of wine, inhaling its fragrance and waiting as Magaidh took a sip of her own.

"You have to understand that it wasn't easy for your mother being who she was, bearing the memories she had from Pencraig, and being chosen by the Moonshadow," Magaidh said finally, placing the mug back on the table between them. Orla watched her gaze slide to the corner of the room behind her, where Orla's anamacha waited. Orla didn't dare to look there; she didn't want to look at her anamacha at all.

"Are you saying she *was* the Mad Ceanndraoi, as the Mundoa claim?"

Magaidh waited a breath before replying. "No. Not mad, but troubled. Having to use the Moonshadow certainly affected her and her judgment, especially toward the end. It was a terrible burden for her to bear, and eventually it became too much for her." A pause. "As it might be for you also, Orla."

Orla's hand went to the twin oak leaves around her neck under her torc, her fingers scissoring them. "Greum expects me to fail," she said, the words spilling out of her unbidden. "He *wants* me to fail. He doesn't want me to have the Moonshadow."

Magaidh didn't deny it. She sat back in her chair, folding her hands on her lap, her face placid. "That may be true. But that's not his choice to make at the moment."

"He wants to go to war again."

Magaidh nodded. "I know. That's why he and Comhnall are talking. That's why he sent for the ceannàrd. But as I said, it's not why I came."

"He wants the Moonshadow to go to war with him, but he doesn't want me to be the draoi who wields them."

"That might also be true," Magaidh said. "Were you thinking that Greum Red-Hand wanted me to take the Moonshadow after you failed? No, you don't have to answer; I see it in your face. Even if it were possible that a draoi could voluntarily abandon the anamacha that has chosen her—and I don't know that it is, though perhaps the Red-Hand does—Ceanndraoi Greum would not have wanted me to take the Moonshadow. He is ceanndraoi. He intends to *remain* ceanndraoi—and he'll do whatever he needs to do to achieve that."

Orla drew her head back at the implication. "No . . ." she breathed.

"Aye," Magaidh told her, and Orla thought she heard her anamacha whispering the same word: <*Aye* . . .> "That's why I intend to remain here in Onglse as long as you're here. I swore to your mother that I would find you and look after you, and I'll keep that oath to her. As I was a true companion to Ceanndraoi Voada, I'll be the same for you, if you'll have me." Magaidh leaned over the table to put her hand on Orla's. Her serious eyes searched Orla's own. "You've no reason to trust me, Orla, and you shouldn't. You don't know me, and in your situation you're wise to be suspicious of anyone who professes to be your friend and gives you advice. So I don't want you to answer. Not now. In time, perhaps, when we've both come to know each other better."

With that she leaned back again, leaving Orla's hands cold after her warm touch. Magaidh picked up her mug again and drank. "Now," she said, "let me tell you how I first met your mother . . ."

9

Avoiding the Shadow

WHEN GREUM CAME TO Orla's chambers the following day to continue her lessons, Orla asked Sorcha to tell the man she wasn't feeling well and wouldn't be able to go with him today. From her bedchamber, Orla listened as Greum insisted and Sorcha held firm that Orla was ill and she simply wasn't going to allow Greum to disturb Orla in her bed. Greum sounded extremely unhappy at being rebuffed by someone he obviously considered only a servant, but he finally acquiesced with little good grace, declaiming loudly enough that Orla understood she was intended to hear the statement, "Tell Orla that a draoi who has any hope of being as strong as her mother should be able to ignore her moon-time when she's asked."

She heard Sorcha shut the door behind the ceanndraoi. A few moments later, Sorcha came into the bedchamber, her cheeks still painted with an angry flush. Orla was sitting on the bed fully dressed. "The man's absolutely intolerable and has no respect for anyone. I can see why your mother abandoned him as soon as she could. And to just assume that you're having your moon-time . . . Let *him* deal with moon-times and see how easily *he* can ignore them." She loosed an exasperated huff of air, then nodded toward the outer chamber. "I went down to the kitchens earlier and brought our breakfast back here. Go make yourself comfortable, and I'll get it on the table."

"Thank you, Sorcha," Orla told her. "And thank you even more for putting off Ceanndraoi Greum. I just couldn't bear the thought of seeing him today."

"No need to thank me; I can understand perfectly," Sorcha answered. "You must be hungry. I know I am, but we can't have you going to the dining hall when you're bleeding too heavily to work with the ceanndraoi." Sorcha grinned, and Orla had to smile back at her.

They were finishing the meal of bread, cheese, and a dish of sea buckthorn berries and bilberries drizzled in honey and milk when there was a knock on the door. Sorcha looked at Orla, who shrugged. Sorcha went to the door and opened it a crack.

"Draoi Magaidh," she said and glanced over to Orla, who nodded. Sorcha opened the door wider. "Come in."

Magaidh and her anamacha entered as Sorcha closed the door behind her. The woman smiled toward Orla. Her torc, the knobbed ends polished from her fingers, gleamed in the sunlight pouring through the open window of the room. "You don't look nearly as bad as the ceanndraoi had me believing."

"I just—" Orla began, but Magaidh laughed and held up her hand.

"I don't care whether you're really sick or whether it's actually your moon-time or not," she said. "Let poor Greum believe whatever he wants." Orla saw her gaze slide over to the Moonshadow's anamacha behind Orla's chair. "Have you used your anamacha since you touched your mam and felt the Moonshadow inside?"

Orla shook her head as Sorcha brought a chair over to the table for Magaidh, then took her own seat again.

"And why not?" Magaidh asked as she sat and reached for the bread.

"That's not your concern," Sorcha retorted before Orla could answer.

"Sorcha!" Orla said, but Magaidh was already turning to the woman.

"You're right to try to protect her, Sorcha," Magaidh answered, not unkindly. "She needs friends she can trust, now and in the coming days. But Orla and the Moonshadow *are* my concern, especially since the Moonshadow now contains my own friend Voada, and because I know better than anyone here just how dangerous the Moonshadow can be." Her regard returned to Orla, though she continued to address Sorcha. "I know that better than Orla does herself, but I suspect she now senses the peril. And that's why she's here in her room now and not with Ceanndraoi Greum," she finished quietly.

"Aye," Orla said, nodding. "I admit it—that's the reason I haven't used the anamacha and why I told Ceanndraoi Greum that I was sick. Talking to my mother, meeting the Moonshadow . . . I told Greum that I wasn't afraid of either of them, but that was a lie. The more I think about having to enter their world again, having to listen to all their voices . . ." She shivered as if spiders were running over her skin under her léine.

"You won't have a choice, and Ceanndraoi Greum knows that as well as I do," Magaidh told her. "I'm sorry, but the anamacha won't wait forever for you. They have their own desires, their own needs, and they'll bring you into Magh da Chèo without your consent if you continue to ignore them much longer—and that'll be neither pleasant nor safe."

"Let them go find someone else," Orla said.

"Stop it!" Magaidh said sharply enough that both Orla and Sorcha straightened their spines against the backs of their chairs. "You may *want* to believe that will happen, Orla, but listen to your true heart. If the Moonshadow abandoned you, if your *mother* abandoned you, how would you feel? Close your eyes and think. Grow up, child."

Orla's head snapped back at the insult. "I'm not a child, Draoi Magaidh," she spat. Her fingers curled into tight fists on the table as she glared at the woman.

"No?" Magaidh stroked the brass knobs of her torc with her fingers. "That's good to hear, because that's what Ceanndraoi Greum thinks you are, and that's why he believes you'll fail as a draoi. It's what my husband thinks of you, too, since he listens to the ceanndraoi far too much. They talk of taking the Moon-shadow to war again, but you're not the draoi they expect to be holding that anamacha when that moment comes. For that task, Greum looks to his favorite potential draoi among Menach Moire and Draoi Ceiteag's acolytes. So prove us all wrong. Show us that you have the strength, the will, and the maturity your mother had, that she thought you would have as well." Her voice gentled then, soothing and imploring at once. "Let me help you, Orla."

"You can't," Orla answered. Her gaze was on the table, on the remnants of their breakfast.

"I can't help you control your anamacha, no," Magaidh persisted, "but I can help you learn how to do that. I can be the teacher you need rather than Ceanndraoi Greum."

Orla's gaze lifted from the table to Magaidh. "The ceanndraoi will allow that?" Orla allowed a trace of hope to enter her voice.

Magaidh sniffed. "He won't like it, and he'll rail and complain and fuss, but he won't be able to stop us. My husband, Comhnall, is ceannàrd, and for what he did with Ceannàrd Iosa and your mother against the Mundoa, Comhnall has the respect of the àrds of the clans. And though I'm not ceanndraoi, everyone knows that I was First Draoi among Voada's draoi and your mother's friend. If Greum wants to gather the warriors of the clans against the Mundoa, then he needs Comhnall, and he needs me. He can't risk offending the Mac Tsagairt clan, because then he offends too many of the northern clans who are allied with us. Ultimately he has to look the other way and let me guide you. But he'll only do that if you insist it's what you want."

Orla looked from Magaidh to Sorcha, who gave her a small nod. Her anamacha had glided closer to her as they spoke; she could feel the cold of its presence at her back.

"All right," Orla said. "When do we begin?"

Later that day, Magaidh and Orla walked well outside the ring of standing stones that marked the inner circle of Bàn Cill on

Onglse. When they reached a gorse-laden hollow between two hills, Magaidh stopped, glancing around. "This will do," she said. "Are you ready?"

Orla shrugged. "I suppose."

"No," Magaidh told her, shaking her head. "You can't have any hesitation or doubt. You must be *certain* you're ready to do this, and I need to hear it in your voice and see it in your body, or we'll go back to Bàn Cill."

Orla gathered herself. She nodded firmly. "I'm ready." She hoped her voice sounded convincing.

Magaidh stared at her for a few breaths. "All right, then," she said. "Call your anamacha to you. Go ahead and enter. I'll be with you. Listen to my voice."

Orla opened her arms, and the anamacha holding her mother and the Moonshadow slid toward her, invisible in the sunlight. There was a moment of cold and disorientation, then the storm-wracked, terrifying world of Magh da Chèo enveloped her, as did the flowing presences of the ghosts her anamacha held, all of them whirling around her, surrounding her, calling to her with their cold voices. <*You're not strong enough . . . You can't control the Moonshadow . . . She'll take you . . . You won't survive . . .*> Amidst the cacophony, she thought she heard her mother's voice as well. <*We're here, Orla . . . We'll be with you . . .*>

And there was another voice as well: Magaidh, calling out against the thunder and the wail of the taibhse. "I'm here, Orla."

Orla tried to find Magaidh in the lightning-punctuated darkness and the shrieking of the wind and the ghosts. "I can't see you."

"Don't worry. I can see you. I'm here, close to you. Listen to my voice. Concentrate on that—it's what your mother told me the first time I used my own anamacha."

"I'll try," Orla said. The taibhse within her anamacha continued to dance and flutter around her like autumn leaves caught in a gale.

"Good. Now, it was Iomhar whom your mother used as her conduit most of the time. Have you called Iomhar before?"

"The ceanndraoi told me to use him, and I have."

"Then go ahead and call him to you. If any other draoi within your anamacha approach, even your mother, push them away. Force them to stay back."

Orla shook her head. She could feel her mother as well as the shrouded presence of the Moonshadow, both of them near her. She thought she could see their forms in the storm, could see their faces resolving on the swaying ghosts about her. "I don't know if I can."

"You can," Magaidh's voice insisted. "Go on and call him to you. I'm watching, and I'll pull you out of Magh da Chèo if I need to."

Orla took a long breath. *<Iomhar!>* she thought into the storm. *<Come to me!>* She saw the shade that she thought of as Iomhar separate from the others, but she also saw her mother's taibhse start to approach. Worse was the sense of a powerful presence coming closer as well: the Moonshadow, like a mountain lurking behind a screen of smaller hills, all of them ready to move aside if she came closer.

<No!> she shouted in her mind to both her mother and the Moonshadow. *<Only Iomhar may approach. The rest of you stay back! Stay back!>*

<Orla, let us come to you, daughter . . .> Her mother's voice wailed in distress, but Orla shook her head, refusing to even look at her. The Moonshadow's presence still loomed, but it was no longer approaching though she could feel it waiting among the other spirits inside the anamacha. She thought she heard a woman's deep voice laughing.

<So you think you can succeed where your mother failed? She ended up here like the others. As you will, too. You'll need me, and you'll call for me . . .>

<Not yet,> Orla answered. *<Not now. Stay back!>*

More laughter answered, but the Moonshadow receded in her mind, sliding back into the darkness of the Otherworld. Iomhar's shade was near Orla, and she opened herself to him, letting his presence touch her.

"Good," Orla heard Magaidh say. "Now use him. Create a spell—it doesn't matter what—and weave the spell cage to hold it. Go on. Release the energy once it's full, then step away and leave the anamacha. You're doing fine, Orla, but I'll stay with you."

Orla's hands began to move of their own accord, weaving the knots of a spell cage in the air before her as Iomhar pulled the threads of energy from the storms around them. She could feel their fire burning against her skin. *Create a spell*, Magaidh had said, but she had nothing in mind. <*Remember . . .*> a voice from the anamacha called to her—her mam's voice—and suddenly Orla's mind filled with the image of the temple she'd known as a child on the top of the bluff in Pencraig. She'd helped her mother clean the temple many times, the two of them talking in hushed tones about when it had been the temple of Elia, before the Mundoa had arrived and placed the horrid bust of Emperor Pashtuk in Elia's place on the altar. Orla remembered the temple, and the gilded sun-paths made of tiles, and the four windows marking the sunrises and sunsets of the solstices, and how she had seen her mother guide her father's lost soul, his taibhse, to the sun-path toward Tirnanog. She remembered standing next to her mother, and both of them seeing the Moonshadow's anamacha gliding through the temple's shadows, and neither of them realizing what it was or what it would come to mean for them.

Orla realized with a start that the spell cage was full and could hold no more of the power Iomhar was feeding her. The fury of it was already straining the knots she had created. With a cry of "Cuimhnich!"—*Remember!*—Orla opened her hands and released the power. At the same time, Orla heard someone shout angrily behind her in the real world, "Who said you could do this?" It was a deep male voice: Ceanndraoi Greum's.

The spell went careening away as Orla took a step backward, releasing the anamacha entirely. Her shoulders sagged, and her knees nearly collapsed under her from the strain of casting the spell, but she forced herself to remain standing.

Orla turned her head to see the ceanndraoi standing there behind Magaidh, who had also left her anamacha. "Draoi Magaidh? Draoi Orla? I demand an answer!" His face was flushed, but Magaidh was staring at something behind and above Orla. Greum looked to the same spot, and Orla saw the anger drain from his cheeks, replaced by a look that seemed more shock than anger. "By Elia . . . what have you done, girl?" he said.

Orla followed their gazes.

Atop the northern hill, gleaming in the sunlight, was a small temple, one whose lines were entirely familiar to Orla: the temple at Pencraig as it existed in her memory, only now seemingly solid and real, looking as if it had been created from the face of a glowing moon. Orla started to move up the hill toward it. "Orla!" she heard both Greum and Magaidh call, but she ignored them, climbing the hill as quickly as she could, grasping at bushes and rocks to pull her up toward the temple.

Her clothes streaked with mud and brambles, her hands filthy, she clambered up to the summit of the hill to stand in front of the temple. She'd thought it only a dream image, but she placed her hand on it and found it to be solid stone, the same white marbled facade she remembered touching many times as a child. The open doorway beckoned her and she stepped inside.

The interior was also the same: there were the sun-paths beneath the four windows, laid in gold in the tiled floor and intersecting at the small altar in the center under the open domed roof. And on the altar itself, not a bust of Emperor Pashtuk but a painted and gilded image of the Goddess Elia.

"How . . . ?" Orla breathed.

"How indeed?" Magaidh's voice asked from the doorway. Orla turned to see both Magaidh and Ceanndraoi Greum standing there, their cloaks as stained from the climb as her own. In the shadows of the temple, a trio of anamacha lurked near them. "You did this with *Iomhar*? Not your mother, not the Moonshadow? With *Iomhar*?"

"Aye," Orla said in a whisper. It seemed nearly sacrilege to raise her voice here. "You said to cast a spell, and I didn't know what spell to cast, and I was thinking of home and being with my mam there at the temple when I could no longer hold the power and had to release it." She stopped, her hands gesturing at the space around them. "This is my memory of that place made real."

"It's not possible," Greum insisted. His gravely, overloud voice seemed a desecration.

Magaidh gave a soft laugh. "Not possible, Ceanndraoi? How strange of you to say, since here it is." She stomped her booted foot on the tiles for emphasis, the sound echoing from the hard stone walls. "It seems to me to be entirely possible." Magaidh smiled at Orla. "I think you should be teaching me. Your mam . . . I'm not sure even Voada could have done this. I know I couldn't." She glanced at Greum, scowling next to her. "Could you do the same, Ceanndraoi?" she asked, her voice deceptively sweet. "Could you create a temple from the pure energy of Magh da Chèo?"

Greum didn't answer. His scowl deepened, carving deep canyons in the lines of his face. "You had no right, Draoi Magaidh," he husked out. "No right to claim the girl as your student. She came to me, not to you."

"I'm not her teacher," Magaidh answered. "At best, I'm only a poor guide. But I'm her friend, as I was to her mother. Maybe that's what you should have been—with Voada as well as Orla. Had you done that, maybe everything would have been different."

Greum's face went as red as his hands. He spat on the tiles of the temple and ground it in with the toe of his boot. Without another word, he left. Magaidh shrugged, turning to Orla. "I'm sorry," she said. "I may have just made things worse for you. That wasn't what I wanted, but the man's attitude . . ."

"No need to apologize for that," Orla told her. "I feel the same way."

Magaidh's short laugh rang out in the temple. "I can well imagine that you do." Magaidh looked toward the doorway. "Should we go back with the ceanndraoi so he can chastise us properly in front of everyone else?"

Orla pressed her lips together as she looked around the temple, filled with light and shadow and Elia's figure gleaming in the sunlight pouring through the open roof. It felt as if she'd somehow managed to come home, even though home was empty of the family she had loved. "No. I think I'll stay here awhile longer."

"Then I'll stay here with you," Magaidh said. "And you can tell me about this place and your memories of your mam."

10

Changes Wrought

THE SUMMONS CAME UNEXPECTEDLY a double hand of days later, and Altan had no choice but to answer. He hadn't expected to see the emperor again until the man's departure for Rumeli and Mundoci, scheduled for two days from then. But there it was, and so Altan had Tolga harness the whites so the emperor might notice that his gift was again being used to bring Altan back to the Great-Voice's palace.

When Altan was ushered into the emperor's presence, it was in the emperor's private quarters. Only Pashtuk himself was present, with the exception of two slaves standing stiff-backed in their livery against the wall. Pashtuk was seated in a plush, high-backed chair before which was a plate of fruits and pastries as well as a steaming pot of spiced wine. Pashtuk gestured to an empty chair on the other side of the table and watched as Altan took the offered seat. One of the slaves hurried over to pour him wine.

"You're walking much better, Commander," Pashtuk said. "It seems you heal quickly."

"I've mostly learned to hide the limp better, my Emperor," Altan told him. "I don't want my men talking about how their commander's getting old and slow. I'd rather my sub-commanders didn't get the idea that I'm able to be pushed aside."

Pashtuk chuckled at that. "Now that's a wise decision. Perhaps Empress Damla should have followed your example. But then I wouldn't be emperor, would I?"

Altan reached down and took a slow sip of his wine to give himself a moment to consider that comment. After the death of the unfortunately childless Emperor Hayat, who had ruled for nearly seven long decades, the throne had briefly been claimed and occupied by his already elderly younger sister Damla. The young Pashtuk, a distant cousin of the empress and then a rising, charismatic sub-commander of the elite palace guards, had led a successful coup a hand of years later. Pashtuk had taken the throne from the empress and had her executed.

Perhaps Empress Damla should have followed your example . . . Altan forced a smile to his lips as he set down his cup. "An army officer generally expects to die in battle of one sort or another," he said carefully. "I don't like leading my people from behind."

Pashtuk nodded, stroking his oiled beard idly. "And an emperor generally expects to rule until he dies or someone more ambitious kills him in order to take his place. An emperor will either die peacefully in his bed when the thread of his life is run, or violently and suddenly; there are no other choices. The key to living a long life is to anticipate who has that type of ambition and get rid of them first." He smiled then, slowly. To Altan the gesture seemed somehow ominous. He seemed to feel eyes on his back though there were no guards visible in the room. *An archer or two behind the trellis, waiting for Pashtuk's order to loose their arrows? Or poison in the wine I just sipped?*

"My Emperor, I hope you don't think—" Altan began, then stopped as Pashtuk lifted a hand, still smiling.

"I don't smell any such ambition in you, Commander," Pashtuk said, and Altan felt the knot in his stomach release somewhat. "No, you're where you wish to be in life: at the head of your army and loyal to your emperor. But sometimes where you want to be is not where you will finish."

Altan could feel his brow furrowing in confusion. "I don't understand . . ."

"Tell me, Commander," Pashtuk interrupted, "do you think you can defeat the Cateni?" His dark eyes glittered as they stared at Altan from under olive-toned ledges.

Altan sat back stiffly. He wondered if Pashtuk somehow knew what he had already set in motion. He answered carefully. "With the troops you're sending me, yes, I believe I can take Onglse, and that will strike a terrible blow to the Cateni."

Pashtuk's smile lingered, then dissolved. "That's an interesting response. What I want to know is whether taking Onglse will defeat the Cateni entirely. Will it make them good, obedient, and productive members of my empire? Will it end the northern clans' rebellions?"

"You're asking me to foretell the future, my Emperor. I'm just—"

"Yes," Pashtuk broke in. "You've said it before: you're just a soldier, so I shouldn't expect you to be a seer. That's the answer of someone who doesn't wish to offend his master. I've already told you that I don't see you as dangerously ambitious. Give me the truth as you see it, Commander, not a carefully phrased avoidance of it."

Altan hesitated for a breath, wondering if truth was actually what Pashtuk wanted or if his comment was designed to make Altan say something that would doom him. *I'm a poor warrior in this kind of battle. Give me a spear and Tolga in my chariot's harness and the enemy arrayed before me. As for the genuine truth—he won't take that well.* Altan took a breath.

"No," he said at last—just that single word. Then the rest of it tumbled out. "This is how I see it, my Emperor, from a soldier's perspective. If we attack Onglse, the clans will rise up again and oppose us every step of the way. When we take the island—and with the additional troops, we *can* do that—the uprisings still won't end. Clan warriors and draoi may come across the River Meadham once more. They'll oppose every one of our attempts to establish or control towns in the north. If they can't defeat us directly, the clan àrds will take their people and retreat into hidden mountain holdings, springing out from the very rocks to attack us whenever they can. You would have to send enough soldiers to cover every stone in their entire land to root them all out. Your grandchildren will still be fighting them long after we're both gone."

Pashtuk's face remained impassive. He reached down and plucked a grape from the table, turning it before his eyes as if fascinated by what he saw. "That's not what Great-Voice Utka believes. He would say that you're a frightened and already-beaten commander. He'd say you actually *admire* these Cateni."

Pashtuk was still staring at the grape. *Ah, well. I might as well die casting the poor weapons I have . . .* "Great-Voice Utka—if you'll pardon my bluntness, my Emperor—is giving you the answer of someone who doesn't wish to offend his master."

Altan fully expected to hear the groan of leather bowstrings at full draw and feel the harsh impact of arrows in his back. But instead Pashtuk let the grape drop as he slapped his thighs with both hands, leaned back in his chair, and roared with laughter. "Ah, you are indeed a treasure, Commander Savas. I can see why Great-Voice Utka despises you." Then the amusement vanished as quickly as it had come, and Pashtuk leaned forward again. On either side of him, the slaves looked carefully straight ahead as if they'd heard nothing at all. "So *do* you admire the Cateni, Commander, as the Great-Voice claims?"

Altan shrugged. "'Admire' is a strong word. As a military commander, as someone who has fought them in battle, I have great *respect* for them, my Emperor. I'd be a fool to say otherwise. Their warriors are the equal of the best Mundoan soldiers, if less disciplined, and the draoi . . . our sihirki are a poor jest against them. Compared to the least-talented draoi, our most accomplished sihirki is a toddler against a full-grown adult. A good commander *has* to respect a competent enemy, because to underestimate them is to inevitably fall to them. But admire?" Altan shook his head. "I'm not sure that's the word I'd use."

Pashtuk sniffed at that, his eyes narrowing. "Great-Voice Utka has made his decision, and that is for you to take Onglse as soon as the troops arrive here and are ready. He is the Great-Voice and *my* voice here on the island of Albann. I expect obedience from you, Commander."

"As I've already told you, I'm loyal to my emperor." Altan raised his chin until his gaze met that of Pashtuk. "And I would insist that I was also being loyal to you, my Emperor, when I disobeyed Great-Voice Vadim and abandoned the assault of Onglse to confront Voada. My loyalty is to the throne and what is best for the empire; if the Great-Voice's orders endanger that, then I'll always—*always*—choose to serve the throne in Mundoci. If that's not sufficient for the emperor, then all you need do is ask is for my resignation or my life. You may have either, freely."

"You're at least consistent in your impudence, Commander. We'll make an agreement, you and I. For the time being, you'll do as Great-Voice Utka asks and take my army to Onglse." Pashtuk's finger prowled his beard once again. "I leave in two days; the troop ships should arrive within the moon if the winds have been good. Know that I'll be watching Albann very carefully, Commander, and if necessary, I'll do what *I* believe is best for the empire in Albann." Again the vague smile lurked within the whiskers of the man's beard. "Commander, it may be that eventually you'll end up somewhere a simple soldier wouldn't expect."

Again Altan wondered at meanings hidden behind the emperor's words. *Is he suggesting that I become Great-Voice?* Altan wondered if that was something he wanted, but he had no answer within himself. "I'll serve wherever you wish, my Emperor," Altan answered.

There seemed no better way to respond.

Sorcha brought a tray with a steaming wine flagon, two mugs, sweet bread, and a jar of honey from Bàn Cill's hives into Orla's bedroom. She set it down carefully on the bed, and Orla smiled at the woman. "What this? You don't need to act like my servant. You're my dearest friend."

Orla saw Sorcha return the smile at that. "I thought you might want this. You were so tired when you came back last night . . ." Orla saw Sorcha glance quickly to the window of the bedroom, where the temple Orla had created could be seen through a gap in the shutters, gleaming white against a deep blue sky. Sorcha shook her head. "Orla, I can't imagine creating that. An entire building. It's such a gift you have . . ." She stopped again, and her movement caused the mugs on the tray to rattle against the wood.

"You're so good to me, Sorcha," Orla told her. "Here, let—"

They both reached for the wine at the same time, and Sorcha's hand closed over Orla's on the flagon's handle. The touch lingered, then Sorcha drew her hand back. "I'm sorry," she said.

"Sorry? For a simple touch? I don't understand."

Sorcha's nut-brown eyes evaded Orla's gaze. She stared at the hand in her lap, the hand that had touched Orla. "Do you . . . ?" Sorcha began before taking a long breath and starting again, her gaze coming back to Orla's. "Do you miss being with someone? I mean, truly being *with* them?"

Orla shrugged. She poured out the wine, drizzled honey over the bread, then handed one slice to Sorcha, noticing that the woman was careful not to allow their hands to touch. "I had the normal childhood feelings about a few boys, but I was only four-teen summers when Bakir"—she paused, grimacing at the pain-ful memory—"took me. I'd never known anyone that way before him, and with Bakir it was more torture than anything. Every time. Rape and lust, not love. Not even friendship or affection. And if that's the way it always is between men and women, then I don't care if I'm ever with a man again." Orla sipped the wine. "*Is* it always that way?" she asked Sorcha.

Sorcha gave a barely noticeable shake of her head. She cupped the mug between her hands, holding it on her lap. "Not always. Alim . . . I suppose he could be gentle enough when he was in a good mood, but that wasn't often, and with the few other men I've known, it was always quick and secretive because it had to be. There was nothing more than just the moment. Except with . . ."

Orla waited, but Sorcha didn't elaborate. "Except with?"

"It doesn't matter," Sorcha said. Her face was flushed, and she brought up the mug and drank quickly. "I'm sorry for what Bakir did to you. You deserve far better."

"We both do," Orla told her. "Maybe we'll find it sometime."

Sorcha's smile appeared twisted and uncertain. "Maybe," she answered.

Those in Bàn Cill were calling Orla's creation "the Moonshadow's Temple." That wasn't, however, a name that the draoi, the aco-lytes, the warriors, or the servants dared use when Ceanndraoi Greum was within earshot. In fact, they avoided mentioning the new temple at all around Ceanndraoi Greum, though Orla was fairly certain it had been an intense subject of conversation among the Red-Hand's confidants.

A hand of days after its creation, the temple Orla had brought into existence still gleamed in the dawn atop the hill just outside Bàn Cill. The edifice was visible to anyone who glanced in that direction from the grounds as long as the Great Temple itself didn't block the view.

Orla walked into the new temple now after leaving Sorcha and Bàn Cill, listening to the echo of her footsteps against the pale stone that mimicked the appearance of a full moon. The Moon-shadow's anamacha glided with her silently, though Orla thought she could sense a certain quiet satisfaction in the faces that flit-tered across its shadowed countenance.

She'd come here every day since she'd made the building and found it the same every time.

She had noticed the differences between the temple at Pencraig and this memory she'd somehow plucked from the energy of Magh da Chèo and made solid. The altar seemed to flow without a seam from the tiles of the floor. The statue of Elia was far more realistic than other images she'd seen of the goddess, and if it was paint that gave the statue its color, she could see no brushstrokes at all on the surface. Orla reached out and placed her fingertips on the statue's cheek, and despite the fact the day was overcast and the sun wasn't yet high enough to touch the altar through the open roof, she found the surface of the statue warm, as if she'd touched the flesh of a living body.

"I overheard the acolytes whispering that you're intending to leave Bàn Cill and live here," Orla heard a voice say from the open doorway. A shadow swept over the floor, and Orla turned to see Magaidh walking toward her, accompanied by her anamacha. Orla thought that she looked older than usual; the lines around her pale-ice eyes were set deep, and in the morning light Orla could see the gray-white that was beginning to invade the blonde strands around her temples. She wore a simple blue-dyed linen bog dress without adornments and no jewelry other than the brass torc gleaming around her neck.

"People say all kinds of foolish things," Orla answered—though in truth, it was something she had considered. There were two small rooms to the rear of the temple that, in Pencraig, had been used for storage, but the larger one could serve as a bedchamber, and the smaller one could easily be converted into a kitchen with a hearth for cooking. There was a clear, bright spring running under the bracken not a dozen steps from the doorway and a bog at the bottom of the hill where one could cut turves of peat. And the view from the hilltop—she could see the green-blue waters of the strait to the east, and on a clear day, the distance-hazed hills of Albann Bràghad beyond. To the west were the rounded hilltops of Onglse marching toward the Storm Sea, the stone walls and forts that protected the island from invaders running along their spines.

It would be tempting to live here, indeed. And it had the added attraction of making it far less likely she'd randomly encounter Greum Red-Hand. Orla smiled at the thought, and Magaidh laughed as if she understood what Orla was thinking. "So you *are* considering it," the woman said. "I can't say I blame you. The view is beautiful up here."

"Did you come up here to appreciate the scenery?" Orla asked her, and Magaidh shook her head.

"No." The woman's expression faded quickly into a somber one. "I asked Sorcha where you were, and she said you'd left just a stripe ago and that I'd probably find you here. You and I are to meet with Ceanndraoi Greum and my husband in the gathering hall of the temple."

"Meet about what?" Orla asked, and Magaidh shrugged.

"We'll find out when we get there. Have you broken your fast?"

"I've had wine and bread. Nothing else."

"Then we'll stop at the kitchens first and coerce Cook into giving us something," Magaidh said. "You'll need the strength. And you should probably get word to Sorcha not to expect you for the midday meal."

"How long will we be in this meeting?"

"I don't know," Magaidh told her. "Comhnall suggested that it may be a long discussion. We aren't the only ones invited, either. Most of the senior draoi will be there as well as some of the clan àrds. If that's the case, Ceanndraoi Greum may be planning to feed us. In fact, I'll insist on it."

Orla frowned at that, puzzled. "So many people? I don't understand—if Ceanndraoi Greum wanted me to be there, why didn't he tell me about it before?"

"He didn't tell you because he didn't invite you," Magaidh said flatly. "I did."

"Oh." The single syllable was all Orla could muster. Her mind conjured up an image of Greum's reaction to her walking into a meeting of the draoi that she had deliberately not been asked to attend. It wasn't a pleasant image. "Magaidh," she began, but the woman was already shaking her head to cut off her protest.

"I know you think Ceanndraoi Greum hates you, but understand this, Orla. It's not hatred you're seeing; it's fear." Magaidh put her hands on Orla's shoulders, her pale gaze not allowing Orla to look away. "Your mother claimed the title of ceanndraoi and proved that she deserved it far more than Greum Red-Hand, and every draoi knows that to be true. He looks at you and instead sees Voada with the Moonshadow's anamacha alongside her, and he's afraid that he'll lose his title yet again. He sees what you've been able to do with little training—like creating this temple—and he trembles. He doesn't hate you; he's *terrified* of you and afraid to show that fear to the others."

Magaidh's fingers pressed hard against Orla's cloak. "If you're to become what your mother was and more—and I believe you are—Greum Red-Hand has good reasons to feel threatened by you," she said. "Just look around you. I *know* Voada couldn't have made this temple."

With that, Magaidh released Orla, and Orla slowly turned from her, taking in the temple's gleaming interior. The sun had lifted higher, peering through broken clouds; shafts of light lathed the white stone with a brilliance that made Orla shade her eyes. When she turned back, she saw that Magaidh had already gone to the entrance of the temple.

"We should go," Magaidh said. "Remember what I've said, and hold your head up when we walk into that meeting. Let the ceanndraoi and *all* of them hear your voice."

When Orla and Magaidh pushed open the doors of the Gathering Hall, the muffled voices inside went abruptly silent. There was a loud rustling as those assembled in the crescent of chairs turned to stare at them. The ghostly, dim presences of the anamacha were arrayed behind their draoi, seeming to glow in the twilight of the hall. The àrds sat uncomfortably on hard wooden seats, wrapped in the colors of their respective clans. Ceanndraoi Greum Red-Hand stood alongside Magaidh's husband, Ceannàrd Mac Tsagairt, in the hollow of the crescent. He turned to glare at the intrusion, leaning on his walking staff as his red cloak swirled around him. His own anamacha glided closer as if expecting to be called to him.

"Sorry I'm late, Ceanndraoi," Magaidh said into the quiet. "I went to fetch Draoi Orla, as I suddenly realized you'd forgotten to invite her to hear what you have to say. I found her at the Moon-shadow's Temple. The view there, I have to say, is wonderful, and the temple itself exquisite. Quite impressive. You really should visit it again to marvel at it, as many of the other draoi have. Wouldn't you agree, Ceanndraoi?"

Orla felt Magaidh link her arm through hers, shepherding her toward the empty chairs at the crown of the moon-horn. Greum's scowl carved shadowy furrows in his face as he watched them approach and sit, though Comhnall Mac Tsagairt ventured a small smile under his white beard. "Please continue, Ceanndraoi," Magaidh said to Greum, waving a hand toward him. "We didn't mean to interrupt. What were you saying?"

Orla thought for a moment that the man was going to refuse to respond. Around his beard, his face had gone nearly as red as his hand. Finally he stopped staring and turned back to the others. "I was saying that I've had word from my contacts in the south, and I've come to the decision that we can't wait here. We can't permit what happened before to happen again. Sitting here and waiting for the Mundoa to make the first move, I'll admit, was a mistake that nearly cost us Onglse and the north last time." He glanced toward Orla and Magaidh. "In that, Draoi Voada was correct."

"You mean *Ceanndraoi* Voada?" Magaidh interjected, her voice disarmingly pleasant and neutral.

Ceanndraoi Greum didn't have a chance to reply, as Comhnall spoke up first, with his own warning glance at his wife and a barely perceptible shake of his head. "As ceannàrd of the assembled clans, I agree with Greum Red-Hand," he said. "Emperor Pashtuk has left Albann Deas and returned to Rumeli, but the whispers we've heard from our people in Savur say that before the emperor left, he ordered troop ships sent to Albann. We believe that Great-Voice Utka has ordered Commander Savas to do what he failed to do before: take Onglse. The simple fact is that we've lost too many good warriors and too many draoi to properly defend Onglse against another full-scale invasion."

"It wasn't our warriors and draoi here who kept Savas from overrunning Onglse and taking Bàn Cill, Ceannàrd," one of the àrds insisted when Comhnall paused to take a breath. "As Ceann-draoi Greum has noted, his strategy last time was a mistake. If Ceanndraoi Voada"—the man put decided emphasis on the title, and with that Orla realized that Greum certainly didn't have the support of the entire room—"along with my brave cousin Ceann-àrd Maol Iosa hadn't left Onglse to gather warriors and draoi and attack the south, Commander Savas would have taken the island. Then, despite everything you say, the Mundoa would have pushed north. We'd have lost nearly all our draoi and far too many war-riors in that futile struggle. We'd be fighting them from the mountain fastnesses even now, and the Mundoa would control many of our towns and much of our land."

Magaidh leaned toward Orla, whispering in her ear. "That's Àrd Eideard Iosa, a nephew of Maol Iosa, who claimed the title of clan àrd after Maol's death. Comhnall believes that Eideard would love to have Maol Iosa's old title as ceannàrd as well."

"I've already admitted my mistake, Àrd Iosa," Greum said loudly. "Isn't that enough for you?"

"I only want you to realize that now is not then, Ceanndraoi," Eideard answered. "I question whether repeating Ceanndraoi's Voada's strategy will work a second time. She and my uncle were successful because their move was unexpected and caught the Mundoa entirely by surprise. When Savas realized what had hap-pened and abandoned the attempt to take Onglse, he was able to fight to a bloody draw the army Maol Iosa and Voada Paorach had taken south." Eideard crossed his arms. "Won't Savas actually be *expecting* you to do exactly as you're proposing, Ceanndraoi, Ceannàrd? And with a new full army at his back, won't he smash us decisively?"

Everyone in the room tried to speak at once, many of them rising from their seats to argue with their neighbors. The result-ing cacophony caused Orla to glance at Magaidh in confusion. She could discern little in the barrage of shouts and curses, and even Greum's booming voice was lost. Clenched fists were raised, fingers were pointed, and àrds and draoi alike quarreled amongst themselves. Finally Greum's pounding of his walking stick on the tiles quieted the room enough that he could make himself heard over the ruckus.

"*Enough of this!*" he shouted, and those in the room began to take their seats again, still muttering. Greum's voice took on a scolding, angry tone. "Àrd Iosa, are you proposing that we stay here and wait for Savas' army to come across the River Meadham again? As I've said, we've fewer draoi and warriors now than we had then. If there's defeat waiting for us in Albann Deas, then that same defeat waits here for us as well. Or do you have some better plan to offer?"

"I don't," Eideard answered just as forcefully, standing again. His head turned, and Orla found herself looking directly into the man's piercing stare. "But we do have the Moonshadow with us once more. Perhaps Draoi Orla would give her opinion."

Orla took a gasping breath as her hands lifted involuntarily and she began to shake her head. Those in the room craned their necks to find her, and Magaidh pressed close to her as if to shield her. But Greum had already reacted.

"*No!*" He barked out that single word, as percussive as a thunderclap in the hall. "Draoi Orla and the Moonshadow have no voice in this. I am ceanndraoi, and Comhnall Mac Tsagairt is ceannàrd, and we have already made our decision. This is not a debate."

"If you've no intention of listening to anyone else, Ceanndraoi," Eideard persisted, "then I, for one, see no use in staying here any longer. You've not convinced me that your strategy is anything but folly, and I tell you that Clan Iosa won't be part of it. Perhaps if the Moonshadow's draoi can persuade me otherwise, we might join you. But until then . . ."

Eideard gathered his cloak around him. He stalked toward the door of the meeting hall with several of his lieutenants and a hand of the other àrds following him. "*Iosa!*" Greum shouted after him, slamming the end of his stick on the tiles once more, but the àrd paid no attention. As he passed near Orla and

Magaidh, Orla could see Eideard's earth-brown eyes under the ridge of his brow, the battle scars that marked his face, and the frown that twisted his mouth. He nodded to Orla as he passed, his long, braided hair—nearly the same color as his eyes but touched with strands of red—falling in errant strands over his forehead. She wanted to speak to him, to tell him that she wasn't Voada, that she was afraid to call up the Moonshadow or her mother in her anamacha, and that she knew nothing of war except for her time in the encampments. But he was already past and striding down the corridor of Bàn Cill before she could find the words.

Magaidh touched her shoulder, and Orla looked back to the hall. Greum was staring at her, his lips pressed together until they vanished under his beard and his eyes narrowed to slits.

"Come with me," Magaidh whispered to Orla. "Let's go back to your rooms. We don't need to be here any longer either."

Orla could only agree.

Magaidh and Sorcha were with Orla when Ceanndraoi Greum and Ceannàrd Comhnall came to her rooms following the meeting. Sorcha rose from where she was sitting at the small dining table with the other two women. She curtsied to both of the men and wordlessly left the apartment, shutting the outer door firmly behind her. No one spoke until the door thudded into the jamb and Orla went to swivel the wooden privacy bar into its brackets. The two men watched her as she returned to her seat; Comhnall had taken Sorcha's seat next to Magaidh, but Greum Red-Hand remained standing, leaning on his walking stick and ignoring the other chair at the table.

"Ceanndraoi?" Orla said, gesturing to the chair. "Would you like some wine? I've another mug Sorcha could bring for us."

"That won't be necessary," Greum said. "I'll be blunt, Draoi Orla. Did you and Àrd Eideard plan that little scene earlier?"

Orla was already shaking her head before Greum finished his

question. "No, Ceanndraoi. I didn't even know who Àrd Eideard
was before this afternoon. Truthfully."

"And that's as I told you, Ceanndraoi," Comhnall interjected.
He placed his hand on Magaidh's; Orla saw the two exchange
knowing smiles, as if they each knew what the other was thinking. "Magaidh would have said something to me had that been
arranged. Eideard is ambitious. He'd like the title I carry." With
his free hand, Comhnall touched the torc of the ceannàrd.

Greum sniffed. The expression on his face made Orla wonder
if he believed either of them. His angry gaze went from Comhnall
to Orla. "I've warned you about the Moonshadow and your mother's shade within your anamacha. You've not engaged with either
of them?"

Again Orla shook her head. "No, Ceanndraoi." She could feel
her anamacha moving close behind her, the coldness of them
penetrating her cloak.

"That temple you created—how could you have possibly done
that without the Moonshadow herself?"

"She didn't use the Moonshadow, Ceanndraoi," Magaidh interrupted. "She's already told you that, and I was there with her in
Magh da Chèo. It wasn't the Moonshadow that she used or Voada
either. Only Iomhar."

"Bah," Greum spat. His stick lifted and struck the tiles again.
"Iomhar alone? That's simply not possible."

"Are you now calling both of us liars, Ceanndraoi?" Magaidh
asked. "Because if you are, perhaps the ceannàrd and I will take
Draoi Orla with us back to Clan Mac Tsagairt and let you fight the
Mundoa without us and without the clans who would follow the
ceannàrd. Why, given what happened today, Clan Iosa would undoubtedly join us . . ."

As Magaidh was speaking, Orla felt the anamacha enter her,
and the storm clouds of Magh da Chèo overlaid her sight. A single
shade stood before her, the others within the anamacha holding
back. She knew the ghost's face. <Orla, our daughter . . . Listen to
us . . .> It was her mother's voice, clear and bold as she remembered it, and the shade spread her arms as if to hug her. Orla

nearly sobbed at the emotions that wracked her, and if she recalled Greum's admonition not to listen to her mother's presence,
she ignored it now. She embraced the ghost, spreading her own
arms and feeling the presence fill her.

". . . and their allies as well," Magaidh was saying, her voice
hard to hear against the roar of the anamacha's world.

"Listen to me," Orla said loudly. Her voice was overlaid with
that of Voada, filling it with an authority that wrenched around
the heads of everyone in the room to stare at her. She knew that
Greum and Magaidh at least would see that she was with her
anamacha. Voada's voice whispered to her as she spoke. "Ceanndraoi, my mother was doing what was best for the Cateni when
she took the title of ceanndraoi and went south with Ceannàrd
Iosa. She nearly succeeded in ridding Albann of the Mundoa,
but in the end she couldn't contain the Moonshadow. *But I can,*"
she told them, her voice rising. "With my mam's help, with her
experience, I can. With Draoi Magaidh's help, with Sorcha's
help, I can. And I'll also tell you that my mother believes that
Eideard's right: the strategy you're proposing now would be a
mistake."

Greum scoffed. "Brave words from a half child still struggling
to control her anamacha. Is that you talking, Draoi Orla, or is that
Voada?"

"It's both of us," Orla answered, "as you already know."

"So you wish to be named ceanndraoi, and Eideard Iosa would
be ceannàrd?" Greum sniffed again, hammering the butt of his
staff on the floor. "Well, neither of those things is going to happen. I am ceanndraoi, Comhnall is ceannàrd, and we *will* follow
the plans I've given to the àrds and the draoi, and those who fail
to follow can be damned by Elia for their cowardice. So, Draoi
Magaidh, Ceannàrd Comhnall, Draoi Orla, are you cowards like
Eideard Iosa, or will you join us when Savas makes his move?—
and he *will* move, and soon. All the signs point to it. War is coming whether we want it or not. Will you fight, or will you cower in
the mountains of the north and hope that the Mundoa can't find
you? Those are your choices. Those are your *only* choices."

<Smash the arrogant pig . . . We will help you do it. Smash him and claim his title . . . Become what you must become . . .> Her mother's voice crooned the words, and Orla heard the others within the anamacha speaking in unison with her, the vibrant, compelling voice of the Moonshadow loud among them. Orla ignored them, blocking them from her mind as she listened to the trio of people in the room with her.

"We'll fight with you, Ceanndraoi," Comhnall said easily. "Those of Clan Mac Tsagairt aren't afraid to spill their blood. We proved that with Ceanndraoi Voada, and we'll prove it again. Magaidh?"

The draoi was shaking her head. "I've not yet heard Ceanndraoi Greum's answer to my question," she said. "Are you saying that both Draoi Orla and I are liars, that she didn't do as she said she did when she created the Moonshadow's temple? I won't follow someone who believes that I lie, nor will I suggest that anyone else I know follow such a person, including my husband."

Greum's eyes narrowed further, his voice no more than a mumble. "I was angry," he said. "I only wondered if you were mistaken in your assumption about Draoi Orla."

"Then you believe that *I* lied, Ceanndraoi?" Orla said. <Smash him . . .>

"Would it matter?" he asked, turning toward her.

"There was no lie. It was only Iomhar's power that I used to create the temple," she responded. "What I suggest you consider is this: can you imagine what I might be capable of with my mam's shade or the Moonshadow herself? Be careful what you say, Ceanndraoi, because if you insult me, you insult Leagsaidh Moonshadow, you insult Iomhar, you insult my mother, and you insult all of those who dwell with them. They are listening to you right now. They howl at me, and if you could hear what they tell me and what they say about you, you wouldn't stand there so arrogantly. Do you think your anamacha more powerful than mine, Ceanndraoi? Do you think you could have stood against the Moonshadow and prevailed when my mam held it? Would you be willing to make that mistake now? Voada is with me, and she says to tell you that if I want the torc of the ceanndraoi, I should simply take it now."

Greum took a step back from her, his breath a hiss as he touched the silver-wrapped brass torc around his neck with a ruddy hand. "You're the arrogant one, if you believe you'll fare better with the Moonshadow than she did."

<Now! Kill him before he calls his own anamacha . . . Make him an example. Become the ceanndraoi as we were . . .>

But Orla pushed Voada back further in her mind. *<No,>* she told her. *<That isn't what I want. Not now. I have to find my own path, Mam.>*

"Ceanndraoi," she said, her voice now only her own, "here's the simple truth. I don't want your title unless it's freely given to me. I know little of war, and so regardless of what my mother believes, I don't *know* whether you and the ceannàrd are right or whether Eideard Iosa is. But I spoke the truth about the temple. I trust those who believe me. I trust Sorcha above all, who helped me escape from the Mundoa. I trust Magaidh, who has shown me more than you could about what it means to be a draoi. Beyond those two . . ." Orla shrugged. "Let me ask you this, Ceanndraoi: what would it mean if the Moonshadow's anamacha were with your army? Is that a weapon you want, or are you willing to leave it behind? It all depends on how you answer me now. Do you believe that I spoke the truth to you?"

Her mother's voice and the other voices in the anamacha shrieked their fury at that. *<Be quiet,>* she told them. *<This is my decision to make.>* Again she pushed them back, and back even more, until she felt the anamacha slip from her entirely and the winds of Magh da Chèo receded from her mind. Her vision clearer, she held Greum's gaze, waiting patiently for him to answer, her head cocked slightly to the side.

Finally Greum gave her a bare hint of a nod. "I believe you," he said, "and the Moonshadow is a weapon we need."

"Then you'll have it, Ceanndraoi," she said.

"Good," Greum managed to say. He looked to Comhnall. "The

ceannàrd and I should go and talk to the àrds and draoi before they leave Bàn Cill. If you'll excuse us, Draoi Orla, Draoi Magaidh . . ."

Comhnall rose from his seat and kissed Magaidh on the forehead. The two men left the room, and Orla let out a deep, long sigh. Behind her, she heard Magaidh take a sip of her wine, the pottery scraping against wood as she lifted it. Orla rose and opened the inner door. She smiled, seeing Sorcha standing on the other side, where she'd obviously been listening to the conversation.

"I hope you don't believe that apology," Sorcha said quietly. "The man still doesn't believe you." Behind them Magaidh chuckled at the comment.

"I know," Orla told her. "It doesn't matter."

Sorcha cocked her head to the side, her long hair sliding from her shoulder. "You're changing. The Orla who left the Mundoan encampment wouldn't have stood up to Greum Red-Hand as you just did." Sorcha's hand covered Orla's, and she leaned forward. Her soft voice was breathy, close to Orla's ear, the words warm against the side of her neck. "I think it's a wonderful change. And necessary."

Orla hugged Sorcha, her arms around her waist.

Magaidh's chair scraped against the tiles, and Orla heard the rustle of linen. "I'm going to find Comhnall and try to learn what Greum's really thinking."

Orla released Sorcha, stepping back. "You don't need to go, Magaidh," she said. "Stay, and the three of us will drink the rest of the wine."

Magaidh smiled, her gaze moving between Sorcha and Orla. "No," she said, still smiling. "I think I'll leave the wine to the two of you." She moved to the room's door. Her hand on the leather pull loop, she paused. "Sorcha's right, Orla. You're changing and becoming stronger, and I'm glad to see it. You do remind me of your mam, and I'll be here for you as I was for your mother. There's still more I want to show you: how to be a war draoi, how to cast your spells from a moving chariot."

"I'll need that," Orla told her.

"Then we'll start tomorrow." Magaidh nodded, then pulled the door open and stepped into the corridor beyond. The door swung slowly shut as they heard her footsteps fade.

"I'll also be here for you," Sorcha said. "Always."

Orla hugged the woman again. "And I need that, too," she answered. "More than you know."

PART TWO

YEAR 24 OF
PASHTUK'S REIGN

11

Against the Storm

ALTAN TOOK WHAT ADVANTAGE he could of the endless delays, hoping that Great-Voice Utka wouldn't notice the Cateni couriers he was sending north and west. Storms delayed the arrival of the trio of troop ships by an entire moon and more. Training the new cohorts—mostly younger and inexperienced soldiers who had tasted battle only in a few border skirmishes in Rumeli—took longer than anyone had hoped. Another moon passed before Altan and his sub-commanders were satisfied they could take them into battle against Cateni warriors and their draoi. Then the weather turned foul, the roads became muddy morasses, and Altan sent a message to the Great-Voice that he planned to wait for better weather.

Utka was furious when he learned that and called Altan into his presence. "Your soldiers aren't capable of fighting in poor weather?" he asked before Altan had even finished making his obeisance. "Does their armor melt in the rain? Are the soldiers Emperor Pashtuk has sent you so frail that a bit of Albann's weather gives them lack-breath? Do you say to your enemy 'Oh, let's wait until the sun is shining before we engage'?"

The Great-Voice's guards chuckled at the jest, and Altan forced a tight smile to his lips, pushing down the rush of irritation at

Utka's sarcasm. "It's the roads, Great-Voice," he answered. There was no chair set before the Great-Voice's throne, so Altan stood there, the rain from the downpour outside dripping from his woolen cloak and puddling on the tiles at his feet. "I've fought battles in worse weather, but we've a long march in front of us. With the mud and flooding, the supply train wagons are going to have trouble keeping up with the infantry and the mounted troops, and the sihirki generally ride with the wagons. Our war chariots are lighter, but may also bog down. If we happen to encounter Cateni forces early, then having the supply train a day or more behind could be disastrous. As soon as we begin to move, we have to assume that word will go out to the clans. I'd like us to be moving faster than those rumors. In my opinion, Great-Voice, waiting another hand or two of days will make a great difference to our chances. Besides, that will give the shipwrights more time to complete their tasks."

Great-Voice Utka stroked the oiled braids of his beard. "Is that why you want to linger here, Commander, or have you simply lost your taste for battle in the last year? Perhaps I should talk to Sub-Commander Musa or Ilkur and see if one of them is less worried about a little mud and rain."

Altan bowed his head toward the man. *He sits there: a noxious, lazy lizard.* "I serve at the emperor's pleasure," he answered. "My scribe would be happy to write a letter of resignation to the emperor for me to sign, if that's the Great-Voice's wish." *And you can deal with the emperor's response*, Altan thought, knowing that Utka would also be considering that.

"I do *not* wish that!" With the half shout, Utka slammed his fist down on the arm of the throne. The gilded brass bracelet on his wrist cracked hard against the marble, the report of metal against stone echoing in the hall. The guards on either side of Utka glanced at one another, hands tightening on the shafts of their spears. "What I wish is to see the northern clans finally under the rule of Emperor Pashtuk. What I wish is to see the island of those accursed draoi taken as it should have been long ago and their temple there razed. I want to see the bones of their warriors white on the fields. That's what I *wish*, Commander, and you seem to be telling me that the damned *weather* prevents me from having that wish fulfilled."

Altan thought that the Great-Voice sounded like nothing more than a petulant child throwing a tantrum. Unfortunately he was a child who could order Altan's head removed from his shoulders if he wished, and the emperor was no longer there to stop him. "Then as the Great-Voice wishes," he said, careful not to put too much emphasis on the last word, "I will have the troops arrayed, the wagons supplied, and we will leave Savur at sunrise tomorrow regardless of the weather. If you'll excuse me, Great-Voice, I have much to do . . ."

Altan could see Utka's eyes—*like those of some fat sow*—narrow as if the man were trying to decide whether to let Altan go. Altan made a deep bow and swept his cloak back over his shoulder, sending droplets flying with the motion. He half expected Utka to bark something at him as he started to back away, head down, toward the reception room's doors. But Utka only grunted as Altan retreated. "Our commander's terrified by a bit of mud," he heard Utka say *sotto voce* to the nearest guard, who gave a dutiful laugh at the jibe. Altan pretended that he hadn't heard. The door wardens swung the door open behind him with a quiet protest of hinges; Altan gave the Great-Voice a final bow and finally turned to stride away.

It was worse than Altan had expected. Great-Voice Utka, against Altan's express wishes, had insisted that the troop ships assigned to transport the army to Onglse be harbored in Muras on the River Meadham rather than at the better but more distant harbor of Gediz on the Storm Sea. The plan had been to follow the main road west along the southern bank of the River Iska from Savur to Trusa, crossing the Iska there at the former capital, then traverse the Great North Road to Muras and the River Meadham.

The first four days, the rain was persistent and torrential, pelting down and turning the roads into nearly impassable quag-mires. The boots of the soldiers were packed with heavy mud up to their knees as they marched along miserably. Altan rode in his war chariot in the midst of the line with Tolga driving the pair of horses from the traces—not the emperor's gaudy whites, which had been left behind in the stables of Savur, but their well-trained gray-and-black warhorses. He cursed loudly as the hooves of the horses tossed clods of mud into the air, painting his body with brown streaks. The wheels were caked with the same mud, and the chariot had twice sunk halfway to the axle; the troops had needed to help the horses pull it loose again.

Worse, the Iska was leaving its banks. The trees along the river ascended from brown pools, and the fields nearest the river were shallow lakes.

In good weather, they would have easily been in Trusa in a hand of days, but Altan figured they were still three or more days away at this pace. As for the army's supply train, it was mud-coated and straggling somewhere in the distance.

"We're not going to get to Onglse any quicker than if we'd just waited in Savur for this to stop."

Sub-Commander Musa's chariot had come alongside Altan's. Under the shelter of his helmet, his thick black eyebrows were lowered as rain dripped from the ridges of battle scars on his brown skin. "All we've done is show our hand," Musa continued. "By now the rumors are traveling faster than we are."

Altan knew that to be true; in fact, he was counting on it. "I have my orders, Musa," Altan told him, and Musa tapped his cui-rass in response.

"I understand completely, Commander." He glanced around to see if anyone other than their drivers was within earshot. "But between us, the Great-Voice has made a mistake, and I just hope we don't end up being the ones to pay for it."

Altan gave no reply to that. "Did you send out the scouts I asked for?"

"I did, and they just returned. That's what I came up to tell you. They say the Iska's completely overrun its banks near Trusa and that the bridge crossing the tributary of the Big Muddy might not be safe. They said that the locals have heard rumors of the Great Bridge at Trusa also being closed due to the Iska's flooding."

Altan sighed at the news. "Send our best engineers forward to inspect the Big Muddy's bridge. If it's truly not safe, then have them make it so—we don't have any choice unless we want to travel overland around the entire tributary system of the Iska and waste an entire season doing it. We have to have the bridge crossable—and the Great Bridge as well, though we'll deal with that when we get there. We'll figure on camping today on this side of the Big Muddy and crossing over tomorrow. Pass the word along, and get those engineers working."

Musa nodded, sending raindrops spattering from the plume atop his helm. His driver yanked hard on the reins of the horses, and Musa's chariot moved quickly toward the rear of the line. "I know this isn't what you planned for, Commander," Tolga commented as Musa left.

Altan wondered just how much Tolga knew of what he'd planned. Tolga might be his lover, and he trusted the man, but he'd still been careful not to tell him everything. He wondered if perhaps he'd been talking in his sleep. "No, it's not," he admitted. "None of it is. Everything's shifting."

"I'm sure you've made excellent contingency plans, then, Altan." Tolga glanced back over his shoulder.

Altan resisted the temptation to snap at Tolga for his presumption, especially here in the open. But there was no one around to overhear, and Altan suspected that most of the men were aware of or suspected their relationship and kept a judicious silence about it. Certainly both Musa and Ilkur had known about Tolga's predecessor, Lucian. Altan swallowed his irritation, knowing that it was at least partially induced by the damned unrelenting rain.

"There are plans," Altan answered. "As to whether they're excellent or not . . . Take us forward, Tolga. I need to see things for myself."

The Big Muddy was living up to its name; what Altan saw was a torrent of opaque brown water strewn with logs, uprooted trees, and other floating debris. What was generally a shallow and relatively tame river was now raging, fast-moving rapids, unfordable anywhere along its swollen length. The debris the river carried was crashing into and stacking up against the stone pilings of the bridge, the water sluicing in an angry froth through what remained of the open space under its single span.

But the engineers thought the bridge still sound enough to cross. "She'll hold, Commander," was the judgment of Halim, a stout, short, tree trunk of a man with gnarled fingers that looked as if they'd been encased in ancient worn leather. Without helm or hood, his dark hair dripped constantly down the oilcloth cloak he wore. His hands clenched and unclenched as he stared at the bridge, scowling gap-toothed at the structure. A small, dilapidated farming village huddled around a small knoll on the far side, the buildings dripping forlornly in the rain. The residents weren't visible, though trails of gray-white smoke from the chimneys and the smell of burning peat indicated that they were there, safely inside. "I've been on her, and the beams are shaking from all the stuff in the water hitting her, but they're still sound. I've had my people shoring up the upstream structure to slow down the erosion of the banks. If this rain keeps up, I won't guarantee she'll still be standing in two days, but right now . . ." A shrug. "She'll hold. But if we need to cross, I wouldn't wait, were I you."

As Altan watched from the eastern bank just above the bridge, what appeared to be part of the thatched roof of a small cottage came twirling down the river, spinning in the current, hit the stone piers of the far bank, and shattered into a maelstrom of sodden straw.

Altan glanced back down the road. "And the supply train?" he asked.

"The bridge will hold for now, as I said. Today. Probably to-morrow. Whether she's still standing by the time the supply train catches up to us is in the hands of the One-God and the weather," Halim answered. "I wish I could give you a better answer, Com-mander, but I can't."

"Then we'd better start praying to the One-God to listen and do something," Altan said. "I appreciate the honesty, Halim. Thanks for your work here."

"I'll make sure the bridge stands, Commander, for as long as I possibly can."

"Do that," Altan told him, clapping the man on the shoulder. "In the meantime, I'm going to have the chariots, the mounted troops, the archers, and infantry cross. We'll make our evening's camp on the other side rather than waiting here." With that, Altan splashed through the puddles and mud back to the road where Tolga waited with his chariot and climbed in. "Back to the line," he said to Tolga. "We'll lead everyone across."

Altan squinted against the searing light. "By the emperor's hairy balls," he growled sleepily, "is that actually the *sun*?"

"It is," Tolga answered. His body was a black shape against the glare coming from the tent flaps. "The rain stopped during the night, too. It's a clear dawn. The camp's still a swamp, though."

Altan yawned and stretched. "Doesn't matter. We can move on to Trusa. Marching in sunlight will feel like a reprieve after all the wet and gloom. Tell Musa, Ilkur, and the other sub-commanders to get their men ready to move on, then get my chariot ready. Any news on the supply train?"

"They're still at least a day behind, but the bridge at Big Muddy is still holding. Hopefully they'll be able to cross and won't be stranded on the other side."

"That's even better news," Altan grunted. "Let me get dressed, then."

"I could help," Tolga said, smiling. "If you wish, Commander."

Altan laughed. "Only if you promise that you'll help me dress rather than undress. I intend to get to Trusa by day's end."

"I won't delay you *too* long, Commander. I promise." Tolga gestured to the light behind him. "But we really should let the sun dry off the road a bit first, don't you think?"

"You're becoming a bad influence, Tolga."

"I merely want my commander to be happy," Tolga answered.

"Then come here," Altan said with a low growl. "We need to be quick . . ."

12

A Game of Fidhcheall

GREUM RED-HAND CALLED THE DRAOI and àrds together two days after the initial meeting. Orla entered alongside Magaidh. The morning light slanted in through the windows, pouring down on a fidhcheall board and figures set on a table between Ceanndraoi Greum and Ceannàrd Mac Tsagairt. Both men arose as the draoi and àrds slowly filed into the hall.

Greum gestured toward the board. "The pieces have begun to fall into place," he said, looking at all who'd entered. "We've had word from several dependable sources that Commander Savas is moving slowly north with his army, though the weather has been against him. He should be in Trusa by now. Our contacts among the Cateni conscripts inform us that the army is ultimately heading toward Onglse. The ceannàrd and I believe we should meet them long before that happens. They also say that the plan is to move from Trusa toward Muras via the Great North Road, where Savas intends to split the army. The main assault force will ship down the Meadham and up the coast; the rest will cross the Meadham and travel overland toward the coast and set up encampments there in order to stop Onglse from receiving reinforcements from the clans. We've seen furious shipbuilding going on in Muras, so we expect our information is correct."

"That could simply be a feint," Àrd Eideard Iosa interjected. He'd returned to Onglse upon hearing that Orla and the Moonshadow's anamacha would be part of the ceanndraoi's army. He swept an arm through the air for emphasis. His long hair was falling out of the ties of his braid, and red-brown strands whipped over the scars on his face. "They could still take the Stormwind Road from Trusa to Gediz and board ships there to Onglse. That's how Savas returned from Onglse the last time. If we bring our army to Muras and find that Savas has gone west, Onglse would be entirely open to them until we could retreat back to the island. They'd be there before we could return."

"But if that happens," Magaidh's husband answered, "we could push south, as Voada did. Savas would be forced to abandon the attack on Onglse once again."

Eideard gave a scoffing laugh. "We also know Great-Voice Utka hasn't made the same mistake as his predecessor and left the south open to invasion; the emperor sent several troop ships, and not all of them are heading north. If we push into Albann Deas, there will still be an army there defending it—a smaller one, admittedly, but dangerous. We won't be sacking Trusa or Savur while Commander Savas takes Onglse, as Voada Moonshadow did. We'd be walking into a trap with Mundoan troops at our front and Savas ready to come at us from the rear once he's burned Bàn Cill to the ground. There'd be nothing but ashes left where we're standing right now." He looked directly at Orla then, the challenge in his stare causing her to take a step back. "Since she holds the Moonshadow, what does Draoi Orla believe is the right strategy?"

Orla expected Greum Red-Hand to interrupt or Ceannàrd Mac Tsagairt to speak. Neither did. The silence in the room made the air feel thick and heavy, and Orla found herself wanting to retreat. Nearly all the àrds and draoi in the room were staring at her. She could feel Magaidh's supportive warmth at her right side, and on the left . . .

The cold of her anamacha pressed into her skin, and she heard their massed and contradictory voices overlay the quiet of the hall. <*You must answer them . . . This is your moment to seize, Orla . . . It's your death they want, so one of them can claim us . . . Ignore them; they have no authority over you . . .*>

She also felt a presence rising against the voices, and that one's voice was stronger than any of the rest. <*Orla, my daughter . . .*>

<*Mam!*> Orla thought back to her, a complex surge of emotions accompanying the word: sadness at the memory of her loss; the love for her mother that she'd never lost; joy at being able to speak to her again. And fear—for Orla felt another darker and stronger presence lurking behind Voada, and she knew that was the Moonshadow herself. <*I don't know what to say to them.*>

<*Here . . .*> The voice was not just her mother's; Orla could feel another voice reverberating in the single word as the Moonshadow pressed closer to her. <*Look into the shadows . . .*>

A vista opened before Orla, as if she were a hawk banking in the wind high above the world. She could feel cold air moving around her. The movement and the height made her momentarily dizzy, but she fought the nausea, narrowing her eyes. Below she glimpsed a river glinting in failing sunlight, and on its banks sat a massive walled city. Around and through the city, an army moved: a plague of armored insects crossing the bridge that spanned the wide river, moving through the city's great lanes, and exiting through the gates on the far side. The army crawled forward on the road leading away from the city, spilling out well to either side, the shapes of men, horses, war chariots, and wagons spreading long, dark shadows across the land at their right hands. *Look at the shadows*, the anamacha's voices had told her— her mother's voice strongest among them—and Orla suddenly realized what they had meant.

A sun setting in the west, the shadows racing eastward away from them . . .

"Savas' army is marching north," Orla said aloud, and with the words the vision faded. Orla blinked, the cold presence of the anamacha leaving her. "Not west. North. Ceanndraoi Greum is correct. They're heading for Muras."

Orla and Sorcha were eating dinner in Orla's rooms when someone knocked urgently on the door: three hard, demanding raps. Sorcha's eyebrows lifted, and Orla shrugged. Sorcha pushed her chair back from the table and went to the door, opening it a crack to peer out. "Àrd Iosa," Orla heard Sorcha say. The woman glanced back at Orla, who nodded. Sorcha opened the door fully. "Please come in. Draoi Paorach is at dinner at the moment, but . . ."

Eideard said nothing. He stalked into the room like a thundercloud pushed by a harsh wind, a scowl on his face. His gaze found Orla's, and the scowl deepened. "Was your intention to humble me before the ceanndraoi and ceannàrd? Are you now allied with them? Is that the game you're playing?"

Orla set down her spoon. She gestured to the chair across from her. "Are you hungry, Àrd Iosa? Sorcha, would you get a plate and a knife for our guest?"

Eideard sniffed. "I'm not hungry. I asked you a question."

"You may not be hungry, but I am. Sit. Have some mulled wine, if nothing else, and we can talk." When Eideard still didn't move, Orla gestured again at the chair. "Please, Àrd. Sit."

The scowl deepened yet further, but Eideard took two quick strides to the table and slid into the offered seat. Sorcha padded to the cupboard to place a mug in front of him, then curled her fingers around the handle of the clay pot on the table and poured steaming spiced wine into the mug. Placing it down again, she slid a crock with a spindle toward him. "Honey?" she asked. Eideard didn't answer. Sorcha gave Orla a glance and went silently into the next room, leaving the two alone, though she didn't shut the door.

Eideard was glaring at Orla, his dark eyes like black stones glittering in twin caves. Orla forced herself to hold his gaze, afraid that he'd think her weak if she looked away. The tableau held for several breaths, then Orla broke off a small piece of bread and dipped it into the stew in the bowl before her. She chewed the bread and swallowed before she answered. "I simply told the ceanndraoi and ceannàrd what I saw in the vision the Moonshadow and my mam gave me. In it, I saw Savas' army going north to Muras. If I'd seen them going west, I would have told them that, and I would have told them that their strategy was flawed. But that's not what I saw."

"So now you're an expert on military strategy?"

"Hardly," she told him, an anger flaring in her that she wasn't entirely able to dampen. She wished Magaidh were here; she would know what to say and how to handle the àrd's questions, but Magaidh was in her own rooms. *What would my mam say? How would she respond?* Orla tried to imagine her mother's voice emerging from her own mouth. "But I'm not as stupid as you seem to think I am either."

The words came out more sharply than Orla might have spoken on her own, and the rebuke caused the scowl on the man's scarred face to vanish for a moment. Orla saw his shoulders drop slightly. "I apologize, Draoi Orla. I never meant to imply that. It's just . . ." His hand rose, palm upturned, then dropped again. "The ceannàrd means well, but he's old and too tied to Ceanndraoi Greum, and everyone has seen how you and his wife have become close. As for the ceanndraoi . . . well, I assume my opinion's obvious enough to you, and I suspect it's one we share—at least I thought so until this morning."

"I'm not sure what you want me to say, Àrd Iosa, or why you're here. You're right—Ceanndraoi Greum and I are hardly friends. Even though he was my teacher in the arts of the draoi until Draoi Magaidh came, he doesn't seem to like me. He knew my mother and the anamacha that's chosen me, and I suspect that's why." With that, she saw Eideard's gaze travel the room as if searching for the Moonshadow, though, like Sorcha, he obviously couldn't see the anamacha standing just behind Orla's chair. Orla brought his gaze back to her as she picked up her spoon, twirling the wooden utensil in her fingers. "Because of my mother, he has his reasons to distrust me, I suppose. No, I don't *like* the ceanndraoi or even particularly trust him. But I still have to respect him."

"Enough that you'll be silent if you disagree with him?"

Orla gave a quick exhalation of a laugh at that. "I won't be silent. But he knows war far better than I do, and I won't oppose his strategies merely because I don't like the man." She stared at Eideard across the small table. "Is that what *you're* doing, Àrd?"

His scowl returned for a moment, then the lines of his face eased, and he suddenly chuckled. "That's a fair question, I suppose. And maybe there's a grain of truth in it."

"I think more a sackful than a grain," Orla told him. "But you were right to say that taking our army to Muras would be a terrible mistake if Savas instead went west. It would be, but I tell you I *saw* Savas' army on the northern road toward Muras."

"And you can trust that vision?"

Orla felt the anamacha touch her back like a cold northern winter breeze and heard the whispers of their voices. "The vision came from my mam; she wouldn't lie to me."

Again Eideard's gaze traveled the room as if searching for the unseen. He shook his head.

"Just because you can't see them doesn't mean they're not there," Orla told him.

"Maol Iosa could see the taibhse, I was always told." <*Yes . . .*> whispered her mother's voice at that statement. <*I remember that . . .*> Eideard shrugged. "I'm blind and deaf to all the ghosts around us."

"Consider yourself lucky, Àrd Iosa," Orla answered. "Then they can't insist that you help do their bidding. Sometimes I think it's more curse than blessing."

"They say trying to contain and use the Moonshadow—" Eideard began, then stopped.

"Drove my mother mad?" Orla finished for him. "There's often truth buried in gossip. Is that what worries you? Do I appear mad to you?"

"No," Eideard answered, his voice flat and inflectionless. "Just terribly young and naïve."

<*Maol Iosa was a talented warrior, and ambitious . . .*> Her mother's voice crooned to her amid the others in the anamacha. <*That*

is why we worked together well. I used his talent and his ambition to make him do my bidding. This Eideard is very much like him . . .> "I won't argue with you," Orla said. "What is it you want from me, Àrd Eideard? Surely you didn't just come here to berate a terribly young and naïve draoi for stopping you from making a terrible fool of yourself."

"A terrible—" he started to say before his lips pressed together in the familiar scowl. "Fair enough," he said. "Yes, I was angry. I thought . . . I was *certain* that Savas would avoid Muras."

"Because it's what *you* would do if you were him?" Orla asked with mock innocence. She could hear the massed laughter from her anamacha at that jibe. Eideard drew in his breath, cocking his head to one side. She thought he was going to shout, but instead, surprising her, he laughed.

"*Tha!*" he exclaimed. *Yes!* "You understand me all too well, Draoi Orla. Yes, I would do exactly that, and *not* taking his army west as I would have done is a mistake, as Savas will now learn. Because of you." He nodded to her.

<He's very like his uncle,> Orla heard her mother whisper among the other voices. *<Proud, but willing to admit when he's wrong . . .>* Another voice seemed to join that of her mother, a deeper and stronger one. *<He would make a good ceannàrd for you . . .>*

"I don't need a ceannàrd," Orla said aloud, and Eideard's eyes narrowed.

"You will one day," he told her. "You see, there are things that I know without having the Moonshadow whisper them to me. One of those is that you're right not to trust the Red-Hand. I'm sorry for disturbing you, Draoi Orla, and for doubting you and thinking you merely the ceanndraoi's lackey. That's a mistake that I won't make again." Eideard inclined his head to Orla. "My uncle and your mother found each other good partners in war, if nothing else. Perhaps we were destined to be together in the same way." He didn't wait for an answer—not that Orla could formulate one for that statement—but pushed his chair back from the table, rose, and left her quarters. The door closed softly behind him.

When Eideard left, Sorcha emerged from the other room, softly applauding. "There are more important things to learn about than simply being a draoi, Orla," she said. "I think you've begun to learn those lessons just as well as those Magaidh's been teaching you."

Orla could only shake her head at that. "I hope you're right, Sorcha."

"Is there anything you need, Orla?" Sorcha asked from the door of Orla's bedchamber. "If not, then I'll retire to my own chamber . . ."

"Stay," Orla told her. "I'm not tired yet." She patted the quilt that covered her. "Sit here for a bit and talk to me."

Sorcha hesitated, then moved to the bed and sat. "What do you want to talk about?"

Orla wasn't sure herself; it really wasn't talk she wanted, just the comfort of Sorcha's presence. "I don't know. What do you think of Eideard?"

Sorcha pressed her lips together, looking at the shuttered window of the chamber before answering. "I think he's arrogant, but an àrd has to be strong-willed and sure of himself if he wants to survive. I hear that he's had several proposals from other àrds trying to marry him to their daughters or sisters, but so far he hasn't accepted any of them. He'll be a good match for the right person." Sorcha's gaze came back to Orla. "A good match for a strong draoi, for instance."

Orla was already shaking her head. "Me, you mean? No, that's never going to happen. After Bakir . . . well, you know."

Sorcha looked toward the closed window again, her back to Orla. "Still, why not? Look at Magaidh and Comhnall. Not every man is like Bakir."

"I know, but . . ." Orla reached out, putting her hand on Sorcha's back and letting her fingers trail down the woman's spine. She felt Sorcha shiver as her hand dropped away. Sorcha turned so that she was looking at Orla again.

"I should go," Sorcha said, but she made no move to leave.

"You told me Alim was never the person you wanted to share a life with," Orla said. "But you said that with others you wouldn't name . . . Who were those others, Sorcha? Why can't you name them?"

"Don't, Orla," Sorcha said. "Please."

"I think I know who they were, Sorcha, and it doesn't matter to me. I understand."

She saw Sorcha's hand start to move on the quilt, and she slid her own hand toward it until their fingers interlaced.

Closing her fingers around Sorcha's, Orla pulled the woman toward her.

13

Fire in the Sky

TWO DAYS LATER, Ceanndraoi Greum—with Orla, Magaidh, and most of the other draoi, the àrds, and their warriors—crossed the narrow strait between Onglse and the mainland of Albann Bràghad in a small fleet of Cateni vessels. They were met on the shore by several other warriors and àrds as well as many of the clan draoi, all of whom had come at the ceannàrd's summons and the verification that Commander Savas and the Mundoan army were on their way northward.

Àrd Iosa approached Orla as they landed on the mainland, his chariot seeming to charge at her as she stepped down onto the shore with Sorcha just behind her and Onglse a fog-wrapped lump well out to sea. Eideard gestured to his chariot and his older driver, Tadgh, standing in the traces. The two horses, night black, blew white clouds from their flaring nostrils as they pawed impatiently at the pebbled beach. "Since Draoi Magaidh has started to train you as a war draoi, you should ride with me to get used to the feel of my chariot, Draoi Orla," Eideard said. The man's smile and the tone of his voice told her that he expected her to comply.

She lifted her chin, pulling up the hood of her red cloak. She felt for the twin oak leaves around her neck, under her torc. "Thank you, Àrd," she said, "but Sorcha and I have made other arrangements."

Eideard's smile collapsed. For a moment Orla thought he was going to argue, but the man only said, "As you wish, then." He tapped Tadgh on the shoulder; the driver pulled at the reins, calling to the horses, and the chariot's wheels spun against the rocks as it rattled off. Eideard didn't look back.

"Was that wise?" Sorcha asked.

Orla could only shrug. "Wise or not, it's done. Come on, we need to find horses to ride."

Orla and Sorcha rode alongside Magaidh in Ceannàrd Mac Tsagairt's contingent near the head of the line that seemed to grow with every passing stripe of the candle. Small bands of clan warriors emerged from the steep hills and the valleys to join the swelling ranks as they marched toward Muras. The north side of the River Meadham was marked by tall pine-studded hills with deep stream-cut valleys between them, descending from the higher, mountainous regions that dominated the central spine of Albann Bràghad. The roads wound like aimless sheep paths through the wrinkled landscape. A trip that a crow could take in but a few stripes of the candle by flying in a straight line might take a full day or more on the ground.

Magaidh was riding in Ceannàrd Mac Tsagairt's chariot; Orla and Sorcha had appropriated a pair of sure-footed brown-and-white Onglse ponies, with Orla's anamacha drifting alongside her like a desultory shadow. By midday Orla wasn't sure that had been the best choice; her rear end was sore and bruised despite the extra padding Sorcha had placed on the saddles.

From the amused expression on Magaidh's face, she understood immediately. "You'll get used to it," she told Orla. "Though on the whole, for a draoi being in a chariot is the better choice."

"You might have warned me," Orla told her.

"People learn best from their mistakes," Magaidh answered. Orla heard multiple laughter at that from Ceannàrd Mac Tsagairt, from his son (and Magaidh's stepson) Hùisdean, who was the chariot's driver, as well as a loud snicker from Sorcha. Orla cast a glance over to Sorcha, who shrugged while still laughing.

"I used to ride Alim's horse back in the women's camp," she said. "*I'm* used to the saddle."

"I'm not sure I ever want to be."

"Then ride with Àrd Iosa, and you won't have to," Ceannàrd Mac Tsagairt told her. He rubbed at the gray stubble on his chin. "Your mam rode with his uncle. Àrd Iosa's a good man, despite his arrogance and"—Mac Tsagairt glanced around before continuing—"despite Ceanndraoi Greum's opinion. Àrd Iosa's driver is Tadgh, who was once Maol Iosa's driver as well, so he knows combat and the needs of a draoi at war better than any. During battle you'll be put in one of the chariots anyway, so you might as well get used to it. Make your choice before the ceanndraoi makes it for you."

Orla could see Magaidh watching Orla's face for her response and nodding to her husband. Magaidh glanced pointedly farther down the line of the army, where Orla could see the Iosa clan's banner—a green-and-blue tartan adorned with an eagle's claw—fluttering in the breeze. The Iosa clan warriors rode horses or walked behind Eideard's chariot. "It'd be good to get your footing in the chariot before your first battle," she said. "Casting spells from a moving, bouncing chariot is far different from doing so while standing on solid ground, and I'll help you practice that as we're traveling. Otherwise the ceanndraoi might put you in the rearguard with all the minor draoi to bother the Mundoa with storms, and no doubt neither your mam nor the Moonshadow would be pleased with you playing such a minor role."

Orla's anamacha slid closer to her at Magaidh's comment, and she could faintly hear their voices in the coldness along her side. <No . . . *Our place is at the front . . . We lead; we do not follow . . .*> Orla wanted to argue with them but found herself without words. She stared back at Eideard's chariot and imagined her mam in a similar chariot, howling and chanting, her hands moving to create spell cages. She imagined lightning and flame erupting from her hands and slamming into the enemy in front of them as the spiked wheels of Maol Iosa's chariot tore into the Mundoan lines and Maol cast spear after spear into their ranks, screaming his own challenges. The image was nearly real, and she knew it came from her mam's memory.

"You'll help me learn this?" Orla asked Magaidh.

"I will, as your mother taught me. The skill comes quickly, especially when you know a battle is coming."

<Yes! That is what we were meant for . . .> Orla wasn't sure whose voice she heard: her mam's, the Moonshadow's, or her own. Her blood pounded in her skull with the vision, her breath came fast, and her fingers clenched white-knuckled around the reins of the pony she rode. She blinked it away, forced herself to take in a deep calming breath and loosen her grip on the reins. Magaidh was watching her, and she knew the woman could see the anamacha pressing against her side, insistent.

"Listen to your own heart," she heard Magaidh continue gently. "Do what it tells you. I'll be here for you, as I was for your mam and she for me."

Orla realized that Sorcha had already pulled her pony to the side of the road, stopping and allowing the line to move past her. Orla gave Magaidh a nod and did the same. They waited, watching the army slowly move past them, until Eideard's chariot approached. The àrd gazed at the two of them, questioning. As his chariot came alongside—the driver Tadgh also eyeing them curiously—Orla kicked her pony to keep pace with the chariot, Sorcha slapping her own pony's reins to follow behind.

"I'm surprised to see you again, Draoi Orla. I thought you'd be riding with Ceannàrd Mac Tsagairt or Ceanndraoi Greum." Orla couldn't determine whether the smile that seemed to lurk on Eideard's bearded lips was amusement or disdain.

"Àrd Iosa," Orla told him, "I shouldn't have turned down your offer to ride with you so abruptly. That was . . ." She hesitated, then pushed forward again. ". . . rude of me."

"So you would have turned down the offer anyway, only not rudely?" he asked.

Orla blinked. "No. I'm only saying—"

She had no chance to say more. With the suddenness of a snake striking, he leaned over the rail of the chariot, plucked her from her saddle as easily as someone lifting a child, placing her on the wooden planks of the chariot before she could protest. She heard Tadgh chuckle as he held the reins of the chariot's horses, balancing himself in the webbing of the traces.

Sorcha rode quickly forward to take Orla's pony's abandoned reins. The chariot lurched over the uneven ground as Tadgh growled at the horses, and Orla grabbed for the rail to steady herself. "There," Eideard said. There was a smug satisfaction on his face as he regarded her. "That's where you should be, ready to ride into battle." He grinned as the chariot lurched again; Orla gripped the rail harder, but Eideard only shifted his weight easily with the motion as Orla imagined a sailor might do on a ship. "Don't worry, you'll get used to how the chariot moves—and it's far better to do it now than when someone's trying to kill you. I'm sure Draoi Magaidh will help you with that also." He cocked his head toward her. "And sitting on a chariot's bench is, well, *gentler* on tender body parts than a saddle." His face split into a smile, and Orla found herself returning it. She saw Sorcha watching them and gave her a quick nod of reassurance.

"You assume too much, Àrd Iosa," she told him, but her smile robbed the words of any true heat.

"Perhaps," he answered, the amusement vanishing from his face. "Tadgh has told me how Ceanndraoi Voada fought from this very platform. Look there." Eideard pointed to the planks below them, and Orla noticed brown stains caught in the grain of the wood. "That's the traces of the blood my uncle and your mother shed in the Battle of Suras, where they both fell. When I took Tadgh as my driver, they expected me to keep my own chariot, but I wanted *this* one, that same chariot Tadgh drove from the field of battle. I wanted to honor my uncle and Ceanndraoi Voada when we meet Savas again, who killed them both. I wanted the commander to see this chariot and know that it holds his doom in the form of the nephew and the daughter of those he fought before. What do you say, Draoi Orla? Is that what you want also?"

Orla had moved her feet away from the stains as Eideard spoke. *My mother's blood? Is that true?*

It was her anamacha that answered, as if a wall of ice were pressing against her left side. <*Yes. We remember the pain, the blood, this chariot. We remember it all . . .*> The anamacha gave a startling wail of distress, and Orla shuddered from the impact of her mother's voice. <*Savas . . . He threw the spear, and our power was drained from the battle . . . We couldn't stop them . . .*> The wail came again, as if the ghost of her mam were experiencing her death once again. Tears gathered involuntarily in Orla's eyes.

Both Eideard and Tadgh were watching her—appraisingly, she thought—and Sorcha as well from alongside the chariot. Orla brought her head up, pressing her lips together but not caring that they could see the tears tracing the slope of her cheeks.

"Aye," she told them. "This is what I want."

Eideard nodded. Tadgh turned his attention back to the horses, and Sorcha looked carefully ahead.

"Then we'll find Savas together," Eideard said. "And we'll have our revenge on him."

A jagged ridgeline of wooded hills just north of the River Meadham's floodplain shielded the Cateni army from being seen by anyone in Muras, which perched on the Meadham's south banks. The town's confines spread out to include a large island in the center of the river. A wide wooden bridge ran from the northern bank of the Meadham to the island, and another connected the island to the town proper on the southern bank.

This, Orla knew, had been the site of her mother's and Maol Iosa's first victory. Voada's army had taken the town in the initial skirmish of her war against the Mundoa, and much of the town had burned to the ground in the wake of that battle.

But Muras had slowly risen from the ashes over the last few years, though scars were still visible. Orla could see the blackened, still-unhealed wounds of ruins as she stared at the town from the heights, only a ride of a few stripes away over a grassy flatland dotted with pastures and farms.

Greum Red-Hand directed the army to encamp well off the road leading north out of Muras, generally sparsely traveled in any case by Cateni going into Muras to purchase Mundoan goods or to sell their produce and livestock at the market there. Ceann-àrd Mac Tsagairt sent a few couples out in plain, ragged garb to scout Muras and report back. They said that several ships capable of ferrying troops were moored on the southern bank of the River Meadham and that the shipwrights' crews were preparing two more—signaling that Commander Savas was definitely intending to invade Onglse, as the gossip around the town confirmed. Food and other supplies for the army were stockpiled in Muras' warehouses. The garrison, most importantly, appeared to be ready and on alert, with more and better-trained Mundoan soldiers and sihirki than there had been when Orla's mam had taken the town.

What pleased Ceanndraoi Greum and Ceannàrd Comhnall the most was that the scouts reported no rumors of the Cateni force moving toward Muras. It seemed the clans were keeping that news to themselves and not sharing it with the Mundoans across the river—and the Mundoa had always been reluctant to venture across the river on their own.

"We'll begin our attack before dawn tomorrow," Greum Red-Hand said to the assembled àrds and trusted draoi. Orla had again pointedly not been invited to this strategy meeting, but Magaidh had brought her along despite that. Ceiteag was there too, standing next to the Red-Hand and staring out over the assembly. "We'll have the minor draoi send a fog down to conceal our approach."

"That's exactly what Ceanndraoi Voada did," Magaidh interjected. "I was there, if you remember, Ceanndraoi, and so was my husband. She sent a fog out ahead of our chariots and warriors to hide us, and we were among them before they knew we were there." Greum Red-Hand's face soured at Magaidh's use of the ceanndraoi title for Voada. Orla could see that he liked what she said next even less. "Don't you think, Ceanndraoi Greum, that given that history, if they see a strange fog coming toward them, they'll understand what it means and respond accordingly?"

"Draoi Mac Tsagairt is right." Eideard spoke up loudly before Greum could answer. "Savas isn't a stupid man. If he knows that we've put together an army—and I don't care what our scouts have said, Savas *must* know from spies in the north that we've left Onglse—then he also knows we're expecting him to come to Muras. He'll have warned his troops about what happened last time. Ceanndraoi Greum, Ceannàrd Mac Tsagairt: to simply repeat what Voada and my uncle did is—" Orla saw his lips start to form the word "foolish" before he stopped himself. "—unlikely to be successful," he finished.

"And what would you have us do, Àrd Iosa? Simply ride up to the bridge and ask them nicely for permission to cross?"

Orla could feel her anamacha move closer to her. *<This is stupidity . . . Listen to us. Let us guide you . . .>* Orla forced their presence away from her mind, answering them with a sharp *<No! I know what to do.>*

Eideard's face flushed under his beard. "I'm only saying—" he began when Orla interrupted, causing Eideard's mouth to snap shut and everyone's heads to turn to her.

"There's no need for us to burn Muras to the ground again," she said. "We only need to stop Savas from receiving the boats he needs to reach Onglse. We can accomplish that *without* attacking the town with our entire army."

"Girl, you don't need to lecture the—" Ceiteag started in a scolding, dismissive tone, her ancient face screwed up in anger. This time it was Comhnall who spoke up to interrupt.

"Let her speak, Draoi Ceiteag," the ceannàrd said. "Ceanndraoi, Draoi Orla's not wrong. Go on, Orla. What are you saying?"

"It depends on what you and the ceanndraoi want," Orla said, turning from Ceiteag's unrepentant stare. "We've reached Muras before Savas; he must be a day or more behind. What is it that you intend? If you only want to stop Savas' army from reaching Onglse easily, then all we need do is destroy the ships they've built for him. As we leave, we can also take down the bridges across the River Meadham so he can't cross his army here."

"I would still set Muras afire once we did that," Comhnall said. "We don't want him to use the quays and shipwrights there to rebuild the ships. We want him to retreat all the way to Gediz, where he'd have to build new ships, while we go back to Onglse and prepare."

"That's certainly a choice we could make," Orla said. "As for the ships, you don't need an army to destroy them; you only need a few draoi who could walk into Muras without being challenged and escape in the chaos afterward. I'm willing to be one of those. If I take off my torc and put on a bog dress, then I'm just a peasant girl come to town to buy goods. But whatever we do, we have to do it *now*, before Savas' army arrives."

That started an uproar as several people attempted to talk at once.

"She may be young yet, Ceanndraoi, but she has the wisdom and far sight of her mother and the Moonshadow in her," Comhnall roared, his voice sending the others into temporary silence. "Draoi Orla's talking sense, Ceanndraoi. Destroy the boats, and Onglse is safe for the time being."

Greum's face was a scowl. "Perhaps. But she also wants us to destroy the bridges," Greum said. "I say that's a mistake. Our army's already here. Maybe Draoi Orla can stop Savas from reaching Onglse easily, but I for one still wish to engage him. I say this: let Draoi Orla take out the ships if she believes she can, but we'll leave the bridges up so Savas has to use them to cross the river. Let the battle between us happen *here* rather than on Onglse. We have the river's escarpments and hills as cover until we reach the floodplain, and the bridge will act as a funnel through which Savas' forces will have to pass."

There was a murmuring amongst those in the meeting at that. Comhnall nodded. "The bridge over the Meadham here at Muras could indeed be a trap for Savas. If we show him our army when he arrives, he either has to engage us here or move a double hand of days east along the river to find a decent ford, knowing we can shadow him all the way and still harry him at that crossing."

Orla felt Greum's stare on her. "You can do what you claim, girl? You can take out the ships in Muras?"

"I can," she told him. "With a few draoi to help. No more than that—we don't want to be seen as a threat to Muras, just as peasants entering the city on normal business, as I said."

Greum grunted. He looked around at the other àrds and chief draoi, and Orla knew he saw little support for himself there with the exception of Ceiteag. His fingers tightened around his walking stick, then plunged the tip of it into the ground. "Then so be it," he said. "Destroy the ships, and leave the bridges. We'll bring Savas and his army to battle."

The draoi approached the first bridge in the late afternoon. The foothills that crept down to the River Meadham were swaddled in the gray wool of clouds, with the distant mountains hidden behind them. A mist beaded on the plain cloaks the draoi wore, dampening their hair. They'd removed their torcs, shed their usual Onglse cloaks for the tartan of local clan farmers, and left all their weapons behind but for a few knives. They'd also brought a hand of sheep and a dog borrowed from a local farm. They pulled a small two-wheeled cart of vegetables, now caked in mud from the road.

Just a clan family heading to town to sell what they'd raised and grown: three women and three men. Four of them were draoi: Orla, Magaidh, a man called Niall, and an older female called Caoimhe. The other two men were younger warriors there as additional protection in case someone in town could see the anamacha that accompanied the draoi and raise an alarm.

As they approached the northern end of the bridge, they saw a quartet of guards emerge from the drystone guardhouse set to one side of the bridge on the northern bank. Orla watched their faces carefully, but none of them reacted to the ghost-like presences with the group. The officer moved toward them, his men sliding out to either side of the road with their pikes ready while the officer straddled the muddy ruts, his arms crossed. The visor of his helmet dripped water, the leather armor he wore was untied and askew, as if he'd hastily donned it, and the expression on his face indicated that he wished for nothing more than to return to the guardhouse next to the bridge entryway, where there was presumably a fire against the drizzle.

Magaidh glanced back at Orla, who nodded. The older woman stepped forward, her arm interlaced with that of Niall. "Good day," she said to the officer in heavily accented Mundoan. "We're from Clan MacDonoghue. We've sheep to sell and some lovely fresh vegetables."

"You're two days late for the opening of market, woman."

"I know, but my man here was out hunting and didn't get back in time. I'd let himself tell you, but he doesn't speak Mundoan beyond a few words."

The officer grunted, standing his ground and blocking the road. "I doubt you'll find buyers today. They've already bought what they can, and the weather's foul."

"You may be right in that," Magaidh told him. "But surely you're not going to deny us the chance. We'll take what we can get."

The guards had spread out among them, poking through the produce on the cart. One of them nodded to the officer, who grunted and inclined his head toward the island at the other side of the bridge. "I suppose you know where the market is?"

"Across the island, just over the second bridge," Magaidh answered. "We've been there many times, sir."

"G'wan with you, then."

"Many kindnesses on your head, sir," Magaidh said, "and may the sun shine on your back today."

The officer sniffed at the expression, wiping at his thin Mundoan nose. "That's about as likely as you selling those lice-ridden sheep," he told her, but he stepped aside. Orla could feel the soldiers watching them as they passed, but none of them said anything or moved until the sheep were on the bridge and their cart was rattling the wooden planks underneath their feet. Orla found herself holding her breath until they reached the island. Glancing back, she saw the soldiers entering their guardhouse again, already talking among themselves, and Orla allowed herself to breathe once more.

The island was occupied mostly by inns for travelers and a few stores. The island was also where the shipyards of Muras were located, along the southern bank. As the draoi neared the second bridge, they could see a hand and four of ships moored there, far larger than any Orla had ever seen before, with two masts with fine canvas sails lashed around each and two hands of oars on either side for when there was no wind. "Savas' army must be huge," Niall said softly as they stared. "Those ships alone could carry twice as many warriors as Greum has."

Orla shivered, thinking of the Mundoan army. She'd traveled with it in the wake of her hated husband, along with First Wife Azru, and their children, little more than a slave and a convenient body for him to use as he saw fit when he was in the camp. Through her mam's memories, she'd seen the army of the Mundoa sprawling over the land, and she'd seen it broken and shattered after the Battle of Siran. <We did that,> she heard voices say, and realized that her anamacha had pressed close to her. <We were there, and we nearly took them. This time, this time . . .>

<Be quiet,> she told them. <We're not here for battle. Not yet, anyway.>

<That will come.> This time it was her mother's voice dominant in the chorus. <Then we will remind them of what we were.>

<Be silent!> Orla shouted at them in her mind, and the anamacha slid away from her. She glanced up at the clouds; the hidden sun was marked by a lowering brighter spot to the west.

"Let's get to the market and set up," Magaidh said to the group. "The rest can wait a few stripes until it's dark."

They continued moving south along the lane toward the bridge entrance leading from the island to the town of Muras proper.

The bridge let them out in the main market square, where there were stalls set up, though only a few sellers were behind the planks and fewer buyers strolled the area. Across the square was the Muras garrison, a two-story stone structure protected in front by a second wall. There were dark scorch marks on the granite wall of the garrison, and some of the stones had obviously been shattered and replaced with new-cut ones. Magaidh pressed close to Orla, whispering, "Your mother did that, casting her spells from the chariot of Ceannàrd Iosa when we came here and took the town. That was a glorious day and our first victory."

Orla stared at the garrison, then shook away the vision of her mother sending fire and destruction into the midst of battle. She pointed to an empty stall near the bridge entrance. "Let's take that one," she said. "We'll get things set up and at least pretend we're interested in selling what we have. . . ."

By the time the light had failed and the torches around the square had been lit, they'd sold one of the sheep and a few of the vegetables, haggling for prices half-heartedly with a mixture of well-dressed Mundoa and shabby Cateni—giving far better prices to the Cateni. "It's time," Magaidh said as the last of the torches was lit. Already the market was largely deserted except for the out-of-town sellers who would be sleeping in their stalls; the locals had already packed up and left for their own homes.

"You know what to do," Magaidh said to the two warriors. "We'll see you on the island."

Magaidh, Niall, Caoimhe, and Orla left the warriors and walked back over the bridge to the island, skirting around toward the western quays and the masts that speared the twilight sky like a forest of limbless trees. The small lane along which they walked fell steeply downhill toward the rushing currents of the ever-widening river; Orla stopped there, where they could easily see the quay and the ships. The workers on the quay had gone home. Firelight glimmered behind the shutters of the houses nearest them while the low voice of a singer drifted from an inn's open door where the lane met the docks a quick walk away.

There was no one else visible along the lane.

Orla took a long, slow breath. *I can do this. It's no different from what I did with Greum and Magaidh. This will be easy. . . .*

"Can you reach the ships with a spell from here?" Magaidh whispered; Orla, Niall, and Caoimhe nodded. "Let's do this, then," she told them.

"I can take the three ships on the right," Orla told them.

"So many?" Magaidh asked. "You're certain?"

Orla nodded. With a deep breath, she called the anamacha of the Moonshadow to her, opening her arms to allow them to fully enter her. She was immediately caught up in the chaotic storms of Magh da Chèo, feeling the cold wind and seeing the rocky landscape illuminated by stuttering lightning from the racing thunderheads, while the real world became a faint underlying shadow. The ghosts of her anamacha surrounded her, calling out to her, and she looked for her mother among them. The Moonshadow herself remained hidden and distant, though her dominating presence seemed to touch each of the other dead draoi within the collective. She could feel her mother emerging from the crowd of spirits around her, but she suddenly felt frightened by her approach. <*Give me Iomhar,*> Orla called into the Otherworld's winds. <*Iomhar, come to me!*>

<*No . . .*> her mother's shade insisted. <*Iomhar's too weak for this. You need us. Don't be afraid. We—I—wouldn't hurt you. Let us help you, my daughter.*>

Orla swallowed hard. She pushed the fear to the back of her mind and nodded. <*Come to me, then.*>

Voada's shade slid forward, her face prominent within the shifting features. <*We're here . . .*>

<*I need you now,*> Orla told her. <*Fire. I need fire.*>

<*We hear you . . . Here . . . Take the power we give you . . .*>

Orla could feel the crackling of the energy of the Otherworld, the hair on her arms lifting in response. Her hands began to move, to make the spell cage to hold the energy her mother's spirit was feeding her. She absorbed it as a furious, angry blaze spilled into the spell cage before her, snarling and fuming, the bright lines of the cage shivering and threatening to snap apart. Iomhar's power had never been so strong, so difficult to handle. Orla redoubled her concentration—*so this is what my mam had been capable of, even without the Moonshadow*—and tried to keep the vision of the real world before her and not become lost in Magh da Chèo.

She concentrated on the ships she'd chosen, gauging the distance and how she needed to spread the energy she'd gathered from her mam. She lifted her hands, raising the spell cage, and shouted the release word as she flung it toward the ships: "Teine!"

As if angry at its confinement, the spell cage shattered as the flames arced away from her, breaking into three distinct fireballs that sent shadows racing across the buildings around the quay and spreading over the water beyond the ships. The fireballs hurtled toward the quay, each striking a different ship. Orla could see the hulls shudder with the impact, the fire spreading along the planks, hissing and crackling audibly even at a distance. As she sagged with the exhaustion of the spell, letting Voada and her anamacha slide away from her, she saw more fireballs impact the other ships, and to the far left of the docks, a foaming, impossible wave lifted the remaining ships on its white crest and hurled them over the quay and down onto the land, masts snapping and timbers cracking.

But that wasn't all. Orla heard cries of pain and surprise; there were crews—workers and sailors—sleeping aboard the ships. As she watched, men with clothes afire ran from the hatches and plunged into the water, screaming. Orla saw them fall, pushing and shoving each other to get away from the inferno of the ships. Some of them were screaming not in Mundoan but in Cateni.

She felt them die. Because of her.

"No!" she called out aloud, the denial raking her throat.

People ran shouting from the buildings and houses in the area into the sudden light and heat of the burning ships. Orla watched the flames climbing higher as the smell of charred wood and melting tar spread on the easterly breeze fanning the fires. The draoi gazed down at glorious, growing chaos. Townsfolk, both Mundoan and Cateni, were running wildly about, some toward the fires, others away. More doors were opening all around them. The lane was beginning to fill with people, though none seemed to pay much attention to their quartet, just another group gawking at the scene before them.

"Orla!"

Orla stared, her mouth agape. This wasn't the same as sending fire at some inanimate target. This wasn't the same as creating a temple from the energy of the Otherworld. This was genuine pain and blood and death happening to people she didn't know, who had done nothing at all to her.

Burned and injured and dying because of her . . .

"Orla! We have to go!" Magaidh shouted against the growing noise and clamor. "We're done here. Orla!" She felt Magaidh take her shoulder and shake her, pulling her back and away, turning her from the sight of the destruction they'd caused.

Orla stumbled away with them, away from the docks and back to the main lane, with Magaidh leading them. They had to stand aside as several Mundoan soldiers dressed in full armor came running from the main street down toward the quays, but the soldiers paid no attention to the draoi. Once the squadron was past, Magaidh quickly led them away, pushing through the curious spectators who were coming to see the fiery uproar. The two warriors were waiting for them there in the swirl of the crowds, and the six of them moved quickly toward the northern bridge.

For Orla it was as if they moved in a dream landscape. Nothing seemed real. Nothing seemed solid.

The bridge's guards, pikes and swords in hand, were at the island end of the span, staring toward the glow spewing smoke on the western end of the island. The officer who had spoken to them earlier was still on duty, staring outward as if uncertain whether he should take his men to the blaze or stay at their post. His gaze snapped around as the Cateni approached, and his face twisted in a snarl.

"*You* did this," he said, the realization lifting his eyebrows. "It was you." He gestured toward them. "Take them!" he shouted to the guards.

The guards rushed toward them. Orla knew she should call her anamacha back to her; the warriors with them had only cudgels and knives for defense. She should enter Magh da Chèo again, take its energy, and kill these guards before they could attack. She could do it.

But she didn't move. The sound of the dying men on the ships was still ringing in her ears, and her hands lifted too slowly. The guards were nearly upon them.

"Teine!" she heard Magaidh shout, and Orla felt the heat of flames rushing past her, a wall of fire that slammed into the officer and his men, scorching clothing, armor, and flesh. They screamed in agony, falling and writhing on the ground as the spell-fire engulfed them.

Then everything was still except for the flames that still licked at the grass on either side of the road. Blackened corpses lay smoking on the cobbles. "Quickly! Over the bridge before others come," Magaidh said. "We're done here." Orla felt Magaidh's hand on her shoulder again. "Orla, come on!"

Orla followed them. She tried not to look at the charred corpses as they passed, but she could smell them all too well.

"Did you somehow think you were going to fight a war without ever killing anyone?"

Orla looked up to see Magaidh standing at the tent opening. Sorcha let her arms drop away from Orla, taking a step back from her. Orla could see Magaidh watching the two of them, the light of the oil lamp gleaming in her pupils.

"Magaidh . . ." Orla began, but the older woman only shook her head.

"No, just listen," she said. "I understand, believe me. You're Voada's daughter, but you're not her. Your mother . . . well, she killed easily, probably too easily. She was driven by revenge and hatred. That suited the Moonshadow well, and she used that to shape her. But you, Orla . . ." Magaidh stepped fully into the tent. She took Orla's hands in her own, her pale eyes searching Orla's. "You've never used your power to kill anyone before, but now you have. It wasn't as easy as you thought it would be, was it?"

Mutely, Orla shook her head. On their return to the Cateni encampment, she'd asked Magaidh to report to Ceanndraoi Greum and Comhnall of their success. She hadn't wanted to face them. Instead she'd returned to her tent. When she started to tell Sorcha what had happened in Muras, she was suddenly, violently ill, vomiting bile when her stomach emptied. Sorcha held her hair, stroking her back and wiping her face with a cool, wet cloth when the nausea finally passed, leaving Orla's stomach muscles sore. She could still taste the sickness in the back of her throat.

Magaidh's lips tightened in a mirthless smile, still holding Orla's hands. "That's what happened with me; the first time I was in battle, I was sick afterward too," she said. "But it gets easier each time. Honestly, that's the sad part. If you survive, if you continue to be a war draoi, you get used to the killing, and eventually you don't even think about it. That's what will happen to you, too— that's what *must* happen. If it doesn't, the Moonshadow will consume you and you'll just be another minor forgotten voice lost in the anamacha, nowhere near as powerful as your mam. As I said, you're not your mam, but I'll also tell you what she once said to me." She paused, her gaze holding Orla's. "She said it was *you* the anamacha of the Moonshadow were searching for when they first came to your village. Not your mam. *You*, Orla. But you were stolen away by the Mundoa before they could become one with you, and so it was your mam who finally merged with them."

Magaidh let go of her hands, and Orla heard Sorcha release a breath behind her. Orla glanced at her anamacha, standing in a corner, faces of the dead draoi within flickering across their face. She saw her mam there, who nodded once and was gone again. "That's true?" she asked.

"*Tha,*" Magaidh told her. "Your mam will tell you the same.

Those in the Moonshadow and the Moonshadow itself saw something in you that even your mam didn't have. As I do. As Sorcha also does." Magaidh took a step back toward the tent's entrance flaps. "But if you're to be the draoi of the Moonshadow, you have to understand that more people will end up dying at your hand. Many more. There's no way for you to escape that, not in these times."

She smiled again, this time with a softness that Orla could feel. "Let Sorcha comfort you for now," Magaidh continued. "I told the ceanndraoi and ceannàrd that you were exhausted and that you'd come and talk to them after you'd slept. They'll expect you at dawn."

Orla felt the bile rising again and forced it back down. "Thank you," she managed to say against the burning in her throat. "I'll be there."

Magaidh nodded once and opened the flaps of the tent.

"Magaidh," Orla said, and the woman turned. "I'll think about what you've said. I appreciate your honesty."

Magaidh gave another nod and smile and left.

14

A Battle Won and Lost

ALTAN HAD SEEN THE FIRES: a glowing orange smudge on the horizon as the army approached Muras and set up camp for the night. An officer from the Muras garrison riding a lathered and exhausted horse came down the road from the north just before dawn, leaping from the saddle as his mount collapsed.

"Sir," he said, clasping his fist to his chest in salute and breathing hard as he was ushered into Savas' tent, "our ships at Muras . . . they're gone. Destroyed. Every one of them. It was the draoi and their spells." The man took a slow breath, swallowing hard. His eyes were wide, as if anticipating a violent reaction from Savas.

"You're certain this was draoi handiwork? Not some careless cooking fire that got out of control?"

"Yes, Commander." The man took another breath, and Altan gestured for Tolga to bring the rider a cup of wine. He gulped it down gratefully in several quick swallows, then handed the goblet back to Tolga. "I've talked to those who saw it happen. They said fireballs exploded against most of the ships all at once while at the same time a huge wave rose from the river and sent the rest crashing into the rocks of the island. I saw the ships afterward, sir, and there was nothing natural about what happened to them. The fires burned even while water was being thrown on them, and the ships were destroyed down to the very keels. While they were still burning, the draoi killed the guards at the northern bridge with another spell and fled back across the river. Burned the poor soldiers to death where they stood. Two people in the nearest houses told me they saw a hand and one of people crossing the bridge and running toward the foothills and the forests. I sent out two hands of scouts from the Muras garrison to chase after them. Only a single soldier came back; he was badly wounded, with a Cateni arrow in his back. He said there's an entire Cateni army in the foothills with more campfires than he could count, waiting. Everyone in the town is terrified, and the Voice of Muras asks that you come right away. He believes that the Cateni will attack the town today."

"He does, does he?" Altan sighed. "So these draoi didn't take down the bridge to the island? It's still standing?"

"Yes, sir. They left it up."

"That's an invitation," Altan told him. "Not a prelude to invasion."

"Commander?"

"Never mind," Altan said. "I thank you for the report. Go and get something to eat and rest while you can. I'll send word to Sub-Commander Ilkur to have the men start to break camp immediately. We'll have a long and fast march as soon as it's light."

The officer saluted again and left them. Tolga secured the tent flaps behind the man as Altan stretched and yawned. "An invitation?" Tolga asked as he turned back to Altan.

"If our ships are destroyed, then the only way to cross the Meadham is over the bridges from the south. Had they taken down the second Muras bridge, we'd have been trapped on the south side of the river. We'd have had to march days east to the fords near the River Yarrow in order to cross, or take the army south and west to Gediz and wait several moons until the shipyards there could build enough ships for us to attack Onglse. No, they left the bridges up as a challenge for us to use them."

It's also not what I was told to expect. This is an aggressive move for the Red-Hand, which is not like him. Something must have happened with the Cateni. What is going on there? Altan was glad now that he'd sent messages west as well as north. It seemed that those contingencies might have been necessary.

"Tolga," he said, "I should have Cateni messengers from the north returning soon. Make certain they're brought to me as soon as they arrive and that the seals remain unbroken until they're in my hands. I'll let Musa and Ilkur know as well."

"So we won't cross at Muras?"

Altan gave Tolga a tight smile. He wanted to protect Tolga in case the plans failed, though he had little hope that Great-Voice Utka would leave any of his inner circle alive if that happened. Still, it was better that Tolga had only a glimpse of the truth. "Have you ever known me to back down from a challenge, Tolga?" he answered. "No, we'll reach Muras on tomorrow's march, and we'll see just how good an army the ceanndraoi and ceannàrd have managed to raise. Maybe we can end this war there."

He'd once thought that was actually possible. Now he wasn't so certain.

Under a failing sun, Greum called together the clan àrds and draoi.

"Our scouts tell us that the Mundoan army is marching quickly toward Muras. They'll likely be encamped there tomorrow. We should be in battle with them the day after." Standing on a boulder in the middle of their encampment, the troops and draoi gathered around him, Ceanndraoi Greum smiled as he made the last statement. There were cheers of agreement, though not from Orla or Magaidh, nor from Eideard Iosa or his warriors. Orla glimpsed Ceiteag standing just to the right of Greum, staring up at him raptly with her gap-toothed mouth open in acclamation. "They'll be unable to get their forces over the bridge quickly, and we'll be waiting for them with warriors and draoi. We will descend on them as a storm. They will be met by our war draoi's spells, by our archers, by our pikes and swords and chariots. It will be slaughter. The greatest Cateni victory ever awaits us. The fields along the Meadham will be nourished by the blood of the Mundoan dead and their rotting corpses."

Greum Red-Hand thrust his walking stick hard against the boulder on which he was standing, the brass ferrule ringing and sparking with the blow. More cheers arose.

"And what does Ceannàrd Mac Tsagairt believe?" Eideard shouted into the chorus of affirmation. "He's met Commander Savas on the field before. Does he think that Savas will be blind to the trap set for him? Does he think Savas is foolish enough to step into it?"

The ceannàrd took a step toward Greum's boulder. Hùisdean—his eldest son and Magaidh's stepson, and also the driver of Mac Tsagairt's chariot—helped him up to stand alongside Greum. "Commander Savas is no fool at all," Magaidh's husband said, glaring in Eideard's direction, "and anyone who acts on the field of battle as if he is will end up feeding the crows."

"Then why would he come here at all?" Eideard persisted. "Surely he knows by now that his ships have been destroyed and that the only way to the north is via Muras Bridge, which will hinder his troop movements. If he's not a fool, then we need to ask ourselves what we've missed." Eideard glanced over to Orla; at the same time, she felt her anamacha slide close to her side, so close that she could hear the whispers of the voices inside. "After all," Eideard continued, "only a few years ago, Savas would have taken Onglse if Ceanndraoi Voada and my uncle hadn't left to attack the south, and yet he managed to defeat the Moonshadow and her army. I can't believe he's going to enter the trap you've set for him, Ceanndraoi, Ceannàrd."

<*You will avenge us . . .*> Orla heard in her head: her mam's voice, the Moonshadow's voice, the voices of them all as a chorus. <*You will kill him . . . We will give you that power . . .*> But she had no chance to answer them.

"Pah!" Greum scoffed at Eideard's statement, rapping his stick against the stone again. Alongside, Ceiteag also glared at the àrd. "Had the Mad Draoi stayed as she'd been told, had your uncle not listened to her honeyed lies about glorious battle in the south, we would have defeated Savas on the island. We would have sent his head back to the emperor, and we wouldn't be facing him again now." Greum's gaze, like Eideard's, was on Orla. Orla felt Magaidh grip her shoulder, her fingers pressing hard.

<*Answer that fool Greum!*> the anamacha screamed in Orla's mind, but Magaidh's voice whispered close to her ear, and it was to her that Orla listened. "The ceanndraoi has his own view of that time, and it's not the true one," she said. "Comhnall realizes that as much as I do, and I suspect the Red-Hand knows it as well. Remember that."

Even as Magaidh spoke, Orla saw the ceannàrd shake his head, a scowl deepening the lines of his face.

"This bickering between us is useless," Comhnall said, his voice loud with anger. His white hair gleamed in the last light of the day. "Ceannàrd, with respect, Onglse would have been *lost* without Voada and Maol Iosa raising the northern clans around them, and nothing you say changes that fact. Everyone here should realize that Savas would have overwhelmed the island with sheer numbers and razed Bàn Cill. You simply didn't have enough draoi or warriors to resist him. Remember that I was at Siran, where the Moonshadow had far more draoi and warriors than you'd gathered on Onglse, and even those weren't enough."

Mac Tsagairt glared at Greum as if daring him to contradict what he'd said, then the ceannàrd turned to Eideard. "And you, Àrd Eideard—whether you think the ceanndraoi's plan foolish or not, it's still our best defense against Savas and the Mundoa. With Draoi Orla, Magaidh, Caoimhe, and Niall's efforts, we've already destroyed the ships Savas was depending on for his invasion. We'll learn what Savas intends when he gets here, and we'll respond as best we can. What's *foolish* is fighting amongst ourselves beforehand. I've heard enough arguments. We'll know what Savas might or might not do when he arrives, not before. For now we should rest and prepare for the battle to come, which is what I intend to do. I suggest everyone else do the same."

The ceannàrd gestured to Hùisdean, who stepped forward to help his father down from the boulder. Ceanndraoi Greum remained standing there, saying nothing, his face grim and unreadable. Eideard shrugged and gestured to his warriors, all of them walking away from the gathering and back toward the tents.

The Moonshadow's voices were still yammering in Orla's head. *<With our help you can destroy Greum. You can be ceanndraoi, as you should be . . .>* "No," Orla said aloud. She stepped away from the anamacha so she could no longer hear them. Many àrds were beginning to leave even though Greum was still standing on the boulder, but none of the Onglse-based draoi had left.

Orla turned to Magaidh. "I'm going back to my tent," she said. Magaidh simply nodded. Together they left as the sun touched the horizon, leaving the forest in shadow and gloom.

Word came to the Cateni encampment the evening of the next day that the vanguard of the Mundoan army had arrived. Commander Savas and his entourage entered Muras while the army set up camp in the fields outside the southern gate of the city wall. If Greum Red-Hand expected Commander Savas to move immediately, he was disappointed.

Two full days passed, two days in which Greum Red-Hand moved the Cateni army from the shield of the forest, down the foothills, and onto the Meadham's northern floodplain: a plainly visible challenge to Savas. The ceanndraoi had the draoi send storms down upon Muras and the encampment. Lightning crawled across the river on legs of fire, and rain turned the earth to mud under ever-present, unmoving clouds. Orla was among the draoi set the task of keeping the army miserable, uncomfortable, and in fear of being struck down by the lightning, though Greum Red-Hand pulled her from the task late that night, telling her to rest.

There was activity, though, in the Mundoan encampment. From the heights, the *faicinn fada*—those gifted with long sight among the Cateni—could see soldiers working, though at what they couldn't discern. The bridge end on the northern side of the Meadham was barricaded and blocked, with Mundoan troops stationed there, allowing no one to cross over onto the island or the town, nor allowing anyone from the town to cross the river, which meant that any Cateni sympathizers within the town couldn't get word to the army.

Eideard came to Orla's tent not long after she returned from her spell-work. Sorcha let him in grudgingly and stood glaring at him as he spoke to Orla, who was eating a cold dinner. "The battle will be coming soon," he said. "As I told you, I would be pleased if you'd ride with me in my chariot, as your mam did with my uncle: the Àrd of Clan Iosa and the Moonshadow's draoi together as they once were."

He lifted his bearded chin as he spoke as if imagining himself as the avatar of his uncle. Orla glanced at Sorcha; she returned the look impassively, her face unreadable, and Orla turned back to Eideard. The major war draoi typically rode into battle in warriors' chariots; that was the long-standing custom, after all. Magaidh would be riding with her husband, Ceannàrd Mac Tsagairt, and Greum Red-Hand would be with his clan's àrd. Eideard might be arrogant, might be temperamental, but there was little doubt about his ability as a warrior, at least according to the whispers Orla had heard. The memory of the sickness she'd felt in Muras after hearing the dying screams of the sailors remained with her, but she also knew that what Magaidh had told her was true: there was no way for her to escape this war or this battle if she wanted to be a draoi. And Orla had already practiced casting spells from Eideard's chariot.

This was the fate she'd chosen when she first embraced the Moonshadow's and her mother's anamacha. The anamacha glowed nearby in the gloom of the tent, but she didn't have to call them to her to know what they would tell her.

"*Tha*," she told Eideard. "I'll ride with you."

He nodded as if that were the answer he'd anticipated. A faint smile lifted the corner of his lips. "Then I'll see you soon enough," he said. "Rest, and be ready." With that he clasped a fisted hand to his chest, bowed his head, and left the tent.

Orla could feel Sorcha's gaze on her. "You find the àrd . . . attractive?" Sorcha's words hovered between question and statement, uncertain. Orla could hear the fear laced with jealousy in

Sorcha's comment, and she understood that. Even though they'd become intimate, even though Orla understood that Sorcha had accepted lovers who were women before, such attraction was new and strange to Orla—it made sense that Sorcha would be uncertain of Orla's feelings. The woman's shoulders were hunched, her head down. She seemed to be staring at the table and their half-eaten meal, her finger trailing along the edge of a wooden platter.

"Sorcha . . ." Orla said, and that lifted the woman's head. Her lips were pressed together. Orla took two quick steps to her and gathered her in her arms, embracing her tightly as she kissed her neck. Her lips at Sorcha's ear, she whispered, "Don't worry. I ride with him because I trust him to bring me back to you. That's the only reason. You've nothing to fear."

Sorcha's arms tightened around her, and Orla smiled, inhaling the scent of Sorcha's hair and hoping that what she had just said would be true.

The battle, when it came, opened before dawn with a cry from the pickets the ceannàrd had set out. "They're already across the river! The Mundoans have crossed!"

The riverbank was alight with flashes of lightning from the spell-storms of the draoi and with the yellow light of Mundoan torches. There were far too many soldiers to have crossed the single bridge that was to have been a funnel and a trap for the Mundoa. Their torches crawled over the floodplain like some impossible glowing creature, spreading out as the Cateni watched. In the pre-dawn glow, the task Commander Savas had given his engineers became apparent. Four temporary bridges had been placed well to the sides of the existing stone bridge, two upriver and two more downstream: wide, wooden structures set on anchored barges that served as supports, and over which several cohorts of the Mundoan had already passed quietly before dawn. Now, Commander Savas opened the barricade to the stone bridge as the sun peered over the eastern horizon.

It seemed that the plan to slow the Mundoan assault through the funnel of the bridge had already failed. Miserably.

Orla awoke to the trumpets sounding alarm. The Cateni encampment was a hornet's nest stirred by a foolish child's stick; angry, wild shouting seemed to come from every side as Orla and Sorcha hurriedly dressed. "Draoi Orla!" she heard Eideard call, and she saw him at the tent flaps dressed in armor and helm. Beyond him she glimpsed his chariot and his driver, Tadgh, the horses tearing at the grass in their impatience as Tadgh pulled at the traces. "Come! We must hurry!"

He grasped Orla's arm and pulled; she shrugged him away and quickly hugged Sorcha. "Don't worry," she said to her. "I promise I'll be back." With that, she strode past Eideard with a glare. Tadgh reached down as she approached the chariot and pulled her up onto the platform; Eideard leaped into it a moment later.

"Go!" he told Tadgh. "Let's see if we can find Commander Savas. Orla, tie yourself to the rail and ready your spells." Eideard plucked a spear from the holder along the rail and hefted it. He grinned.

Their chariot was among the flood rushing down the slope toward the river. Orla could see the various clans' banners flapping madly on the lead chariots in the wind of their charge. Just to her right was the ceannàrd's chariot with Magaidh lashed to the rails, her hands already weaving a spell. Mounted warriors followed by Cateni warriors on foot flowed behind them in a wild, shouting wave.

And ahead of them, waiting, were the phalanxes of the Mundoan army, their own banners—all emblazoned with the Mundoan hawk—fluttering. Two of the new bridges were aflame, but the spell-storm of the draoi had ended with the start of the engagement so as not to strike their own forces. A red dawn sent shafts of light through shredded and broken clouds to shimmer from the pikes and swords of the Mundoan troops. Orla tightened the lashings that held her to the rails of the chariot as it bounced and jolted over a plowed field. She opened her arms in invitation, and the Moon-shadow's anamacha entered her, overlaying her world with the dark realm of Magh da Chèo.

She could feel the shades of the dead draoi crowding around her and hear their voices calling. This time she didn't want Iomhar. "Mam!" she cried into their wailing. "Mam, come to me!"

<We're here . . .> she heard her mother's voice say, though there was the sense of a greater, darker presence nearby: the Moonshadow herself. Orla ignored the Moonshadow, looking toward the ghost that was her mother. <It's battle, then,> the ghost said, and there was a strange eagerness in her voice that made Orla shiver.

<Tha!> she answered in her head. <I need you, Mam. Lend me the strength I need.>

In her doubled sight, she could see a forest of pikes set in the ground before Eideard's chariot, with grim faces behind them. They were plunging headlong toward them, their chariot now ahead of even Greum's and the ceannàrd's. Eideard shouted back to her over his shoulder. "Now, Orla! Take them!"

Orla could feel the power gathering, drawn by her mother from the storms of Magh da Chèo, and she forced herself to thrust away all the doubt and the memory of her guilt after killing the sailors and workmen in Muras.

I have to do this . . . She began to chant, her hands moving to weave the net for the spell. She took it in, gathering more and more until a new sun sent shadows racing from between her fingers, burning. When she could hold it no longer, she flung it away with a word: "Teine!"

A ball of fire arced from the chariot, growing as it raced toward the Mundoans and dribbling a trail of fiery rain behind. It struck the line of pikemen with a fearsome roar and thunder, sending the pikes to ash and tearing a great hole in their ranks. Men screamed as they were burned, as they died, their terror ringing in Orla's ears as Eideard's chariot surged through the opening she'd made—as other chariots down the line did the same. The opposing lines of the armies smashed into each other with a din unlike anything Orla had ever heard: cries of rage and pain, the clashing of metal on metal and blade on flesh, the screaming of horses maddened with the smell of blood.

Orla heard Eideard's yell of triumph. <Tha!> her mother shouted in exultation, and the other shades shouted with her, even the Moonshadow. <*We will pay them back for what they did to us!*>

Tadgh pulled on the reins, and their horses reared, smashing down on the soldiers before them with metal-clad hooves as the bladed axles of the chariot chewed at the pressing Mundoan troops around them. Eideard's mouth was open as he thrust again and again with his spears at the nearest enemy soldiers, his armor and body flecked with red. <*Again!*> Orla's mam's voice roared along with the others inside, feeding her power so that she had no choice but to weave another spell to contain it. This one was different: not fire, but a blue and cold light more frigid than any winter storm she'd ever felt. She held it until she couldn't bear the pain anymore, spreading her hands as she screamed the release word her mother gave her: "*Deigh!*"

Glass-like shards of hard ice shot outward like a deadly flight of arrows, and the Mundoan soldiers around the chariot went down in response, grunting and writhing as the ice penetrated through armor, flesh, and bone. Now it was Eideard who shouted "Tha!" in response. "Tadgh! Forward!" he ordered as Orla sagged in the ropes that held her upright, exhausted from the effort of casting the spells amidst the chaos.

<*You have to be stronger . . .*> she heard her mother say. <*This isn't over; it's only begun.*>

But the screams and cries still sounded in her ears, and Orla screamed with them, the sound tearing at her throat.

<*You must find your strength, or you will die . . .*> Not her mother's voice this time, but the Moonshadow's dark tenor. <*We chose you. We know you. Find the iron within you. It's there . . .*>

"The Moonshadow . . ." a breathless messenger said to Altan as he stood in his chariot, desperately trying to make sense of the welter of men and banners before him. "Sub-Commander Ilkur said you should know that the Moonshadow has returned to battle. The draoi who holds the Moonshadow opened our line and has already killed hand upon hand of our soldiers. The formation's broken, and the Cateni are pouring in behind her. The subcommander is trying to hold the lines, but we're being pushed back. They say . . ." The messenger swallowed hard. "The subcommander said to tell you that the Cateni say it's the Mad One's daughter who holds the Moonshadow now, and she rides with the new àrd of Clan Iosa, Maol Iosa's nephew."

Sudden dread filled Altan with the news. "You're certain it's the Moonshadow and the Mad One's daughter?" The messages he'd received from Onglse told him not to be concerned about Orla's presence at Bàn Cill or the reappearance of the Moonshadow. The notes that had come to Altan from the north had claimed she would never be able to wield the Moonshadow as her mother had. *Was that information wrong? Was it all a deliberate lie? If I'd known before the Battle of Siran that I had the Mad One's daughter nearly in my grasp, perhaps I could have bargained with her mother, or even the daughter after the battle. Now she rides with Iosa's àrd, as her mam did. Have I made a terrible mistake? Is Greum Red-Hand even in control of his draoi anymore?*

He shook away the thought; the truth had come to him too late. Too late. The very ghosts of the past had risen to assault him and shatter the plans he'd made.

"Yes, Commander," he heard the man answer. "We could hear the Cateni shouting her name. And the power of her—I've never seen the like."

Too late . . . Altan cursed aloud, causing Tolga to glance at him over his shoulder. From the chariot alongside Altan's, Sub-Commander Musa spoke. "We still have surprise and numbers, Commander. They weren't prepared for us. Let me send three of my experienced cohorts to help Ilkur on the left flank while we take the right. We'll crush them as we did at Siran, even if the Moonshadow's truly here."

"Siran was hardly a victory," Altan reminded Musa. Ahead and to the left he could see the banners of the ceanndraoi and ceannàrd on their chariots. He wanted nothing more than to order Tolga to plunge into the fray, to lose himself in the furious confusion of battle. *If the Red-Hand has decided that he can truly win here, he's a poor tactician; no, he'll retreat as he should, and we'll parley. Ceannàrd Mac Tsagairt is old and never had Maol Iosa's flair. They've already made a critical mistake assuming we only had one avenue of attack; they'll make another. This will still work.*

"I agree, Musa," Altan said. "You command the right flank. I want you to push forward hard, try to break their line, then close with Ilkur against their front. I'm going with your three cohorts to Ilkur."

"Sir!" Musa responded, saluting. "Flaggers!" he shouted, holding up three fingers and pointing to the west. The flagger signaled to the cohorts in reserve, and men and mounted officers began to move in response.

Altan nodded to Tolga, who in turn slapped the reins down on the backs of their warhorses, shouting to them. The chariot turned violently, and they raced off behind the lines. As they approached, Altan caught sight of the ceanndraoi's banner, with that of the ceannàrd and Clan Iosa close by and Ilkur's banner before them. He could also see the flashes of spells being cast, followed by the shouts and screams of the dying and wounded. Even as he tapped Tolga on the shoulder and pointed toward Ilkur's banner, he saw a new spell cast from the direction of Iosa's chariot: a fireball brighter than the rising sun rushed outward, and the pure, terrifying *whoomp!* as it exploded in the ranks of the Mundoan line nearly made him clap hands over ears. Altan felt the concussion in the air pound at his chest, the echo thundering belatedly from the hills to the north.

He knew that power. He remembered it all too well, and he knew that he'd been told a lie: Voada's daughter was *at least* the equal of her mother. The Moonshadow had found a new and unfortunately competent draoi. Altan cursed under his breath. Ahead he saw Mundoan foot soldiers fleeing the front lines, running toward them as they pushed forward. Altan snatched a spear from the rack, brandishing it and shouting at those retreating. "Turn and fight, you cowards!" he cried. "You shame the emperor! Back to your lines!"

Some of them, seeing their commander's chariot as well as the cohorts that were following him, shamefacedly halted and began trudging forward again; others kept running south, open fear on their faces as they dropped weapons and armor in their flight. Altan had no time to worry about the defections as his chariot, leading the new cohorts, plunged into the melee.

Altan was appalled by what he saw as he approached Ilkur's chariot: the field before them was strewn with Mundoan bodies, some of them still writhing on the ground, and the air was thick with the ugly smell of charred flesh. There were clusters of fighting between Cateni warriors and Mundoan soldiers, but a terrible stillness followed where the chariots moved along the front with their draoi. Altan waved the cohorts forward, their officers screaming orders and putting them into ordered phalanxes that advanced over the broken and bloodied ground. Tolga pulled Altan's chariot alongside Ilkur's. Ilkur shouted to the archers behind the lines: a cloud of arrows arced over them to fall amongst the Cateni, who raised shields against the deadly rain.

Even as Altan tried to make sense of what he was seeing, another spell flashed out, this one from the ceanndraoi's chariot, hurtling into the ranks trying to reform and tearing open a hole that rapidly filled again as more soldiers pushed forward.

So the Red-Hand has come to think he might prevail here. So much for our agreements.

"Commander! Thank the emperor you've brought the cohorts we need!" Ilkur cried. His face was bloody, and there were soot marks on both his chariot and his armor. The spear he held dripped blood and gore from the leaf-like blade. "The draoi are concentrated on this flank, and our sihirki are worse than useless against their spells. I've tried to hold as best I can, but our lines broke and ran when the draoi-fire started coming. I'll have each of the cowards' damned heads for desertion when this is over."

"We knew that was likely to happen when we sent the emperor's new troops forward and kept back the experienced men, Ilkur," Altan told him. "Too many of them are new to Albann and battles here. They've never seen what the war draoi can do; now they have. Next time they'll hold their lines, or I'll have the archers shoot them down from behind. The cohorts I've brought are old hands. They remember what it's like; they're not going to run."

"They'd damned well better not," Ilkur grunted. "And us, Commander? You told me to stay back, but I'm growing tired of watching the Cateni chariots moving about so freely."

"So am I," Altan told him. *My plans can burn in the pits of Pamukkale now, for all I care, and the Red-Hand will pay for his hubris.* "Musa will be one end of the pincer; you and I will be the other. You take the ceannàrd's chariot; I'll take the ceanndraoi's."

"And the Moonshadow, Commander?"

Altan could only shake his head at that. "To kill a two-headed beast, you must cut off the heads. The Moonshadow's dangerous, but she's only part of the body. Iosa's nephew isn't the ceannàrd, and Voada's daughter isn't ceanndraoi. Not yet, anyway, and we have to hope that they never become that."

"Then the ceannàrd it is." Ilkur saluted Altan, then shouted to his driver, pointing to Mac Tsagairt's banner as his chariot lurched forward.

Tolga glanced over his shoulder at Altan. "The ceanndraoi?"

Altan nodded. Tolga slapped the reins down on the horses as Altan hefted the spear in his hand.

I will pay the man back for his betrayal. . . .

Her mam continued to feed her energy from Magh da Chèo without heeding any of Orla's protests of exhaustion.

<*You can do this . . .*> her mam cried. <*You* must *do this . . .*>

Orla had lost count of how many times she'd had to weave a spell cage to snare the power and cast it away again, lest she be injured or killed herself. In between she sagged against the ropes holding her upright in the chariot. The frightening realization was that she *could* go far beyond what she thought were her limits, that it was actually becoming *easier* to control the energy and use it.

Eideard cast spear after spear into the Mundoans around them, sometimes leaping from the chariot to engage them with a sword until Tadgh circled around to pick him up again. The floorboards of the chariot under Orla's feet were slick with blood, some of it from Eideard but mostly from Mundoan bodies. To Orla, the battle had shrunk; her world consisted only of Eideard's chariot and the press of soldiers around it that she kept back with fire and ice, all of it overlaid with the dark landscape of the anamacha's Otherworld. The din was no longer something of which she was truly aware: the cries; the screams; the shouted orders; the hissing of spells being released; the clatter of blade against blade—it was all just eternal background noise that made no sense to her.

Through her doubled vision, she saw two Mundoan chariots: one racing toward the ceannàrd's banner, the other toward the ceanndraoi. Eideard saw them as well; he shouted to Tadgh, pointing, then looked back at Orla. "You have to do something," he said. "We can't reach them in time."

<Tha! . . .>, she heard her mam shout in affirmation as she felt the anamacha begin to scour energy from the Otherworld once more. <Look—that's Savas' banner . . .>

Orla blinked, trying to clear her vision. They were nearest to the ceanndraoi's chariot, and Commander Savas' chariot was bearing down on it. The ceanndraoi's hands were moving to form a spell cage, but as Orla watched, the commander threw a spear. The warrior in Ceanndraoi Greum's chariot raised his shield, but too late—the spear slid past the edge and into Greum Red-Hand's shoulder. The ceanndraoi roared in pain; the spell cage he was weaving shattered, and the energy inside flew off in a hundred directions in a shower of angry blue sparks. Orla saw Greum look around desperately; she knew he saw her readying to cast another spell, and the Red-Hand looked with wide eyes toward Savas, who had snatched up another spear.

But Orla had also seen Magaidh just beyond the ceanndraoi. She appeared as exhausted as Orla, and Comhnall struggled to lift his own shield and spear as the chariot of the Mundoan sub-commander raced toward them. The Mundoan sub-commander hurled his own spear, and though the ceannàrd managed to raise his shield in time, the impact sent Comhnall sprawling on the floorboards as his shield fell from his hand, leaving both Magaidh and the ceannàrd helpless. The sub-commander plucked up another spear to throw. As Comhnall tried to rise, Orla saw his left arm hanging limp at his side.

Orla's spell cage was glowing full; she raised her hands and shouted the release word.

<*No!*> her mam shouted, aware of where she intended to cast the spell. <*What are you doing? That's not Savas!*>

The fireball flared and hissed past Greum's chariot, slamming into the earth just in front of the sub-commander's chariot. The ground exploded, taking down the horses and overturning the chariot. Both the sub-commander and his driver spilled out onto the ground. From the floor of her chariot, Magaidh lifted her hand in salute to Orla while the ceannàrd struggled to rise again.

Commander Savas' chariot had stopped; she saw the man staring toward her. Greum Red-Hand glared at Orla, blood streaming down his clothing. He shouted to his driver, who jerked the reins hard, sending the chariot careening onto two wheels as it fled the field of combat. As Greum's chariot abandoned the battle, the ceanndraoi sent a flaring orange light arcing and hissing high into the morning sky.

The voices of the anamacha were all screaming at her as the carnyx, the Cateni war horns, began to sound the call of retreat—in response to Greum's signal, Orla realized. At the blare of horns, the Cateni warriors turned and began to run northward, back toward the hills beyond the floodplain. The ceannàrd's chariot turned to follow that of the ceanndraoi. Orla saw a look of disgust cross Eideard's face. "The bastard Red-Hand's given up!" he shouted. "We can't stay here alone." Eideard then called to Tadgh to follow the retreat. The chariot bounced over the broken, shattered field, jarring Orla in her bonds.

She looked back to see Commander Savas watching them closely, but he did not pursue.

15

Licked Wounds

"**H**OW IS THE CEANNÀRD?" Orla asked Magaidh. The encampment was furious with movement and sound: warriors having their injuries cared for; wives and husbands keening over the loss of loved ones who hadn't returned from the battlefield; the terrible screams coming from the archiaters' tents; people hurriedly readying animals and packing in anticipation of further retreat back into the folds of the high green mountains to the north.

"Comhnall's shield arm is broken. He's in pain, but hopefully the archiater has set the bones well," Magaidh answered. "But he won't be fighting again for some time." Her face was drawn, her hair and skin flecked with dried blood; she appeared drained and exhausted, but then everyone looked much the same. Magaidh reached out and pulled Orla to her in a quick embrace. Orla heard Sorcha, standing alongside her, draw in a breath. Magaidh's own breath was warm on Orla's ear. "My son Hùisdean took an arrow in his arm as he drove the horses, but he's young and will heal quickly. All three of us would be dead if it weren't for what you did, Orla. And for that my family will always be in your debt, both myself and Comhnall."

She released Orla, still holding her by the shoulders. "Take good care of your draoi," Magaidh said, glancing at Sorcha. "Without her, the battle today would have been entirely lost. She saved us. She saved all of us."

Orla shook her head, though her cheeks reddened at Magaidh's praise. The exhaustion still hadn't left her, even after several stripes of the candle, and now that the battle was over, the images and sounds of what she'd done were returning to her, making her feel sick. If Savas and his army attacked the camp now, she wasn't certain she could trust herself to cast even a single spell. The very thought made her shiver. Orla hugged herself, as if she were cold. "I did nothing you wouldn't have done for me," she said. "And what of the ceanndraoi?"

Magaidh grimaced. "The archiater who attended him thinks he'll recover from his wounds." She glanced around, lowering her voice. "At least the physical ones. As I'm sure you understand."

Orla nodded. Eideard had been vocal about his feelings even as they abandoned the battlefield. *The man sounded the retreat unnecessarily. We had the advantage of the field and would still have taken them, but the Red-Hand was only concerned with saving himself.* She'd heard many of the other àrds muttering in agreement on their return to the encampment.

Orla had seen Commander Savas' banner and his chariot; she still remembered that he'd stared at her as if he knew who she was and whose anamacha she held. She was certain he would have come after her if they'd not retreated, and she didn't know what would have happened then. *Eideard would have welcomed that chance, but . . .*

"What's going to happen?" Orla asked Magaidh. "The ceannàrd injured, the ceanndraoi . . ." She paused.

"That will depend on the draoi," Magaidh answered. "Those of Onglse who are close to the ceanndraoi might stay with him: Ceiteag, Moire, several of the others in his inner circle. But the other draoi, those of us who live out with the clans . . . well, I don't know if they will still look at him and see someone they want to follow or who deserves their respect. Not after taking us from a battle we might have won."

"And you, Magaidh? Does the Red-Hand deserve your respect?" Orla asked.

Magaidh didn't answer beyond a tightening of her lips.

"They respect *you*, Draoi Magaidh," Sorcha interjected. When Magaidh and Orla looked toward the woman, she continued. "I hear the other draoi talking when they think no one is listening. They think that the person Voada chose as her First Draoi would make a better ceanndraoi than the Red-Hand, who refused to follow where Voada led, who was never part of her victories, and whose inaction may have caused her defeat in the end."

Magaidh gave a quick shake of her head. "The ceanndraoi should be the best of us, the most powerful, and that's not me. It *was* once Greum Red-Hand, but that changed when Voada left Onglse and took the title for herself. And now . . ."

Magaidh didn't finish the thought. Orla felt the touch of winter as the Moonshadow's anamacha pressed close to her. <*We are the strongest. . . . We are the First . . .*> She couldn't tell whose voice was predominant among them.

"No," Orla said: to Magaidh, to Sorcha, to her anamacha. "You're implying that it should be me, but that's not what I want. I'm not ready."

<*We will make you ready . . . All you must do is give yourself to us . . .*>

"Sometimes you're not given a choice," Magaidh said. "Sometimes the title chooses the person, not the other way around. But I agree with you; you're not yet ready. The àrds and draoi have called for a formal conclave as soon as possible, and they've told the ceanndraoi and ceannàrd to be there. I was sent to make sure you attend as well."

"A conclave?"

"Aye," Magaidh said, then added more gently, "I don't know what's going to happen. None of us do. There will be a lot of shouting and arguing, that much is certain, but as to how it will end . . . ?"

She lifted a shoulder and let it fall again.

"Commander, you requested that the Voice of Muras and the chief shipwright meet with you . . ."

Altan looked up from his field desk and nodded to Tolga, standing at the entrance to his tent. Tolga had already set two chairs in front of the desk. "Fine. Send them in," he said.

Tolga saluted and stepped back. Two men entered the tent; Tolga let the flap close behind them and remained in the tent himself. The chief shipwright was gray-haired with a face that showed hands upon hands of years in the sun and a body that displayed the scars of hard work with saws and chisels. He was short and muscular and at least half Cateni, Altan suspected, despite his Mundoan name of Sabri.

The Voice of Muras was Demir, a nephew of Great-Voice Utka. He was dressed in royal purple, his black hair oiled and perfumed, his heavy-lidded eyes adding an air of languid disregard to his presence, as if the man were habitually bored. The resemblance between Demir and his uncle was enough to give Altan an immediate dislike for the man.

The Voice's eyebrows lifted slightly as he stared at Altan, still seated behind his desk. With a barely concealed sigh, Altan rose (his knee protesting), saluted, and bowed his head to the man. "Voice Demir, thank you for coming. If you'd like wine . . ." He nodded toward Tolga, who approached holding a tray with three wooden mugs; he handed one to each of the men and set Altan's down on the desk. "Please sit," Altan told the two, gesturing to the chairs facing his desk. Sabri hesitated, obviously uncomfortable being in this company, but Voice Demir gathered up his robes and sat as if placing himself on a throne, arranging the folds around him. He sniffed at the wine, frowned as if the offering were beneath his station, and set his mug on the nearest corner of Altan's desk.

"Commander Savas," Demir said, as if it had been he who had called for the meeting. "Congratulations on your victory this day.

All of Muras is grateful. I'll send my uncle my report once I've had the chance to compose it, but I have to wonder why the cohorts the Great-Voice gave you aren't out pursuing the ceanndraoi and ceannàrd and their army and destroying them entirely."

Altan glanced at the Voice's hands, as soft as a child's. *He's never held a weapon, never fought, never had to do manual labor. He'd piss himself if he were ever in a battle.* He swallowed his irritation at the Voice's barely hidden scorn. "I follow the emperor's and Great-Voice Utka's orders," he said. "I was told to take Onglse and the north. I can't accomplish that by chasing the army of the clans into the mountains—that would only waste the good troops the emperor sent me. Fighting the clans on ground that they choose and I don't know is a hopeless task, as I'm sure Voice Demir can understand. And I already have too many good soldiers to send to the flames and many more who need to heal, including my sub-commander Ilkur, who was very nearly killed. I appreciate your congratulations, Voice Demir, but to me this wasn't a victory. It was at best a draw, and came close to being a terrible defeat." *And I still don't know why the ceanndraoi called for the retreat. Worse, I felt the Moonshadow's presence again, and that terrifies me more than anything.*

Demir seemed to shake himself, as if he'd only half heard Altan's answer. "Of course," he said, waving a hand. "Certainly. But yet, to remain here . . ."

Altan could hear the unspoken words. *If the army stays here, Muras will have to feed and supply it.* Altan could see the man totting up expenses in his mind.

"I don't intend to remain here a moment longer than I must, Voice Demir," Altan said, and Demir could not hide the relief on his face. "But to complete my task for the Great-Voice and the emperor and conquer the north, I need to take Onglse, which is the heart of the draoi. Both the emperor and the Great-Voice realize that. And to invade Onglse, I need ships that can reach it, which is why I asked the shipwright to come here. Shipwright, how soon can you replace the ships that the draoi burned?"

Sabri, the shipwright, gaped for a moment, obviously startled at being addressed. "Commander," he managed to say, stuttering a bit, "most of the ships we'd built were burned down to the waterline. The others were smashed by the terrible wave one of the draoi sent. I might be able to salvage the keels, but little else. Replacing them . . . that would take several moons, and I only have a hand and two of good craftsmen—"

"I don't have moons," Altan interjected. "But I do have men: good engineers and experienced builders who know woodworking and the like. Men who have sailed. I can send you as many hands as you require. If you need more than I can supply, I'll have them sent to you from the yards at Gediz. How *soon*, Shipwright, if you had as many workers as you could handle?"

The man sputtered wordlessly, looking from Altan to the Voice. "Well . . . I don't know . . . A hand and four of ships . . ." Sabri tapped at his forehead with a forefinger, his eyes shut tight. "With enough skilled men, a large crew for each ship, people to cut down and bring in lumber, several good foremen to direct them . . . Two moons, maybe—"

Altan didn't let him continue. "Good! You'll start immediately, then, and work as quickly as you can," he said loudly, clapping his hand down on the desk. "Send me your requirements by this evening, Shipwright, and you'll have your crews ready to start work tomorrow. In the meantime, Voice Demir, my army will remain camped here on the northern side of the river to protect Muras and keep the draoi from burning down *these* ships."

Demir managed a wan smile; Sabri seemed lost in thoughts and calculations. Altan rose, gesturing to Tolga. "Thank you both for your cooperation," he said. "You should return to the town and your families; I'm sure they're waiting for you. Good evening, Voice Demir, Shipwright Sabri."

Altan watched Tolga usher them from the tent. When he could no longer hear their footsteps outside, he turned to Tolga. "I need three messengers. I have a letter to send to Great-Voice Utka in Savur, another to send to the Voice of Gediz, and the third messenger will ride north under a flag of truce."

"Gediz? North?" Tolga asked. "But—"

Altan lifted his finger to stop the protest. "You and the last two messengers are the only ones who are to know about their missions. Send me the messenger for the Great-Voice first, wait for half a turn, then bring the messenger who'll be riding to Gediz, then finally a trustworthy volunteer willing to ride north. Go now." Altan patted Tolga's cheek affectionately. "And remember, say nothing. In the meantime I have those messages to prepare."

Magaidh had said there'd be shouting and arguments. In the end, there would be more of both than Orla had thought possible.

For two full hands of days, little happened at all. The Cateni remained in the hills; the Mundoan army remained on the northern floodplain of the Meadham. Anyone attempting to enter Muras on foot from the north was stopped and turned back. The River Meadham was blocked with chains well east of the town; no boats were permitted to pass that weren't flying the flag of Mundoa, and even those were searched. There were occasional skirmishes between the two armies, but for the most part, an uneasy peace reigned.

The unease extended to the feelings between the àrds and the draoi. Orla overheard tense and angry arguments, which occasionally—especially between the warriors—turned into physical altercations that the àrds quickly broke up.

It was four days later that Ceanndraoi Greum finally bowed to the demands for a conclave.

The meeting took place in a hollow nestled between the ridges and the foothills, a clearing ringed by ancient oaks half a stripe's walk from the encampment. The air was cool and sweetly scented, and the green canopy overhead dappled the mossy earth with sunlight. The branches of some of the oaks held clusters of mistletoe, and Orla brushed the glossy, stiff green leaves as she passed. She felt that she was entering an ancient, sacred temple, and she heard the whispers of the Moonshadow's voices in her head.

<Like the sacred grove of Onglse at Bàn Cill and its blackstone circle, these trees were planted and cared for by the race that was here before the Cateni and whose bones sleep deep in the ground . . . I felt its power even then, when our people passed through while fleeing to the north from the carnage of the White Ships . . . I was simply Leagsaidh of Clan Mac Cába then, but on Onglse, the Moonshadow would emerge from the blackstones and merge with me, making me the First Draoi. We came back here afterward with an army at our back, and we performed the ritual of oak and mistletoe here before we went south again to drive out those who came in the White Ships . . . We remember . . .>

Orla pushed away the Moonshadow's voices as she, Sorcha, and Magaidh entered the natural amphitheater, which was already crowded with the various clan àrds and draoi. Anamacha shimmered in the shadows like wisps of softly glowing fog near their chosen draoi. Both the ceannàrd and ceanndraoi were already there, seated on stumps in the center of the ring and evidently in the midst of a private argument. Orla could hear their raised voices amid the general hubbub, if not the actual words they were exchanging, and the two men were gesticulating violently, both one-handed and obviously in discomfort.

The leaders were hardly the only ones in the clearing caught up in discussion—Orla could see Eideard not far from them, his dark eyes glimmering underneath a furrowed brow as he and a trio of other àrds spoke, their heads together. He caught sight of Orla and nodded to her. Orla wondered how anyone would be able to bring everyone together when she saw Ceiteag step from underneath the shadows of a tree. Her long and unbound white hair was bright in the sunlight; she was dressed in a simple undyed linen bog dress, her only ornamentation the torc of the draoi around her thin neck and bracelets of horn around her wrists. She looked around the clearing as she entered, holding a large polished brass bowl in her hands. Her gaze seemed to pause momentarily as she found Orla's eyes; she might have nodded toward her, though Orla thought that might have been her own imagination. Ceiteag moved to where the ceannàrd and ceanndraoi were seated and set the bowl on a boulder thrusting up from the grass between them. From her belt she took a small leather-wrapped wooden beater and struck it against the bowl: once, then two more times. Three clear, high, ringing notes sang out, riding easily over the noise of the conversations. By the time the notes slowly faded, everyone had gone silent.

"This conclave of the àrds and draoi has begun," she intoned in her high, quavering voice. "Who will ask the first question?"

"I'll ask what all of us want to know," Eideard called out without hesitation. Orla could see the storm cloud rage in his face, the same expression she'd seen on the battlefield. "Why did Ceanndraoi Greum call for retreat too early? The battle wasn't yet lost, not nearly so, and I was about to engage Commander Savas himself. Draoi Orla had just removed his sub-commander from the fight, and the ceanndraoi must have seen that—certainly the ceannàrd did. Draoi Orla and I would have done the same with Savas and ended it. I say that the battle would have been ours had the ceanndraoi not pulled back our warriors and draoi and left us without support."

Shouts of agreement and dissent erupted all around the clearing until Ceiteag struck the bowl again. "Quiet!" she barked. "Allow the ceanndraoi to speak and answer Àrd Iosa's question, unless you are afraid to hear what he has to say."

Greum Red-Hand had risen stiffly from his seat, glowering at the people arrayed before him and especially toward Eideard. He waited until the shouting had subsided once more, leaning more heavily than usual on his walking stick. Orla could see pain mingling with his expression, and the bandages around his shoulder and chest were bloodstained. Greum lifted his chin.

"I wasn't the one who called for us to withdraw," he said. His voice was slower and less forceful than usual, but it still carried throughout the ring of oaks. "Yes, you all saw the light I sent into the sky, but that wasn't intended to signal a retreat. It was only a failed spell I was unable to properly cast. I was sorely wounded at the time, but I saw that Draoi Orla had chosen to protect the ceannàrd and Draoi Magaidh rather than her ceanndraoi." Orla drew in her breath at that; Magaidh shook her head as if warning

Orla to stay silent. "I was laying half senseless in the chariot, and I thought I could muster one more spell to send toward Commander Savas, but my hands couldn't complete the spell cage, and the power escaped me. My driver thought me dead or dying, and so he turned the chariot away. That, along with the carnyx-players on the hill seeing the spell-light in the sky, caused the retreat to be sounded and our army to turn. Nothing more. The retreat wasn't deliberate; it was purely Elia's will."

There was more grumbling around the clearing, but everyone went silent as Ceiteag lifted her beater again in warning. "Is your question answered, Àrd Iosa?" she asked.

Eideard gave a mocking cough of a laugh. "It's answered, though I find it interesting that the ceanndraoi seems to spread the blame like a pat of butter on stale bread, even to Elia Herself. But I have another—"

Before Eideard could speak, Ceannàrd Mac Tsagairt also rose. "I know the question," he said, "and I have your answer. I failed, and I should no longer be ceannàrd." The grove went entirely quiet with that pronouncement; only the rustling of oak leaves in the breeze could be heard. Orla turned her head to look at Magaidh, who was watching her husband with eyes that shimmered with unshed tears. *She knew he was going to say this . . .*

Mac Tsagairt touched his left arm, bound tightly to his chest. "I've seen more years than most here, and I have fought too many battles. At my age, this arm will take seasons to heal, if it ever does completely. The army of the clans deserves a younger and more vital ceannàrd. My time is done."

With that, Comhnall nodded to his son Hùisdean, who stepped forward, took hold of the ends of the silver torc of the ceannàrd around his father's neck, and bent it enough to remove it. He gave the torc to Comhnall, who, with his good hand, placed the torc on the stump on which he'd been sitting.

Ceanndraoi Greum was shaking his head, his gaze furious as he watched Mac Tsagairt. Orla could see a tear sliding down Magaidh's cheek; both Sorcha and Orla put their arms around her.

"Let someone else here take my burden around their own neck,"

Comhnall finished. In the silence that followed, Mac Tsagairt walked slowly from the grove, escorted by Hùisdean. The warriors moved aside to let him pass in respectful silence. As Comhnall came near Eideard, he paused; a look passed between the two men, and then Comhnall walked on, striding through the ring of oak trunks and into deep emerald shadow.

"Iosa . . . Iosa . . ." The call started as a single voice, which was quickly joined by others until the chant rang loudly in the clearing. "Iosa! . . . Iosa! . . ." Eideard bowed his head as the shout grew louder, then strode to the clearing's center, brushing past Greum Red-Hand. He took the torc of the ceannàrd from the stump and lifted it. The clan àrds roared their approval. Eideard pulled the torc open more and placed it around his muscular neck as the acclamation washed over him.

Greum said nothing, not even looking at Eideard until the tribute faded.

"If you expect me to do the same as our former ceannàrd, all of you can wait until the rain turns this boulder into a mere pebble." Ceanndraoi Greum's voice brought everyone's attention to him. He tapped the boulder on which Ceiteag's bowl sat with the end of his walking stick. The bowl rang softly with the impact. "*I am still ceanndraoi.* I will remain ceanndraoi. No mere *warrior* can take that title from me." Now he looked directly at Eideard, then spat on the ground between them for emphasis. Eideard's face flushed under his beard, but he made no move.

Cold seeped into Orla's back: the Moonshadow's anamacha. <*We should be ceanndraoi . . . As we've always been . . . We should claim the title, not the Red-Hand . . .*>, the voices inside the anamacha whispered in her head. In the dimness of the grove, Orla could see Greum's anamacha, Dòrn, shimmering alongside him, as near to him as the Moonshadow was to her. She wondered what his anamacha might be whispering in his head. Greum looked at those around him, his regard lingering for a moment as it passed Orla and Magaidh.

"Do the draoi believe they need a new ceanndraoi?" Greum

said. "If so, let them declare it. Let someone challenge me. Any of you. Even injured as I am, I'm ready."

Orla felt Magaidh's hand grasp her wrist. She said nothing, only shook her head once, then released Orla's arm. The rest of the draoi were silent as Greum's gaze swept over them. "I thought not," he said finally, then he looked at Ceiteag. "Ring the bowl a last time," he told her. "This conclave is over. I'll meet with our new ceannàrd this evening, and he can give me his wise advice." The look he gave Eideard made it clear just how valuable he thought that advice would be.

Then, as the bowl chimed three more times, Greum—leaning heavily on his stick for support—made his slow way from the ring of oaks.

16

A Meeting of Enemies

AFTER EIDEARD IOSA AND Greum left the clearing, Orla waited as nearly all the other draoi and warriors followed them. She felt them staring at her as they did so; she wondered what they were thinking, especially the draoi. It wasn't until then that she stirred

The walk back to the camp seemed far too long. Orla trudged alongside Magaidh and Sorcha, her head down and her thoughts whirling around what had happened. It was Magaidh who broke the silence between them. "Eideard was so eager to take Comhnall's title," she said. "I hope he's ready for all that it means."

"So you knew Ceannàrd Mac Tsagairt no longer wanted the title before the conclave?" Sorcha asked her.

Magaidh nodded. "Comhnall was reluctant to accept the title in the first place after Ceannàrd Maol Iosa's death, but Greum insisted—he knew he had to make some concession to the northern clans after he and Onglse had failed to support Voada and Maol Iosa, and he felt Clan Mac Tsagairt was the best choice, since Comhnall was already Ceannàrd Iosa's First Àrd. Comhnall believed himself too old even then. And after this injury . . ." Magaidh gave a bitter laugh. "There's a certain sense of justice in

178

knowing that the Red-Hand will be dealing with another Ceann-àrd Iosa who dislikes him even more than his uncle did."

Orla listened to their conversation without speaking. She could feel that they were speaking around her, avoiding the subject of the ceanndraoi and his defiance. *Should I have taken his challenge? Is that what I was supposed to do? Is that what Elia wants of me?*

She knew the answer her anamacha would give her. The Moonshadow remained a careful few steps away from her, far enough that she couldn't hear the yammering of the voices inside. She saw the faces flickering across its visage, her mother's face among them, and thought she saw disappointment in the ghostly features.

She noticed movement to their right from a converging path and saw Ceiteag emerging from the oaks, carrying the bowl and beater. "Wait a moment," the woman called out. Magaidh—and belatedly, Sorcha and Orla—halted to let the older woman catch up to them.

"Draoi, may Elia be with you," Sorcha said to her. Ceiteag nodded to Sorcha and Magaidh, then her rheum-laden and wrinkle-netted eyes snared Orla's gaze.

She stared at Orla for two long breaths, not letting Orla look away. "I want you to know this," she said. "A little more than two years ago, I stood with Greum Red-Hand on the cliffs of Onglse as we watched the last of Commander Savas' ships leaving for the south to do battle with your mother. I told Greum then that he was making a mistake: that those of us on the island should join with your mother; that he should acknowledge her openly as ceanndraoi and send what aid we could to her. He refused. He said the southern clans who had risen up with Voada and Maol Iosa would have to deal with their own mess and that the Moonshadow had driven your mother mad. He was furious that she dared to give herself the title of ceanndraoi. What I didn't say to him—and perhaps I should have—was that she'd been given that title by the clans for what she'd accomplished and that she deserved the title because of that. But I held my tongue, and I too stayed at Bàn Cill when Greum remained on Onglse."

Her gaze flickered over Orla, over Magaidh, over Sorcha. "I know the man better than any of you. He understands what he's doing and has made deliberate choices, and he holds the interests of the Cateni in his heart, even if you think otherwise. Anyone who says he doesn't is being blind and foolish."

Ceiteag licked dry, cracked lips with the tip of her tongue. "He refused to let go of his title then as he's refusing now," she continued. "His pride, perhaps, has always been stronger than his reason. It still is, and that's not going to change. Ever. But I ask you to trust him, especially now. You don't understand all that he's done and is doing."

"I don't agree with you, Draoi Ceiteag," Magaidh told her. "I think his pride has overwhelmed him entirely. I believe he thinks only of himself and the power he holds, not of the Cateni."

Ceiteag's mouth pursed. "As I said, then you're the fool. I suppose you think this child"—she nodded her head toward Orla—"is fit to be ceanndraoi just because she's not yet as mad as her mam."

"I only worry that's it's too soon," Magaidh said flatly. "Orla's not ready."

"And in that, at least, you're right," Ceiteag answered. "I knew Voada before she learned how to join with her anamacha. I taught her first. I was a poor teacher, as Greum would tell you, but I was afraid for her even then. She'd suffered too much already in her life and I wanted nothing more than to give her my friendship and comfort. I did that as best as I could in our time together. But I knew—I *feared*—that the Moonshadow would be too strong for her." Ceiteag's gaze came back to Orla. "As I'm afraid it will be for you," she finished. "I don't hate you, Draoi Orla. But I have little hope for you."

"I've made no challenge to the ceanndraoi," Orla answered. "I don't even know what this challenge that the ceanndraoi spoke of might be." Her throat was dry and parched; the words were difficult to shape, her voice hoarse.

"Then you don't *need* to know what it is, do you?" Ceiteag answered. "I can tell you this for certain: Greum Red-Hand will never voluntarily give up the title of ceanndraoi while he lives. He certainly won't give it up to Voada's daughter."

"Then he can keep it," Orla declared. "I don't want to be ceanndraoi."

"Neither did Voada, but it was what she became," Magaidh said quietly.

Ceiteag sniffed at that pronouncement. "Until Voada came, Greum Red-Hand had led the draoi well. He was respected as ceanndraoi, and for good reasons. I see two paths for you, Orla: either you can do as Voada did and leave us to become Orla Moonshadow among the draoi you can convince to follow you, or you can stay and give your total obedience to the ceanndraoi. That way, maybe you'll escape your mother's fate."

"I don't want to be ceanndraoi," Orla repeated.

Ceiteag laughed at that, showing her gap-toothed mouth, which Orla found strange. "You sound so much like her," she said. "Just like you, your mam was certain she understood the shape of things. And she was just as wrong."

Ceannàrd Eideard came to Orla's tent with the morning sun. Orla opened the flap of the tent to see him, Sorcha at her shoulder. His chariot rattled and clattered, and his horses neighed, their breath steaming from flared nostrils. Tadgh was in the traces, reins in his strong hands as the horses stamped at the muddy earth.

"Come ride with me, Draoi Orla," he called out. "We need to talk, you and I."

Less than a stripe of the candle later, she stood with Eideard on the edge of the escarpment, looking south toward the River Meadham and Muras, with the waving banners and tents of the Mundoan army spread out on the floodplain before them.

"The ceanndraoi is a fool who cares far more about himself than the welfare of the Cateni," Eideard began. Despite his insistence that they needed to talk, that was the first thing Eideard had said beyond polite pleasantries when she'd stepped into the chariot with him. He wasn't looking at her but at the landscape spread out below. Eideard waved an arm to take in Savas' army. "He listens to no one but himself. If he had, we would have driven the Mundoa back across the river and sent them fleeing south."

Not certain how to reply, Orla remained silent, waiting for him to say more. Eideard heaved a dramatic sigh. "It's obvious to me and to other of the àrds that Greum Red-Hand shouldn't be ceann-draoi. Not anymore. I wager that most of the draoi feel that way as well, even if they won't openly speak out against him." Now he glanced at her. "Is that your feeling too, Draoi Orla?"

"You're asking someone too new to the torc," she answered, touching the brass circlet around her neck. It seemed to her that it was heavier now than when she'd first put it on. "I never knew the ceanndraoi until I came to Onglse a few months ago, and I never really knew that I was menach or draoi, though my mother said I might be because I could see taibhse. I never understood anything of the northern clans or Onglse. For three years I lived with the Mundoa as an officer's lowly second wife, and all I knew of the world was that and the gossip I heard in the camps."

"But now you've seen how the Red-Hand is. You've fought and argued with him yourself."

"Yes," she admitted. "As a person, he's cold and stern. I would never choose to be his friend or be with him. I haven't agreed with all of his tactics. But none of that means he's a poor ceann-draoi, does it?"

Eideard sniffed. His hands prowled his beard, tugging at the oiled strands. They could hear Tadgh giving water to the horses and talking to them, a double hand of strides back from the escarpment. "If the Red-Hand were a *good* ceanndraoi," Eideard said, "he'd have known or suspected what Savas was preparing in Muras, and we'd have kept them in the funnel trap of the bridge as he himself suggested, rather than letting them cross in a wide line—though I don't think the Red-Hand's was the best strategy in any case; why stay where your enemy can easily strike at you? If he were a *wise* ceann-draoi, he'd have listened to Ceannàrd Mac Tsagairt's counsel and had us burn down Muras while we had the chance, take down the bridges entirely, then head back to Onglse to prepare a reception for Savas when he eventually arrived there. Greum did none of those things. Now Savas sits in Muras like some obstinate turtle in the middle of a stream, and we sit here and watch. We have no sense of what he intends, and it's imperative for us to know that if we're to make our own plans. Last night, when I spoke with the Red-Hand, I asked him if we've tried to send spies into the town or contacted any of the Cateni living there. I can tell you the answer. He's done *nothing*. He sits and waits, and he listens only to his own advice."

Eideard bent down, plucked a stone from the edge of the bluff, and threw it over the edge as if he could strike down the nearest Mundoan. They both listened to the stone crash futilely into the underbrush below.

"From what Magaidh's told me of my mother, she was also someone who only listened to her own advice," Orla replied. "Which sounds exactly Greum. Like the Red-Hand, she could also be cold and stern, and dangerous besides, even to those she loved. Yet your uncle thought of her as the ceanndraoi, and he chose to follow her even though that led them both to death."

"To *honorable* deaths," Eideard answered. "Death in battle against the enemies of the Cateni. Maol Iosa has gone to Tirnanog and the Hall of Warriors as his reward, while your mother lives on in the Moonshadow."

"But they're still *dead*," Orla insisted, "and only Elia knows what they might have accomplished had they taken a different path and lived longer."

Eideard shook his head, the braid of his long hair moving as he stared outward again. "You have the Moonshadow. I've seen what you can do with it. Your mother was ceanndraoi; you could claim the same title. That's what Greum Red-Hand is afraid of. I know it even if he won't say it." Orla could hear the echo of Ceiteag's voice in Eideard's. She shook her head at both of them.

"I've only seen three hands and three of summers," Orla said. "Magaidh said that I'm not ready. I may never be. When my mother joined with the Moonshadow, she was three double hands and more old. Yet she couldn't contain Leagsaidh Moonshadow—that personality within the anamacha, *my* anamacha, consumed her. I haven't yet allowed the Moonshadow to touch me; I don't know what would happen if I tried."

"Maybe your mother was *too* old. Maybe a younger, stronger person—"

"Maybe, maybe, maybe," Orla repeated mockingly. "You're full of maybes and could-have-beens, Eideard Iosa, but you don't *know*. You *can't* know. In the end you're no different from Greum Red-Hand. You only care about how you can use me—or rather, how you can use the power of the Moonshadow. I don't believe there's *honor* in dying in battle, Ceannàrd. It's just *death*."

"How can you say that, Orla? You have to hate the Mundoans more than most for what they did to your family."

Orla gestured toward the Mundoan army as Eideard had a few moments before. "I hate what the Mundoa did to my family, and I'd love to see them gone from all of Albann. But when you know the enemy—"

He scoffed, stopping her from saying more. "Are you saying you didn't hate the Mundoan you were forced to marry?"

"It would be easy to say yes to that. Bakir . . . the man made me watch while the soldiers under his command beat and kicked my mother until I believed she was dead, and that same night he forced himself on me. But in my time with him, I also saw that Bakir genuinely loved Azru, his First Wife, and his children. I hated what he'd done, but the man himself? He had some good qualities, even if he rarely showed them to me. For that matter, Azru protected me from Bakir as much as she could, and I loved her and her children in turn. It was Azru who helped Sorcha and me escape when Bakir died, when the other Mundoan wives might have turned on us. Am I supposed to hate her simply because she's Mundoan? And Commander Savas? My mother met him in Pencraig while she was still the Voice-wife, and she said he treated her and my father extremely well. He might have become her enemy, but she didn't hate him. I *know* that because she's told me herself." Orla nodded toward her anamacha, then realized that Eideard couldn't see the apparition or understand what her gesture meant. "Neither do I," she told him.

"Altan Savas killed your mother. He killed my uncle—how can we *not* hate him for that?"

"My mother and your uncle would have killed Savas just as certainly had that been the fate Elia chose for them. They'd have killed him not with hatred but because it was their duty to do so to protect the Cateni people. You and I may want the same thing, Ceannàrd, but we want it for vastly different reasons."

"I don't understand you, Orla," he said. She could hear genuine confusion in his voice, not simply disagreement, and it softened what she might have said. She managed a fleeting smile.

"I know you don't," she told him. "I'm not entirely certain I understand myself."

"Now Savas sits in Muras like some obstinate turtle in the middle of a stream, and we sit here and watch. We have no sense of what he intends, and it's imperative for us to know that if we're to make our own plans."

Orla lay in her tent, Sorcha alongside her. The moon shimmered faintly through the cloth above her, and she stared at the blue-tinged spot in the darkness. She could hear the sounds of the encampment asleep around her: someone snoring loudly nearby, the single-note call of the night thrushes, the trill of fiddle-bugs in the trees, the soft footsteps of the guards on their rounds and the murmur of their conversations. Orla shifted restlessly under the blankets.

"Still awake?" Sorcha whispered sleepily in the dark.

"Sorry. I keep thinking about my meeting with Eideard today."

"Oh." The reply was flat, the inflection telling. Silence. A breath. "He wants you to be . . ." Another breath. ". . . like your mother and his uncle."

"Yes."

"Is that what you want, too?"

Orla closed her eyes. "I don't know what I want." Then she realized what Sorcha had implied, and her eyes opened again, searching for the curve of Sorcha's body in the darkness. "Sorcha, my mother and Maol Iosa were never lovers, and I don't want Eideard Iosa that way either. Never. You don't have to worry."

Sorcha's hand found hers, their fingers intertwining though neither of them spoke again. The touch was comfort enough. Orla heard Sorcha's breath begin to deepen and slow, her fingers relaxing. Orla slid her hand from Sorcha's and rose from their makeshift bed, pulling on a woolen robe and tying it around her, slipping her feet into leather sandals. She opened the tent flap and went out; her anamacha glided alongside her but not close enough for her to hear their voices. She made her way between the tents to the perimeter of the encampment. The guard on watch stiffened and grabbed his pike as she approached, then relaxed as the torc around her neck reflected the light of the torch alongside him.

"Draoi Orla. You're up early. It's a hand of stripes yet till dawn."

"I needed to walk," she told him.

"It may not be safe outside the encampment."

"You don't have to be concerned. The Moonshadow walks with me," she told him. She saw his gaze search the air around her, seeing nothing, even though she could feel the chill of the anamacha at her left side and see their ghostly faces appearing and vanishing again, her mother's among them.

The guard relaxed and moved aside. "Don't go far," he told her. "Stay where we can hear you and respond quickly if you call."

"I will," she told him. "Don't worry."

She went out into the moonlit landscape, the grass wet around her feet and ankles. She found a fallen tree overlooking a creek running down toward the Meadham. The stream's water was loud in the night, rivulets splashing white around the rocks of its bed. The torches of the camp were a glow just uphill as she sat. The voices of others were falling stars in the night, ephemeral and fleeting as she recalled their words.

Ceiteag: "I see two paths for you . . ."

Magaidh: "It's too soon. She's not ready."

Eideard: "Altan Savas killed your mother. He killed my uncle. How can we not hate him for that? . . . Now Savas sits in Muras like an obstinate turtle, and we sit here. We have no sense of what he intends to do. . . ."

A winter snow pressed against her back, sending the thoughts scattering. <Savas is a good man . . . A man of honor . . .> Her mam's voice, its familiarity making Orla's chest tighten.

"I know. I told Eideard that you didn't hate Savas," she whispered into the night.

<We were enemies, but we respected him . . . We had no hatred of him . . . There's a way for you to speak to Savas . . . We did that once, tried to convince him to leave Onglse to end the invasion and all the death, but he wouldn't listen to us . . . He thought me a dream . . .>

"You only tried once?"

<Only that time . . . You could talk to him . . . We can show you how . . .>

"Then show me," Orla said.

<Open yourself to us . . .> Orla saw the anamacha glide in front of her now, and she opened her arms as it approached, allowing it to enter her.

She found herself in Magh da Chèo, its storm-wracked landscape a darkness interrupted by fitful blue lightning. The ghost of her mam was already there, separated from the other draoi and standing before her. The sight of her face made Orla yearn to clasp her in her arms, but there would be no warmth, no body to embrace. Her mam was a shade of light and shadow, no more—as I will be one day, she reminded herself. She faced her mother. <How do I do this?> she asked her.

<First you have to understand that you won't be able to touch Savas or do anything to him. You won't be able to harm him, but he will see you and hear you. Is that enough for you?>

Orla nodded.

<Then begin to make your spell cage, and accept what we give you . . .>

Voada lifted her hands to the sky, but no lightning sliced down from the storm clouds to her fingertips. Instead her mam seemed to grasp the lowering clouds themselves. Orla moved her hands in the pattern she'd been taught, chanting the words to bind the net and pull the energy from her mam to herself. This was different from the other spells, though. The spells she'd cast in the past had been designed for battle; they were harsh and furious, snarling against the spell cage. This spell was more like trying to hold seal oil: slippery, cold, and draining through her fingers. Softer. Quieter.

When the cage she'd woven seemed full, Voada whispered the release words in Orla's head: "*Bruidhinn nam fhochair.*" Speak in my presence.

Orla repeated the words, and the world changed around her once more.

Magh da Chèo had vanished, but she was no longer in the night meadow outside the encampment. She was . . . honestly, she wasn't sure *where* she was. In a house, it seemed, on an upper floor; from the open window, she could look out westward over Muras toward the quay where she'd burned the ships, the river shimmering in the moonlight. There were lanterns lit on the wharves, and men moved through the light, carrying timber and tools. She could hear the faint sounds of hammers and saws and the quiet commands of the shipwrights as they directed the work. At least two ships appeared to be nearly ready to sail again. *They're rebuilding what we destroyed,* Orla realized. *That's why Savas hasn't moved his army . . .*

There was the sound of a sword sliding from its scabbard behind her, and Orla turned to see a half-naked older man sitting up in his bed, the sword in his hand and the blankets pooled around his waist. His chest hair was graying along with that on his head, the body still retaining the shadow of what once had been a muscular, toned one, now crisscrossed with scars. There was a younger man asleep in the same bed, but he didn't wake—Orla wondered if that was part of the spell. The man with the sword was staring directly at her; she wondered what he saw.

<Altan Savas . . .> Orla heard her mother say, the name echoed by other voices within the anamacha.

Almost as he had heard the voices, Savas spoke. "Voada?" His voice was husky and low with sleep. The man alongside him didn't stir.

"No," Orla told him. "I'm Orla, Voada's daughter."

Savas blinked heavily. "Yes, the face . . . you have some of her appearance, but younger. I saw you in the chariot with the Clan Iosa banner, and I knew I'd felt that draoi's power in the past. You nearly killed my sub-commander Ilkur. Why are you troubling my sleep, phantom?"

"I'm not a phantom," Orla told him. "My mam said she spoke to you this way once before, when you were both on Onglse."

Savas' eyes narrowed at that, and he lifted the sword, pointing it toward her though he didn't move from the bed. "I'd almost forgotten that. Her appearance startled me so much that I cut her with this sword, and the blade only passed through her like smoke. I thought her a strange and lucid dream, talking of peace and truce, especially since she never came to me again. That truly *was* her?"

Orla nodded. "It was. She was no dream. Neither am I. And your weapon is unnecessary. You already know you can't touch me, but neither can I touch you."

Savas placed the sword across his lap, though his hand didn't leave the weapon. He glanced at the man sleeping next to him. Orla recognized the stubbled face—the driver of Savas' chariot. Were they lovers? The Mundoa Orla had known considered such relationships at best shameful and at worst an abomination, and the Cateni were generally the same. Neither culture admitted openly that some people might be attracted to their own gender. *Do we share that affliction, Savas and I? Do we both keep the same secret?*

"Maybe my sword can't touch you . . . or maybe it can," Savas was saying to her. "What does Voada's daughter want that she'd haunt my sleep? Revenge?"

<Tha! . . .> the voices shrieked as one in her head. <Yes!>

<Be silent, all of you> she shouted back at them. "No," she told Savas aloud. "I only thought . . . I thought I should know the person who is supposed to be my enemy."

"That's a good trait for someone in command, but dream or real, you look rather young to be ceanndraoi. Or are you telling me that the Red-Hand's been deposed at last?"

His voice held a strange inflection she couldn't quite understand, and his eyes narrowed as he said the words, as if the idea that Greum might no longer be the ceanndraoi worried him.

"No," she answered, but Orla's voice lacked force. Yes, her mam—or rather the anamacha as a whole—wanted her to hold the title. The Moonshadow wasn't content being a mere draoi under another's command. She wondered if that was why her mother had made the decision to leave Onglse and attack the south on her own without consulting Greum Red-Hand, if the Moonshadow and those within the anamacha had known that by doing so they would become ceanndraoi by default—and so they'd forced their will on Voada.

<We are First . . .> The voice that Orla thought of as Leagsaidh Moonshadow dominated the chorus. <We will always be First . . .>

"I'm almost surprised at that," Savas was saying.

"Why?" Orla asked, then stopped, the word only half spoken as she looked at his face. "No, I know why. You feel you would have lost the battle had Ceanndraoi Greum not sounded the retreat. That's why you didn't pursue us, and that's why you thought Greum would lose his title."

Savas lifted an eyebrow. "Perhaps, Dream," he said, but the way he said the word made her wonder if she'd spoken the truth or if there were some other reason she was missing. Surely Savas hadn't known how exhausted Orla had been or that Magaidh and the other draoi had felt the same. He couldn't have realized how many of the Cateni warriors had already fallen, that there were no reserves waiting, that the Cateni had staked all they had on that battle. Had Greum Red-Hand stayed, had he not fled, it might have been Savas who called for retreat. "However, battles can't be refought," Savas continued. "Every battle is a new one, even when on the same ground with the same opponents. You may tell Greum Red-Hand that we're prepared for him if he wants to try us again."

"You don't intend the battle to be here," Orla told him, gesturing to the window. "You're rebuilding the ships we destroyed. You, the Great-Voice, and Emperor Pashtuk want Onglse. You want it because of what taking the island would represent to the clans, the draoi, and all Cateni."

Now both Savas' eyebrows were raised, and his fingers tightened around the leather-wrapped grip of his sword, then slowly relaxed. He yawned. With one hand he nudged his bed companion, who still didn't wake. Savas looked back to Orla. "So we both dream . . . Why are we talking, Dream Orla? If you want to know your enemy, you already do."

"Perhaps we shouldn't *be* enemies."

"Yet we are. I told your mam this when she came to me as you have: I'm a simple man, a soldier who obeys his orders. Nothing more."

"My mam didn't agree with that. She thought you clever—and dangerous, yes, but also someone she respected, even as an enemy. She hoped there might be a way to find peace."

"If there was, I didn't see it then, and I don't see it now. So tell me, Dream Orla: are *you* like your mam?"

"I don't know," she answered honestly.

"Do you think you can defeat your enemy where your mam failed?"

"I don't know that either."

That seemed to amuse Savas. She thought he nearly laughed. "Somehow I suspect we're to find out."

"Perhaps we will," she told him. Orla could feel the spell fading, the room growing fainter around her. She didn't try to hold it but instead let the vision fall away entirely. She found herself still standing in the moonlit meadow, the grass dew-wet around her feet. The fires of the camp were yellow stars at the top of the hill behind her.

She turned and began walking toward them.

After the Dream Orla vanished—no, she couldn't have been a dream, for Altan was as awake now as he'd been when Orla had been standing like a glimmering specter at the foot of his bed— Altan placed the sword back in its scabbard and put it alongside the bed. He shook Tolga's arm again, and this time the younger man blinked and yawned, a hand over his mouth.

"Altan?" Tolga grumbled. "It's not morning yet. Is something the matter? Can't you sleep?"

"A strange dream woke me," Altan said.

Tolga ran his hand down Altan's chest and lower. "A good one, I hope."

Altan grabbed Tolga's hand and brought it back up. "I was talking to the dream—to Orla, Voada's daughter, the draoi with the Moonshadow. You heard nothing?"

Tolga shook his head. "Nothing. She was *here*?" He looked around as if expecting to see her ghost lingering in the corner of the room. "She didn't . . ."

". . . try to kill me?" Altan finished for him. "No. I don't think she could. But I also think that wasn't what she wanted."

"What did she want, then?"

Altan laughed. "To see if there was another way to end the war, evidently," he said musingly. "Her mother made much the same offer to me once. But unfortunately, that was something I couldn't give Voada at the time. Now her daughter has arrived and muddied the waters again." Altan sighed. "It's been three hands of days now. The Red-Hand has had his time to keep our bargain. We've waited long enough."

17

Confronting the Moon

"**S**HE'S NOT READY." MAGAIDH'S VOICE.

"*Just like you, your mam was certain of the shape of things. And just as wrong,*" Ceiteag seemed to answer in her head. Then Eideard's voice drowned them both out.

"*Your mother was ceanndraoi; you could claim the same title. That's what Greum Red-Hand is afraid of.*"

And last came Savas' comment: "*Why are we talking, Dream Orla? . . . So tell me, Dream Orla: are you like your mam?*"

The statements, questions, and opinions echoed and danced and argued inside Orla's head, but she could neither refute nor answer them. Orla stared at her anamacha. The features of the draoi captured inside flitted across its face: male, female, old, young, smiling, scowling, furious, and sympathetic. All of the spirits who were once alive, once just like her. She didn't know most of their names—she'd never called them to her, had never heard their stories. Their voices were simply part of the hidden chorus.

She feared she would soon be just another of them, her own name and life forgotten. *Not like Leagsaidh herself. Not like Iomhar. Not like your mam. Their names will always be remembered because of what they accomplished.*

On her return to the camp, Orla had told Eideard what she'd gleaned from Savas. Eideard had immediately gone to Greum Red-Hand; he's still with him, as far as Orla knew. Orla had wandered outside the camp again, out to the ring of oak trees under a sky that mirrored her gloom. She hadn't spoken to Sorcha, to Magaidh, to Ceiteag, but their voices were with her.

"Sometimes you're not given a choice," Magaidh's memory whispered to her.

Choices. "How can I choose when I don't know enough?" Orla said to the air.

"Then learn what it is you need to know." The voice sounded like Sorcha's, enough that Orla turned around to see if she was there. But there were only the oaks, the grass, and the songs of the birds.

And her anamacha, barely visible under the canopy of an oak tree, staring at her. Waiting. The anamacha wore a single face, not multiple fleeting ones. A woman. Orla knew immediately who it was: Leagsaidh Moonshadow.

Impulsively, Orla opened her arms. "Come to me," she said. The anamacha obediently—and eagerly, too eagerly—glided forward, sliding into Orla's body and bringing with it the noise and clamor of the Otherworld it inhabited. The shades within the anamacha crowded around her, their voices shrill.

<We know why you've called us . . .>

<You're a fool, a child . . .>

<You'll be with us soon . . .>

She saw Iomhar, who only shook his head sadly at her. Then the shades scattered like frightened birds as her mam strode through the crowd of them, her ghostly face stern. *<No . . .>* she said simply. *<We won't allow it. You're not ready. I* wasn't *ready . . .>* The use of the singular rather than the plural made Orla shiver, made her want to cry. This apparition felt like it *was* her mother, not just some ghostly representation overlaid with all the other presences within the anamacha.

"Mam," she began, "I have to know what I can do. I need to know if I'm strong enough."

<The Moonshadow will make you part of her, as she did me . . .>
Lightning sliced the sky at the mention of the name, visible
through the figure of her mother, the following thunder drum-
ming against Orla's chest. <It's her bidding that you'll do . . . You'll
die . . . You'll be lost in here, just one of many . . .>

The chorus returned, agreeing. <Tha! . . . Like me . . . And like
me . . . Lost . . . Forgotten . . . Listen to Voada . . . She knows, even
though she was one of the strong ones . . .>

"Mam, it's useless for me to hold the Moonshadow if I can
never dare to use her."

Her mam's face became more solid for a moment, more clear,
and Orla saw the deep sadness in her eyes and caught the glint of
remembered emerald in the irises. The eyes shimmered, but there
were no tears; Orla wondered if it were even possible for a taibhse
to cry. Voada's hands stretched toward her, and Orla grasped for
them, but it was as impossible as holding smoke.

Voada's lips didn't move, but Orla heard her mam's voice. <I
thought I was simply using her power. I thought I was in control. I was
wrong. In the end, I wasn't strong enough . . .>

"Then tell me how to avoid that, Mam. Tell me how—" Orla's
voice caught in her throat. Her mother was drifting back into the
crowd, fading into the mist of bodies. All their voices had gone
silent. Another presence was moving forward, one whose existence she'd only glimpsed distantly in the landscape of Magh da
Chèo. The apparition's long, unbound hair flowed behind her as
if in a wind off the ocean, the color of chestnuts streaked with
pale gold, and her eyes were the color of the sea under a cloudless
sky. She radiated power—it seemed to crackle in the air around
her—and when she spoke, the chorus of the anamacha spoke
with her.

<I am Leagsaidh. I hold the Moonshadow, and the Moonshadow is
within me. You called me.>

"No," Orla began, but the woman only gazed at her, and Orla's
denial faded away, unheard in the thundering of Magh da Chèo.

<We would have taken you in Pencraig, but Voada wouldn't allow
that . . .>

"I was too young."

Leagsaidh laughed at that, a bitter sound. <*Youth might have protected you. It might still. Your mam was older and brittle—though I was even older when I came to Onglse and found the blackstones. Here . . . Let me show you . . .*>

Leagsaidh reached for Orla, who backed away. "No," she said, but the apparition moved too suddenly and rapidly, the misty presence wrapping around her, and she was suddenly somewhere and someone else. . . .

She *was* Leagsaidh, listening to the long-dead woman's thoughts and feeling her emotions, the touch of sun and wind on her skin, the fabric of her tattered bog dress scratching along her knees, but she was also Orla, a silent observer inside. She stood at the rim of a valley, looking down at a place both familiar and unfamiliar to her. Below, the valley was ringed by a stand of large oak trees. Beyond the oaks was an inner ring of tall blackstone menhirs capped with granite slabs, and at the center of the ring on the valley's floor stood a single, smaller blackstone column.

The part of her that was Orla knew this place. This was Bàn Cill on Onglse, the sacred place of the draoi, but a Bàn Cill without people, without the walled ring of protective forts around the valley's lips, and without the temple that now enclosed the central blackstone. This was Bàn Cill untouched, as it had been before any draoi walked there.

Leagsaidh/Orla stared at the sights and marveled. This was unlike anything she'd experienced before. The moons-long diaspora of her people had taken her to many places outside the realm of her knowledge, but this . . .

Since the last winter solstice, the clans had fled north and away from the invaders who had emerged from the fleets of white-sailed ships, who had pillaged and murdered and raped their way through the fields and villages of Albann Deas. Leagsaidh's own daughter, thirteen summers old, had been staying with an aunt who had just given birth; she'd been killed when the invaders had landed near Darende, where the aunt lived. Leagsaidh tried not to imagine what she must have endured before she died. Leagsaidh's husband, the àrd of Clan Mac Cába, had fallen in battle near Ladik along with Leagsaidh's two sons. After that defeat, the warriors of the clans had been unable to muster a concerted resistance, instead retreating across the River Meadham for safety. Leagsaidh had come to the island of Onglse with the weary remnants of her clan and a few others.

She'd come across this valley while following the small flock of sheep they'd acquired. The sheep were wandering among the stones now, her black-and-white dog barking as he tried to herd them back up the hill toward Leagsaidh, but Leagsaidh was paying attention to neither dog nor sheep. This place . . . it felt impossibly *ancient*, as if it had been here since the Nameless God pulled up Albann and the other lands from the endless waves. The Nameless God then tore itself asunder on the knives of the mountain peaks of Albann Bràghad, giving birth to Elia and her brood, the gods who took the Nameless God's spilled blood and used it to bring all life to Albann and then to the entire world.

Leagsaidh could feel the power throbbing in the bones of this place, beating in time with her own heart.

She walked down through the ring of oaks to the blackstone ring. Her hand, brushing against the stones as she passed, caused sparks to erupt from deep within, the cold fire gleaming under the polished, night-black surface like stars as it traced the path of her fingers, a fire visible even in the sunlight. She passed through the ring of blackstones; the air felt heavy and oppressive as if a storm were about to break even though the sky above was blue and empty of clouds. Her ears were ringing, as if hearing some sound both too low and too high to decipher. She approached the central stone, sunlight flashing from its glossy facets, causing her to shield her eyes from the glare.

There was something *moving* inside the stone. Leagsaidh could almost see it, almost hear it. She reached out her hand and placed it on the stone. The glassy surface was cold, as if she'd plunged her hand into a snowbank, and she tried to snatch away, but it refused to move. The stone was holding her in place.

Then she felt it: a Presence rising from the depths of the stone and sliding into her as if she were a vessel to be filled. She screamed in fear, still trying to pull her hand away from the stone, her entire body shaking with the sense of being inhabited by another. She heard laughter, as if the Presence were mocking her terror.

And she heard its voice, deep and throbbing. <*I've waited so long . . . So long . . . Finally . . .*> With the voice, she felt her hand drop from the stone, and Leagsaidh's and Orla's twinned awareness fled into a dark, storm-plagued landscape.

<*That was how I became the First Draoi of the Cateni . . .*> Leagsaidh said as the winds of Magh da Chèo howled, as the other ghosts in the anamacha surrounded them. The Moonshadow's hand was still on hers. <*And this . . . this is how it ended . . .*>

Orla's perception went whirling away once more into Leagsaidh's memory. Now she was in the midst of a battle, with a ruddy twilight sun illuminating a coastal dune field strewn with bodies. Out on the horizon she could see ships under sail, and she knew that they were the White Ships fleeing the carnage of Ìseal Head and returning home. She could feel the exhaustion of her body from having cast spell after spell, and a fury and blood-lust that blocked out every other response. The Presence—the Moonshadow, Leagsaidh called it—was with her, and the emotions she felt were that of the Moonshadow. Leagsaidh herself cowered inside her own head.

A scar-faced man in armor spattered with streaks of blood and gore was screaming at her, spittle flying from his bearded lips: a Cateni warrior. She knew him: Tuathal of Clan Leask, ceannàrd of her army. There were others behind him, all pleading with her: Cateni warriors, the draoi whom she'd helped to bring their own presences from the blackstones, those whom she'd taught to control the half gods that were now part of them. She'd shown them how to hold the power drawn from Magh da Chèo, how to shape it and use it. She knew some of them were already calling her mad. Too consumed with revenge. Too lost in the Moonshadow that gave her power.

She didn't care what they said or what they thought: she'd led them from the north to the south coast of Albann, chasing those from the White Ships and driving them before her army in battle after battle, and now it was so nearly finished . . .

"Stop this!" Tuathal shouted. "Ceanndraoi Leagsaidh, stop! We've won. They've surrendered. They're beaten. You must stop!"

"No!" Moonshadow/Leagsaidh/Orla shouted back to him, her voice tearing at her throat. "Look, Ceannàrd! They're still *here*!" She pointed with a trembling finger toward the beach, where the last soldiers from the White Ships were huddled, calling out in desperation to the ships that had already left, some of them waist-deep in the waves or swimming out toward the few vessels still anchored in the bay. The pebbles of the beach were littered with abandoned weapons, armor, and banners. "I want them all dead, *all* of them—for what they did to me, what they did to us, what they did to our land!"

The Moonshadow was already pulling more energy from the Otherworld, and she began to move her hands instinctively to create a spell cage to hold it. Tuathal continued to argue with her. "This isn't necessary, Ceanndraoi. You've won. *We've* won. These are just the remnants of them, and they're leaving."

Leagsaidh didn't answer. The rage was rising in her as the power of the Otherworld filled her spell cage. Tuathal reached for her hands, trying to stop her from casting the spell; with his touch, her fury and anger overtook her. The Moonshadow rose up inside, and she shouted the release word, not caring that Tuathal and the others stood directly in front of her. She saw Tuathal's eyes widen in sudden terror as she loosed the power, a sun exploding outward and hurling broken bodies away from her. Cateni bodies. Uncaring, she strode through the gap she'd created toward the beach and the White Ships: as she heard the screams of dying Cateni to either side; as she smelled their charred and burning bodies; as she heard the cries of outrage from the warriors and draoi around her.

"She's gone mad," someone cried.

"Stop her, or the Moonshadow will kill us all!" another shouted.

She didn't care. She was focused only on the beach and her enemies, their very presence a mockery.

She felt the first touch of another draoi's spell; a burning flame blistered her skin, though the Moonshadow immediately sent a cold wind that blew away the flames. She heard the creaking of bows being pulled back, and she turned angrily, the same gale sending the arrows flying wildly. She snarled at them all. "Let me do what I must, or I'll kill you instead," she grunted, her teeth bared like a wild animal. They were closing in around her, and she no longer even attempted to contain and shape the strength that the Moonshadow ripped from Magh da Chèo and fed to her; she simply let it flow through her unchecked and undirected. Lightning flared around her, fire spewed from her fingertips, burning her as much as those surrounding her, wind howled, and hard rain hammered the ground.

Leagsaidh screamed as a spear ripped into her side, turning to face the warrior who'd thrown it only to feel another thrust into her spine. She went to her knees in pain and shock, the energy still flailing madly around her. A sword cut her; spells pummeled and burned her. She tried to rise, tried to shape another spell, but her legs refused to move, and she could no longer see the Otherworld or the Moonshadow within it.

"Why?" she screamed at them. "Why are you doing this to me? I saved you! I saved all of us!"

There was no answer as she spiraled away into darkness, hearing the Moonshadow's deep voice as she fell.

<*Now you join with me . . . Now we will be as one forever . . .*>

Orla still felt the pain and heard the growl of the Moonshadow's low voice, but she was back in Magh da Chèo, and Leagsaidh's ghost was staring at her. "Why did you show me this?" Orla asked, managing to husk out the words through the remembered agony of Leagsaidh's death. "Did you do this to my mam, too?"

Leagsaidh shook her head. <*No,*> she said. Orla tried to focus on the woman, but it was difficult. There was a darkness behind her—not the dark of storm clouds, but a void of utter blackness that hurt her eyes when she tried to look closely at it. A looming, human-shaped nothingness. <*No. Not her. She wouldn't have understood. But you already do, don't you?*>

"No, I . . ." Orla began, then stopped. The continuing pain made concentration difficult. She felt as if her body had been pummeled, then burnt. She wanted to fall to her knees, wanted to drop to the ground and sleep. Her gaze went to the darkness behind Leagsaidh, then quickly away. She drew in her breath. "There's no 'Leagsaidh,' is there? It's not Leagsaidh Mac Cába who drives mad the draoi who hold this anamacha, only the creature she drew from the blackstone. You've become one. Leagsaidh Moonshadow. One being, not two."

Leagsaidh laughed, a bright sound in the storm. Orla thought she heard an echoing and much lower laugh as well, and it tore at the agony of her body, nearly making her double over. She straightened slowly. <*I knew you'd see it . . . One doesn't merge with a demigod and remain who they once were. Certainly not easily, and perhaps never . . .*>

"Elia is my god," Orla answered. "*Our* god."

Leagsaidh snorted her bitter amusement. <*If you think of Elia as a good and gentle parent, you're a fool. Elia made the Moonshadow and the other cores of the anamacha. They're of Her, all of the other gods, terrifying or otherwise, and Elia doesn't care . . . After you know the Moonshadow, you'll know . . .*>

"I don't believe you."

<*Believe or not as you wish. I don't care. Most of the draoi here never dared call on me. A few did in great need, then never attempted it again because they feared falling to the madness. Your mam . . . She called me once, then again and again, but she never understood. She was never the one we wanted, never the one we were searching for, even back in Pencraig.*>

Orla shivered at that, knowing who Leagsaidh meant. Or perhaps she shivered from the fever that was wracking her; it was impossible to tell.

<I was the First,> Leagsaidh continued, though Orla found it difficult to concentrate on the words. <I merged with the Moonshadow because there was no one else. And yes, it ripped and tore open my mind, but it also gave me a gift: the strength to do what no one else could and drive away those of the White Ships. And my own people killed me for that . . .> Her voice went bitter and cold. <They turned on me as they'll turn on you, Orla. They'll call you mad and possessed, and they'll condemn you . . . because you know that you must call on me to do what you want. Iomhar can't help you. Neither can Voada. They're both too weak. You've already called me forward, whether you know it or not. I'm here. The Moonshadow wants you as it wanted me . . . To be One with us.>

Orla collapsed, unable to stand any longer. The gray stones of Magh da Chèo tore at her knees, grinding into her skin. She saw her arms in the flickering lightning, and she gasped; her skin was red and blistered, cracked and bloody. The wind was like a file tearing across the wounds.

<You've called us, and we've come . . . We're here . . . We're always here . . . You're now marked as ours . . .>

"No!" Orla screamed in denial, still huddled on the ground. She couldn't look up, but she felt Leagsaidh and the Moonshadow close by her, and she heard their combined laughter.

18

Mark of the Moonshadow

"**O**RLA?"

The voice seemed to come from a terrible distance. "Orla, can you hear me?"

Something cool and wet yet too rough touched her forehead and her cheeks: a cloth? She tried to open her eyes but closed them again quickly against the light. She lifted an arm; it moved sluggishly, the muscles aching. "Oh, thank Elia, you're awake. Orla, what's happened to you?"

She realized it was Sorcha's voice. She eased her eyelids open again a slit. She was in their tent. She could hear the activity around her and saw venison stew cooking over a nearby fire. A shimmer in the corner of her vision was her anamacha; she looked away quickly. The tent smelled of boiled herbs, incense, and the venison. "How did I get here?" Orla managed to ask. Her voice sounded graveled and tired, as if she'd been screaming.

Sorcha leaned over her again with the wet cloth—just soft linen, but it felt like broken and jagged stones were being dragged over her forehead. "Magaidh came to look for you after the ceann-àrd and ceanndraoi met. When she couldn't find you, she sent people out searching; they found you collapsed outside the camp

203

and brought you back here. You've been lost in a fever for over a day."

There was something in the way Sorcha gazed at her—the way she'd look at her face, then look away again—the set of her mouth, the forced smile . . . "Sorcha, what's wrong?"

Sorcha didn't answer. Instead she moved away, and Orla lifted her head to see her rummaging in her pack. She brought back a polished disc of copper: her mirror. Silently, she held it up before Orla. The image trembled in Sorcha's hands, then steadied. With a gasp, Orla let her head drop back down.

You are marked as ours . . .

Her face was reddened and scarred, most of her hair burned away. Fragments of memory came back to her: the battle at Ìseal Head, the draoi and warriors attacking Leagsaidh after they tried to stop her from continuing the assault . . . She had *been* Leagsaidh in that memory. She'd killed her own people in a blind rage. She'd felt the agony of the spells, the spears, the swords raised against her.

You are marked as ours . . .

The breath went out of her.

Sorcha took the mirror away, then sat on the blankets alongside her. Orla heard the cloth being dipped in a basin of water again, and she turned away as Sorcha tried to place it on her forehead. "The archiater said . . ." Sorcha's voice broke then, and she stopped. "She said that what happened must have been spell-fire, since this isn't like any burn she's seen before. She's left an ointment for you. She thinks the burns will heal, but . . ."

"I'll be scarred. A horror."

"She doesn't know. She can't know," Sorcha answered.

"*I* know," Orla told her. Then: "Go away. I want to be alone."

"Orla, let me stay. Please."

"Go away. Please." Orla closed her eyes. A few breaths later, she felt the bedding shift as Sorcha stood.

"I'll be back in a stripe. I'll bring some stew," Sorcha said.

Orla didn't answer. She listened to Sorcha's footsteps as she left and the rustling of the tent flaps. She opened her eyes; the multiple faces of her anamacha watched her from the far corner of the tent. "Why?" she asked them, but of course there was no answer.

She lay there and wondered if she could still cry.

"Here's your stew. You need to eat."

Sorcha held out the bowl to Orla. She kept her gaze on Orla's face, her chin lifted slightly as if in defiance. "I'll feed you if you don't feel you can do it yourself."

"Give it to me," Orla told her. She sat up in the bedding and took the bowl and spoon, grimacing both at having to support the weight and the way the movement pulled on the burned skin of her arms. She placed the bowl in her lap. Sorcha was still watching her, so she dipped the spoon into the broth and managed to bring it to her mouth. Opening her mouth wide enough to sip the broth hurt, and the heat of the stew was painful against her lips; she struggled not to show it. "Good," she said.

Sorcha nodded. "Magaidh, Ceiteag, and Ceannàrd Iosa are outside. They're waiting to see you."

"What do they want?"

"What they always want. Magaidh is afraid she may have failed you the way she fears she failed your mam. Ceiteag wants to scold you for not listening to her warnings. And Eideard wants to see if you might yet be the ceanndraoi so that he doesn't have to deal with Greum."

Orla could hear bitterness and perhaps jealousy in Sorcha's voice. "And what do you want?" Orla asked her.

"I want to be with you and help you, however I can. Nothing more." Her chin lifted farther. "That's all I've ever wanted, ever since—" She stopped. "Eat your stew. What do you want me to tell them?"

You have to face them eventually . . . "Tell them they can come in. Briefly."

"Finish your stew. I'll fetch them, and I'll make sure they don't stay long."

Sorcha left, and Orla could hear muffled voices outside, Sorcha's raised against the others. Orla ate a few more bites of the stew, but her stomach was rebelling, and she set the bowl on the ground. The voices subsided, and she heard footsteps. The tent flap opened, letting in sunlight; she saw figures against the glare, then the flap dropped again, with Sorcha staying outside the now-crowded tent. Orla drew in a long breath and faced the trio, steeling herself as she felt everyone staring at her face.

It was Magaidh who spoke first. "Oh, Orla. My poor dear . . ." she husked out, dropping to her knees alongside Orla. Magaidh's anamacha remained well behind as if not wanting to approach. Magaidh started to reach for Orla's hands, then stopped before touching the cracked, savaged skin there. "Who did this to you?" she asked.

"I did this to myself," Orla told her. "I called Leagsaidh Mac Cába, and I met the Moonshadow."

"*They* did this to you? Why?"

Orla didn't answer. Couldn't answer. She glanced at her own anamacha, silent and impassive.

"It's because she awoke what she should have kept asleep," Ceiteag interjected. She was standing near the tent entrance, her anamacha close by her. "I told your mam, as I told you: the Moonshadow is terribly dangerous. Greum warned her too. Trying to control the Moonshadow warped and eventually killed your mam, and now . . ." Her voice trailed off. The old woman half turned, no longer looking at Orla.

"None of that matters," Eideard said loudly. He'd moved to the other side of Orla. He looked at her face unflinchingly. A finger traced the line of one of the battle scars on his own face. "Those who fight always bear the marks of their battles. They are marks of honor and bravery, and we all have them. No warrior will care if the ceanndraoi carries hers too."

"I'm not ceanndraoi," Orla protested.

"You *will* be if you've brought out the Moonshadow and survived. The Red-Hand and Draoi Ceiteag both know it. Every draoi fears the Moonshadow, but our enemies fear her even more. Ask Magaidh if that's not true."

I don't want to be ceanndraoi only because of fear, Orla thought, but she was too tired to argue. She looked over to Magaidh, whose regard was now on Eideard.

"Aye, our enemies fear the Moonshadow," Magaidh agreed. Her gaze returned to Orla. "And so do some of our own draoi and warriors as well," she added. Then, more softly, "But I was never afraid of your mam. Never. I was afraid *for* her because of the pain I knew she was enduring. But afraid *of* her?" She shook her head. "No. I put the same trust in you, Orla. I always will. I hope you know that."

Ceiteag sniffed in the twilight of the tent. "You're fools," she muttered. "All of you."

Eideard grunted. "Fool or not, I want no one other than Draoi Orla in my chariot when we go into battle."

"Because you imagine it's the ceannàrd and ceanndraoi riding as one, the way Voada and your uncle did," Ceiteag scoffed. "Is that the glory you're imagining in that head of yours, Eideard Iosa? Then you should think about what happened to them. Only fools find glory in defeat. I was Voada's friend, and I wanted only for her to succeed and be happy, but she chose a different path. I wish only the same for Orla, but I see her walking her mother's path."

"A true friend would have followed Voada, not the Red-Hand," Eideard snapped back at her. "Only a frightened old draoi would have hidden away in Onglse while the real ceanndraoi was fighting the Mundoa in the south."

The tent flap opened, letting in light that hurt Orla's eyes. "That's enough!" Sorcha snapped, her figure a silhouette against the glare. "Stop this. All of you."

"Sorcha's right," Magaidh said. "This bickering isn't helpful. Orla, what do you need from us?"

The Moonshadow's anamacha moved with the question, gliding toward Orla until she could feel its icy touch along her side.

Orla saw Magaidh and Ceiteag watching the movement while Ei-deard's gaze remained on her.

<*Everything . . . We will demand everything of them and more . . .*> The Moonshadow's voice, supported by the chorus of other draoi inside. Orla tried to find her mam's voice in the mix but failed.

"I need to get up. I need to walk," she said simply. She held out her hands to Sorcha. "Help me."

Her legs were unsteady, and the bog dress felt like a rasp being run over her flesh, though she didn't lift the hem to see if they had been burned like her arms. Her feet looked normal enough in the sandals she'd put on. She concentrated on placing one foot in front of the other. Magaidh walked on her left, Sorcha on her right, both ready to catch her should she fall, while Ceiteag and Eideard walked a pace behind.

The wind was cold on her face, which at least eased the burning.

As they walked through the lane between the tents, those in the camp stopped to stare at her. Orla kept her head up, her chin lifted, her mouth set in a line as if she didn't care what they were thinking. She could hear whispered conversations around them, none of them loud enough to understand what people were saying.

<*Let them stare . . . Let them call you names that they won't say to your face . . . It won't matter once they see what we can do . . .*> The voices of the anamacha gave her little consolation.

Ahead there was a man in draoi robes and torc standing in the lane, watching their approach. The sun was behind him so that Orla had to shade her eyes, but she knew who it was by the cane the man grasped in his left hand, leaning heavily on it: Greum Red-Hand, his expression stern.

"Draoi Orla," he said in his low voice as they came within a few paces. She saw his eyes widen as he took in her appearance. "I heard the news of what happened to you. Is it true that the Moonshadow did this to you?"

She nodded silently, and he echoed the gesture.

"I'm sorry," he said. He lifted his right hand, the one that shone red-orange in the light. "Do you know how I came by this?" he asked, then continued without waiting for an answer. "A few of the old draoi know the story, but most of them are gone now, and I haven't told the tale in a long time. The truth is that we both have anamacha with great potential, Draoi Orla. There's a reason that the ceanndraoi is most often someone who is bonded to one of the earliest anamacha, and I'll admit the Moonshadow is the First and thus the most powerful. But mine . . . mine was the next to emerge from the blackstones after Leagsaidh opened them, when she brought other Cateni to Bàn Cill to see if they, like her, could merge with those who were caught in the blackstones. For my anamacha, it was Iseabail of Clan Buccleugh. She became one with the demigod who slipped from the second of the blackstones, and it . . . it is nearly as powerful and difficult to control as the Moonshadow."

Greum took a long, deep breath, staring at his own hand. "When the anamacha claimed me," he continued, "I was like most young and foolish draoi, and my teacher, like most, tried to convince me that I should use only the least of the draoi caught in the anamacha at first. I thought I could delve far deeper than that, so I called up Iseabail, and with her came the creature at the heart of the anamacha, whom she called *Dòrn*, the Fist." Greum fisted his hand and let it fall back to his side. "The Fist marked me for my arrogance, and I was forever after 'Greum Red-Hand,' a symbol to my fellow new draoi not to search all the way to the cores of their anamacha. It seems we have a new symbol now. I wonder what they'll name you: Orla the Burned, perhaps?"

There was no mockery in his voice, only a resigned sadness.

"Tell me, Ceanndraoi," Orla said. "Afterward, were you able to reach all the way to the anamacha's heart and use Iseabail Dòrn?"

"It was too dangerous," he answered. "I never tried again."

<*He was too afraid* . . .> Orla heard her anamacha declare as it touched her, her mam's voice predominant. <*Are you now as*

fearful of us?> Orla didn't answer the anamacha. Greum cocked his head to one side as if waiting for a response from Orla.

"I will," she told him. "I have no fear of the Moonshadow now. It has done the worst it could do to me, and I've survived it."

"You still believe you can control the Moonshadow and not succumb?" Greum scoffed. "Then you're as much a fool as your mam."

"The Moonshadow itself wouldn't agree with you, nor would Leagsaidh," Orla told him. "And truthfully, I don't care what you believe."

"Is that a challenge, Draoi Orla? Does Orla the Burned think she should be ceanndraoi?"

<Tha! . . .> the Moonshadow whispered with a hundred voices. *<Yes! . . .>* Orla could feel the others around her waiting for her answer: eagerly for Eideard, fearfully for Ceiteag.

"I leave that in Elia's hands and yours," Orla said to them all. And with that she nodded again to Greum. "Enjoy your day, Ceanndraoi. Sorcha, I'd like to return to my tent now and rest some more."

19

Deceptions and Departures

T HE NEWS TRAVELED RAPIDLY through the Cateni camp, spreading from tent to tent. It was Magaidh who brought it to Orla, entering her tent without calling out first. "You must come to the escarpment," the draoi said breathlessly. Her gaze went from Orla to Sorcha, sharing her bedding, though she said nothing. Orla noticed that Magaidh's gaze kept slipping aside from her savaged face and coming back, as if constantly expecting to see it somehow restored to what it had once been. "The ceannàrd is asking for you, as is the ceanndraoi."

Orla sat up with a groan and a grimace as muscles and burned skin protested. Sorcha yawned and blinked, pulling the blanket up over her body as she realized someone else was in the tent.

"What's happening?" Orla asked.

"It's best that you come see for yourself," Magaidh answered. "Hurry and get dressed. I'll wait outside for you."

When they'd put on clothing, Magaidh led them to the escarpment through a camp that was chaotic, with warriors, draoi, servants, and camp followers all bustling about and talking excitedly amongst themselves. The walk itself nearly exhausted Orla; more than once she felt Sorcha's hand at her arm to help her, but she ignored the pain and forced herself to keep moving.

At the escarpment were the ceannàrd and ceanndraoi along with Ceiteag, many of the senior draoi, as well as most of the àrds. As Orla approached the lip of the steep bluffs, she saw immediately what had caused the uproar.

The Mundoan army had filled the floodplain below just the day before, but there was no army there now. It was gone, vanished. All that remained were a few tents and scorched circles where fires had burned. "The sentries said that the campfires were burning all night, so they didn't suspect anything," Magaidh said to Orla. "The night was moonless and clouded, and they could see nothing but the fires and a few people feeding them; they didn't see or hear the troops leaving. It wasn't until dawn that they realized the camps had all been abandoned."

"That's not the worst of it," Eideard added. "The two ships you saw, that you thought nearly rebuilt? They're gone too, and we can't see anyone working on the others at the docks. I sent scouts down onto the plain; they tell me that there's still a cohort of Mundoan troops holding the bridge, but otherwise Savas has abandoned Muras."

Orla shivered, feeling the Moonshadow's anamacha pressing close to her. <You know what he intends . . . 'I'm a simple man, a soldier who obeys his orders' . . .>

"He's going to Onglse," Orla said. "He wants the island and Bàn Cill."

"No, he's not," Greum insisted. Orla drew her head back.

"He is," she insisted. "I know it."

"You can't be certain of that." Greum turned from the view to glare at Orla. He studied her face intently. "We don't know where they've gone yet, and two ships of troops are hardly enough to allow Savas to mount an invasion of Onglse."

"I know what he said to me," Orla insisted. "His orders are to take Onglse, and he obeys orders. Send scouts westward along the river and you'll find his army."

"I've already done that," Eideard said. "Savas may be on one of the ships, but the great bulk of his army has to be traveling on foot. Even at a forced march, they can't be that far away. If they're following the Meadham, our rider I've sent out will see them."

"Your scouts won't find them, Ceannàrd Iosa," Greum said. "I believe Savas has gone back to his Great-Voice to crow about his victory here at Muras and spin a tale of how he singlehandedly stopped the Cateni army. We've already won here. The war is over for now, and we can hope it will remain so for another year or more."

<*Greum Red-Hand singlehandedly stopped his own army . . .*> the anamacha howled in Orla's mind. <*Why? Why?*> Orla ignored the yammering, though she still wondered at that herself.

"But assuming you're right and Savas still intends to attack Onglse," Greum continued, "that means Savas is taking the army to Gediz—as you've suggested, Ceannàrd—expecting to build the ships there that he needs to transport his army. And that would take *moons*."

Eideard shrugged. "Either way, Muras is standing open before us," Eideard said. "We could take it in a hand of days, maybe less. We should do exactly that—sack Muras for the wealth it can give us, free the Cateni in the town for a second time, then burn the town to the ground so the Mundoans can't ever use it again to threaten us."

There was a rumbling of agreement from those around them, but Greum was shaking his head. Orla's anamacha continued to scoff. <*Fool . . . We were First. We should be ceanndraoi, not this man . . . There is something wrong here, some deception . . .*> Orla could hear the Moonshadow's voice loudest among the many.

"Muras is a baited hook being dangled in front of a hungry fish," Orla shouted against them all, though the effort seemed to tear at her throat. She could feel her burned skin pulling around her mouth and neck, and the pain made her want to moan.

Greum laughed derisively. "Ah, Burned Orla is now an expert on Mundoan strategy? Has the Moonshadow gifted her with knowledge beyond her own? Or don't you think Savas capable of making a mistake, or that I could be right and he's gone back to the Great-Voice to convince him that we Cateni are no longer a threat?"

Orla pushed the pain to the back of her mind so she could speak. "As I've already said, Altan Savas is a soldier who obeys orders, and his orders are to take Onglse. That's what he'll try to do. I don't know *how* he intends to do that, but I know he'll try. Ceanndraoi, Ceannàrd—at a fast march, how many days are we from Onglse?"

Eideard shrugged. "We're a hand and four days to the coast. Maybe a day less if Elia blesses us with good weather and we leave the camp train behind. What of it? Savas' army can't travel any faster than ours, and from this side of the river we can cut overland directly to the coast. They can't—even if they *had* remained on this side of the Meadham, they don't know the land as we do. They have to follow the river."

"Perhaps, but once we're at the coast, we still have to arrange for Cateni ships to take us across the strait. That will take several more days, assuming, as you say, Elia blesses us with good weather for the crossing. So it's likely two hands of days or more for us to be back on Onglse, and you're considering having us dawdle here for another hand of days in order to take Muras." Orla didn't try to disguise the scorn in her voice. "Meanwhile, the ceanndraoi seems to want us to declare victory and simply disband the army. Savas has two ships crowded with as many soldiers as he can cram into them. Those ships and the soldiers on them could be at Onglse in a hand of days, then return to the mouth of the Meadham to pick up more men. Who defends Onglse and Bàn Cill? A few minor draoi? A smattering of warriors? A ring of half-empty forts? Savas doesn't *need* his entire army to begin the invasion of Onglse. Ceannàrd, Ceanndraoi, we should head back to Onglse *now*."

<*Tha! . . . Spoken like the ceanndraoi you need to be . . .*>

"I'm still ceanndraoi," Greum said. "You can't possibly know what Savas intends. He could as easily be sailing the two ships down to Gediz, or entirely around Albann Deas back to Savur. His army could be *anywhere*. And until we *know* where Savas is, I see no reason for us to move."

"For once I agree with the ceanndraoi," Eideard said, "especially when a prize sits there below, ripe for the taking."

"Muras is hardly a prize worth taking," Greum answered, pointing down toward the town. "And we will ignore it." He swept his robes around him, struck his cane on the stones of the bluff, and stalked away back toward the camp. Ceiteag and most of the other draoi followed. The warriors looked to Eideard.

<Fools . . .>

Eideard hadn't moved. His gaze remained on Orla, his head slightly cocked as if waiting for her to speak. "I know Savas," she told him. "I know him because my mam knew him and she's here in my anamacha, and I know him because I've spoken to him myself."

Eideard nodded. "I understand why you would believe that. But if the Mundoa are, as you say, moving toward the mouth of the Meadham, then my scouts should know within a day. We can afford to wait one more day to know which one of the three of us has guessed correctly."

"I hope you're right," Orla told him. "I just hope we don't regret not having that day."

He continued to stare at her. "Then become ceanndraoi, as you should be," he told her. "Then you can give us the order to leave, and I will obey it."

<Yes! . . . Become what you know you must . . . What we deserve . . .>

Orla moved her arm as if to wave away the anamacha, and pain shot through her shoulder at the movement. Her whole body was throbbing; she found herself wanting another infusion of the archiater's herbs. *As soon as we get back to the tent, I'll have Sorcha make some . . .* "I can't," she said, as much to the Moonshadow as Eideard, Magaidh, and Sorcha. "I don't know if I'm strong enough. And I don't know if it's what *I* want."

"Then we wait," Eideard told her. "For a day, at least."

Altan had to shade his eyes as he gazed out over the widening river toward the estuary of the Meadham. He thought he could glimpse the flat horizon of the Storm Sea in the hazy distance, with the sun just beginning to touch the ocean through a screen of dark clouds from a storm well out over the water. There were gulls flanking the ship, banking on a wind that already smelled of brine and kelp. The tide was running out, and the ship's prow carved twin white trails in the water under the bellying sail. The officers of the ships called out orders to the sailors, who scurried to respond.

The only other boats they'd seen on the water had been the small fishing boats called *currachs*, rowed by two to eight men and favored by the Cateni. The fishermen had stared at Altan's pair of much-more-massive vessels with their masts and sails, but no more. Beyond the single ship that accompanied them, Altan had seen no other sails as yet, but he hoped to do so soon. "Perhaps tomorrow," he said aloud, which caused Tolga, leaning over the ship's rail, to glance at Altan.

"Sir?" he asked. Tolga's face was pale, and he wiped at his mouth, spitting once over the side. "Ships are an abomination," Tolga said. "People were never meant to leave solid land. Have you been below decks in the men's sleeping compartment, Commander? The smell there is vile beyond description."

"Everyone's sickness will pass, Tolga. I promise."

"It isn't fair that you don't feel it."

Altan chuckled at that. "Fair or not, if all goes well, we'll all be back on land again in a few days, and we'll have more to worry about than our stomachs. There are ships coming from Gediz to meet our cohorts at the coast, and the emperor's troop ships should also have made the trip around Albann Deas by now. If the One-God wills it, we should have a proper fleet with which to attack Onglse."

"While the Cateni will be gnawing away at poor worthless Muras."

Altan shrugged at that. At this point, none of his plans had been achieved. It was as if the One-God were deliberately trying to stymie him. *Did I misjudge Greum? Has the Red-Hand decided that gaining the Moonshadow has changed everything? Or is it because*

Iosa's become the ceannàrd? "Perhaps. Or perhaps not. It depends on the ceanndraoi and ceannàrd." *And on whether they listen to Orla Moonshadow.* The waking dream with Orla still haunted him. Was she going to be another incarnation of her mother? Or worse? Voada had nearly brought the Mundoa to their knees. *But she's not her mam. Not yet, anyway . . .*

Altan shook away the thoughts. He heard Tolga retch again and hurriedly lean over the rail to dry heave. Tolga spat and wiped at his mouth again. "The Voice of Muras wasn't happy with your leaving," Tolga said when he'd recovered. "I'm sure he'll complain to the Great-Voice."

"Let him," Altan replied. "He didn't want us to stay, and he didn't want us to leave. Either way the man was doomed to be unhappy. If he's intelligent enough to read the cards, he'll be taking his family on a trip to see Trusa. And if he's not, then he deserves his unhappiness. However, the Great-Voice was emphatic about what he wanted."

Altan looked again to the west and the estuary. The sun had slipped halfway down the horizon, sending shafts of yellow light through the silhouetted clouds. "You should go see how the horses are faring before the light fails," he said. "We'll need them in good shape when we land. Then we'll take our supper."

Tolga nodded. "I'll do that. I suspect the horses are doing better than me. And as to supper, my appetite is gone. You'll be eating alone, Commander."

Orla walked back to the camp between Sorcha and Magaidh. Neither of the women spoke to Orla as she walked, alone with her thoughts and the nagging voices of the anamacha, which remained close to her.

Their voices were contradictory: some of them encouraging, some taunting.

<*You're weak . . . You'll be here with us very soon . . .*>

‹Voada was strong enough to have challenged Greum, had she wished to . . . So are you . . .›

‹You're a mere child . . . You will be lost if you try . . .›

‹Do what your heart tells you to do, and we will help you . . .›

Orla searched for her mam's voice in the cacophony. She couldn't distinguish it.

But the strongest voice among them was Leagsaidh Moonshadow's, and it made itself heard.

‹We can give you the strength you need . . . Just bring us forward . . .›

"I need to know," Orla said. "What does it mean to challenge the ceanndraoi for his title? How does a draoi do that?"

"Orla," Magaidh answered, "you're weak and hurt, and you're so young. I'm not sure—"

"Just tell me," she said.

She thought for a breath that Magaidh was going to remain silent, but the draoi finally spoke. "I've never done this, nor did your mam—she didn't challenge Greum for the title she took; it was given to her by others. But I'm sure someone in your anamacha must have challenged for the title; you should have them tell you."

"You can't?"

Magaidh stepped in front of Orla, forcing her and Sorcha to stop. She took Orla's hands in hers gently. "I won't, because it's out of my experience. It's easy for Ceannàrd Eideard or others who aren't draoi to tell you to challenge Greum, because they know nothing about the cost and can't do it themselves. Eideard probably thinks it's the draoi equivalent of a swordfight. I'll tell you this much: it's worse, which is why it's so rare for a ceanndraoi to actually be challenged and why Greum feels confident that you won't. Draoi have died in challenge or damaged their minds so severely that they might have preferred death. Do I think you should be ceanndraoi? Aye, in time I think you should. But now? No. But I won't stop you from trying if that's what you want to do, and I'll help you as much as I can."

Her fingers pressed Orla's hands once, then released them. "That decision's yours alone," she continued. "It has to be."

That evening, Sorcha lay cuddled against Orla's back, her arms around Orla, her body warm and comforting in its solidity. Her lips touched Orla's neck just below the ear, and her hand brushed Orla's stiff and damaged hair. From the other side of the tent, Orla could see her anamacha gleaming though it shed no light, faces appearing and vanishing on it like cloud shadows racing on the mountains.

"I don't want to lose you, Orla," Sorcha whispered in the darkness. Her breath was sweet. "I couldn't bear it. I don't need you to try to be ceanndraoi; I only need you."

"Even as I look now?" Orla asked her, then stopped. "No, don't answer. That wasn't fair of me." She found Sorcha's hand, intertwining their fingers.

"I need you as you are, however you are," Sorcha answered. "And I'll be here for you whatever you decide."

"I know that too, and I love you for it. I just . . ." Orla let her voice trail off.

"Just sleep for now. The morning may bring news to help you decide."

"It might," Orla agreed, but the thought gave her no comfort. They fell into silence then, and not long after, Orla heard Sorcha's breath deepen and slow. She lifted Sorcha's hand from around her waist and slid out from under the blanket around them. She put on robe and sandals, trying not to groan with the effort of the movements, closing her eyes more than once against the painful stretching of healing wounds. She left the tent, the Moonshadow's anamacha following her as she sought out the meadow just beyond the camp. The sentries only nodded at her as she passed their torches, their faces averted. They said nothing.

In the meadow she opened her arms in invitation to the anamacha, letting it enter her. Magh da Chèo enveloped her in storm as the souls of the dead draoi crowded around her, all of them trying to speak to her at once. <Mam . . .> she thought. <Come to me . . . I need to find Savas once more . . .>

<We're here . . .> A single figure became more solid before her as the others faded back, and her mother's familiar, sympathetic

face tore a sob from her. <*Take the power from us and hold it . . . We'll guide you the rest of the way . . .*>

The figure of her mam lifted her arms to the sky of the Otherworld, and lightning flickered down to her as Orla began to shape the spell cage. As before, she found this energy difficult to contain; it kept wanting to slip away from her, and the weaving of the spell cage needed to be tighter and more compact. When she thought it full enough of what her mam drew from Magh da Chèo, she uttered the released words— "*Bruidhinn nam fhochair!*"—thought of Altan Savas, and found herself . . . elsewhere.

The floor was swaying and rocking in her vision. Looking down, Orla saw her feet alternately slipping through the wooden planks and rising above them. The sight made her momentarily nauseous, and she quickly looked away. *I'm on a ship.* The room she found herself in was small and cramped, and this time Altan Savas was sleeping alone. There was a small window in the cabin with the shutter open; she went to it and looked out. She could see the headlands of the River Meadham dark against the moon's glow, the waves of the Storm Sea lashing the rocky cliffs ahead, but what made her stop and gasp was the sight of other ships in the estuary—a double hand of them at least, all flying the imperial banner of Emperor Pashtuk, stooping hawks descending with talons open against a field of blue that looked black in the moonlight. She realized then how wrong they'd *all* been: ships had been built at both Gediz and Muras, and the building must have started before Savas' army had left the capital city.

We're already too late . . .

"Is that what you expected to see, Dream Orla?" she heard Savas say from behind her. She turned to see him sitting up weaponless in his bed, his scarred chest bare. "Have I put a dagger of fear in the ceanndraoi's heart? I hope so. He deserves it for his betrayal of our compact."

Orla was glad she couldn't hear the voices in the Moonshadow respond to that declaration. She also realized what the commander wasn't saying. "You didn't *need* the ships at Muras," she answered, still looking at the armada on the river. "Ever. You only intended to draw the ceanndraoi's army as far away from Onglse as possible."

Savas smiled almost ruefully. He rubbed at his heavily grayed beard. "You're clever enough, Dream Orla, but you still have it wrong. A shame for the Cateni that Greum Red-Hand shares that quality. Oh, I won't lie— the draoi destroying *all* the ships we had ready at Muras was painful. I had promised the Great-Voice that we'd lose only two, at most three. But it was hardly a fatal wound, because it wasn't my only strategy."

Orla turned to him, and she saw his eyes narrow as he took in her ravaged, changed features. "And now you go to Onglse?" she asked.

He didn't answer the question, only asked another. "Is your spell a poor one tonight?" he asked. "Your face looks . . . damaged."

"That's none of your concern, Commander," she told him.

He nodded. "As you say. Let me ask you, then: where are you and your warriors and draoi, Dream Orla? Are you still at Muras?" He clucked his tongue, shaking his head. "We should both be pleased. In the end, that means fewer people, both Mundoa and Cateni, will end up dead."

"Why should you care? You told me before—you're just an obedient soldier. Your duty is to kill the enemy."

"You're a draoi," he answered. "In war, killing people is also *your* duty. But that doesn't mean either of us has to enjoy that duty when it falls to us. I threw the spear that killed your mother because it was my obligation and because otherwise, she would have killed me. Whether you believe me or not, I took no joy from the deed. She was a worthy adversary, and I respected that. If you and I meet again in battle one day, I'll feel much the same about Draoi Orla." In the faint light, she saw a wry smile brush his lips. "Or have things changed more than that? Is it Ceanndraoi Orla now?"

Orla shook her head. "No?" Savas continued. "That's a shame; Greum Red-Hand hardly does justice to his title. If you were ceanndraoi, then perhaps . . ." He stopped, not finishing whatever thought he had. "As I was saying, should you and I meet in war,

I'll take no pleasure in what happens." He stopped and gave a quick, sarcastic chuckle. "Especially if I end up being the one lying dead on the field."

"We *will* meet, Commander," Orla said, the words coming to her unbidden. They tasted true even as she spoke them. She felt the spell beginning to fade, the ship's cabin becoming indistinct and the landscape of the meadow appearing through it. Savas must have noticed a change as well, as he lifted a hand to her in farewell.

"Then I'll expect to see you one day soon," he said. "We'll both sleep as well as we can until then."

Orla started to reply, but Savas was already gone, a mist scoured away by a wind, and she was sitting again in the meadow alongside the stream. She turned toward the torches of the camp and began walking, the Moonshadow pacing alongside her.

PART THREE

YEAR 25 OF
PASHTUK'S REIGN

20

Defending Onglse

ORLA STOOD ON THE BLUFF across from Seal Point, looking across Onglse Strait toward the mainland, hazed by distance and mist even here at the narrowest point. Well to the south, she could just make out the shapes of the Mundoan troop ships anchored near the smaller islands of Eilean Mòr—one of them, undoubtedly, the ship on which she'd met with Savas. Had the weather been kinder, she might have also been able to see the imperial banners that adorned too many of the forts along the stone wall that ringed the island.

Below her on a pebbled, narrow curve of a beach, several currachs were being offloaded of warriors, draoi, chariots, horses, and equipment, having fought the strong tides and currents to one of the few landing places on Onglse not under control of Savas' forces. A treacherous journey at the best of times; a hand of currachs had foundered during the multiple crossings, drowning three àrds and as many draoi as well as a hand and three of warhorses. Given their already thin ranks, that was a loss they could hardly afford.

We were all blind, myself as much as anyone. Savas has outmaneuvered us at every turn. By the time we finally moved, we were nearly too late. We may still be too late.

Orla still shivered at the memory of the angry confrontation between Eideard and Greum after she'd returned with the tale of Mundoan ships in the estuary of the River Meadham. She'd thought the two might come to blows as they argued about what the Cateni should do next. She'd been certain Eideard would either draw his sword to kill Greum or that Greum would conjure up a spell and destroy Eideard where he stood. She'd had to put herself between them, scolding them like she'd once scolded Bakir's children when she was watching them for Azru, threatening to use her own anamacha if she must. *"This is exactly what Savas wants to see,"* she'd told them, *"the two of you at each other's throats. Onglse is in peril. The clans are in peril. If you want Bàn Cill to fall, then all you need do is stand here and shout accusations at each other instead of acting."*

By the time dawn broke, Greum Red-Hand grudgingly agreed to Eideard's plan, though Orla found herself wondering why Greum objected to what seemed a reasonable course of action. Eideard sent the àrds—as well as the ceannàrd, each with his chariot carrying one or two of the draoi—racing overland to the coast ahead of the foot soldiers and the camp supply train, there to find boats to take them across the strait to Onglse. They wouldn't be able to stop the initial invasion—it was already far too late for that—but they'd be able to reinforce the warriors and draoi there. Eideard's strategy was to employ minimal resistance at first and permit the Mundoa to take the outer defensive ring, pulling most of their warriors and draoi back to the smaller, tighter second ring. Eideard intended to hold the second ring until the rest of the army and draoi arrived with Comhnall Mac Tsagairt.

Hold. From what Orla had already seen, she thought that might be an impossible task.

She heard footsteps approaching from behind her. "That's the last of them," she said without turning around, knowing it was Eideard. "No one else will be coming to help until Àrd Mac Tsagairt and the rest of the warriors finally arrive."

And Sorcha and Magaidh with them . . . It had pained Orla to leave her lover as well as Magaidh behind, but she knew Sorcha would be better protected and safer with the bulk of the Cateni warriors around her. Orla worried more about Sorcha's safety during the crossing of the strait, but that would be in the hands of Elia.

For her part, Magaidh had chosen to remain with her injured husband and serve as additional protection should they be attacked during their march. *"I'm sorry,"* she'd told Orla as they parted. *"Part of me wants to go with you, but one more draoi is unlikely to make a difference. Comhnall's my husband; he's hurt and needs my help. I'll keep Sorcha safe for you. And you . . . keep yourself as safe as you can. We'll be there to rejoin you as soon as possible."*

"They'll be days yet," Eideard muttered. He came alongside her to look down at the beach. "I'm afraid we'll be defending the second ring without them."

"Then that's what we do."

From the corner of her eye, she saw Eideard nod. Still gazing down at the currachs, he spoke to the air. "I hear things, Orla. Some of the draoi are openly saying that the ceanndraoi no longer deserves his title. He was wrong about Muras; he was wrong about Savas. You . . . you were right."

Orla felt the Moonshadow slipping closer to her with that comment, and she stepped back—she didn't need to hear the voices; she didn't need to listen to them argue about what she should or shouldn't do, didn't need to hear Leagsaidh tell her again how she was the First and so they should be ceanndraoi. The wounds the Moonshadow had given her were still tender but healing, though she realized that her face would forever be scarred and disfigured. She hadn't used her anamacha since she'd gone to Savas; she feared what would happen if the Moonshadow forced its way forward again.

You'll have to use the Moonshadow soon. You won't be able to avoid it.

"It's not the time for that," she told Eideard. "We don't need to be fighting amongst ourselves with the larger enemy at our door. What Greum Red-Hand holds is only a title. Nothing more."

"But you and I together—" he began.

"Eideard, you've demonstrated that you're a fine, brave warrior. You understand war and its tactics. I admire you for that, and so do the others. You deserve the title you've taken, and you *have* it because the other àrds insisted that you take it. Magaidh told me that Comhnall gave up the title because he knew it would pass to you."

"You think most of the draoi wouldn't do the same for you? They understand the power you hold better than I do. And after Muras, the respect they once had for Greum Red-Hand is gone." Orla didn't respond. She heard Eideard exhale loudly as he turned to her. "We'd have beaten Savas at Muras except for the ceann-draoi. You wouldn't have made that mistake if you'd had the silver torc."

"Eideard, I was already empty and exhausted when we fled the field. Only Elia knows what would have happened. We might have prevailed, but we also might have lost everything."

"When will it *be* time, Orla? When Greum makes a fatal mistake that costs us Bàn Cill?"

"It's not time," she repeated. "Not yet."

The first of the Cateni were just reaching the bluff from the winding path leading up from the shingled beach. Eideard waved toward them. "I think of you as the ceanndraoi whether you have the silver torc or not," he told her. "So do many of the others. But let's get this group settled. It won't be long until we're all tested."

Savas moved more slowly than they expected. Ceanndraoi Greum and the others arrived before the attack on the inner ring commenced. It was a small comfort. Comhnall Mac Tsagairt and the bulk of the army, though, had yet to reach Onglse, still marching through the mountains of the mainland.

Onglse was protected not only by the sea and the strong currents of Onglse Strait but also by two rings of stone walls punctuated by tower fortifications, at the center of which sat Bàn Cill with its much smaller third ring. In its history, the much longer outer coastal ring had been broken sporadically by enemy invaders, most recently by Commander Savas in Voada's time, only a hand of years before. Savas had actually opened a breach in the second ring's defenses before he'd turned back south. Now Savas' forces held the great bulk of the southern arc of the coastal ring but not yet any of the forts of the second ring.

In all history, the smallest third ring had still never been breached.

The fear was that this might be that moment the sacred grove and temple of Bàn Cill itself was open to being overrun. The sun was shining down from a nearly cloudless sky, so bright that the anamacha were entirely invisible alongside their draoi, though Orla could feel the Moonshadow's presence. Staring out from the crenelated tower of the southernmost of the second ring's forts, she looked out over a sequence of furrowed hills that lay between the two defensive walls. Several sheep wandered the landscape, grazing. The land before her was stony and heather-clad, streams running through the boggy bottomland between the hills. The tall grasses, sedges, and thistles atop them punctuated the landscape with the colors of red fescue, sea plantain, sea pink, marram grass, and buttercup. Scattered here and there were stands of pine, yew, whitebeam, buckthorn, and oak, all of which would impede and slow the lines of an invading army.

The land of Onglse itself was their ally here.

They could see Savas' army beginning to form their lines on the first hill inside the coastal wall, the imperial banners flying from the chariots, and their battle horns—brighter-sounding and more shrill than the bronze carnyx used by the Cateni—blaring signals that caused the sheep to lift their heads briefly. Orla expected that Commander Savas himself would be riding in his chariot, though from this distance Orla couldn't distinguish his from the others. Eideard had already taken his chariot out, riding just out of bowshot from the Mundoan front lines, calling for Savas to emerge and challenge him directly.

<Savas won't respond. We know him too well . . .> Her anamacha

remained pressed close to her side, and her mam's voice was loudest among them. Eideard evidently realized the same; he and Tadgh had already turned back, the gates below Orla creaking open to allow him entrance to the courtyard crowded with other chariots as well as mounted and unmounted warriors. More warriors and draoi waited in the nearest towers to the east and west to engage the terrifyingly long Mundoan line on their flanks.

Ceanndraoi Greum was also standing at the tower's summit in company with Ceiteag and several of the other draoi. His shoulder wound had largely healed in the intervening days; his arms moved as he called out. "I couldn't reach them with a spell from here," he said too loudly. "I don't believe any of the others could either. Though of course the *Moonshadow* . . ."

Orla started to protest, but Greum gave her no chance to speak. Since his return, he had resumed command of the Onglse forces. Orla had seen messengers—not Cateni she knew, and neither warriors nor draoi—entering the fortifications and going to Greum's apartments. She assumed they were bringing word of Savas' movements. Leaning on his staff and letting his bad leg swing around, Greum turned to the courtyard as Eideard's chariot entered. He leaned the staff against the inner wall, pulled his robes about himself, touched the silver torc around his neck, and called out to those below as he lifted his hands.

"Today, we honor those who gave their lives holding back the invaders in order to give us time to return to Onglse. Without their sacrifice, Savas and his horde would already be in Bàn Cill, cutting down the oaks and burning them, desecrating the sacred temple of Elia, replacing her figure atop the central blackstone altar with a bust of Emperor Pashtuk: an insult to every draoi, every àrd, every clan, and every Cateni." Greum pointed southward, toward the Mundoan army. "We are all that stand before them now, and we must not allow the lives of those warriors who have earned their place in Tirnanog and those draoi who now dwell in Magh da Chèo with their anamacha to be wasted. We must stand here, and we must *hold* this line of defense for Onglse: until the rest of our warriors and draoi can return to help us;

until the clans of the north send us every last son and daughter to help us cast out the Mundoa and send them back across the Meadham; until we have washed this soil with the enemy's blood and our own. Will you do this?" he shouted, and was answered by an affirmative roar, the clashing of spears against shields, and the metallic bleating of the carnyx. The other draoi on the rampart shouted with them, Orla joining them.

As the cheers faded, they could hear the sound of the Mundoan horns accompanied by the steady thudding of boots, horses' hooves, and iron-clad wheels on the landscape of Onglse. Savas' army had begun its advance. The sheep scattered before them.

"Ceannàrd Iosa, do the warriors understand their orders?"

"They do, Ceanndraoi," Eideard answered. "We know what's expected of us, and we're ready as soon as the draoi join us."

Greum nodded. "Then it will begin soon. Open the gates; it's time for us to fight or to fall. Archers, draoi: take your positions on the walls. You draoi who are with the chariots, go to them now." With that, Greum grabbed his walking stick and turned back to face the Mundoa. Most of the other draoi moved with him. Orla and the few other draoi who would ride with the chariots went instead to the tower's interior staircase leading down to the courtyard. Orla ran to Eideard's war chariot, accepting the hand he extended to help her up.

"Are you ready, Ceanndraoi?" he asked her, grinning.

"Don't call me that," she told him. "And why are you smiling?"

"Because Savas is waiting for me, and I have my uncle to avenge. Why are you so solemn?"

"Because I don't delude myself about what we're facing." Orla tied a rope around her waist to the back rail of the chariot, pulling it tight. She could feel her stomach roiling at the thought of what awaited them. "I'm ready," she told him. It was a lie, but Eideard nodded, tapped Tadgh on the shoulder, and the chariot jolted forward through the fort's gates and outside.

Orla found her view constricted compared to what she'd been able to see from the tower. Aside from the jolting ride of the chariot, she was now low to the ground. The second wall largely

followed a ridgeline and the tower itself had a large meadow
fronting it; the meadow sloped rapidly down to a boggy winding
stream, and the Cateni had made that as impassable as possible.
For two days the minor draoi had been constantly chanting rain
spells, swelling the stream until it overflowed its banks. The
flooding had left nothing but blankets of thick mud for several
strides on either side of the stream itself. A chariot's wheels would
become hopelessly mired, the hooves of cavalry horses would become heavy, and foot soldiers would become slow-moving targets
for the archers on the ramparts, who could see down to the
stream.

Their hope was that the Mundoa would realize that crossing
the bottomland and ascending the hill to the waiting chariots and
warriors would cost them more than they were willing to spend.
None of the Cateni expected Savas to abandon the assault on the
ring, but a retreat to assess and adjust their tactics would gain
the Cateni a few more days: more time for Àrd Mac Tsagairt and
the rest of the army to arrive. *And Sorcha and Magaidh with them,*
Orla thought.

However, at the moment, those waiting for the attack couldn't
easily see past the next hill ahead of them. Orla couldn't see the
front line of Savas' army at all, as it had yet to ascend to the summit of the ridge in front of their own. The second ridge back—out
of range of either spells or arrows—was lined with chariots and
yet more soldiers under imperial banners.

They could *hear* the front line, however: the jangle of livery,
the calls of the officers keeping the lines together. As Orla
watched, the banners of the line began to lift above the green hill,
gold thread in the cloth glinting in the sunlight.

"We'll wait for them," Eideard called out to the other chariots
and warriors who had followed them from the gates, closed again
behind them. They could see the long line of foot soldiers nearing
the crest. "Keep to the meadow here—let them founder in the
bottomland. The archers and draoi will deal with them as they
come up the hill, and we'll make short work of any who make it
up to us."

Even as he spoke, the first volley from the archers in the fort arced over Orla and those around her. Shields flashed up from the Mundoan line to catch most of the arrows, but the line's advance was staggered as several of the Mundoan soldiers went down. The arrows were followed immediately by the first spells of the war draoi in the ramparts, Greum's voice the loudest as he shouted his release word. Fireballs hissed across the hills, lighting flared from sudden clouds; amidst the smoke and flames, gaps became visible in the Mundoan line, with bodies strewn across the hilltop and spilling down into the ravine ahead.

"Shields up!" Eideard shouted suddenly. A dark flock of arrows from behind the Mundoan line lifted over the hill, seemed to hover in the air momentarily, then fell. Orla heard arrows thunking into the meadow grass around them as Eideard put his shield over the two of them; when he brought it down again, it had been liberally feathered, as had Tadgh's shield. The thick leather armor over the backs of their horses was scarred with the marks of arrowheads.

Horns blared behind the Mundoan lines, and signal banners waved from the second ridge; with a massed battle cry, the front line began to rapidly descend the slope. "Now!" Eideard called to Orla and the other draoi in the chariots. "Tadgh, take us forward!"

Tadgh shouted to the horses, slapping the reins down on them so that the chariot lurched toward the slope's verge, allowing them to see the soldiers charging toward the stream and the bog at the bottom of the valley. Orla opened her arms, allowing the Moonshadow's anamacha to enter her. Her vision was overlaid with the landscape of Magh da Chèo, and she fought to keep her focus on the onrushing line. Her breath shivered; she feared that the Moonshadow itself would force its way into her mind, and she wouldn't be able to stop it from sending her reeling into madness and memory again.

<Mam! Come to me,> she called, and from the crowd of ghosts around her, Voada's shade slid forward. If the Moonshadow was present, it remained well back.

<We're here,> her mam said. <Make your spell cage.>

As Voada began to tear energy from the Otherworld, Orla's hands moved in the now-habitual patterns, taking in and holding the power her mam fed her. Heat and light flared between her hands. The spell cage bulged, threatening to tear apart and release itself, but as Orla started to speak the release word, a new voice intruded: a doubled cry from Leagsaidh and the Moonshadow itself. *<No! Not yet. Let the spell cage expand. We will give you more . . .>*

<Mam!> Orla shouted in her mind, desperate, but her mother was gone. Before her in Magh da Chèo was only Leagsaidh and a darkness looming behind her, clawing at the Otherworld's storm and hurling the bright shreds toward her. *<I can't hold this!>*

<You can. You must. Trust us . . .>

<I can't . . .> But she had no choice. She continued weaving the spell cage, making the strands longer and thicker, forcing her hands to move faster so that nothing escaped. The other draoi were already releasing their spells; fireballs, lightning, howling wind, and jagged balls of hail all plunged into the Mundoans. The glare between Orla's hands became that of a new sun, sending shadows fleeing even in the sunlight. Eideard glanced back at her, and she saw his eyes widen.

<Now!> Leagsaidh/Moonshadow shouted. *<Now!>*

Orla spoke the release word—"Teine!"—and hurled the inferno toward the Mundoan advance, already beginning to fall apart from the other spells as the soldiers reached the swampy morass of the valley. Orla's spell exploded in the midst of the line, sending bodies flying with terrible screams, gouging out a crater from the slope behind them and sending clods of mud, rocks, and shattered bodies raining down on the soldiers still trying to advance. The line broke, soldiers with liquid fire clinging to their armor attempting to flee back up the slope against those who were still descending. Others threw themselves into the water of the stream, rolling in the mud in a vain attempt to put out the flames, or tried desperately to pull themselves up the side of the crater.

The advance morphed into a rout all at once, the Mundoan soldiers still on their feet scrambling back up the slope, pulling at the brush and grass for support, some of them crawling on all fours. The slope was littered with abandoned weapons and armor torn from their bodies; the wall of the crater slumped as Orla watched, sending a landslide of rocks, mud, and soldiers' bodies toward the valley floor. At the top of the ridge, the Mundoan officers pushed in vain at the retreating soldiers to turn them back. The Mundoan signal flags waved frantically, and their horns sounded: a trio of notes that Orla had never heard before. The Mundoa began to retreat, the chariots on the second hill vanishing behind the slope, the banners lowered.

Eideard shouted in triumph, waving a spear at the backs of the Mundoans, his voice joined by the roar of the other warriors in the meadow and those watching from the ramparts. Orla pulled herself away from the Moonshadow. She found she couldn't join the cheers; instead she looked at her hands, the hands that had held that terrible spell. She thought they should be burned and blistered, but no, they were unchanged. The screams of the dead and dying Mundoan soldiers still echoed in her ears, and she could see them writhing in agony in the valley below her. Some of the Cateni warriors were half sliding, half walking down the slope, swords in hand, to dispatch the wounded.

Eideard looked over his shoulder at her, his face split in a wide smile that accentuated the white battle scars he bore. "It was your spell that turned them, Orla. They felt the Moonshadow's presence, and they fled."

Still staring at the carnage below, Orla shook her head. <*They were your enemy,*> she heard the Moonshadow's chorus whisper. <*They would have killed you if you hadn't killed them.*> "This isn't over," she told Eideard, told the Moonshadow. "This is just the beginning."

"*Tha*, you're right," Eideard answered; unheard by anyone but Orla, those in her anamacha added their agreement. "No one could have done what you just did. Not even Greum Red-Hand." He paused. "Ceanndraoi," he added.

21

The Taste of Defeat

"**H**OW MANY DID WE LOSE?" Altan asked his two sub-commanders. He was seated at a scarred and battered table in the room he'd commandeered in the last tower they'd taken in the coastal ring. Like most of the fortifications along the coastal wall, it had been poorly defended. The few warriors and draoi holding it had fled toward the center of the island after only a token resistance, and the tower had become the base of operations for their push toward the inner defenses of the island.

Now Ilkur and Musa stood before Altan with their *krug* armor still muddy and filthy, their hair sweat-matted and disheveled. Altan gestured for the two men to take chairs and sit; Ilkur was still limping from the injuries he'd sustained in the battle at Muras.

"By our count, we lost *dört yüz* and more," Musa answered: four hundred. "That's just the count of the dead. The injured total nearly double that, some of whom will also die while many will never be fit for battle again. The Cateni arrows and spells were partially responsible, but most of the dead and injured came from being mired in the accursed bog the Cateni created and from that terrible spell from the draoi witch."

"Too many." Altan shook his head, but nothing could drive out the memory of that final explosion and the sight of well-trained soldiers running away in sheer terror. "This is my fault," he told them, knowing they wouldn't understand just how true that was. *This wasn't what Greum and I agreed to. This wasn't the way the battle was supposed to end. Now there's only one path, and that's to do what the Great-Voice and Emperor ordered me to do in the first place.* "We knew the Moonshadow was here, but after how easy it was to take the outer defenses, even with the draoi they had . . ."

"You couldn't have known, Commander," Musa said. "None of us could. We all believed an open frontal assault would prevail again."

"We fought the Moonshadow with Voada, and she eventually fell," Ilkur added. "But this . . . Voada never showed anything like what we just witnessed. The daughter's more dangerous than her mother."

"We all underestimated her," Altan agreed, "but I'm ultimately responsible. Onglse needs to fall and fall soon, and neither the Great-Voice nor the Emperor are likely to care what our excuses might be." *Or my head will pay for that failure, and both of yours might roll as well for being associated with me.* Altan didn't need to voice that addendum aloud; they all knew it.

"Pushing troops forward isn't going to work against that second ring. Even without the damned Moonshadow, we'd have lost too many soldiers in the bog they'd prepared for us. We need to take out as many of the towers and as much of the wall as we can, along with their warriors and draoi, before we commit good men forward again. Ilkur, set the carpenters to preparing bridges and ladders; you know what we need. Tell them to scavenge wood from the ships if they need to—if we fall here, we won't be needing them anyway. Musa, tell the engineers that we must have ballistae capable of casting stone and fire over two of these ridges, and I want them tomorrow. Voada was able to throw spells a long distance, so we'll have to assume Orla can do the same or worse, but none of the other draoi can match that. They might be able to make us miserable with rain and storms, but we'll do the same in return with boulders and flaming pitch. A few days of that and we'll have worn them down enough to try again. All right—the two of you know what you need to do, and I have a report to write that Great-Voice Utka and the Emperor are not going to enjoy in the slightest when it reaches them. Dismissed. Clean yourselves up and get some food."

Musa and Ilkur stood, clasped fists to chests as they bowed their heads, and left Altan's chamber. Altan put his elbows on the table, kneading his forehead with knobbed fingers. The beginnings of a headache pounded in his temples. *Greum promised me they would retreat again as soon as we reached the wall. We should have had more time—and we would have without Orla. Everything has changed with her presence. . . .*

Greum Red-Hand wouldn't have sent chariots and draoi hurrying to the coast to Onglse's succor. No—Greum was supposed to have taken the lure of Muras, giving Altan an excuse to return to the mainland, giving him the opportunity for the sacrifice he was willing to make for the good of the empire and his men. But now . . .

Altan's scribe knocked a few moments later, bringing in ink and parchment and seating himself across the table from Altan. "Are you ready, sir? If not, I can come back later."

Altan rubbed his temples, frowning. "No," he said. "We'll do this now. The report needs to be sent to Emperor Pashtuk and Great-Voice Utka . . ."

The tower's interior courtyard as well as the grounds around it had been converted into the archiaters' facility. Altan, accompanied by Musa and Ilkur (with their chariot drivers, including Tolga, just behind), walked among the cots and tented areas in the dying light of the day, stopping to speak for a moment to each of the wounded soldiers.

"I will tell the Great-Voice himself how well you fought . . . Your efforts and your sacrifice weren't in vain . . . Your bravery didn't go unnoticed . . . The archiaters will bring you back to full health . . . Those towers in the distance will be ours soon, you'll see . . . Heal quickly; we need you . . ."

The platitudes and compliments flowed from Altan's lips; he'd said them too often over the years in victory as well as in defeat, but they were never easy. He looked his soldiers directly in the eyes as he spoke. He grasped their hands, patted their shoulders. He saw their pain, saw injuries that he knew would likely end their lives in days or moons, or leave them crippled forever. He also saw how they responded to his words with a resurgence of animation in their faces, a look of mingled hope and belief.

Their pain is my fault. All of it is my fault. He hated their admiration and faith when he had none to give himself.

It was several turns of the glass before he was finished, drained and exhausted. Outside the archiaters' makeshift hospital, the night and the stars were banished by the glare of a trio of gigantic pyres, as the dead were first prayed over, then cremated. The pyres had been erected on a hillside overlooking Onglse Strait, but the wind sent the smell of smoke and charred flesh back to them. Altan and the others stared at the fires, unmoving, as whirling towers of glowing sparks spewed into the sky from each of them. Finally, as the pyres collapsed, Altan embraced Musa and Ilkur, thanked them for being with him, and went to the small bedroom of his quarters.

He undressed and waited for the soft knock he knew would come. When it did, he opened the door slightly and allowed Tolga to slide in. They embraced and kissed quickly, then Altan stepped away from his lover.

"Seeing the men, the pyres . . ." Altan said, shaking his head. "So many hurt, and so many to be burned."

"Your men all know you won't waste their lives unnecessarily," Tolga said. "You had to order the retreat or three times as many might have died, with no guarantee that we'd have taken the tower. You did what you had to do."

"Did I? You don't know everything, Tolga." *And I can't tell you.* "What I *had* to do was break the second wall ring so we could get to Bàn Cill. That's what I *had* to do. I didn't succeed in that, and despite what I told the men, I wasted lives in the attempt. The Moonshadow . . . I should have known. We saw the currachs crossing the strait in the north; we—no, *I*—didn't understand what that meant." *And I should have known. Word should have come to me, but it didn't.*

"We all believed it was the northern clans sending over what few warriors they could spare. That's what the injured warrior we found told us."

Altan scoffed. "A dying old warrior who knew his time was done? That's what the man was *ordered* to tell us before he died. I should have suspected the truth even if I didn't know, and I should have prepared for the advance as if those suspicions were truth." Altan's hands were waving in self-disgust, and Tolga grabbed them. When Altan scowled in irritation, Tolga released his wrists, holding up his own hands and stepping back.

"Stop this," Tolga said. "Stop it now."

"Tolga! You dare—"

"Dare what? To speak to you not as soldier to commander but as a lover? A friend? Or are you angry because I'm telling you what you already know? Altan, you can't blame yourself."

Altan wanted to rage at Tolga, to order him away, but he closed his eyes and took a long breath. *He loves you, and if you don't love him the same way, you at least consider him a friend. So be that to him.* He forced his voice to quiet, though he continued to protest. "Who else should I blame? You? Ilkur? Musa? Great-Voice Utka? Emperor Pashtuk?" *The blame is largely Ceanndraoi Greum's. It must be.* But he couldn't say that. That was something he couldn't share with Tolga.

"Fine. Blame yourself if you want. Or blame the Pale Ones who serve the One-God for not stepping in. It doesn't matter. 'The past is done and can't be changed; all that matters is the future.' Isn't that what you've always told me a good officer needs to remember?"

Altan managed a tight smile at that. "So you're going to throw my own words back at me?"

"You want more? I've been listening to your conversations with your officers for several years now. I have a full quiver of your advice just waiting to be used. Why, here's another—"

Altan lifted his hand. "Spare me. I've heard enough. You're right, Tolga. What matters is the future. I won't underestimate the Cateni or Orla Moonshadow again."

Or trust the Red-Hand's word again. I especially won't do that.

22

Ceanndraoí

GREUM WASN'T PRESENT WHEN Eideard and Orla returned to the courtyard to the cheers of the Cateni. Nor was Ceiteag. Orla could see neither of their faces among the archers, warriors, and draoi arrayed along the ramparts, applauding and shouting at their routing of the Mundoan attack. Eideard noticed as well; he leaned close to Orla. "Greum Red-Hand saw what everyone else saw. He can feel the silver torc slipping from his neck."

"I'm not challenging him, Ceannàrd."

Eideard's face twisted; she wasn't sure if the expression was a smile or something else. "After today, I'm not certain you have a choice."

Their chariot was swarmed by cheering people as Tadgh guided the horses into the courtyard and the tower's gates swung shut behind them. The noise was tremendous; Orla caught snatches of praise from hundreds of open mouths around her, and she heard the title "Ceanndraoí" shouted toward her more than once. She, Tadgh, and Eideard were lifted from the chariot and carried above the crowd. Hands raised them up to a balcony on the inner wall of the courtyard—the balcony outside the rooms that were currently the ceannàrd's, Orla noted. The adjoining balcony was that of the ceanndraoí's quarters. The cheers continued unabated until Eideard lifted his arms. His voice rang from the walls of the courtyard.

"We have gained a powerful victory here." He paused while the cheers rose again, waiting until they faded once more. "But let's not mistake it for more than it is, because I know Commander Savas won't. This was simply one small battle. The war for Onglse has just begun in earnest; there will be many more battles to come, and their outcomes are in the hands of Elia, the bravery of our warriors, and the skill of our draoi. For now, celebrate and rejoice, but don't forget that while the Mundoa lost far more lives than we did, we still paid a high price in Cateni lives. Honor the memories of those who fell here. Pray that their souls find Tirnanog as we burn their empty bodies tonight; the menachs will be watching for them." He hesitated, looking out over those in front of him. "And remember this also: the Moonshadow has returned to us, and Orla Paorach wields her anamacha as well or better than Voada did." Orla grasped Eideard's arm, but he ignored her. "Without her, we might still be fighting this battle, and many more Cateni lives would have been lost."

With that the cheering erupted again, and this time the chant arose: "Ceanndraoi! Ceanndraoi! Ceanndraoi!"

"Do you hear, Orla?" Eideard shouted over the din. "They already know who you are and who you should be."

Orla shook her head in denial, but the chant continued. She didn't know where Greum Red-Hand might be or what he was thinking, but she knew that wherever he was, he also heard the chanting.

Orla was washing herself in her chamber, her bog dress down around her waist, when a familiar voice spoke behind her. "Draoi Orla." Ceiteag. Covering her breasts with a hand and arm, Orla turned to see the older woman standing near the door. "He wants to see you," Ceiteag said.

She didn't need to add who "he" was. "Why?" Orla responded.

Ceiteag only sniffed at that. "Are you coming, girl, or do you want me to tell the ceanndraoi you refuse?"

"I'm coming. Just let me dress . . ."

Ceiteag didn't move, watching without speaking as Orla dried herself and pulled up the top of her bog dress, tying it again around her neck. She adjusted her torc and the twin silver oak leaf pendants she wore. Ceiteag opened the door as Orla approached, letting her pass, her hollow, ancient eyes watching as the Moonshadow's anamacha followed her. The narrow stone hallway was busy and crowded, but everyone stood aside to let the two pass. Whispers followed them.

"You shouldn't have allowed them to call you ceanndraoi," Ceiteag said as they walked down the corridor toward the ceanndraoi's quarters.

"I didn't ask for that, and I certainly didn't encourage them," Orla responded, irritated by the statement. "And exactly how was I to stop them? What would you have had me do?"

"You don't know what Ceanndraoi Greum has tried to do for the Cateni. There can't be two ceanndraoi," Ceiteag answered. "You know that."

"There were two ceanndraoi after Mam left Onglse with Maol Iosa," Orla told her, knowing the statement would only antagonize Ceiteag, but she was too tired and exhausted to care, and she still needed to attend the lighting of the pyres before she could rest. Eideard had insisted she must come, and she had agreed—it was her insistence that they quickly return to Onglse, after all, that had led those warriors to their deaths. The least she could do was to honor their sacrifice.

"I warned you that the Moonshadow was dangerous," Ceiteag snapped. "I warned your mam as well, and she ignored me. The Moonshadow drove her mad. Look what it's already done to you. Why, your poor face—" For a moment, Orla thought she saw sympathy in those eyes, then Ceiteag's wrinkled mouth snapped shut, her cheeks collapsing. "We're here," she said, stopping at the door painted with the image of a silver torc. She knocked; they heard Greum call for them to enter. Ceiteag opened the door.

"Draoi Orla is here, Ceanndraoi," she said, then stepped aside to let Orla enter the room. Ceiteag didn't follow; she shut the door behind Orla.

Greum was standing with his hands clasped behind his back, his cane dangling behind like a wooden tail. He gazed out through the slatted doors of the balcony toward the courtyard where only a few stripes ago Eideard and Orla had been cheered; the last rays of the setting sun striped his form with gold light. Greum turned at the sound of the door closing, bringing his hands forward and supporting himself on the cane. Orla thought his black hair had grayed significantly since Muras. He scowled at her through his beard, though his gaze quickly left her face, straying somewhere past her.

"There can't be two ceanndraoi, Draoi Orla."

"I've heard that said already today. You say it like it's simply impossible, and we both know that's a lie."

His face soured even further at her statement. His eyes flicked back to her and away again. "Your mam falsely claimed the title after she abandoned us at Onglse. She heard people calling her ceanndraoi, and even though I was still ceanndraoi, she allowed them to call her by *my* title and treat her as if she were actually ceanndraoi. She severed and diluted the authority of the ceanndraoi so that no one knew whom they should follow."

Orla felt the brush of her anamacha against her side, and she stepped away, not wanting to hear the voices. "Mam didn't *abandon* Onglse," she told Greum. "She saved Onglse from falling by taking an army south so that Savas had to break off his invasion."

"No, no, no!" Greum shouted, banging his cane on the floor in emphasis with each denial. "We would have *held* Onglse if she had listened to me, if she'd stayed, if she hadn't seduced Iosa and taken him with her. I would have *won*."

Perhaps it was her exhaustion from the day and everything that had happened. Perhaps it was Greum's hubris and his twisting of the truth that she knew from her mam and Magaidh. Perhaps it was because he avoided looking directly at her face. Perhaps it was because she knew that the dead draoi inside the

Moonshadow would be howling in outrage at hearing Greum's statements. Perhaps it was knowing that she still had much to do before she could afford to sleep.

Whatever the root causes, Orla felt anger rising up inside her as she looked at the self-righteous man standing before her. The vision obliterated any timidity left inside her.

"You would have lost back then," she told him. "Just as you lost at Muras, just as—had Ceannàrd Iosa listened to your advice after your premature retreat—we'd have *already* lost Onglse because none of us would have been here today to stop Savas. You're an incompetent fool, Ceanndraoi Greum. You might have the title; you may even once have deserved it. But you don't deserve it now."

"And you believe you do." Scorn dripped from his voice.

Orla let out a sigh of frustration. "I don't know whether I do or not. There may be others better suited. Maybe Magaidh should be ceanndraoi. I only know *you* shouldn't."

"You have no idea what I've done as ceanndraoi. You have no idea what you've ruined since you arrived, you and the Moonshadow."

She saw him glance toward his anamacha, standing so close to him that she knew he must be able to hear the voices within. She pointed to the misty presence. "After today, do you still believe that your Dòrn is stronger than the Moonshadow?"

"Ah, so you *do* want this," Greum said in answer, a forefinger sliding along the silver torc around his neck. "You've started to believe all those fools shouting your praise earlier and the lies Eideard and Magaidh have been whispering in your ears. You know they all did the same with your mother—at first. Then they started calling her the Mad Draoi, and after Siran and her death, they cursed her for failing them. Voada *failed*. And that will be your fate, too, Orla Moonshadow. I accept your challenge."

Orla stepped back in surprise. "But I haven't—"

Greum's arms opened suddenly, and with alarm she saw his anamacha slide into him as his hands began to weave a spell cage. In the same moment, she felt the shock of the Moonshadow entering her of their own volition. Orla was plunged into Magh da Chèo, its torn, dark landscape overlaying the ceanndraoi's room. They were *both* there: she could see Greum standing a few strides away. Someone—*something*—was standing next to him, its form shifting back and forth: a woman in a flowing red robe; a writhing, smoking fume. The answer to her unspoken question came in the voices of her own anamacha.

<*That is Iseabail with Dòrn . . . I remember her . . . I showed her how to bring Dòrn out from the blackstone, how to become one with it . . .*>

Orla turned toward the sound of the voice. A similar vision stood alongside her: the figure of Leagsaidh and the aching void that was the Moonshadow. She could feel both Dòrn and the Moonshadow clawing at the Otherworld, sucking in its power. Lightning crackled and hissed all around them.

<*Iseabail, your draoi is an old, frail man . . .*> Leagsaidh Moonshadow called out.

<*And yours is just barely a woman and terribly inexperienced . . .*> Iseabail Dòrn answered. <*But what does it matter, Leagsaidh? They all die in the end . . . They all eventually become part of us . . .*>

Without warning, a whip-like snarl of blue light snapped from Iseabail Dòrn toward Orla and Leagsaidh Moonshadow. The impact was stunning and painful, sending Orla sprawling on the stones of the Otherworld even as she howled in pain. But Leagsaidh and the Moonshadow seemed to feel nothing. They took in the light, held it, and sent it back toward Iseabail and Dòrn redoubled, a strand of orange fire added to it. This time it was Greum Red-Hand who screamed, collapsing to his knees, though again neither Iseabail nor Dòrn seemed affected.

Orla struggled to her feet; she saw Greum trying to rise as well. A raging storm loomed above the two anamacha, and once more lightning flared between them . . . and once more both Orla and Greum were flung to the ground. Thunder boomed, so loud that the impact of it was like unseen fists pounding at Orla. Jagged stones tore into her skin, blood seeping from the gouges. The torc around her neck felt hot, and when she reached to touch it, she had to snatch back her fingertips with a gasp from the burning metal. She started to pull it from her, but Leagsaidh's voice shouted in her head: <No! You must not! You are draoi . . .> She forced herself to release the torc, grasping instead the oak leaf pendants her mother had given her. The silver felt cool, almost cold, in her palm, and she closed her fingers around them for the comfort they gave her. Lifting her head, she looked for Greum in the chaos.

His bloodied body lay near the roaring gale around Iseabail and Dòrn, as battered as Orla's. He too was clawing at his torc. Eerily, she could see the knobbed ends of his torc closing around his throat, compressed by invisible hands. Greum dug at the constricting band, his fingers desperately trying to get underneath it and pull it apart. His nails were tearing long, deep scratches into his skin, blood running down his neck. Tendons stood out like taut ropes. His chest heaved with his struggle to breathe, his mouth gaping like a fish and his eyes protruding, his face as red as his hand.

Greum was dying. Orla could feel it. She heard the laughter of Leagsaidh Moonshadow and an answering wail from Iseabail Dòrn. Thunder continued to pummel them all.

"Stop this!" Orla screamed: at Leagsaidh and the Moonshadow, at Iseabail and Dòrn, at Greum. "Stop!"

<The challenge . . . It's not over yet . . .> Leagsaidh said. <Only a few more breaths . . .>

"No!" Orla shouted again. "End this now!"

<This isn't over . . .>

"It is now," Orla answered. "Leave me!" She could feel the Moonshadow resisting as she turned her mind away from Magh da Chèo, as she pushed the ghosts of the draoi away from her. She felt Iseabail watching, felt the hesitation in the other anamacha as well.

<This is a mistake . . .> Leagsaidh Moonshadow protested, their twinned voice snarling. <You don't leave an enemy alive . . .>

"I said leave me!" she ordered the Moonshadow again, and the Otherworld vanished, the thunder quieting and the storm clouds fading into nothingness. Her torc was no longer burning. She was on her knees back in the ceanndraoi's rooms, her anamacha standing an arm's length away, the faces of multiple people passing over it and looking at her with accusation, with understanding, with anger, with sympathy. She briefly caught her mam's face among the many, then it was gone again.

And Greum. He was here as well, sprawled on the carpet over the worn wooden boards. At first Orla thought he was dead; his face was pale now, his eyes closed. But she saw his chest rise with a breath, and his anamacha was still present, standing near him. "Ceanndraoi Greum?" Orla called, but there was no response, no movement.

The door to the apartment opened. "What have you done, girl?" Ceiteag cried, and Orla turned her head to see the old draoi, her mouth open in soundless grief as she hurried to the prone Greum. She went to her knees alongside him. "He's alive," she said to Orla in a growling rasp of a voice. "You didn't let the Moonshadow—"

"Kill him?" Orla finished for her. "No."

"He would have killed you. You know that."

Orla could only nod her head. She had no strength left for more. Ceiteag turned back to Greum, stroking his hair; the man still didn't move. Orla allowed the silence to lengthen, recovering her breath as she slowly started to regain her own strength. She finally pushed herself up from the floor, standing shakily. She looked at her anamacha, watching the faces come and go.

"This was nothing I wanted," she told all of the dead draoi inside, not caring if Ceiteag or Greum could hear her also. "I don't care what you think I should have done. It was my decision to make, not yours."

"You should have finished this," Ceiteag told her. Her eyes shimmered with unshed tears. "It would have been kinder."

"Will he . . . do you think he'll recover?"

"Maybe," Ceiteag answered. "Or maybe not. He's somewhere far away. I'll send for the archiater, but his fate's in Elia's hands now, and his anamacha . . . it's trapped now. The anamacha can't find another draoi while he lives."

Orla had no answer for that. She gazed down at Greum and Ceiteag, then took a tentative step toward the door. Ceiteag's voice stopped her.

"Wait," she said, her voice breaking on the word. Her withered hands found the end knobs of Greum's torc and pulled them desperately apart until the torc hung loosely around his neck. Ceiteag removed the silver torc from Greum's neck, holding it one hand. As if he were aware of what was happening, Greum took in a long, loud breath like a drowning man, though he remained unconscious. Ceiteag waited, continuing to hold out the silver necklace of twisted, ornate metal toward Orla. Orla hesitated for a breath, then stepped toward the woman. She pulled open her own bronze torc enough to slip it from around her neck, but didn't hand it to Ceiteag or take the one she offered.

"You're certain this is what you want?" she asked. "Is it what Greum would want?"

"The Moonshadow was stronger than Dòrn, and you were stronger than Greum," Ceiteag answered. She blinked, and tears ran down the time-worn channels of her face. "Eideard and the others were right; you should be ceanndraoi." Still on her knees, she extended the torc toward Orla. Orla began to reach for it, but Ceiteag held onto it, her fingers closed around the cold silver. "This will bring you no pleasure, Orla," she said. "This isn't a gift; it's a curse. You have no idea what his title has cost him, and you've no idea what you ruined for *all* of the Cateni. You've no idea. No idea at all."

"I believe you," Orla told her. "And I'm sorry." She extended her own torc to Ceiteag and took the torc she was proffering. She placed the silver torc around her own neck as Ceiteag put the bronze one on Greum, pushing the ends together to tighten them.

Orla did the same. The silver torc of the ceanndraoi was significantly heavier than the bronze and more resistant to being pulled open or pushed closed. It hung heavily on the ledge of her shoulders. She could see Ceiteag staring at it.

"I'll need your help with this burden," Orla said, and Ceiteag's gaze went from Orla to Greum and back.

"Tha, you will. More than you realize," Ceiteag said, then repeated the words. "More than you realize, Ceanndraoi Orla," she said, her voice quavering. The title sounded strange to Orla's ears, as if the woman were addressing someone else.

Orla inclined her head to Ceiteag. She watched as Greum took another shuddering breath before she turned and left the room.

Orla went to her own room, wishing Sorcha were there for the comfort she would have brought. Exhausted, she lay down on her bed, falling asleep without intending to do so. She was awakened sometime later by a soft knock on the door. She opened her eyes to find the room dark except for the low blue flames of the peat fire in the hearth and an open window lending a bit of light from the crescent moon peering through broken clouds. The Moon-shadow's anamacha gleamed in the far corner of the room opposite the door, waiting and silent.

"Orla," she heard Eideard's voice call through the door, "it's time for us to light the pyres."

Orla rubbed at her eyes with the backs of her hands. "A moment, Ceannàrd," she said. She put her feet on the floor and tried to stand. There was a strange and unaccustomed weight on her neck that upset her balance. She sat back down as her fingers found the braids of the torc, tracing its pattern around her neck. Sighing, she stood again. From the chest at the foot of her bed, she took out a well-worn brown cloak and swept it around her shoulders, bringing up the hood so it mostly hid the ceanndraoi's torc—her torc now. She went to the door and opened it. "Come in," she told Eideard. "I'm nearly ready."

He slipped inside, taking in her appearance. He nodded to the flash of silver around her neck. "So the rumors are true. Draoi Ceiteag hasn't been allowing anyone into Greum's rooms, but she summoned an archiater . . ."

Orla nodded.

"Is there another body we need to place on the pyre tonight?"

"Greum's alive," she said. "At least I hope he still is."

Eideard's eyebrows raised at that, but if he thought that a mistake on her part, he said nothing. "Then, Ceanndraoi, we should go and send our warriors to their rest."

She walked with him to the courtyard, where he stopped and pointed southward. There was a bright glow in the sky there, reflecting from the bottom of the clouds. "The Mundoa are doing the same," he said, "but they have far more bodies to burn. I count at least three pyres there."

"One pyre is more than enough," Orla told him.

"There will be many more pyres before you and I are finished here."

"And that's also my fear."

Their pyre had been constructed well inside the wall, between the tower and the grove of oak trees that marked the boundary of Bàn Cill. It was several levels high with bodies laid reverently on each level. Orla could smell the oil-soaked wood as she and Eideard approached. She also began to hear the whispers from the warriors, draoi, and others gathered to watch.

The torc. Look, she wears the torc. The rumors are true. Orla is now ceanndraoi.

Orla tried to pay no attention to the comments, her gaze firmly on the pyre before her. "Ceannàrd. Ceanndraoi." Two of the clan àrds stepped forward holding torches. They handed one to Eideard, but Orla shook her head when the other was offered to her. The àrds exchanged glances, then stepped away.

<*Come to me, Mam,*> she thought, opening her arms. Her anamacha obediently came toward her, ice touching her skin so cold that Orla drew in a breath. Voices called to her as the Otherworld drifted over her vision of the pyre, though she noticed that Leagsaidh and the Moonshadow were not among the ghosts of the draoi. They remained hidden in darkness. <*No,*> she told the voices. <*I want only my mother. Only Voada.*>

<*We're here . . .*> the voice of her mam said, and her form emerged from the crowd as the other draoi moved away. <*We know what you need, my darling . . .*> Her voice sounded sad, and

the specter's eyes seemed caught by the torc around Orla's neck. <*Begin . . .*>

Orla started to weave the spell cage as Voada fed energy to her. This was a simple spell, little more than the first lesson that Greum had taught her what now seemed long ago, when she was just learning to control her ability. Flames leaped into existence in the open air between her moving hands, but she didn't let the fire linger there. "Teine!" Orla shouted, and cast the flames toward the pyre. They hit the timber supports, dripping down slowly as if they were liquid, then the flames ignited the oil. At the same time, Eideard tossed his torch into the wood piled under the pyre. The light caused them both to lift their arms to shade their eyes, and the heat drove them all back a step, then another and another as the entire pyre came alive with dancing, hungry flames. The menachs began to chant the Prayer of the Worthy Dead, and the shadows of the Cateni were thrown long and black over the rolling landscape.

It was nearly dawn before the pyre finally collapsed to send a swirling tornado of glowing sparks high into the sky. Orla imagined each rising ember as the soul of one of the fallen, ascending to Tirnanog and their final peace.

23

Reunions and a Dream

WHEN THEY RETURNED TO the tower, weary and exhausted from their vigil at the pyre, Eideard stopped before the door marked with the silver torc. He opened the door and gestured for Orla to enter.

"These are Greum Red-Hand's quarters," she protested.

"Not now. I sent word to Ceiteag that she was to move him while we were at the pyre. He has your torc; now he has your room. And this is yours, as it should be. Next to mine, so we can meet whenever we need to."

Orla frowned. "Exactly what does that mean?"

"Nothing more than what you want it to mean," Eideard answered. He bowed his head to her. "The ceannàrd and ceanndraoi have to consult on strategy, if nothing else. Surely you don't believe that Savas is going to leave Onglse because we beat him once. You *don't* think that, do you?" he asked with a comically shocked face, his features so distorted that Orla responded with a helpless laugh. "There," Eideard said. "I knew you could still smile. You should never forget how to do that."

"I'll bear that in mind," she told him, though the smile had vanished like hoarfrost in the sun. "And now . . . It's been far too long a day. I need privacy, and I need sleep, so if you don't mind, Ceannàrd . . ."

"Not at all," he said. "Enjoy your new quarters. You should find everything of yours already here. I had one of the acolytes take care of it. Everything's ready for you. I'll see you later today. *Much* later for both of us, I suspect."

Orla closed the door behind Eideard, and the movement of air brought the scent of oily smoke from her clothes. She sorely missed Sorcha; she would have been here to comfort her, to soothe her, to tell her that all her efforts and her exhaustion had been worth it, that she'd done the right thing.

But Sorcha wasn't here; she was somewhere with Magaidh and Comhnall, though hopefully she'd be here soon. Orla wondered whether she should use the Moonshadow to go to her in a dream, but she was too exhausted to consider that.

Orla shuffled into the bedchamber and stripped off her clothing, setting it aside to give to one of the acolytes to wash in the morning. She opened the chest—*her* chest, she noticed, though the bed wasn't hers; this one was larger and more sumptuous— and took out a nightdress.

Her anamacha was standing at the foot of the bed, watching her.

She wondered if anything had changed with Greum, wondered if she should go to her old rooms and ask Ceiteag, but the bed beckoned. She pulled down the quilt and crawled in. Every muscle in her body seemed to ache and protest. She lay on her side, her free hand touching the unfamiliar torc around her neck and the much more familiar and comforting shapes of the oak leaves on their chain.

She was asleep before she finished her next breath.

A woodpecker was tapping on the trunk of the oak tree under which she was reclining. She could hear the spines of the leaves rustling in the wind, could smell the scent of the heather on which she lay as she watched clouds scudding across the sky. A black squirrel was sitting on the branch above her, clutching an acorn between its paws.

"Ceanndraoi?" it said. The woodpecker was knocking again, but the oak tree was now a currach with the Onglse Strait gray and foaming around it. She could feel the hull rocking under her, but there were no oars with which to row or steer, and she could not sit up. Something was pressing heavily against her body, not allowing her legs to move. Her anamacha sat in the prow, looking back at her.

"Ceanndraoi?" their voices said.

Orla's eyes opened, then closed against the assault of sunlight. She was in Greum's bed—no, *her* bed now—in his—no, *her* bed-chamber, and the knock came again from the entrance door in the adjoining room. She shook her head, trying to clear it of confusion. "Just a moment," she called out. She flipped the thick quilt away from her legs and feet, swinging them down. She gathered the nightdress around herself and ran fingers through what remained of her damaged, straw-like hair. "I'm coming."

Leaving the bedchamber, she went to the entrance room, slid the iron bolt from its holder, and opened the door.

"Sorcha!"

Sorcha grinned. "And look who I've brought with me," she said, stepping slightly aside so that Orla could see the woman behind her. "Magaidh. May we come in . . ." She paused, grinning. ". . . Ceanndraoi?" she finished.

Orla opened the door wide, taking Sorcha into her arms as she entered and kissing her. Magaidh came in behind Sorcha, and Orla released Sorcha to embrace her as well. "When—?" Orla began.

"We came over early this morning," Magaidh said. "It's midday now, in case you wondered. The bulk of the army's still being ferried across. The Mundoa saw us and sent their ships north through the Strait to intercept us, but I had the draoi send a storm their way. We've managed to keep them bottled in the south and even wrecked one of their ships on Innis Holm. We'll get everyone over safely by nightfall, I hope." Magaidh stepped back from Orla, though Sorcha still clung to her. She tilted her head, gazing at Orla's neck. "Things have changed since we last saw each other."

Orla's free hand went involuntarily to her torc. "Perhaps too much," she said.

"The Red-Hand's dead?"

Orla shook her head and shrugged simultaneously. "I don't know. When I last saw him, he was still alive but not responding to anyone around him. Ceiteag's with him; you'd have to ask her."

Magaidh crossed her arms under her breasts. "Was that wise, leaving him alive? It means we've lost a powerful anamacha for now."

"Wise or not, I couldn't let the Moonshadow kill him." Orla put her arm around Sorcha's waist, pulling the woman to her for the comfort it would bring; she noticed that Magaidh gave a brief smile at the sight. "I didn't want to challenge him, Magaidh, but he gave me no choice. Ceiteag and the archiaters are nursing him in my . . . in other quarters here."

Magaidh and Sorcha glanced at each other. "And you?" Sorcha asked. "How are you after all this? Everyone is saying we won a great battle because of you."

The soldiers screaming, the bodies strewn across the ground . . . The memories assailed her, and Orla found herself trembling in Sorcha's arms. "We've turned them back for the moment," she said simply. "How was your journey?"

Neither of the women pointed out her clumsy attempt to deflect talk of the battle. "Mostly uneventful," Sorcha told her. "We stayed on the north side of the Meadham, so we were in Cateni territory the entire time. We kept hearing how many of the àrds and draoi had already passed through on the way to Onglse, so we knew you'd come through safely as well—at least as far as the coast. We saw the remnants of the pyre as we came here."

With the words, the smell of the burning oil, wood, and dead bodies seemed to rise around Orla again. The faces in the Moonshadow's anamacha laughed at her discomfiture. "Have the two of you eaten?" Orla asked. "I don't know when I last ate, and I should talk to Eideard. Magaidh, would Comhnall join us?"

"I'll ask him," Magaidh said.

"Good. Come back here in a stripe, and we can break our fast here. I'll have the kitchen staff send a meal to us and set a table."

"So the new ceanndraoi is already getting used to her position," Magaidh commented.

Orla's head lifted, uncertain of what Magaidh's tone might mean. "I'm sorry," she began, but Magaidh raised her hand to stop the apology.

"Don't. Take a lesson from your predecessors, Greum and Voada: no one expects the ceanndraoi to apologize. We expect the ceanndraoi to lead and to act."

"You make it sound simple."

Magaidh smiled at that. "It is. But simple has never meant easy."

The meal had been finished, the dishes pushed aside, a few slices of bread and meat still on the serving tray. Flagons of dark ale sat before each of them, a pitcher on the side table. Eideard took a long pull from his flagon, gave a satisfied sigh, and wiped his beard and mouth with his sleeve. "I'm glad to see you back, Àrd and Draoi Mac Tsagairt. We desperately need the warriors and additional draoi that you've brought. You give us hope, as does our new ceanndraoi. I tell you, you should have seen Orla during the battle yesterday. She was simply magnificent—she set the Mundoa running for their lives."

Eideard was sitting to Orla's right, and he reached over to touch her shoulder as he finished his compliment. Orla saw Sorcha watching the gesture from across the table, though the woman said nothing. Orla smiled, but she also leaned away from Eideard. "The Mundoa retreated, but they'll return," she said. "They didn't realize that we had as many draoi and warriors as we did and didn't understand how we'd prepared for them. Savas won't make the same mistake twice."

Eideard scoffed at that. "It doesn't matter. Now we have the rest of our army here. We'll not only hold here, but we'll push them back and off Onglse entirely."

Orla heard the voices of her anamacha, which had approached her unnoticed. Her mam's voice was predominate. <*He understands your power, but he still sees you as an inexperienced young woman and a possible conquest . . . He thinks about how much power he'd wield if the ceanndraoi were also his wife . . . You need to take control here . . . He wants to use you, but he doesn't want to be second to you . . . You must be the ceanndraoi and his superior, as I was with his uncle . . . Speak now! . . .*>

"That's brave talk, Ceannàrd," Orla interjected, "and a thought we certainly all applaud." She took a breath as if she were about to say more, then stopped.

Eideard drew his head back. "Ceanndraoi?" he asked.

"As I've already told you, Savas won't make the same mistake twice. When he comes next time, he'll be better prepared and ready. We know he saw the boats ferrying our troops across the Strait, so he knows that we've been reinforced. He also still holds the bulk of the outer wall—what if he chooses to attack at an entirely different and more susceptible point on the second wall this time, or if he attacks in more than one location at once? He may well consider taking this tower too costly to attempt attacking it again."

Orla could see the annoyance on Eideard's face at her comments, but before he could answer, Comhnall spoke up. His left arm was still bound tightly to his chest, still useless.

"Ceanndraoi Orla's right, Ceannàrd," he said. "You've done well strengthening this post with the resources you had, but what about the other towers and the rest of the wall? You shouldn't underestimate either Savas or the Mundoa. That's what happened to us at Muras—a mistake that both Ceanndraoi Greum and I made, and it's a mistake *we* can't repeat."

To Eideard's credit, Orla saw him considering their objections seriously, though she thought it was mostly due to Comhnall's comments, not her opinion. "You're entirely right, Àrd, Ceanndraoi," he said, a finger circling the lip of his pewter drinking vessel. "Àrd Mac Tsagairt, you were First Àrd under my uncle Maol Iosa. I wonder . . . would you be willing to be my First Àrd as well?" He lifted a hand against the objection that Comhnall began to speak. "No, I know what you're going to say. You can't fight as you once did, but I could use—no, I *need*—your knowledge, your experience, and your counsel. I think I would benefit greatly from that. That's more important than your ability to fight from your chariot."

<*Notice he doesn't mention you . . . . 'I think I would benefit greatly' . . .*>

<*Be quiet,*> Orla thought to the anamacha. She wondered if Comhnall would agree, having been Ceannàrd so recently. But she saw Magaidh touch her husband's arm and smile gently at him. After a breath, Comhnall lifted his flagon from the table with his good hand. "Ceannàrd, I will serve you as I served your uncle and as I served our ceanndraoi's mother," he said. "As First Àrd."

"Then we should all drink to that," Eideard answered. He lifted his own mug. Around the table the others followed suit. After the mugs clattered back down onto the table, Eideard nodded to Comhnall. "First Àrd," he said, "you will take charge of distributing our new resources along this wall. If, as you suggested, Savas changes his point of attack, we can't have our forces concentrated here."

"In that case, Ceannàrd, I need to send *faicinn fada* volunteers— those with the long sight—to approach the Mundoan line as closely as they dare, so we can see where they are and what they're doing," Comhnall said. "We don't know enough yet; I need more information before I deploy the warriors."

"And if I can make a suggestion, Ceanndraoi?" Magaidh added. (<*She at least remembers what we are . . .*>) "We have enough draoi here now that we can set a few groups of them to bring foul weather to the Mundoa to hinder their movements and lower their morale. Your mam used that tactic herself, as did Greum when Savas invaded Onglse the first time."

<*Speak! Don't let this meeting become the ceannàrd's . . . Be their leader . . .*>

"Then we'll do that as well," Orla said loudly. "Will you oversee

that, Magaidh, as my First Draoi?" Magaidh nodded her accep-
tance, and Orla rose. "Then we're done here for now. We all have
work to attend to, and we have very little time to prepare. Let's
begin."

"Ceanndraoi," Eideard began, but Magaidh and Comhnall
were already standing.

"Eideard, Magaidh, Comhnall: we'll meet here again at dusk
and discuss where we are with our plans," Orla said. "Until
then . . ."

Eideard picked up his flagon, drank down the ale left in it,
then slammed it back onto the table. "As the ceanndraoi wishes,"
he said, and pushed his chair back from the table. He bowed
somewhat drunkenly and was the first to the door, staggering a
bit as he did so. Magaidh and Comhnall also made their obeisance and followed Eideard out. Sorcha went to the door and shut
it behind them.

Leaning against the wooden planks, her hands fisted tight at
her sides, she turned to Orla. "And what am *I* to do, Ceanndraoi?"
She looked pointedly at the table and the remnants of the meal.
"Ceannàrd Iosa, First Àrd Comhnall, Draoi Magaidh: they all have
skills you need, and you've set them tasks. How do *I* serve the
ceanndraoi? What is it that I'm to do? Clean up after our meal?"

The rebuke in Sorcha's voice stung Orla. She could see tears
shimmering in Sorcha's eyes. When Sorcha blinked, twin tracks
of moisture slid down her cheeks, though she kept her hands at
her sides and lifted her head defiantly.

"Sorcha . . ."

"No," Sorcha broke in, shaking her head and sending more
tears flowing. "I'm not a draoi, a menach, or a warrior. I was taken
from my family as soon as I began my moon-times and given to
Alim as a wife—a man who despised Cateni women like me and
used me whenever he wanted. I was mother to his children, and I
loved them despite Alim, but I've had to leave them behind. I
have nothing . . ." Her voice broke in a sob. ". . . to offer . . .
you . . ."

Orla went to her, gathering the woman into her arms and

pressing her head to her shoulder. She stroked her hair, kissed her neck. "Nothing to offer?" she whispered. "Sorcha, you are my heart. Without my heart, I can't survive."

"Eideard, he—"

"Eideard only wants my power. He doesn't want *me*. If I weren't Orla Moonshadow, I'd be someone he'd entirely ignore, disfigured and ugly and not worthy of his attention. He'll never have me—not in that way. I promise."

Sorcha sniffed, wiping at the tears. "Still," she said, "I can't help you like the others."

"You can," Orla told her. "You will. Greum Red-Hand had people like Ceiteag to control who he talked to and set his schedule. I need you to be my voice and my face when people come saying they need to talk to me or when I need something done and can't do it myself. And most of all, I need you to just *be* with me. Be my friend. Be my lover. Tell me what no one else would dare tell me—because I know I can trust you to be honest. Would that be enough?"

Orla felt Sorcha's nod against her shoulder. "Good," she said. "Then we won't talk about this anymore. After all, we still haven't had time yet to properly say hello to each other again."

"I sent forward a double hand of *faicinn fada* who volunteered; a hand and one returned," Comhnall said after they ate their late dinner. From the open shutters of the balcony, they were touched by the last of the sun's red and failing light, but it lent no warmth. Orla's hands and face felt cold despite the roaring peat-and-wood fire in the apartment's large hearth. To the south, they could see low storm clouds cloaking the coastal wall where Savas' troops huddled. A map of Onglse was spread out in the middle of the table.

Orla's anamacha stood near her; she ignored it as best she could, not wanting the dead draoi to hear her thoughts. The prospect of facing a long war with the Mundoa made her stomach roil and complain. She wondered how warriors like Eideard, Comhnall, and—yes—Savas could take such pleasure in battle and death.

She wondered if that was what had driven her mam mad. She wondered if it did the same to all warriors.

"From what our long-sighted ones could see," Comhnall continued, "Savas is intending an attack on a wider front this time. There are cohorts of Mundoan soldiers massing at three of the towers along the southern wall—here, here, and here." He pointed to three locations along the coastal wall directly opposite their own tower on the inner wall. "The largest number of cohorts is still posted at the middle tower, to which they retreated and which Savas seems to have made his headquarters. Ceannàrd, I've placed the warriors from Clans MacGowan, Kilmahew, and Chrom here at the tower to our left"—he pointed again, this time to the inner wall—"and the warriors from Clans Ayrshire, Dubh-ghlais, and Cuinneag to the right. The remainder I'd advise keeping here."

Eideard nodded at that. "I'd agree, given what you've told us. Is there more?"

Magaidh answered him. "Since we have most of the clan draoi here with us now, we don't have to worry about exhausting the most effective war draoi. At the ceanndraoi's suggestion, I've set those with skill at weather spells to making the Mundoa miserable, rotating them in and out as they become tired. The Mundoa won't be seeing the sun at all, and the rain should mire them down even more. While the minor draoi can't actually direct the lightning from the clouds, Savas will still lose a few men to the bolts, and that will keep them jumpy and nervous."

Magaidh was looking at her, and Orla realized that they were all waiting for her to respond. "Good," Orla told her. "Thank you, Magaidh. That will help a great deal. Is there more we need to know?" she asked those around the table.

Comhnall nodded. "The *faicinn fada* tell me that there's a fair amount of engineering work going on. I don't think we have long to wait: another day, maybe two. But I worry we still don't know enough. The Mundoa used to have Cateni conscripts in their ranks, and we could often learn things from them, but that practice has been stopped. They still use Cateni servants in their cities, and"—with an apologetic glance at Orla and Sorcha— "their soldiers still take Cateni women as wives. But neither the Cateni wives, servants, or conscripts are here on Onglse."

Orla saw Sorcha withdraw at the comment, staring out toward the empty courtyard and the dark storms over the coastal wall, hugging herself as if she were remembering her time with Alim and her lost sons. "This former wife might be able to learn more," Orla told them. "I'll go to Savas myself tonight as I did at Muras, and we'll see what I can learn."

"Is that wise?" Eideard asked.

Orla shrugged. "It's just a spell. I can't touch him; he can't touch me. But I can see his room and his surroundings, and we can speak to each other. Maybe I'll see something, or he'll say something . . ." She shrugged. Sorcha had turned around to look at her. "It's worth the effort. I'll try tonight, and I'll let you know if I find out anything worthwhile," Orla told them, and the others nodded.

She wondered if they'd be so agreeable if they knew what she intended to ask Savas.

24

Preparing to Kill

SAVAS WAS SLEEPING NEXT to the same younger man she'd seen before, and now she recognized him as Savas' chariot driver. Orla saw Savas nudge him with an elbow, though the younger man didn't stir. The voices in the Moonshadow's anamacha all laughed mockingly at Savas' attempt, but Orla was the only one who could hear them. "My spell keeps him asleep, Commander," Orla told Savas. "You should remember that you can't wake him."

Orla was standing near the window of Savas' bedchamber, but the shutters were closed tightly. She scowled—she'd hoped that she'd be able to see the grounds around the tower the Mundoa held, but she couldn't touch or affect solid objects through the spell. She saw Savas respond to her irritation at the closed shutters with a smile. "What's the matter, Dream Orla? Can't see what I have my men preparing for you? Give me *some* credit for learning from mistakes; after last time, I expected this. I never should have allowed you to see the ships. If you hadn't, perhaps you wouldn't have been on Onglse yesterday, and I wouldn't have lost so many good men."

The Moonshadow's voices barked with laughter. Orla heard her mam's mocking laugh in the chorus. <*The bastard will lose more . . . We'll have his life as well . . .*>

"Then I suppose I should be grateful for your initial mistake, Commander."

Savas seemed cynically amused by Orla's comment. He smiled as he left his bed, uncaring about his nudity. She noticed that he grunted with the effort as he lifted himself from the bed, that he had a decided limp, that his body was covered with scars and wounds both new and old, that his stomach was more a paunch than Eideard's firm, narrow waist. With the observation came the realization of just how old the man was—easily the age her own father had been when he'd died.

"Isn't that the goal of every war leader—to kill more of the enemy than they kill of your people?" Savas asked as he cocked his head, his eyes narrowing as he stared at her image. "I believe I see a different torc around your neck tonight, Dream Orla. Am I correct in thinking you've finally become the ceanndraoi? The damage to your face I recall seeing before, though."

"I'm ceanndraoi," she acknowledged, "as was my mam before me. As for my face . . . that's another story."

"Then I'll look forward to hearing it one day. Congratulations, Ceanndraoi. Your mam was a worthy and dangerous opponent. You're obviously the same, and I look forward to the challenge." (<*This time we will prevail . . . We look forward to that moment also . . .*>) "Oh, and I assume the incessant rain and lightning is the doing of your draoi? I remember that also. The mud is an inconvenience, I must admit, and the lightning a deadly little addition. But in the end, it won't make any difference; as I suggested, I do learn from my mistakes, and our last battle was one of those. Ceanndraoi, I find I still have the same question for you: why are we bothering to talk? Your mam came to me only once, but you . . . It seems you intend to make a habit of these little talks."

"I've come because I don't take any pleasure in killing people, Commander, but I have to do whatever I can to protect my people and my land. What I wonder is whether there's any path you and I can follow to stem the bloodshed."

<*No!*> Orla heard a single voice shriek: the Moonshadow, or perhaps Leagsaidh, echoed by other dead draoi. <*They must pay!*

We must nourish our land with their blood . . .> It was the same re-action she'd expect Eideard, Comhnall, Greum Red-Hand, and perhaps even Magaidh to have if they heard her statement. Orla shook her head, ignoring the anamacha's voices and keeping her attention on Savas, whose amusement deepened to a full laugh.

"I told you before: I'm just a simple soldier, Ceanndraoi. Great-Voice Utka and Emperor Pashtuk give me my orders, and I obey them. I've been told to take Onglse, and that's what I intend to do."

"You were ordered to do that before," Orla interjected. "Yet when my mam left Onglse with Ceannàrd Maol Iosa, you chose to ignore those orders and came back to defend the south. Had you been just a 'simple soldier' and instead followed your orders, taking Onglse wouldn't have mattered, because we Cateni would be holding many of your cities in the south and have burned the rest to the ground. So forgive me if I find that I'm not entirely convinced by your argument."

"That wasn't a choice I made lightly, Ceanndraoi. It nearly cost me my head despite the outcome. So you'll understand if I'm re-luctant to repeat the experience."

"I am more powerful and more dangerous than my mam ever was," Orla declared. "I can touch the Moonshadow and use it in ways she couldn't. You can believe that or not as you wish, but you won't win here, Commander." The voices of the anamacha called out their agreement. *<No . . . We won't allow it . . . We will sweep them into the sea . . .>* "We won't allow it," Orla said, echoing their voices.

"That may be, but forgive me if I can't take your word for that."

"I'm very serious, Commander. The losses you suffered yester-day will be nothing if you go forward again. You and I should look for ways to negotiate an end to this conflict."

<No . . . There is no negotiation, no parley . . . There is only blood and more blood . . .>

Savas hesitated, and for a moment Orla felt hope. But his smile turned wry and sour. "Negotiate? The only 'negotiation' the Great-Voice would accept is your surrender. Is that what you wish to do, Ceanndraoi? Surrender to me? Or do you think that the

Great-Voice would be willing to surrender to you because you've claimed that you're more dangerous than your mother?"

<There . . . You have your answer . . . There is only one solution . . .>

"You won't negotiate? We can't parley?"

He gave a slow shake of his graying head. "I don't see how that's possible. I thought I might be able to trust Ceanndraoi Greum's word, and I found that he doesn't keep his vows. I'm learning from my mistakes, remember?"

"I'm sorry, then," Orla told him. "I'll take no pleasure in what will come, but you'll see the truth of what I've told you, Commander."

"Perhaps," Savas answered. "But we each have our duties and our burdens. You're Cateni. You should understand that there's no shame in a life that ends with an honorable death."

"You and Ceannàrd Eideard Iosa think alike," Orla told him. "And *that's* the shame. For both Cateni and Mundoa."

With her answer, she let the spell dissolve, and found herself back in her quarters in the tower.

Altan didn't wake Tolga after Ceanndraoi Orla left. Instead he wrapped himself in a blanket and sat in the chair at his desk, musing on this encounter and watching the fitful glow of ashes in the room's hearth. He found himself troubled by much of what she'd suggested.

We barely managed to survive Ceanndraoi Voada; she burned down a hand and more of southern cities, and she would have done the same to the rest if we hadn't stopped her. Her actions had the Cateni rising up everywhere. She managed to kill Great-Voice Vadim and sack Trusa, and we're still dealing with the consequences of that. If Orla's even the equal of her mother, trying to take Onglse could end in disaster, and Great-Voice Utka isn't going to be able to contain her with the troops he has. Orla could finish what her mother set out to do.

And if her boast about being even stronger than her mother is true . . .

More and more since that final battle with Voada the Mad, Altan was feeling old and tired. In his younger days he'd found the prospect of a coming battle exciting; he'd yearned for the excitement, for the thrill of defeating those who dared stand against the emperor and the Great-Voices Altan had served. But in the last few years. . . the incessant battles with the Cateni and, worse, the internecine political battles that accompanied them had aged him far more than he wanted to admit. He found himself thinking more of the pleasures of simple comforts: good food, good wine, staying in one place and watching the world move past him, returning to Rumeli and seeing his children again. Being with Tolga.

When Ceanndraoi Orla spoke of parley and peace, he'd found himself wishing that were possible.

It's what I thought I'd arranged with the Red-Hand: a ploy that might end this war. It's what I'd hoped to accomplish, but Muras and the presence of the Moonshadow ended that hope. Maybe I should have resigned when the Great-Voice asked. Perhaps Musa or Ilkur should already be in my place.

Altan scowled at the thoughts. He picked up a small polished-brass mirror that lay on his desk and stared at his wavy reflection. Tired eyes with deep wrinkles in the corners stared back at him from the metal. "Have you made a terrible mistake?" he asked his reflection.

There was no answer in those eyes.

"Altan?" a tired voice called from the bed. Altan laid down the mirror. Tolga was sitting up, yawning as he stared at Altan. "Can't sleep?"

"No," he answered. "Too many ghosts tonight."

Tolga's eyebrows raised. "You're seeing ghosts?" He let his gaze travel the room as if expecting to see spectral presences.

"Not here. Those that live in my head."

"My father always said that ghosts didn't have the ability to hurt the living." Tolga rubbed at his sleep-tousled hair. "But he said that sometimes they carried a message to us from the Pale Ones who serve the One-God. Premonitions and predictions. Did your ghosts tell you anything?"

You won't win here, Commander. Orla's words.

"Nothing I'm willing to believe," Savas said to Tolga. He pushed himself up from the chair, groaning as he did so. "My body aches," he said.

"Lie down here, and I'll give you a good rub-down. That'll make you feel better and drive the ghosts from your head. We need you ready to lead the cohorts to victory, after all."

"Yes. We need that, don't we?" Altan answered. As Tolga poured pungent oil on his back and began massaging his shoulders, he tried to banish the doubts and worries from his mind.

But the wisps of those ghosts proved obstinate and stubborn.

Orla awoke to find herself wrapped in Sorcha's arms. She said nothing for a time, just enjoying the feel of the woman's body against her back. Finally, she stirred and stretched, and Sorcha released her.

"I was beginning to wonder if you were ever coming back."

"I was never gone. Weren't you holding me the entire time?" Orla asked.

"Yes, but . . ." Sorcha padded over to the hearth. With a towel, she swung the crane from over the peat fire and poured water into a teapot on the table. "So did you learn anything? Should I wake the ceannàrd?"

"Let the man sleep. I'm exhausted from the spell myself."

"Did you talk to Savas about . . . ?" Sorcha let the rest of the question trail off. She poured a mint infusion from the pot into two mugs and brought them over to the bed, handing one to Orla.

"He only gave me the same answer as before: he's just a soldier performing his duty. He won't parley. He won't consider negotiation or a truce." Orla sipped from her mug and shook her head. "No, we've no choice but to fight them. And if that's what we have to do . . ." She pulled in a long breath. "He'll regret the choice. But so will the Mundoa and Cateni who will die as a result, as well as their families and those who love them." Orla looked at her anamacha, standing at the foot of the bed and watching the two of them. She knew what they would say. <*The Mundoa came here and killed and enslaved us . . . Don't weep for them . . . They deserve death . . .*>

Part of her agreed with that. She remembered the terror of the day of her father's funeral: the way Bakir and his soldiers killed all the Cateni in their house without remorse, without pity; how she and her brother, Hakan, were taken away as the soldiers turned to her mother; how Orla screamed in terror as they beat and kicked Voada. When Bakir took Orla's maidenhead that night in his bed, he'd told her that her mother was dead and Voada was a horrible witch who deserved all the pain she'd suffered, and that if Orla didn't want to suffer the same fate, she'd be an obedient second wife and do everything and anything that Bakir and his first wife told her to do.

The rage she'd felt still burned inside her and blunted any sympathy she had for the Mundoa she'd killed and maimed since the Moonshadow had come to her.

Blunted the sympathy, but didn't entirely banish it. There were good Mundoa just as there were bad Cateni. There was Azru, without whom Orla wouldn't be here at all. In any case, it wouldn't be only Mundoa who would die in the coming battle. There would be more pyres and more souls to send to Tirnanog.

Orla handed the mug, smelling of mint and honey, back to Sorcha. "Thank you," she said. "I think I need to sleep now. And if you keep holding me, I know my dreams will be better than my last ones. I'll need that, since I don't think the ceannàrd will be happy with what I intend to do."

Sorcha set the mugs on the floor and stroked Orla's scarred cheek. "Then I'll hold you and send you good dreams," she said. "Gladly."

25

The Battle for Bàn Cill

IT WAS TWO DAYS later that the advance scouts placed by Eideard and Comhnall came racing back to the tower with the news that Savas' forces were stirring. "They have ladders and bridges—it looks like they're expecting to use those to cross the streams and bogs in the bottomlands. The front is entirely foot soldiers with just a few mounted officers, no chariots at all. They must be holding them back until they can establish the bridges across the streams and bogs. And they're coming along a wide front this time, easily spanning three towers of the second wall, with at least six full cohorts involved. There was movement everywhere we looked."

After thanking the scouts and sending word to the *faicinn fada* watchers on the tower ramparts, Eideard started to snap orders to the àrds and draoi. "Àrd Mac Tsagairt, I want you to take command of the tower to our west; Àrd MacGowan, you'll command the east tower. I'll be here in the middle, and I'll have flaggers and carnyx players on the tower for signaling between us. I want the chariots set in front of the gates here, as we did during their last attack—they'll be devastating against those on foot. Magaidh already has the draoi sending them foul weather; they'll be struggling to get through the bogs again. Ceanndraoi, you'll ride with me as before, of course."

"*I do learn from my mistakes . . .*" Savas had said.

Orla spoke then. "No, I won't," she said simply, and the softness of her voice drew their attention, all of them leaning toward her. "That's not what I need to do. Savas isn't that stupid."

"Ceanndraoi?" Eideard asked. She couldn't decide whether he looked angry or just puzzled.

"I believe that our scouts have it wrong. Savas isn't holding back the chariots and horsemen; he's taking them elsewhere. He knows that his first attack on this wall was a mistake. Look at the map." She pointed to the table, where Eideard had laid out a map of Onglse. "The deep furrows in Onglse run east to west in front of us, but they finally bend northward and flatten out a few crow calls past the western tower. He can run his chariots, mounted troops, and ballistae with a couple of cohorts of footmen and archers for support along the ridge from where he is now right up to the wall there, out of direct sight of the west tower. Meanwhile the rest of his army keeps us occupied here. I believe they're already on the move; that's why the Mundoa haven't attacked here yet, to give them time to approach on the longer route. If Savas can break the wall beyond Àrd Mac Tsagairt's forces, he'll be through and behind our line, with very little between him and Bàn Cill."

"You're saying that the movement our scouts saw is a feint?" Eideard said. "Ceanndraoi, with respect, I know battle strategy, and so does the First Àrd. You don't commit that many men to a diversion."

"That's because it's not *entirely* a diversion," she insisted. "If breaking through the wall to the west fails, then Savas is hoping he'll still win at least one of the towers with the same result. With respect," she said, mimicking Eideard's tone, "my mam and your uncle saw the Mundoa and Savas in battle many times, as she has told me. Savas is employing the twin horns of the bull—they've used that strategy before to their advantage. The First Àrd no doubt remembers that."

Comhnall nodded in agreement, but his finger traced the line of the second wall on the map. "We can't spread out our line that far," Comhnall said. "We don't have enough warriors and draoi to hold it."

Orla nodded. "I understand. And that's why I'll be meeting Savas alone."

Orla stood atop the wall. The brash wind was heavy with a cold drizzle. It whipped her hair around and sent the grass-green cloak and gray bog dress she wore to flapping against her. Through the misty rain, she could barely make out Àrd Mac Tsagairt's tower well off to her left and around the curve of the wall; the next tower in line to her right was closer, though still some distance away. Colin, her charioteer today and also a *faicinn fada*, stood next to her. "I can just see them now, Ceanndraoi. You were correct: they're coming, and no one with long-sight in the west tower would be able to see them through this weather." The man sounded nervous, and he looked around as if hoping that by some miracle hands upon hands of Cateni warriors were standing around them. He had also, after his first glimpse, avoided looking directly at Orla's face; he continued to do so now.

It had taken a great deal of argument and Orla's insistence that she would do this whether they wished her to or not, but eventually Eideard, Comhnall, Magaidh, and the others had reluctantly agreed to allow her to come here, when they obviously preferred she stay to defend the other fortifications. Even then, she wasn't sent entirely alone. Eideard had chosen his cousin Colin's chariot to take Orla; the chariot and its driver waited for her just below on the inner side of the wall, along with a double-hand of mounted warriors as additional escorts. If she was unable to deal with Savas or if (as Orla knew Eideard expected) Savas simply never appeared, they would quickly return to Magaidh and Comhnall in the west tower. In addition, Magaidh had sent along Mànas, a young man and minor draoi, in case she required magical help—and to send a fireball flaring into the sky if Orla needed to signal for help and was unable to do so herself.

"Ceanndraoi, we should go down now. They'll be within an archer's reach in half a stripe or less."

"Go on down and tell the others to be ready," Orla told Colin. "Send Mànas up. I'll be staying here. I *want* Savas to see me."

Looking just to the right of her face, Colin bowed and scurried down the ladder to the ground below. Orla found her fingers seeking out her mother's oak leaf pendants, never off her neck under the ceanndraoi's torc. She stroked the ridged surfaces between her fingers. A bit later, she heard the sound of Mànas clambering up, and she released the oak leaves. The draoi was breathing hard as he approached her. He pushed back thick brown hair that had escaped the tie at the back of his head. Though still considered an inexperienced war draoi, he was likely a few years older than herself, she noticed—but then, most of the draoi were older than her. At least he had the politeness to look at her face without flinching. He also glanced warily over to the anamacha of the Moonshadow standing alongside her. "Ceanndraoi, how can I help you?"

"I'm certain that there will be arrow fire on this position from the Mundoa. I need you to take care of that so I can conserve energy for my own spells. Can you do that?"

He nodded quickly. "I can, Ceanndraoi. Don't worry."

"Good," she told him. "Then stay here with me. Commander Savas' people will be here soon."

Already she could see the chariots approaching out of the mist, though none of them was flying the imperial banner that would mark Savas' own chariot. They spread out as they approached the wall where the ridgeline flattened. As Orla had predicted, the bulk of the chariots and mounted soldiers appeared to be with them, along with a significant force of foot soldiers. Behind them, she could make out the towering forms of a hand of ballistae, catapults ready to hurl boulders at the wall. She could hear them as well: the creaking of their great wheels, the calls of the drivers, the cracking of whips on the packhorses that were pulling them, the thudding of boots on the stony ground, the clatter of metal against metal. Behind the chariots and the front line of men, marching before the ballistae were the archers.

The machinery of war was laid out before her.

"Get ready," she told Mànas. "Call your anamacha."

A few breaths later, she saw the archers stop to lift their bows at the command of an officer. Bows curled as the bowstrings were pulled back. Then arrows filled the sky, a swarm of deadly, hissing small birds. She heard Mànas shout his release word, and a new wind fluttered her cloak as it passed her. The arrows plummeting down directly in front of them were swept aside, falling harmlessly to the ground on either side while the rest clattered as they struck the wall or feathered the ground before it. A second flight of arrows met the same fate.

"Good!" she told him. "Be ready to keep that up." Orla felt her anamacha slide close to her, and she opened herself slightly to their voices, calling for Iomhar to come to her. When she felt his presence, she called out, using the power he fed her to amplify her voice so it rang out loudly across the landscape. "Commander Savas! Let us talk! Come forward! I promise your safety!"

She thought for a moment that he wasn't going to respond, then she saw a chariot near the ballistae begin to move, and from it was waving the banner of a stooping, angry hawk on a blue field. The chariot came forward through the lines, stopping just below her. Savas in his mirrored krug armor stared up at her; so did his driver, the younger man who shared his bed.

"Ceanndraoi Orla," he called out. "So you're not merely a dream this time. And you've guessed at my tactics all too accurately, it seems. I have to admit I'm impressed. But where's your army?"

"I'm real enough," she told him. "And I've brought no army with me."

"That would seem, well, *foolish* on your part." He gestured to the array of forces behind him. "I have one, after all."

"I don't need an army, and I'm not a fool," she told him. "What I'm offering you is another chance to avoid terrible bloodshed.

Take your army back from where you came, and I promise that no one will die here, at least."

<*He's laughing at you . . . Can't you hear him?*> the anamacha's voices shrieked at her. <*He thinks you're insane already . . .*>

She could hear a mild mockery in his voice as he answered, "If you surrender to me, Ceanndraoi, I can make the same promise. But I assume that you're not intending to do that. I'd say we're at an impasse."

Orla sighed. "Commander, I want you to order your soldiers to move well away from your ballistae. All of them. And have them move the horses too if you want to spare them."

Savas glanced back at the ballistae, still far away at the rear of the formation, then looked back at Orla, puzzled. "Ceanndraoi, those are well out of the range of even Voada's spells. Believe me, I remember just how far she could cast spell-fire."

There was rumbling laughter from deep within the anamacha at that. "As I've already told you, Commander, I am not my mother. Will you move your people or not? Choose."

Savas leaned forward toward his driver and spoke to him, then jumped down from the chariot as the driver slapped the reins on the two horses and rode back toward the lines. "This will take some time, Ceanndraoi," he said, calling up to her.

"I can be patient," she told him. She watched as Savas' driver rode up to one of the other chariots; she recognized the banner of the sub-commander whom she'd nearly killed at Muras. The two spoke, then the sub-commander barked an order to his own driver and careened away toward the rear while Savas' driver returned to the commander. Not long after, she saw the dark specks of the soldiers around the ballistae moving back and away from the machines and other men leading away the teams of horses.

Orla opened her arms to the Moonshadow, which moved quickly to her. The shadows of the Otherworld fell over her sight, the sky as always speared by crackling blue lightning. She felt her mam coming forward out of the crowd of draoi within the anamacha, but she held up her hand to stop her. <*Leagsaidh Moonshadow,*

come to me . . .> she called into the storms, and she heard her
mother wail in distress.

<No . . . The Moonshadow drove me mad . . . You can't . . .>

But the warning was already too late. Leagsaidh approached,
the Moonshadow looming behind, a darkness that somehow
glowed as if illuminated by a black sun. *<We're here . . . We should
kill them all and be done with it . . .>*

There was tempting power in the words. Orla felt herself wanting to agree with her, to let herself fall under the seductive spell of
their twinned voices. *<No,>* she told them, but the word lacked
conviction, and they laughed at her.

*<Your way won't work . . . You'll never convince them . . . The only
things they understand are death and blood . . .>*

It took all of Orla's will to draw back and shout *<No! Do as I've
said.>*

<As you wish . . .> Leagsaidh Moonshadow answered, and there
was a mocking amusement in their voices. *<In time you'll learn
that we're right . . .>*

She ignored them, waiting, and when she felt them pulling energy from Magh da Chèo, she started weaving the spell cage. This
was not like anything she'd handled before, different even from
her mam's powerful spells. This was raw, undiluted energy that
burned her hands even through the spell cage. She had to squint
against the glare of it. *<More . . . Give me more . . .>* Orla told them,
and the Moonshadow laughed again.

The glow in the spell cage redoubled in intensity, and Orla
closed her eyes. *<Now!>* she heard Leagsaidh Moonshadow shout,
and her mother's voice, and Iomhar's, and the other draoi inside
shouted with them.

"Teine!" Orla cried, opening her eyes as the spell cage shattered and the fireball inside shot away from her, arrowing over
the land, as bright in the daylight as a falling star on a moonless
night, spewing sparks as it roared over Savas' head, over the chariots and infantry and archers, to finally break apart with a thun-
derous *boom* as it approached the ballistae. A single smaller
fireball struck each ballista and exploded, shattering timbers and

sending them flying, turning what remained into instant infernos sending smoke and sparks pinwheeling up into the mist and rain. Shouts of consternation and awe rose from the Mundoa, and Mànas muttered an obscenity behind Orla.

The effort cost her. She wanted to drop to her knees, wanted to close her eyes and sleep. She stiffened her back, refusing to show how the spell had drained her. She couldn't display weakness to Savas, or he would overwhelm her with sheer numbers.

"Commander Savas," Orla called down to him, and she drew on the dregs of the Moonshadow's power to strengthen her voice so that the soldiers behind him could hear her. "Did that convince you of what I can do? You should know that I can do the same to this entire line you've put before me—and I *will* do that if you insist on remaining here. Your sihirki are a joke, your arrows can't touch me, and now you've no ballistae to take down the wall. Do you want your men to die in agony, writhing in spell-fire? I'm offering you the opportunity to retreat. Now. Will you save your men, or do you need to see the reality of what I've threatened to do? It's your decision, Commander, but you need to make it now."

To the credit of Savas' influence over his troops, none of them broke rank, none of them moved. Commander Savas continued to stare up toward Orla, and she worried that he would refuse, that she would need to call on Leagsaidh and the Moonshadow once more when she wasn't entirely certain she'd survive that.

<*You played your bluff . . . Now you'll pay for it . . . You'll be one of us . . . One of us . . .*>

"I'll accept your offer of safe passage back to the outer wall," Commander Savas said, and Orla felt relief surge through her. "You've won here. But the war between us isn't done, Ceanndraoi. We aren't finished. Understand that."

Orla nodded, and Savas said something to his driver, who reached down to pull him back into the carriage as it began to move. Orla watched as Savas spoke to his sub-commanders, as the army turned to march back the way they'd come, past the smoldering ruins of the ballistae. Horns blared, and drums pounded, the clamor slowly receding. Well out in the distance, she could see the Mundoa also retreating from the other towers. Mànas, Colin, and the other men with her were cheering.

She smiled, but that was all she could manage. Savas' words were still in her ears, and so were the voices of the anamacha.

<You shouldn't have let him go . . . You still haven't learned . . . You kill your enemy; you don't let him live . . .>

Orla would learn upon her return that the battle had not gone so easily for those in the towers.

As she rode in Colin's chariot to the west tower defended by Comhnall and Magaidh, her sense of worry increased, especially since she knew that Sorcha had gone there as well, since it was closest to where Orla had stationed herself. That concern grew when she saw workers erecting a pyre well back from the wall and saw the number of Cateni dead laid out nearby.

As Orla's entourage entered the rear gate into the courtyard, they found that the outside gate wall had entirely collapsed. Warriors and servants alike were carrying away the rubble, and the courtyard had become a hospital for the injured, with archiaters moving among the makeshift beds and the groans and cries of those gravely wounded. "It's a shame that you draoi have no spells that can heal a person," she heard someone say as Orla leaped down from the chariot to gaze at the scene. She turned to find Sorcha there, cloth for bandages in one hand and a basin of red water in the other. Her hair was matted with dried blood, and more streaked her forehead. Sorcha gave Orla a fleeting smile and lifted the bandages. "I thought I would do what I could here," she said. "The head archiater says that I have the touch and she'll teach me what she knows. Maybe I'll be an archiater."

Orla hugged her, not caring about the water that sloshed out of the basin or what others watching might think. "You'd make a wonderful archiater," she told her when she released her again. "Were you hurt? All the blood on your face and hair—"

"—is not mine," Sorcha finished for her. "I was helping to bring the injured in here. And there's still too much to do here. Magaidh and Comhnall are waiting to talk to you; they can tell you better than I how the battle went. They're still outside the tower. Go on, now. I'll come and find you later."

Comhnall was standing with Magaidh and his son Hùisdean alongside their chariot, though it was Hùisdean wearing a warrior's armor, and another young man she didn't recognize was in the traces, holding the horses. Comhnall had evidently directed the battle from the tower's ramparts, as expected. His good hand was clutching a sword, though it looked unbloodied, and his left arm was still bound to his side, though someone had strapped a shield to it.

Clouds of steam billowed from the horses' nostrils as Hùisdean stroked their heaving flanks, and the sides of the chariot were covered with gore that caused Orla to quickly look away. Hùisdean's leather armor was liberally spattered with scarlet, and Orla could see wounds on the young man's arms and left side, now clotted with dark blood. Magaidh looked to be exhausted and drained, holding tightly to the chariot's rails.

There were bodies strewn on the ground around them, all in Mundoan armor, all of them unmoving.

"Ceanndraoi!" Comhnall said as she approached, and Magaidh hurried to her, enfolding her in her arms.

"I don't know what you did," Magaidh said, "but we're all grateful for whatever it was. We were holding the wall, but that was at a terrible cost. Yet suddenly the Mundoan banners were waving and their horns were calling, and they disengaged and retreated. We didn't pursue, not knowing what had happened with you. We saw fire and smoke to our west where you'd gone, but there was no way to know . . ." Magaidh heaved a sigh, catching her breath, and grabbing Orla tightly. "I'm just glad to see you, though you look even more tired than me. The Moonshadow?"

Orla nodded silently, and Magaidh hugged her again. "Be very careful," she whispered into Orla's ear. "Please. It was hard enough losing Voada. I've no interest in having to grieve like that again."

"What happened here?" Orla asked, and it was Comhnall who answered. "Savas' people had bridges and ladders their engineers had made. Those allowed many of the foot soldiers to cross the ravines, as well as some mounted soldiers and a few chariots, though Magaidh and the other draoi sent fire down to burn many of them." Comhnall shook his head. "But their line was simply too long for us, and it was impossible to stop the advance. At this tower, they swarmed up the final slope here as well as to the east, overwhelming the warriors I'd arrayed. The fighting was fierce and—as you've undoubtedly already noticed—deadly."

"And once the warriors and soldiers were engaged," Magaidh added, "we draoi were limited in what we could do without also hurting our own people. The Mundoan officers had set heavy ballistae on a ridge just out of draoi range to hurl boulders and fiery pitch at the tower and walls, and though we draoi managed to intercept some of those, they still succeeded in damaging the fortifications." She gestured at the ruins of the gate wall behind them. "Their sihirki tried a few of their own spells"—Magaidh shrugged—"but none of them were of any concern."

"The ceannàrd and Àrd MacGowan—how did they fare?" Orla asked, and Comhnall shook his head.

"We haven't yet heard," he said. "But as far as we can see, the Mundoa seem to have vanished back to the outer wall. Hopefully the ceannàrd and Àrd MacGowan were no worse off than us. And you, Ceanndraoi? How was it with you?"

"Savas isn't an unreasonable man," she said. "He made the right choice after I demonstrated to him what would happen if he persisted. Still, he'll change tactics next time to adjust, and the following battle likely won't go even as well as this one."

"So there *will* be a next time?" Magaidh asked. Orla knew she was asking the same question her anamacha had: *You didn't kill the man?* She shrugged. Magaidh's gaze remained on her. "Oh, my dear girl," she said. "You're exhausted. Comhnall, I'm taking the ceanndraoi to our quarters to rest. She needs to sleep and recover before we do anything else. If Eideard comes here, tell him he's not allowed to bother her."

"No," Orla insisted. "There's still too much for us—" But Magaidh was already leading her away, and Orla found herself too tired and unwilling to resist.

26

Parley and Agreement

"**O**RLA?"

Orla lifted her head against the heavy weight of the ceanndraoi's torc, blinking to clear the sleep and the dreams of battle and death from her head. "Sorcha? Is that you?"

"Aye." Sorcha's voice sounded as weary as her own. Orla wondered how long she'd been asleep and whether Sorcha had been tending to the wounded all that time. "Magaidh said to tell you that the ceannàrd is here and that there's a chariot with a white banner approaching our tower."

"I'll be right there," Orla told her, reluctantly pulling aside the quilt that covered her. She was still wearing the bog dress she'd worn during her confrontation with Savas. It smelled of spell-fire. She tucked the oak leaf pendants under her collar. "Give me a little time, and I'll be there."

"I'll tell them," Sorcha said, and vanished again.

When Orla emerged, she found everyone near the ruins of the gate, looking outward. A chariot with a white cloth fluttering from a pole was approaching; a driver crouched in the traces, and a man in Mundoan krug armor stood behind him. There were no spears or other weapons visible. As Orla reached the group, she heard Eideard call to the archers on the tumbled walls to hold.

The man in armor jumped from the chariot as the driver halted near the broken gate wall.

"Ceannàrd," he said, "I am Sub-Commander Musa. Commander Savas requests that we be allowed to remove our dead from the field so they can be given honorable treatment."

Eideard nodded at that. "We Cateni understand that. Tell Commander Savas that he may do so as long as none of your people are armed or wearing armor."

"I'll make certain of it, and we thank you, Ceannàrd." He started to climb back into the chariot, but Orla stepped forward and called to him.

"Sub-Commander, tell Commander Savas that the ceannàrd and I would like to meet with him tomorrow." Both Eideard's and Musa's heads swiveled to stare at Orla: Musa with an appraising look, as if he were trying to gauge how a haggard and disfigured young woman had managed to cause their earlier retreat, Eideard simply appeared startled and surprised. "No more than two hands of people for each of us, and no weapons," she said. "I'll have a pavilion set up on the ridge between us. We need to talk."

"The ceanndraoi *is* a weapon," Musa commented. "A rather effective one."

"Your commander knows he can trust my word," Orla answered. "Just tell him what I've said."

Musa glanced quickly at Eideard, as if waiting for him to comment, then swung himself up into the chariot. "As you wish, Ceanndraoi," he told Orla. "I'll return with his answer."

As Musa rode away, Eideard turned swiftly to Orla. "Why?" he asked. "Why treat the man we just defeated as an equal? And why weren't *we* consulted about that decision?" He swept his hand around to encompass the others in the group.

"Would you have agreed to it if I'd asked, Eideard?"

"No, which is why—"

She lifted her hand, not letting him finish. "Then you already have your answer," she told him.

His face flushed, his scars standing out white against the

reddened skin. "The ceanndraoi forgets that we're all on the same side here." He spat on the ground for emphasis. "She forgets that I am ceannàrd."

"And I am Ceanndraoi Orla Moonshadow, and the Moonshadow has its own side," she told him. "You'd be wise not to forget that." Then, with heavy emphasis, "Ceannàrd."

She nodded to them and walked away.

Musa returned a few stripes of the candle later bearing Commander Savas' agreement to meet the next morning, though Musa added that Savas wished Greum to be among the attendees. When Orla questioned that, Musa only replied, "Greum Red-Hand was the ceanndraoi that the commander dealt with until very recently, and he wishes to know how the Red-Hand feels about any decision we might make."

"I'm afraid that's not possible, Sub-Commander. Greum Red-Hand was . . . injured, and he currently lies senseless."

"He's dying?" Musa asked.

Orla shrugged. "He may recover, he may not. That's not in anyone's hands but Elia's." *I didn't want his death, as much as I disliked the man. I still don't.*

"The commander was quite emphatic in his wish that the former ceanndraoi attend this meeting."

Orla wondered at that. What possible advantage could Savas see in Greum's presence? "For all we know, moving Greum Red-Hand might kill him," Orla told Musa. "I'm afraid that the commander will have to be disappointed."

"I'll relay that to him," Musa answered, "and if that changes his answer, I'll return with the news."

"That will have to do," Orla told him. "Tell the commander that I look forward to our meeting."

Musa nodded to them, then pulled himself up into his chariot and gestured to his driver. They watched him drive off. Orla turned to the others. "I need to return to the former ceanndraoi's quarters before this meeting," she told them. "Have the parley tent erected, and I'll be back in the morning."

"May I come in, Draoi Ceiteag?" Orla asked the sour face that peered back at her.

"Who am I to refuse the ceanndraoi's wishes?" Ceiteag answered. She opened the door just wide enough to admit Orla. The room beyond looked little changed from when these had been Orla's quarters. Bedding had been placed in the room, and through the open archway to the bedroom beyond, Orla could see Greum's blanket-covered figure. She could see his anamacha standing motionlessly in the corner of the darkened room, as if in accusation.

So he's not dead . . .

"I hear that Ceanndraoi Orla has secured another great victory over the Mundoan army," Ceiteag said. Her voice was flat and emotionless. "You must be very proud of your accomplishments."

"I might be when this is all over," Orla told her. "But it's far from done. How's Draoi Greum? Commander Savas has asked after him."

"Draoi Greum," Ceiteag answered with a strong emphasis on the title, "is as you left him, Ceanndraoi. No different."

"The archiaters . . . ?"

Ceiteag pursed her lips as if she were about to spit. "Worse than useless," she said. "They wanted to purge him and burn their herbs around his bed. I sent them away. I'll take care of him myself."

"May I see him?"

"If you must."

Ceiteag ushered her into the bedroom. Candles burned in the niches, giving off a scent that couldn't cover the stronger smell of stale urine and fecal matter. Greum's face was paler than Orla remembered, and the hands lying on the linen sheets seemed ruddier than before. His lips were cracked and dry, his closed eyes sunken. She could barely see the rise and fall of his chest. A bowl of broth stood on a small table next to the bed, along with a flagon of water, a wedge of cheese, and an uneaten loaf of bread. Ceiteag seemed to notice Orla glancing at the table.

"Every stripe of the candle, I lift his head, open his mouth, and spoon a little water or broth down his throat. If I put food in his mouth, he won't chew it or swallow it; it just sits there, and I have to pull it back out for fear he'll choke." She glared at Orla, her eyes glinting in the light of the candles, her anamacha near her side. Greum's anamacha also stared at Orla, hands upon hands of faces flickering across their head. "Remember how you told me you didn't kill him? You lied. In truth, what you've done is far worse and more cruel than simple murder. He'll die *slowly* now, wasting away from hunger and thirst until his body gives up. Your mother had more compassion than you; she'd have ended his life quickly. Mercifully."

"Ceiteag, I didn't know—"

"No, you didn't know," Ceiteag said mockingly. "You know so very little, Ceanndraoi." She blinked heavily, focusing rheum-wet, white-glazed eyes on Orla. "Why are you here? Are you really concerned with the former ceanndraoi's health? Or is the Moonshadow worried that he might still be a threat to you?"

"No," Orla told her. "Commander Savas . . . he seemed eager to see Draoi Greum again, and I'm wondering why that was. I'm wondering why Greum said that I'd ruined everything by coming to Onglse and by challenging him as ceanndraoi. I'm wondering what I'm missing, and since you've been the Red-Hand's constant companion for the last several years, and because you knew my mother, I thought you might be willing to tell me."

Ceiteag looked away from her, her gaze going to Greum. "You and the Moonshadow ruined *everything*," she declared, still looking at the stricken draoi. Then her head turned back to Orla. Her eyes were cold and angry. "You've no idea."

"Then tell me," Orla said.

"No." The answer was emphatic. "I won't. Let that be the great Orla Moonshadow's punishment for what you did to the man who could have brought peace to Albann. Now get out. He doesn't want you here. Neither do I." With that statement, Ceiteag's ana-macha slid over to her, and Orla saw it enter her. Her own anam-acha responded, coming to her so that the Otherworld began to overlay her vision. *<She's weak . . . Destroy her, then kill the Red-hand as you should have before . . .>* Orla couldn't tell whose voice she was hearing as all the draoi inside crowded around her.

<No. Leave me!> she shouted to them, thrusting out her hands as if to push them away.

<Foolish girl . . .> she heard them reply, but slowly the Other-world began to fade. "I'm leaving," Orla told Ceiteag. "And I'm truly sorry, Draoi Ceiteag. Sorry for what I've done to both of you. You were kind to my mother and to me, and for that I thank you."

She started to leave the room, but Ceiteag called out to her.

"Wait, Ceanndraoi," the draoi said. Orla turned, seeing Ceiteag biting at her lower lip as she looked at Greum Red-Hand in his bed. "You need to know that he wasn't a bad man," she said. "The things he did . . . that he'd agreed to do . . . he thought all of them were the best actions he could take for the Cateni."

"I believe you," Orla told her.

Ceiteag heaved a long sigh, as if coming to a difficult decision. "Then I have something to tell you . . ." she began.

That night, the tent was set up on the ridge between the two en-campments. Orla's entourage, which included Sorcha, Magaidh, Comhnall, Ceiteag, and Eideard as well as a hand of unarmed warriors, set out at daybreak. As they approached, they saw Com-mander Savas, his two sub-commanders, Musa and Ilkur, their chariot drivers, a sihirki, and other officers already waiting for them, though several more chariots and a cohort of soldiers were perched on the ridge immediately behind them. The two groups were to be seated on opposite sides of the long trestle table under the tent on chairs draped with brocaded cloth. Bread, cheeses, and both ale and water flagons had been set on the table by the kitchen staff from the Cateni tower. The servants hurried forward to escort everyone to their chairs: Orla and Eideard were seated at the middle of the table across from Savas, Musa, and Ilkur.

Orla rose after everyone was seated, their mugs filled, and food offered, though most declined. "Welcome, Commander Savas. It's good to meet you again."

"Is it, Ceanndraoi?" Savas asked. "And what is it that you expect us to accomplish here?"

"That's very simple, Commander: I seek an end to this war." There were huffs of disbelief and skepticism from around the tent, from both sides of the table. Orla heard Eideard give a nasal half laugh next to her.

Savas' face, Orla noticed, betrayed nothing of his thoughts. "If that's what you wish to accomplish, Ceanndraoi, then you're talking with the wrong person. None of the Mundoa here have the authority to make such a decision—that lies with Great-Voice Utka and Emperor Pashtuk. You should be talking to them."

"You command the army, and it's your army that wages the war and pays the greatest price. Not the Great-Voice nor the emperor."

"So you're asking me to surrender? Why would I do that, when I still have my army at my back with greater numbers than yours, and when I could send south for yet more troops?" Savas leaned back, folding his arms over his krug.

"Forget the empty threats, Commander. I could strand your army here with a few simple spells," Orla told him. "What if your troops ships out in Onglse Strait burned, as they did at Muras, so you couldn't leave Onglse? Are you and your men going to swim back to the mainland? There's nothing you could do to stop me from doing that, and our draoi and I could do the same to any ships that enter the Strait to replace them or any boats you try to build from the trees here. What does your advantage in numbers matter if you're marooned here on Onglse? Why, we could just leave you here to starve. After you've eaten your horses and the few sheep here on the island, after you've plundered what you can of the food stored in the towers you hold, what then? How long would it be until your troops turned on you and begged you to surrender to us? You can't make a meal of swords, Commander Savas."

Orla could feel everyone's eyes on her as she spoke. There was silence in the tent when she'd finished.

"Now who makes empty threats?" Savas asked, still leaning back in his chair. "You're just as trapped here. You and the draoi won't leave, because we'd raze your sacred Bàn Cill if you did. Your warriors alone wouldn't be able to stop us. And even if you sink the ships the Great-Voice sends—and he *will* send ships, more than you can imagine, because when he stops receiving my reports, he'll know something is terribly amiss—he'll simply raise an army and come north with it, burning down every village and slaughtering every Cateni he finds on the way. I may no longer be here at that point, but is that the result you want, Ceanndraoi? You may be as strong or stronger than your mother, but even the Moonshadow can't stand alone against an army."

"Perhaps not," Orla admitted. "So let's talk about what we *can* do. After all, you were willing to work with Greum Red-Hand. I'm told that the two of you had reached an agreement, one that was abrogated at Muras."

Savas' hands dropped at that statement, and exclamations erupted from around the tent. Eideard stood up, as did Comhnall, and that drew Musa and Ilkur from their seats. Fingers were pointed across the table, and insults were hurled. Orla saw Magaidh start to call her anamacha to her as the meeting threatened to spiral out of control.

It was Savas himself who quashed the fire. "Enough!" he bellowed, standing, his roar cutting through the clamor. "Musa, Ilkur, stand down. Everyone: *sit!*"

The voice of command worked. Musa and Ilkur and the other Mundoa returned to their seats, and slowly the Cateni did the same. "Better," Savas said, still standing. He held out his hand toward Orla. "Ceanndraoi, walk with me, if you would."

27

Revelations

ALTAN REMAINED SILENT AS they walked, as did Orla. He moved deliberately in the direction of the Cateni wall and tower, thinking that going toward the Mundoan line might make Orla suspect an attack. The last thing he wanted now was to rouse the Moonshadow. He felt rather naked without sword or knife, knowing that even though he couldn't see it, Orla's anamacha was walking with her.

When they were well away from the parley tent and the others, he stopped, his hands behind his back. "So you've spoken with Greum Red-Hand?" he asked Orla. He forced his eyes to remain on the young woman's damaged face, though that was difficult.

The ceanndraoi shook her head. "Not Greum; he's still lost in the Otherworld," she said. "There's little chance that he'll live—at least that's what Draoi Ceiteag believes. It was Ceiteag, his confidante, who told me what she knows."

Altan nodded. He knew Draoi Ceiteag was the Red-Hand's closest companion, though in their correspondence Greum had denied that she knew much of the details of their agreement. "And what exactly has she told you?"

"That Muras was to have had a far different outcome. She said that Greum was to retreat when your army arrived without a battle at all, and that some of the clan àrds closest to Ceanndraoi Greum had also agreed to this. The two of you had created a pre-arranged treaty Greum and Ceannàrd Comhnall would sign to end hostilities. The northern clans would agree to send a yearly tribute to the Great-Voice and Emperor Pashtuk in return for being left alone above the Meadham. But because of my presence, because of what I did, the attitude of Ceannàrd Comhnall changed, as did that of the àrds whom Greum had approached and even Greum Red-Hand himself. Greum began to think that he might be able to force further concessions from you by con-tinuing the fight. Ceiteag didn't know what concessions Greum had in mind or know how far he was prepared to take things, but that's what she knew. It's possible Greum even thought that he might prevail entirely."

"And now you think the same?"

"I think that if we had to, we could win the victory that eluded my mother." Altan felt a chill with those words. He started to reply, but Orla continued. "But the cost of that in Cateni lives isn't a price I'm comfortable paying."

"I notice you neglect to mention the cost in Mundoan lives."

Orla merely gazed back placidly at him. "Mundoan lives are *your* concern, Commander. Not mine."

"Is that you speaking or the Moonshadow?"

"Both of us. Though I remind you of what I did yesterday to avoid killing Mundoans. I could have just as easily killed every soldier around your ballistae. I could have just as easily killed you. I did neither of those things."

Altan sighed. "We keep dancing around with words, Ceann-draoi. I should have talked openly with you about Greum Red-Hand and about our agreement before now, during one of those times you came to me in the night. I didn't because I didn't know that I could trust you, especially when I realized that Greum was backing out of our arrangements. For that matter, I was never certain that Great-Voice Utka or Emperor Pashtuk would adhere to such a treaty once I had it in hand or whether it would all fall apart anyway. I'd made my own alternate plans in case, and I followed them. I regret my silence, but I can't change that now. So let me ask you—as ceanndraoi, would you put your seal to the treaty? If you will, I'll take it back to Savur, give it to the Great-Voice, and advocate that he also place his seal on it, no matter what that might cost me."

Orla seemed to be listening to voices that he couldn't hear, her head cocked to one side. *The Moonshadow?* he wondered. *Or perhaps Voada?* "No," she said after a long pause. "I won't. Not now."

"Then just tell me what it is you want, and I'll tell you whether it's something I can give you or not, and we'll both know where we stand."

"I want an Albann where the Cateni and the clans rule themselves."

Altan was unable to stop the scoffing laugh that erupted from him at that pronouncement. "Negotiation is about compromise," he told her. "You're asking for total surrender from us, and you won't get it. Ever. And certainly not from me."

"Why not?" Orla persisted. "What does Emperor Pashtuk want from Albann, Commander? It can't be land; you've enough of that and more in Rumeli. It can't be our people—we've already proven that we're poor conscripts, slaves, and servants. How many rebellions has your empire had to quash here already, leading to increasing resentment and discontent among the Cateni you rule? Here we are right now in the midst of yet another rebellion. What value does Albann give to your empire? Our silver and gold? Our jewelry and crafts? Our iron? Our salt from the Storm Sea? Our crops and farm animals? Our coal? Our timber? Our marble? All of those and more go over the Barrier Sea regularly, mined and created and forged by Cateni hands and taken from us without our consent. I ask you to imagine this, Commander: what if those things *still* flowed from Albann to the empire, only freely? What if Emperor Pashtuk still received from Albann what the empire desires, only without having to keep an army here? You and Greum Red-Hand wanted to end the wars in the north, but perhaps you were thinking too narrowly. What if Albann wasn't a conquered state but an ally of the empire?"

Altan's hand prowled his beard, stroking the glossy salt-and-pepper strands. He wondered if she'd somehow cast a spell without him knowing, for he found himself considering her words rather than simply dismissing them out of hand. *Did I make a mistake trying to deal with Greum? Can I trust her? She's Voada's daughter, but I liked Voada when I met her at Pencraig, before the Moonshadow . . .*

"I don't see how that's possible," Altan answered.

"Perhaps it's not. But it certainly can't happen at all unless someone makes the proposal in the first place." She was staring at him, her eyes trapped in scars; she was too young to have done all that she had, but she had the face of an elder. "You'll die here otherwise, Commander," she told him. "You and all your soldiers. And for nothing at all. If you think that's an empty threat, I'd ask you to remember what I did yesterday. Remember what my mother nearly accomplished, and know that I'm stronger than her because my anamacha contains both my mother and the Moonshadow. I'm asking you for all of us: for the Cateni and for the Mundoa. Let us try to end this together, or I will end it alone in blood."

He wanted to agree. The exhaustion from decades of battles, the aching in his joints and body, his distaste for Great-Voice Utka . . . he wanted to lay down all those burdens.

But he was a soldier, and he had his orders.

"I can't give you an answer here and now, Ceanndraoi," he told her. "Let me consider what you've said, and I'll come back to the parley tent, alone, in the morning with my answer."

Orla nodded at that. "I'll be waiting there for you," she agreed.

Sorcha insisted on accompanying Orla to the parley tent the next morning to await Commander Savas. "I know you've already told Ceannàrd Eideard and Magaidh not to come with you, but I'm going, and I don't care what you say," she told Orla as they dressed in her quarters. Eideard and Magaidh had been difficult to convince, but Orla had insisted, not wanting them to know what she intended to offer to Savas in order to convince him. They would only try to talk her out of it, and she didn't have time for arguments. But Sorcha—it would be good to have someone there who would support her without question.

So Orla chuckled at Sorcha's determination with a smile that felt strange on her face after a largely sleepless night. She'd kept turning over the possible answers Savas might give her in her mind, along with how she was going to respond. The looming dark presence of the Moonshadow had haunted her dreams when she had been able to fall asleep, and its multiple voices had alternately mocked her and laughed at her. *<You know this won't work . . . You're throwing everything away on a false hope. . . You'll end up here inside with the rest of us for the next draoi to hold . . .>*

Sorcha stood back a pace from Orla as she watched Savas' chariot approach and stop several strides from the parley tent. The young driver she remembered from her visits to Savas' bedchambers pulled at the reins with muscular arms, and Savas descended slowly from the vehicle, stiff-legged. As he approached the tent, his gait quickened, and his limp nearly vanished. *Like an old man used to concealing his age*, she thought. He was weaponless, as before. Savas gave her the Mundoan salute as he stood before her, a fisted hand clasped over the breast of his armor. He gave a nod of acknowledgment to Sorcha before his gaze returned to Orla. "Ceanndraoi," he said. "I suspect you've had as little sleep as I've had."

"It's that obvious?" she asked him, and he smiled gently.

"I'm afraid I'm a poor diplomat," he said. "I'm just—"

"I know," she told him. "A simple soldier. You've told me more than once before. But I find you neither simple nor a mere soldier, Commander. So did your sleepless night give you an answer to my question?"

"It did," he said. "As much as I would like to avoid further bloodshed, I don't see how we can possibly achieve what you suggested. I appreciate that you don't think me a simple soldier, but protecting these troops"—he waved a hand toward the far ridge and the outer wall of Onglse—"as well as the holdings of Emperor Pashtuk is my responsibility. Leaving Onglse to you because of what you *might* be capable of doing would mean abandoning my duty and my honor. If that means we must continue the fight, then . . ." He stopped, his shoulders lifting and falling again. "As I told you yesterday, I don't have the authority to do as you asked. Only Great-Voice Utka could do that, or Emperor Pashtuk himself."

It was what she'd expected him to say, and it pleased her to see mingled disappointment and regret on his craggy, scarred face. "I'm sorry, Ceanndraoi," he added. "But it will be an honor to meet you on the battlefield again. To an honorable death, for one of us."

She shook her head. "There won't be a battlefield meeting. I need to go to Great-Voice Utka myself if you can't do this without him."

Savas gave a cough of a laugh. "Ceanndraoi, I can't allow you to take your army south. Your mother did that—"

"Not my army," she said before he could finish. "Only me."

Savas blinked. He tilted his head quizzically. "I don't understand."

"If you had captured me alive on the battlefield, what would you have done, Commander?" she asked. "Would you have killed me, or would you have taken me as captive back to Savur for judgment?"

"I would have taken you to Savur."

"Then take me," she told him. "I'll go willingly, as your prisoner."

"Orla!" Sorcha broke in. "You can't do this!"

Orla turned to her, smiling. "Don't worry," she told Sorcha. She leaned close to her, speaking in her ear so that Savas couldn't hear. "This is the best way. I promise you."

Then she turned back to Savas. "Well, Commander, you have my offer. Take me to Savur so I can make my case to your Great-Voice. If you won't do that, then I'll do as I threatened to do. I'll burn and sink your ships and leave you and your army here on

Onglse to starve, with draoi and warriors across the Strait and on the islands to make certain you don't leave. Then I'll take my army south with me. We'll go to Savur ourselves, and I'll burn every Mundoan city to the ground as I pass. It's your choice, Commander. Do you want me as your captive or unleashed as my mother tenfold?"

"That's hardly a choice," he answered.

"Good," she told him. "Then here's how this must happen . . ."

28

The Prisoner

SAVUR WAS BY FAR the largest city Orla had ever seen. Her birth town, Pencraig, had been small—though Orla had thought it quite large at the time—but Pencraig had still dwarfed most of the clan villages north of the River Meadham. Bàn Cill on Onglse was majestic and beautiful, but it was also small, with rarely more than a few hundred inhabitants except during the solstice celebrations. She'd thought Muras bloated and over-large with its crowds and shipyards. They'd passed through the former capital of Trusa on their way; the partially rebuilt town, rising again from the ashes and ruins in which her mam had left it, had seemed impossibly large and foreboding to Orla's eyes, with its massive encircling walls and stout, dark gated archways through which all visitors had to pass.

But Savur . . .

They had their first glimpse of Savur from the summit of one of the hills that surrounded the Mundoan capital. The vista, bathed in alternating sunlight and shadow from the clouds drifting in the sky, caused Orla to suck in her breath in awe. The city nestled in the arms of seven hills, sprawling in an arc along the glistening waters of the deep harbor, with the many-mouthed River Iska yawning wide into a long bay leading out to the Barrier

Sea, a misty line well out in the shimmering distance. The inner city was crowded with tall buildings, most in the minareted Mundoan style with golden domes sparkling in sunlight. The city spilled well beyond the ancient wall, built long ago by the Cateni who had first laid the foundations of the city, and up the slopes of the hills. A wide avenue arrowed through the city all the way to the harbor, crowded with carriages and people. Even from their vantage point the noise of the city reached them, a cacophony formed by thousands of voices, the rattling of livery and carts, music from the public houses, the hammering of smithies, the bleating and lowing of sheep and cattle being led to the markets, and a multitude of other diverse sounds.

"Ceanndraoi, it's time," Savas said. He held out a length of rattling iron chains. He and Orla were in his chariot, Tolga in his usual place in the traces. Savas' muscular warhorses had been replaced by twin white steeds for their entry into the city. They were accompanied by a partial cohort of soldiers in Mundoan armor, though they were not all Mundoan. Sorcha rode a horse alongside the chariot; Orla heard her take a long breath as Orla held out her hands to Savas, who wrapped her wrists in the heavy, cold chains before closing a large lock through the links to bind them together. He stretched out his arm to hand the key to Sorcha. "Here," he said. "We each have a key. But I can't have the ceanndraoi entering Savur without her hands bound so that she can't cast a spell. In truth, Great-Voice Utka will ask why she still *has* her hands and her tongue when he wants her head as well, but . . ."

"This was the only way, Sorcha," Orla told her. "The only way."

"No, it wasn't," Sorcha answered. Orla could see her blinking away tears. "We all know that. You could have taken victory at Onglse and elsewhere."

Orla lifted her chained hands. "This was the only way we might avoid mass bloodshed."

"Except yours, or perhaps the commander's."

"This was Elia's way," Orla told Sorcha calmly. "I prayed to Her, and this was the answer She gave me."

"And it's the way we're all committed to now," Savas broke in. He nodded to Tolga, and the chariot began to move forward again, its iron-clad wheels loud on the flagstones of the North Road, well-paved this close to the capital. "Sorcha, stay behind the chariot with the soldiers. Ceanndraoi, it may become rough from here; I'll shield you as best I can."

They rode down from the hills toward the city. As they moved between the outlying houses and farms, people began to gawk and point. Most of them wore Mundoan clothing, but Orla could see the occasional Cateni faces among the onlookers. The crowd grew in size and volume as they approached the city gates, and Orla heard the whispers: "Commander Savas! Look, he's captured the ceanndraoi! The Moonshadow is in chains!"

As they passed through a market square near the gates, fruits and vegetables as well as rocks and occasional feces from the horses and dogs of the city began to rain down on the chariot, hurled with curses and insults toward Orla. "Cateni witch! You killed my son! My husband is dead and my children fatherless because of you! Flay her alive! Rip her stomach open, and let the crows feed on her while she screams!"

As he'd promised, Commander Savas raised his shield over Orla as she crouched low in the chariot. Along with the invectives, she could hear the sounds as the missiles struck the shield, spattering her with their shattered, wet fragments. She heard Sorcha screaming uselessly at the crowd, telling them to stop. The soldiers around them spread out along the roadway, pushing back the onlookers with their warhorses. At the same time, the Moonshadow's voices howled in protest in Orla's mind. <*You see! . . . This is not the way . . . You're a fool . . . You've made a mockery of yourself and us . . .*>

Orla found herself in agreement, wishing her hands were free. *I could end this with a spell. I could send them running in fear.*

From under Savas' shield, Orla saw that the guards stationed at the open gates suddenly came to full attention, saluting the chariot that flew the commander's banner. They passed through the shadows of the arch, the rain of abuse ending, and out into sun again along the wide Avenue of the Emperor.

"We're safe enough here," Savas said as he lowered his shield and set it aside, allowing Orla to see the shade trees set along either side of the road and government buildings of white stone and gold-domed minarets placed well back on manicured lawns. Orla found herself both awed and angered by the architectural opulence on display, knowing that it was Cateni slave labor that brought in the raw materials that had gone into these edifices, Cateni stonemasons who had cut and shaped the marble and granite blocks, Cateni forests that had supplied the timber, and Cateni laborers who had milled the logs. It had been Cateni craftspeople who hammered together the boards and mortared the stones, laid the tiles and fitted the doors and windows. It was Cateni gold that adorned the spires and gilded the ornamental touches. These massive buildings were maintained and cleaned and polished by Cateni servants and slaves.

All the riches on display in Savur were stolen goods that belonged to Albann and the clans.

There were crowds along the Avenue of the Emperor—nearly all Mundoan—who shouted insults toward Orla and gave loud cheers for Commander Savas and the troops with him, but there were also soldiers in the livery of Great-Voice Utka stationed along the avenue, keeping everyone back and under control. There were a few Cateni servants in view, but though they watched Orla intently as she passed, they remained silent.

Great-Voice Utka's keep was near the harbor; Orla could smell the sea as they approached; gulls with raucous calls banked across the sky on wide white wings. If Orla had thought the other buildings ostentatious, this one seemed built for a god. They first had to pass along a vast wall that hid much of the keep from common eyes, then they came to huge double gates a hand of men tall that yawned open as they approached, several soldiers pushing on the gilded iron bands that confined the thick oaken timbers in order to swing them open. Tolga turned the chariot into a great courtyard, Sorcha and the soldiers following behind before the gates were closed once more.

A wide expanse of marble steps led up to a columned portico where golden doors opened to disgorge a phalanx of keep guards and richly dressed attendants. They were followed by the Great-Voice Utka himself, wearing a blood-red *entari* over his tunic and a matching *sarik* emblazoned with a golden hawk. Orla could see that the Great-Voice was no military man; the arms that emerged from his entari showed little musculature as he raised a hand glittering with jeweled rings toward Savas. His long beard was oiled and dyed an utter black, plaited with silver and gold threads. Dark, shadowed eyes stared at Orla from under his sarik, lingering on her face and the silver torc around her neck. She hated the feel of his stare.

"So this is Mad Voada's spawn," he said. "She can't use her spells?"

Savas lifted Orla's chained hands so that Utka could see her bonds. "No, Great-Voice."

Utka sniffed as Savas let Orla's hands drop again, the chains rattling. "Hmm . . . I'd have simply lopped off the girl's hands entirely; then there'd be nothing to worry about at all. She's not as impressive as I'd thought she'd be from the reports you sent. I was expecting . . . someone more *dangerous* in appearance, I must admit. Still . . ." Utka waved his jeweled hand. "Bring her in. I want to see our new prize captive."

Great-Voice Utka turned, his lackeys—Cateni, Orla noted—swung open the door of the keep again, and Utka and his entourage went into the darkness beyond. Savas pointed to two of his soldiers, one an older man, the other younger with a dark beard. "Sub-commander," he said to the older, "stay with the men here in the courtyard. You know your orders. You"—that to the younger man— "come with me, and bring two hands of men with you."

With that, Savas leaped down from the chariot as Tolga left the traces to hold the reins of the horses. Savas helped Orla down onto the ground as the uniformed and armored warrior escorts and Sorcha all dismounted. More Cateni servants came forward to take their horses. "Stable the horses," Savas told Tolga and the servants. "I expect we'll be here for a time." Then he leaned close to Orla. "You're certain this is still what you want?" he asked again.

Orla nodded, though part of her wanted nothing more than to flee from this place surrounded by her enemies. "Are you certain it's what *you* want?" she asked him in return.

Savas didn't answer. Instead he pretended to examine her cuffed hands; she felt him slip the key to the lock into her palm. Then he took her arm and—more roughly—walked her up the steps to the keep, with Sorcha and the soldiers behind.

29

A Rising Moon

THE ROOM INTO WHICH Orla was eventually hauled was huge and opulent. The Great-Voice sat on a throne on a raised dais with two steps; Orla thought he looked like a gilded toad sitting atop a mushroom, waiting for flies to pass by. His acolytes stood to either side of the dais, and there were guards armed with pikes and swords on either side as well, with two more at the door of the room. Closed doors behind the dais promised to lead deeper into the warrens of the keep.

Savas guided Orla toward the Great-Voice with a hand on her arm. She could feel Sorcha immediately behind her, while Savas' soldiers spread out in a careful arc in the rear. The Moonshadow's anamacha remained close to her side, its voices clamoring inside her head.

<*We shouldn't be here . . . This is a dangerous ploy, and it won't work . . . You can't trust the Mundoa—none of them . . .*>

And another voice, the loudest: <*Give yourself to us . . .*>

Orla could feel her stomach churning as they approached the dais. She pressed the key in her hand tightly.

"So you're the ceanndraoi now," Utka began as they halted at the base of the dais. She could see his gaze moving from side to side around her, as if searching for the anamacha he'd undoubtedly

304

been told would also be there. "You control this supposedly power-ful Moonshadow that no one else can see. So Greum Red-Hand is dead?"

"Greum Red-Hand was terribly injured in . . . an accident," she told him, choosing the words carefully. "When we left Onglse he was still alive, though barely so. By now . . ." She shrugged, the chains linking her hands together clanking with the motion.

"And you are Orla Paorach, daughter of Meir and Voada Paor-ach, once the Hand and Hand-wife of Pencraig. According to our records, your father at least was a loyal subject of the emperor and of the lamented Voice Kadir of Pencraig."

Orla managed an ironic laugh. "Your version of history is flawed, Great-Voice. You forget that I was there. Yes, I'm the daughter of Meir Paorach, Hand of Pencraig before he died. And I'm also Voada's daughter, and my mam was brutalized and mis-treated after my father's death by Maki Kadir, former Voice of Pencraig whose death was entirely unlamented by my people. As ceanndraoi, Mam gave Voice Kadir and your predecessor Great-Voice Vadim the justice they both deserved before she fell. As to my family's supposed loyalty to the emperor . . ." Orla pursed her lips and spat on the marble of the dais' first step.

The keep guards at the dais stiffened, fingers tightening around the shafts of their pikes. Utka snorted his derision, though he looked at Savas as if he expected the commander to strike Orla for her inso-lence. "Impudent child. At least we have Commander Savas to thank for killing the Mad Ceanndraoi Voada and capturing you be-fore you could match your mother's slaughter and destruction. Your short time as ceanndraoi is now over, I'm afraid."

"You're wrong once more, Great-Voice. I permitted Commander Savas to bring me here so I could offer you an end to the hostilities between Cateni and Mundoa."

Utka slapped the arm of his throne with an open hand as he roared with laughter. "You *permitted . . .*" he sputtered. He grinned in Savas' direction as if they were sharing a joke. From the corner of her vision, Orla saw Savas smile tight-lipped back at the man. "And what is it you feel you have to offer?"

"It's very simple, Great-Voice. We offer continued tribute to the emperor in return for allowing the clans to rule themselves, as we did before you Mundoa came. You and all the Voices will leave your cities and towns and return to Rumeli. In return, gold, silver, and goods will continue to flow across the Barrier Sea to the emperor: payment for our continued freedom."

"It's that simple, is it?" Utka asked, still grinning. Then the grin fell from his face. "You're wrong, however. Tribute *will* continue to flow across to Rumeli, because we'll take whatever we need from the clans. And you, Ceanndraoi? You'll be just a sad reminder of what happens to those who oppose Emperor Pashtuk and his Great-Voice in Albann: a rotting corpse impaled on the city gates for the ravens to pick clean—but only after we've made you scream in agony for every drop of Mundoan blood you've spilled. It's a shame we never had the chance to do the same to your mam."

Utka gestured to the guards at the dais. "Take her below. I'll be down later to deal with her personally." He chuckled again, shaking his head, his chin waggling in amusement. "You *permitted* . . ."

The two guards bowed toward the Great-Voice, then started down the steps toward Orla, who fumbled with the key Savas had given her. It fell, clattering on the tiles. The ringing of the key on the floor sounded impossibly loud in the hall, drawing everyone's attention; Orla saw Utka's eyes narrow in sudden suspicion.

Orla felt more than saw Sorcha rush to her. At the same time she heard the sound of swords being drawn by the soldiers behind her. Someone screamed, and the sycophants near the dais suddenly scattered like roaches in sunlight. "Treachery! Guards!" Utka shouted, rising from his seat as Sorcha twisted her key in the lock of Orla's chains. Orla let them drop to the ground, opening her arms to call her anamacha to her.

<*Mam! Come to me* . . .>

She felt her mam sweeping toward her from the press of draoi in the anamacha, but a shadow fell over them all, hurling aside her mam and the other draoi ghosts. She heard her mother wail as she was tossed. <*Orla* . . . *!*> Then Leagsaidh Moonshadow was there before her, a form of swirling storm clouds and lightning.

<No!> Orla mind-shouted to the apparition. *<You're not wanted.
Let my mam come to me!>*

Leagsaidh Moonshadow gave a twinned laugh, low and high.
<This is finally our time,> it said. *<Give yourself to us . . . Together
we'll show them what we can do . . . Here . . .>*

Orla's world merged with that of Magh da Chèo. She could
hear the metallic clash of sword against sword around her, but
the sounds were simply distractions to which she could pay no
attention. The Moonshadow surged toward her like a vast incho-
ate wave, laughing and hurling energy toward her almost faster
than she could contain it. The power threatened to overcome her,
to send her spinning away to be lost forever. Her spell cage was
alive with fury, with unfocused and unspecific energy she could
take and shape in whatever way she wanted.

But she knew what the Moonshadow wished her to do. She
could feel its yearning and its desires, could hear its double voice
whispering in her head, crooning to her. *<Use what we give you.
Give in to us . . . We can reduce him to ash as he cowers there on the
dais screaming . . . His anguish would be delicious . . .>* The Moonshadow, its voice twinned with Leagsaidh's, was as seductive as a
lover's. *<Do it! Kill him . . . Let us be done with him . . .>*

But Orla was shaking her head. That felt wrong. *<No. What will
yet another death accomplish, even his?>* she asked. She pushed the
Moonshadow away, though it was like trying to contain a flood
with her hands. Instead, she remembered the temple that she'd
erected on Onglse with Iomhar's aid, though she couldn't call
Iomhar to her now with the Moonshadow's energy burning in her
hands. Instead she imagined a smaller but more ornate edifice,
with barred windows and no door at all perched on the dais and
surrounding Utka: a glorious prison.

Utka screamed as the wall of white stone appeared around
him, and Orla also heard the derision of the Moonshadow. *<You'd
play games with what we give you . . . ? Let us show you what we can
do . . . Let us enter you fully . . .>*

<No,> she told them, but they only laughed.

<You have no choice. Not really . . .> But the Moonshadow

receded slightly. Utka was still screaming invectives, and Orla heard the battle around her pause at the same time. She concentrated on taking the energy the Moonshadow was still feeding her, completing the structure around Utka until it was solid, so tall that it nearly reached the vaulted ceiling of the throne chamber and large enough that it dominated the center of the room, minareted as if in mockery of the Mundoan architecture outside. She could see Great-Voice Utka's face at the nearest window, his ringed fingers wrapped around the cold stone bars as he shook them futilely.

The effort of creating the edifice and fending off the Moonshadow had cost Orla; it was far more tiring than simply gathering power and releasing it in much the same form, like most war draoi would do. She wanted nothing more than to let her hands drop to her sides, to stop the Moonshadow from tearing power from the Otherworld and forcing it on her.

But she couldn't rest yet. She turned back to the room and the struggle between the soldiers and the keep's guards. There was blood staining the floor tiles and splashed over the armor of the soldiers, and she wanted no more of it. Orla reshaped the energy that the Moonshadow continued to rip from Magh da Chèo, concentrating as she released it as separate, sharply focused bursts of wind that sent the quartet of Utka's guards and the sycophants who hadn't left the room tumbling over the tiles to the walls. Savas' soldiers quickly relieved them of weapons. *<Leave me now,>* Orla thought to Leagsaidh Moonshadow. *<It's done.>*

<Done?> They laughed at her, the barrage of sound nearly knocking her over. *<Why, it's barely begun . . . Now you'll give yourself fully, as your mam eventually did . . .>*

<We've already won here,> she answered.

<This isn't victory . . . There's no victory until your enemies lie dead at your feet . . . All of them . . .>

The younger soldier Savas had spoken to earlier removed his helm, revealing Eideard's face staring at her in concern as he stood over the Mundoan guards. "Ceanndraoi?" he asked.

Bind their hands and feet for now, she wanted to tell him. *They're not to be harmed.* But the words couldn't come. She couldn't make herself speak. Her mouth opened and shut again. Savas was staring at her, and she wondered at the odd look on his face.

"Savas!" Great-Voice Utka roared from his new prison, his shrill voice sounding as if it came from some impossible distance, no more important that the shrilling of a mosquito. "You're a dead man. You hear me? A dead man. You're *all* dead!"

Orla shuddered as frigid darkness enveloped her, the real world dimming so that only Magh da Chèo seemed solid and genuine. The Moonshadow blanketed her, and its voice roared in her head, though Leagsaidh's voice was now strangely absent. There was only the low, dark rumble of the Moonshadow itself. *<You see . . . We're with you now . . . We are you, and you are us . . . We'll show them why they must fear us . . .>*

With that the Moonshadow began to tear at Magh da Chèo again, ripping energy from that world and sending it flaring toward her. Orla found her hands, unbidden, creating a new spell cage, moving in a complex pattern she didn't know and had never been taught. She could sense that Eideard and Savas were calling out to her, but their faces were faint and nearly lost behind the mist of Magh da Chèo, their voices inaudible over the roaring of the Otherworld's storms. Between her hands there was only blinding, snarling light, so bright that it burned red through her closed eyelids.

<This is our land. This is our home.> Orla found her own mouth opening, her voice speaking the Moonshadow's words; it was the voice of a god, so loud that she imagined everyone in Savur clapping hands over ears. *<You're not welcome here! You must leave! I am Orla Moonshadow, and you will listen to me!>*

Part of her rejoiced in the feeling of power that spilled over her. That part of her *wanted* this as much as the Moonshadow did. She could feel the intense desire, a heat inside her. Still, another part of her protested—*<No! This is wrong!>*—and with the denial she felt the presence of her mother rushing forward toward the Moonshadow, like an angry dog attacking a bear threatening her pup. Voada interposed herself between Orla and the Moonshadow, and the two of them roared at the Moonshadow as one: <*No! You will listen to us!*>

The Moonshadow spat defiance, but Orla shouted back at it, her own voice united with her mother's. <*You will obey me! I hold the Moonshadow, and you are mine to command! Mine!*>

The Moonshadow growled again, but the creature at the center of the anamacha was no longer taking power from the Otherworld and forcing it onto Orla. The spell cage burned and sizzled, too full already, and Orla knew she couldn't hold it much longer. <*You're throwing away your future, Orla! You could be so much more!*> Then the presence snarled like a wounded animal as the Moonshadow slid wordlessly back into Magh da Chèo's eternal night, leaving them alone for the moment.

The spell cage throbbed between Orla's hands; the energy trapped inside was blinding. She could sense the power's desire to be released even as she panted from the exertion of holding it, not knowing the release word. She imagined the spell cage breaking apart, the raw fury of Magh da Chèo rushing over her, reducing her already blistered body to ash and dust. She could feel hands from the outside world grasping at her arms, closing around her waist. Orla gave them only the barest of thoughts, and she felt the hands all release her, flung away from her with faint screams. Her mam spoke again, a single word, and Orla echoed it with the voice of the Otherworld.

"*Pléasc!*" Shatter!

The spell cage burst apart, and the light arrowed out from Orla toward the side wall of the chamber. She was barely able to direct it. She felt the building shudder under the massive impact. Tile and masonry fell in a glassy shower as the energy ripped through the keep, room after room, expanding as it went. When the spell reached the outside wall, it brought down nearly half the keep, tumbling massive marble blocks into the courtyard; men and horses screamed as they were crushed. The spell continued on, sending the stones of the keep's wall hurtling outward into the Avenue of the Emperor as passersby on foot or in carriages shouted in alarm. Orla felt the spell moving like a tidal force toward the harbor, still expanding and growing, starting to weaken but still tearing down buildings and houses on either side of the wide avenue, the awful roar of it growing fainter with distance.

And there was more: Orla could feel the lives caught up in the fiery maelstrom she had created. She heard men, women, and children crying out in agony and terror. She felt the cracking of bones and the snapping of spines as their bodies were battered and broken.

Worst of all, she felt them die: candle flames blown out by a careless, uncaring wind, a wind of her making, though not of her choice. She wanted to collapse, to fall to the tiles in exhaustion, but the residue of the Moonshadow's presence held her up, every muscle in her body trembling with effort.

How many? How many more have I killed? She could hear the faint laughter of the Moonshadow as well as the ghosts of the draoi inside crying out.

<Orla!> Her mam's voice called to her in fear and sorrow. There was no comfort in her words. *<I'm so sorry. I came too late to help you . . .>*

<Now you understand what happened to me, but I couldn't control her. I had no one to help me at all, as the First . . .> Orla knew that voice, too: Leagsaidh, now sundered from the Moonshadow. *<Orla Moonshadow, they'll call you forever . . .>*

<Even with the Moonshadow, I could never wield that kind of power . . .> said Iomhar, marveling.

And hand upon hand of others called to her as well: mocking, laughing, praising, chastising, awed, and aghast all at once.

She could feel the Moonshadow in the darkness, gathering itself again, angry as it pulled at her and tried to insinuate its will into her own once more. *<You and I, Orla, we will level this entire city . . . Then they'll see . . . Then they'll have to surrender to us . . .>* Orla could feel the Moonshadow plucking at her hands, readying them to begin weaving a new spell cage, and she fought to remain still.

<No!> she shouted into the Otherworld. <You'll do as I ask. Mam, stay with me . . .>

The Moonshadow's laughter boomed, a thunder against the Otherworld's storms. <We'll crush them now . . . Together . . .>

<No!> Orla screamed again, but she felt her hands start to move, and she couldn't see her mother at all, lost in the chaos around them. Storm clouds lowered around her; lightning arced. Orla could see the real world fading as she fought against the Moonshadow's control, forcing herself to hold out trembling arms toward Savas, toward Eideard, toward Sorcha. "Use your weapons," she pleaded. "Cut off my hands. You have to stop this. You have to stop me. Do it!"

She wasn't sure they understood, wasn't even certain they could still hear her. The world where her friends stood seemed slowed and distant, disconnected. Sorcha shook her head; Eideard only stared, his eyes wide. But finally she saw Savas nod. He started to move toward her as if through thick water.

<No!> The voice wasn't hers or the Moonshadow's. It was . . . Orla wasn't certain. A woman's voice . . . no, the voices of two women and a man. And more . . . <Wait! None of us were strong enough by ourselves,> they said. <The Moonshadow took each of us alone . . . But you . . . You're not alone . . .>

<Mam? Leagsaidh? Iomhar?>

<Take us in . . . You don't need to resist the Moonshadow alone . . . You can't . . . Let us help you . . . Let us do what we should have done long ago . . .> Her mam's voice. In her vision, she could see her mother's shade standing before her once more, her arms out as if to embrace Orla, and Orla opened her arms in response. Her mother's taibhse slipped into her, the shock of the connection like that of falling through the ice on a winter pond. She felt the others slipping into her behind Voada: Iomhar, Leagsaidh, all of the other dead draoi inside the anamacha. Her mind was filled with them, and she looked at the Moonshadow and saw it as she'd never seen it before. It was no longer ominous, no longer towering over her in Magh da Chèo like a massive storm front. It was

merely another lost taibhse—stronger than any single one of them, yes, but it was only one. Alone.

<*This is how it was supposed to have been from the start. You are no match for us together.*> Orla spoke the words, and it seemed that the Otherworld shivered with them, all of the voices of the dead draoi within her echoing the thought. The Moonshadow tried to draw itself up, to tear at the storms of Magh da Chèo and hurl the power at her blindly, but Orla raised her hand and slapped the Moonshadow away.

<*No!*> The Moonshadow cried its denial, but its voice was no louder and no more powerful than any of theirs.

<*You killed me . . . and me . . . and me . . . You drove me insane . . . and me . . . and me . . . You made me do what I never wanted to do . . . You made me hate myself . . . You made others hate me . . .*> The voices of the draoi hurled accusations at the Moonshadow. <*You used all of us, and now we will finally use you . . . You are our servant; we are no longer yours . . .*>

Orla forced her own voice above the others she held inside her. <*Not yet. But for now we are done with the Moonshadow . . . Go away until we call for you again . . .*>

With a shrill wail, the Moonshadow fled across the pocked, savaged landscape of the Otherworld. When Orla could no longer feel it, she opened her arms again. <*I release all of you,*> she told them. <*But I will call you again soon.*>

The taibhse slid away from her, one by one returning to Magh da Chèo. Her mam was the last, and she turned to Orla with a smile. <*It should have been you from the beginning . . .*> she said. <*It should always have been you . . .*>

Now that the other draoi inside the Moonshadow's anamacha were no longer connected to her, Orla felt the rising of an overwhelming exhaustion. Magh da Chèo faded from her sight as the real world snapped into focus around her, the people there suddenly unfrozen. Her legs collapsed underneath her, and she felt Sorcha trying to hold her up. Then Savas was there helping, and Eideard, and they laid her down on the floor.

"I'm sorry," Orla said, her voice a dry, broken husk. She looked at each of them. "I'm sorry. This wasn't how . . . But it's over now. Over . . ."

But even the real world was fading now, and she allowed the sweeping blanket of night to take her.

Orla fought her way through thick clouds and a terrible weight pressing down on her. Her eyes refused to open. She flailed her arms, trying to escape, and someone caught her hands.

"Shh!" a voice whispered. "It's all right. You're fine. I have you."

"Sorcha?"

Lips pressed the skin of her hand. "Aye," Sorcha answered. "You're in the Great-Voice's bed in the keep. Here . . ." Orla felt a cool, damp cloth press against her eyes, wiping them gently. "That should help. Your eyes were all crusted with sleep."

Her eyelids lifted slowly. It seemed to be night. Candles and oil lamps were the only illumination in the room, casting wavering shadows over the tapestried walls where figures in Mundoan dress swayed. The bedroom was large and lavish, with cushioned chairs against the walls and gathered around a table near the room's hearth. Orla found herself wondering how many people shared the bed and the room with Utka, a thought she quickly shoved away.

Sorcha leaned over her, her long strands of brown hair—black in the night—falling like glossy curtains over the sides of her face. "How long?" Orla managed to say.

"Several stripes of the candle. Are you thirsty? I have water or wine, and there's mulled wine heating at the hearth if you'd prefer."

"Just water for now. Thank you." Her mouth was dry, her throat parched. Orla pulled the thick quilt aside and sat up slowly, taking the mug of water that Sorcha pressed into her hand. "What's happened since . . ." She wasn't sure how to finish the question.

"Very little, honestly," Sorcha answered. "Commander Savas

and Ceannàrd Iosa have made certain that we continue to hold the keep, though with the walls being breached . . ." Sorcha bit her lip, and a stab of guilt went through Orla at the memory that it was she and the Moonshadow who had done that. "Magaidh and other draoi have arrived, though. The Mundoan garrison in Savur seems confused and uncertain how to respond, since they know we hold the Great-Voice captive. Both the commander and ceannàrd, as well as Draoi Magaidh and First Àrd Comhnall, asked me to tell them when you awoke. I can wait until you're sure you've rested long enough . . ."

Orla smiled at the woman, though the gesture was an effort and faded as quickly as it had come. She set the mug aside, rose from the bed, and hugged Sorcha fiercely, the solid feel of her body a comfort against the uncertainty in her head. "No," she said. "Go and bring them to me. We have decisions to make." *And I have an apology to deliver.*

They arrived just as Orla poured some of the warm mulled wine into one of the silver goblets stamped with the imperial hawks on the table; the astringent scent of the spices cleared her head somewhat. She waved all of them to seats near the hearth; Sorcha, unasked, ladled more of the spiced wine into the remaining goblets. They all stared at her, Magaidh especially, as if searching for Voada's madness seared into her scarred face.

"I'm sorry for what happened," Orla told them. "I lost control of the Moonshadow. But I've learned a method to handle it and bend the beast inside the anamacha to my will rather than its own. I promise you that it won't happen again."

"I heard your mam say nearly those same words once," Magaidh said. "I think that's a dangerous promise to make."

Savas and Comhnall both nodded. Eideard's eyes narrowed. Orla tightened her lips: not a smile, not a grimace. "I understand why you would feel that way, Magaidh. I absolutely do. But it's true—and it's a skill I believe I can teach to any of the draoi who are afraid to call up the entity at the core of their anamacha for fear of its power—and that will make all of us stronger draoi. Believe me, I know better than most how dangerous it can be to call up an anamacha's source." Orla gestured to her face. "I wish Mam had discovered what I have; if she had, you might be talking to her now rather than me. And I understand if you feel you can't entirely trust my word on this. I hope that in time you'll see that I can truly be Orla Moonshadow and not simply the Moonshadow's puppet." She caught Savas' gaze. "I never intended to kill any innocents here, Commander, either Mundoan or Cateni. But I lost my initial fight with the Moonshadow."

"We're at war," Eideard interjected before Savas could speak. He gave a snort of laughter. "No one dying? No one hurt? That was never going to happen no matter how much you wanted it, Ceanndraoi. And the commander knows that as well as I do."

"What *does* happen now?" Magaidh asked into the following silence. "That's the real question. For example, what do we do with Great-Voice Utka?"

"Simple," Eideard responded. "We send his head to Pashtuk. That'll have the additional benefit of stopping the terrific racket he's been making in what's left of the reception hall. I swear the man has the lungs of a Gray Wraith."

Orla was already shaking her head before the ceannàrd finished. "I didn't spare the Great-Voice just to kill him. Let him go back to Rumeli and tell the emperor how he lost Albann for him."

"So let the emperor kill him?" Eideard said. "Because that's what will happen."

"The emperor's likely to do far worse to the man than just take his head." Savas spoke for the first time. He glanced around the table at each of them. "Here's what I would like, if the ceanndraoi agrees. Right now my army is still on Onglse, per your request. Let me send word to Musa and Ilkur that we've taken Savur and its garrison and that the Great-Voice is our prisoner. I'll order Musa and Ilkur to take our troops on Onglse to Gediz and await further instructions. As commander, I'll then write an order to be delivered to every garrison in Albann declaring that Great-Voice Utka has surrendered unconditionally to Ceanndraoi Orla, Ceannàrd Iosa, and the army of the clans. All Cateni conscripts are be released from service immediately; all Mundoan-born soldiers have free passage to make their way to Gediz or Savur, whichever is closer, from which they will take ships back to Rumeli. Any soldier with a Cateni wife and family who instead prefers to remain in Albann will be allowed to do so—I suspect there are several soldiers who have made their homes here and would want to stay."

"And for my part?" Orla asked.

"I would like to send a report to Emperor Pashtuk confessing my actions in everything that's happened. I will also tell him that while Albann insists on self-rule, as long as he doesn't retaliate, the clans will continue to send their tribute to the emperor and consider themselves an ally of the Mundoan Empire. Albann will welcome Mundoan travelers and commerce as long as they abide by the customs and laws of Albann. Furthermore, as reparation for the loss of Savur, you will also send back to the emperor his Great-Voice, the soldiers of the Savur garrison, as well as the contents of the treasury Great-Voice Utka amassed here."

There were mutters and whispers around the table as Orla pondered that. First Àrd Comhnall had said nothing during the discussion. Now he set down his goblet of mulled wine and sat up in his chair, groaning slightly as he moved. "And how to do you think the emperor will respond to all this, Commander, should the ceanndraoi agree to your suggestions?"

"I don't know the emperor well enough to even guess," Savas admitted. "It's possible he may simply raise a new army under a new commander and send an invasion force to take back Albann; in that case, I think he'd ultimately regret his decision, as the draoi and all of Albann would be set against him and he'd be without any strongholds here. Or he may agree, if grudgingly, to this compromise—at least for a time—in order to salvage what he can. That's my hope." Savas picked up his own wine, swirling the red liquid as he stared down into the goblet. He set it down without drinking, tapping the side with a fingernail so that the goblet rang like a bell. "One last item: I intend to give my report to the emperor face-to-face. I'll accompany Great-Voice Utka and the soldiers in taking ship to Rumeli."

"And you'd go," Orla asked him, "even knowing that you'd almost certainly be going to your own death?"

Savas lifted his gaze to meet hers. The lines of his face were carved deeper into his skin than before. "I would," he said. "It's nothing less than I deserve for my betrayal and disobedience."

"Because you're just a simple soldier?" Orla asked him, and one corner of his mouth lifted in a fleeting smile at her comment.

"Yes," he answered. "And as such, I will resign my command directly to the emperor and accept whatever punishment he demands."

Orla looked around the table. She felt her anamacha close behind her, an icy presence at her spine. *<This is what you wanted . . .>* she heard her mam's voice say. *<This is what we've always wanted . . . >*

Orla shook her head at the voices and at Savas. "You may go to Rumeli if you feel you must, Commander," she told him. "But you'll also be taking a message from me as ceanndraoi. And you'll tell him that he'd best not disregard the dreams he'll have experienced before your arrival."

"His dreams?" Savas asked, his forehead creasing in puzzlement. Then his forehead smoothed. "Oh," he said. He nodded to Orla. "I'll tell him exactly that."

30

An Emperor's Dream

THE BEDROOM OF EMPEROR Pashtuk was more lavish than that of Great-Voice Utka and far more crowded. Orla knew from sad experience that Mundoan men in power often took more than one wife; there were two women sharing the emperor's bed, one spooned against him under the covers, the other one on her side with her back to him, naked on top of the quilt. Two more women slept on separate beds to either side of the room. Three servants added to the sounds of snoring: a man in the far corner and a young man and woman cuddled together near the hearth and a table laden with the remnants of a dinner. In the hearth, flames licked along the length of a huge log, embers crawling on the blackened wood.

Emperor Pashtuk wore a gown of aching blue with the sigil of the empire embroidered at his breast. His oiled and braided beard lay like a sleeping cat on the quilt over him.

Orla strode over to the bed, standing at the foot. "Emperor Pashtuk," she said loudly.

His eyes opened and found her. He gasped, sitting up in the bed. His movement shook his bedmates but didn't wake them. "Who . . . ?" he sputtered. "How did you . . . ?" Then, finally: "Guards! Get in here! Everyone, wake up! Intruder! Assassin!" He shook the shoulder of the nearest woman; but there was no response.

Orla smiled at him. "Shout all you like, Emperor; they can't hear you. And you can't wake your bedmates either."

Pashtuk lunged for the bedside table. He snatched a long curved dagger from the drawer there. Sweeping aside the covers, he lunged for Orla with a scream. She watched the blade plunge harmlessly through her body. Pashtuk drew back the weapon and stabbed her again with the same result. Breathing heavily, his robe open, he stared at the blade. "You're a spirit. A ghost," Pashtuk said. "Or you're bad meat I was served this evening haunting my sleep."

"I've been called all of that before—well, I've never been called bad meat—but I'm very much alive. Emperor Pashtuk, I am Ceanndraoi Orla of Albann, daughter of Ceanndraoi Voada, and I hold the Moonshadow. It's through the Moonshadow's power that I've come to you."

"You're the Mad Draoi's daughter? This is a spell? An enchantment?"

Orla nodded. "It is. I've come to bring you news. Just listen, for my spell will fade soon enough . . ." She began to tell him all that had transpired. She could see the skepticism on his yellow-brown face growing as she spoke, and when she finished, he spat on the floor between them.

"You expect me to believe any of this?"

"The proof of what I've said is already on its way to you. You'll have it soon enough."

"And if it *is* true, then you dare, you *dare* to name Altan Savas as Great-Voice and the sole representative of my empire in Albann?"

"I've already done so," she answered calmly. Orla saw Pashtuk open his mouth to protest again, and she lifted her hand to silence him. "I also expect Great-Voice Savas to be returned, or you'll have made a mortal enemy of Albann and me, not an ally."

"And if I send you back the traitor commander's head instead?" Pashtuk asked. "What then?"

"Then," she answered, "you should consider that I'm standing in your bedroom without any of your people knowing that I'm here or responding. I'd tell you to imagine what else I might be capable of doing that you could neither prevent nor stop. When he comes to you, ask the former Great-Voice Utka what I did in Savur, and think of that happening here—because it would. I am Orla Moonshadow. I promise that you don't want me as your enemy, Emperor."

She saw him ponder what she said. Her words were pure bluff, but he couldn't know that. "I'm neither dream nor ghost," she continued. "I am entirely real, and the proof of everything I've told you, as I said, will be before you before the next moon comes. I hope you make the right choice, Emperor Pashtuk, or it will be one of your last."

With that, Orla let the spell fall away from her and vanished.

Epilogue

Year 1

ORLA TOUCHED THE TWIN silver oak leaves on their silver chain, then spread her arms to her anamacha, feeling the shock of cold and disorientation as the anamacha entered her body and her vision became doubled with the landscape of Magh da Chèo. The spirits of the draoi gathered around her, and she called them all to her: <*Mam, Leagsaidh, Iomhar . . .*> They came, and she felt their minds link with hers. Then she made the final call: <*Moonshadow, you may come to us . . .*>

She felt its approach like a storm rushing over the landscape. Lightning snapped and snarled, thunder boomed, but she was surrounded by the other draoi, the ones the Moonshadow had rendered mad and killed, and they faced the dark presence together. Not entirely unafraid, any of them—Orla was certain that she'd never completely lose the fear of bringing the Moonshadow forth and allowing it to enter her. <*That would be dangerous and foolish . . .*> she heard her mam answer, as if she sensed Orla's trepidation. <*We won't allow that . . .*>

<*I know,*> she told them. <*But I need the Moonshadow's power again.*>

The Moonshadow's low voice rumbled. <*You will always need me, because you are nothing without me . . .*> it said, its voice mocking. <*And one day I will take you back as my own, as I took the others who guard you now.*>

<*Perhaps,*> she answered, <*but this is not that day. Now be quiet. Send me the energy I want. Fill my spell cage.*>

Sullenly, the Moonshadow turned to the raging storms above them and began to claw at the clouds, lightning shimmering around its hands before it disdainfully flung the energy toward Orla, whose hands were moving in the pattern of the spell cage: a large one, for she would need everything she could possibly hold.

She was standing in the plaza of the Great Temple at Savur: the most Mundoan building in all of the capital city. The plaza had been cleared of visitors by clan warriors under the direction of First Àrd Comhnall, and Magaidh watched with her husband from the plaza's tiled entrance. The Great Temple of the Emperor loomed above Orla, a tall and massive dome atop the three-story facade of balconies and archways, the gold-leafed dome itself set in a forest of minarets.

Over the last month, Orla had set about the work of repairing the damage done to Savur by herself and the Moonshadow. The Great-Voice's keep had been restored, the wall around it rebuilt, the Avenue of the Emperor repaved—it was now called the Avenue of the Ceanndraoi by nearly everyone—and the buildings along the avenue repaired or replaced. Some of that work had been done by Cateni craftspeople, but much of it was the result of draoi spells, the bulk of them Orla's.

But there was no way to restore the lives that had been lost that day. The gold that Orla had ordered given to the families in restitution could never replace the loved ones they had lost, nor did it temper the guilt that Orla would always feel.

Now she wanted Savur to shed its reputation as a model Mundoan city. She would remake Savur in the mold of the Cateni so that travelers who came here would see what Albann and the clans were capable of achieving. She took in the Moonshadow's energy, facing the Great Temple and imagining it as a temple of Elia: one larger and more elaborate than any she'd ever seen, with a ring of blackstones around its perimeter; its dome—she would

allow it to remain golden in memory of what it had once been—
open to the sun and sky, with four huge entrances and great windows of stained glass above them, aligned to the solstices' sunrises
and sunsets. The paths of the solstices would scribe a great X on
the tiled floor, and where the lines intersected a massive blackstone altar would sit, with a smiling statue of Elia atop it, awash
in sunlight or nourished by rain. No more minarets; no more
gaudy architectural touches that the Mundoan loved so much.
This would be simpler, but it would also be grander because of its
very simplicity.

Orla imagined it as she wanted it to become as the energy filled
the spell cage she held, blinding and furious. She held onto the
temple she saw in her head, and she spoke a single word: "Cuimhnich!" *Remember!*

The spell cage shattered and the energy surged out, wrapping
itself around the Great Temple in swirling colors so bright that it
hurt the eyes to see it. The temple seemed to shiver and melt in
the glow, then the light pulsed, flashed, and was gone. Orla
blinked away the blinding afterimages. What stood there when
she could see again was no longer the Great Temple but the Temple of Elia that had been in her mind, now solid and real, with a
new blackstone ring dominating the plaza, the stones a good
three men high.

Finished, Orla sighed, opening her arms to send away the
Moonshadow and the draoi in her anamacha. The sudden release
caused her knees to buckle, her muscles giving way to exhaustion. She stared at the structure she'd just made.

She heard people applauding and shouting around her.

A hand touched her shoulder, and she smelled a woman's per-
fume on the breeze. She turned her head to see Sorcha behind
her with her two children, Erdem and Esra, at her side. Azru was
with them with her own children: Bakir's children, Orla's step-
children.

"Ceanndraoi, a ship is coming into the harbor flying the imperial banner," Sorcha said. She pointed to the east. Beyond the
plaza and out past where the Avenue of the Ceanndraoi met the

harbor in the Bay of Iska, a single ship was visible, entering on the tide.

Orla smiled—she knew that ship, having visited it more than once before its arrival, using the Moonshadow to appear in a cabin there.

"Altan?" she said, staring down at the man in the bed. She'd expected to see Tolga in his arms, but instead there was a woman with dark hair next to him, and sprawled on beds across the room were three children: two girls and a boy. She could see a blend of Altan's features and the woman's in their sleeping faces.

She saw Altan's eyes flicker open, squinting as he stared at her in the swaying moonlight coming through the small open shutters of the vessel.

"Ceanndraoi," he said, throwing aside the covers and standing on the rolling planks. "It's good to see you again. I was afraid that might never happen."

"I told the emperor that I needed him to send back my Great-Voice alive and unharmed," Orla told him. She glanced back at the beds; Altan gave her a tight-lipped smile that seemed touched with melancholy.

"My wife and my children," he said in explanation. "I couldn't leave them behind. Yes, you gave Pashtuk your ultimatum, but he was none too eager to comply. He named me the Great-Voice of Albann because he felt he had no choice, but I'm permanently exiled from Rumeli. The emperor told me that if I ever dare to set foot there again, he'll have me flayed and dismembered alive, after which he'll use my tanned skin for a bedsheet. 'And that will happen no matter what this Orla Moonshadow says she can do. Tell her that,' was his summation." Altan shrugged. "I was afraid of what Pashtuk might do if I left my family behind—though my wife wasn't at all enthused about going to live in Albann. So it seems Albann is now my permanent home and will be theirs as well. I'm to be just a simple bureaucrat."

Orla nodded. "And Tolga?"

"He's in the next cabin." Altan glanced at his sleeping wife. "I'll see

him later. He and I . . . we'll have to be careful. I suspect my wife wouldn't entirely understand or approve of our relationship."

Orla grinned at that.

Orla started to stand, groaning with the effort, though she nodded in satisfaction as she looked toward the harbor and the approaching ship, then back to the new temple before her. The gaggle of children—Sorcha's as well as Azru's—ran across the plaza to her, taking her arms as she slowly stood. "Here, let us help you, Piuthar-màthar . . ."

On her feet, her arms around the children, Orla smiled at Sorcha and Azru before returning her gaze to the ship. "Welcome home, Altan," she said toward the vessel and its fluttering banners, then gestured to Magaidh and Comhnall. "Let's find Ceannàrd Eideard, and we'll go meet our new Great-Voice and his family. We have a lot of work he needs to get started on."

Appendix

CHARACTERS (in order of appearance)

OPENING AND PART ONE:

Pashtuk (PASH-took)	Emperor of the Mundoa
Orla Paorach (OAR-lah POO-rahk)	The daughter of Voada, the Mad Draoi. Protagonist of the novel.
Sorcha (SOHR-eh-kah)	Friend of Orla
Azru (AZZ-roo)	Bakir's first wife and mother of his two children
Erdem	Son of Sorcha
Esra	Son of Sorcha
Bakir (Bah-KEER)	Orla's husband, a Mundoan army officer
Alim (Ah-LEEM)	Sorcha's husband, a Mundoan soldier
Voada Paorach (Voh-AH-dah POO-rahk)	Orla's mother. As ceanndraoi of the Cateni, she had led the unsuccessful rebellion in Year 22 of Pashtuk's reign. Sometimes referred to as "The Mad Draoi."

Altan Savas (ALL-tan SAH-vahs)	Mundoan commander in charge of the war against the northern tribes
Greum (GRAY-umm)	The ceanndraoi, or head mage, of Onglse. Known as "the Red-Hand."
Leagsaidh (LEGK-see) Moonshadow	A long-dead draoi famous in Cateni history. The First Draoi and reputedly the most powerful.
Maol Iosa (MAHL EE-sah)	Ceannàrd (leader) of the Cateni rebel army, killed with Ceanndraoi Voada in the Battle of Siran
Utka (OOT-kah)	Great-Voice of Albann Deas
Vadim III (Vah-DEEM)	The previous Great-Voice, killed by Ceanndraoi Voada in the sack of Trusa
Tolga (TOLL-gah)	Driver for Altan Savas
Ceiteag (Kay-tig)	Draoi and menach on Onglse who was the first teacher of Voada Paorach
Elia (Eh-LEE-ah)	The sun goddess of the Cateni
Moire (MOY-yah)	A menach and draoi on the island of Onglse
Iomhar (EYE-oh-var)	The ceanndraoi of the Cateni at the time of the initial invasion of the Mundoa, killed in the battle of Íseal Head. Iomhar, like Voada, was chosen by the Moonshadow's anamacha. Also called Iomhar of the Marsh.
Beris	Emperor of Mundoa when its armies conquered the Cateni tribes south

of the River Meadham. He was succeeded by his son, Emperor Hayat, followed by the brief reign of Hayat's daughter, Empress Damla, who was deposed and executed by a military coup and replaced by Emperor Pashtuk.

Lucian

Commander Savas' previous chariot driver and lover, killed in battle on Onglse

Frangan MacCraig
(FRANN-gann)

Draoi killed while attempting to assassinate Emperor Pashtuk

Comhnall Mac Tsagairt
(CAHN-ull Mack TAG-gert)

Àrd (head) of Clan Mac Tsagairt

Magaidh Mac Tsagairt
(MAH-ghee Mack TAG-gert)

Wife of Comhnall Mac Tsagairt and a draoi trained by Voada

Eideard Iosa (Edd-erd Ee-sah)

Àrd of Clan Iosa and cousin of Maol Iosa

PART TWO:

Musa (MOO-sah)

Sub-commander in the Mundoan army under Altan Savas

Ilkur (ILL-curr)

Sub-commander in the Mundoan army under Altan Savas

Halim (Hah-LEEM)

An engineer in Altan's army

Hùisdean (OOS-den)

Eldest son of Comhnall Mac Tsagairt, stepson of Magaidh Mac Tsagairt, chariot driver for Ceannàrd Mac Tsagairt

Tadgh (TAHD)

Driver for Maol Iosa, now Eideard Iosa's driver

Niall (NIGH-all) — Male draoi

Caoimhe (KEY-vah) — Female draoi

Sabri (Sah-bree) — Chief shipwright in Muras

Demir (D'meer) — The Voice of Muras, nephew of Great-Voice Utka

Tuathal (TWO-uh-hul) — Ceannàrd of the Cateni in Leagsaidh's time, of Clan Leask

Iseabail (Eesh-ah-bell) of Clan Buccleugh (Buh-Klew) — The first draoi to have Greum Red-Hand's anamacha

Dòrn (Durr-ahn) — Fist; the name of the core demigod in Greum's anamacha

PART THREE:

Colin Iosa — A warrior, cousin of Eideard Iosa

Mànas (MAH-nahs) — A young male draoi

TERMS AND PLACE NAMES (in alphabetical order)

Albann (AHL-pahn) — The large island of the Cateni, now conquered by the Mundoa

Albann Bràghad (AHL-pahn BRAWK-ahd) — The Cateni name for the region north of the River Meadham. The "r" must be rolled.

Albann Deas (AHL-pahn Deesh) — The southern portion of Albann, below the River Meadham

Anamacha (Ah-nah-MAHK-ah) — Literally a collection of souls—the manifested ghosts of dead draoi

	who are the channel through which the living draoi gain their power
Anail (AH-nahl)	Gust or gale
Archiater (ARK-ee-ate-err)	The title for someone who treats injuries and illness. Archiaters are often of the herbalist tradition and may or may not be effective.
Àrd (ARHD)	"Head"—the leader of a clan, group, or place among the Cateni
Bàn Cill (Bahn Keel)	The sacred temple of the Cateni on Onglse. This is where the draoi are trained and where they gather.
Barrier Sea	The channel between the island of the Cateni and the mainland
Beinn (BANE) Head	A headland on the west coast of Albann Bràghad, north of Onglse
Carnyx (KAR-nix)	A bronze trumpet often shaped like the head and elongated neck of a horse or snake, held upright and blown in battle. Creates a raucous and loud sound. Used by the Cateni.
Cateni (Kaw-TEHN-ee)	The collective name for the natives of the island, such as Voada, though there are innumerable sub-tribes or clans
Ceannàrd (KEY-ohn-ard)	Literally "high chief"—the title for a clan leader or military commander among the Cateni

Ceanndraoi (KEY-ohn-dree)	The head draoi of the tribes, usually based in Onglse, where the draoi are largely trained
Clan Mac Tsagairt (Klahn Mack TAG-gert)	One of the northern clans in Albann Bràghad
Cohort	A small subdivision of the Mundoan army, usually consisting of five hundred soldiers or fewer
Cuimhnich (Cuhn-YEEK)	Remember or recall from memory
Currach (CURR-awk)	A small fishing boat (also sometimes spelled as 'curragh')
Darende (DAHR-ren-dah)	A town on the southwestern coast of Albann Deas
Davul	A two-headed drum used in Mundoan music, played with a heavy stick in the right hand and a thin, light one in the left
Deigh (Jaye)	Ice
Doineann (DEN-yunn)	Hurricane
Dört yüz (Dort yooz)	Dört is Mundoan for four, and yüz means one hundred; therefore, four hundred
Draoi (Dree)	The Cateni term for those who are able to use magic
Eilean Mòr (AY-lan Mohr)	"Large Island"—an island in the Onglse Strait
Elia's lamp	The sun

Entari (Ehn-tah-ree)	A rich brocaded cloak worn by the upper classes of the Mundoa
Faicinn fada (Fah-Kin Fahda)	Someone with excellent eyesight, someone gifted with "long sight." A critical quality for archers and those on watch.
Fidhcheall (Fee-kyuhl)	An ancient form of chess
First Maker	The Mundoan creator god
Gediz (Geh-DIZZ)	A town on the west coast of Albann Deas
Gray Wraith	A howling, shrieking ghost in Cateni mythology that sometimes visits people to announce their impending deaths
Great North Road	The road that runs roughly north from Ìseal in the south, through the capital of Trusa, and to Muras on the River Meadham. It crosses the Meadham but ends not far into Albann Bràghad.
Great-Voice	The Voice over all Voices on the island. He lives in Trusa, the Mundoan capital city.
Hand (title)	The person responsible for collecting taxes for Mundoa in a town or city. His spouse is called the Hand-wife. Often this person is a local Cateni.
Hand (counting)	Five. The Cateni count up to four, then from there use "hand" and "double-hand." A "hand and two" is seven; a

	"double hand" is ten. A "hand of hands" is twenty-five, and so on.
Horned Spirit	The gesture of the horned spirit—thumb folded over the middle two fingers with the index and little finger extended—is considered a curse and an insult
Ìseal (Eh-SEAL)	A harbor town on Ìseal Head
Ìseal Head	Location of the first battle with the Mundoa at the Barrier Sea
Ismil (ISS-meel)	A town in Albann Deas
R. Iska (ISS-Kah)	The long and wide river on the banks of which sits the capital city Trusa (Iskameath)
Kavak (Kah-VAK)	A major coastal city in Rumeli
Koruk (KOHR-uck)	A major city in Rumeli
Krug (Kroog)	The "mirror armor" of the Mundoan army officers
Lack-breath	Asthma or shortness of breath
Ladik (Lah-DEEK)	A town in Albann Deas
Léine (LANE-ah)	A long close-fitting smock worn by the northern clans
Magh-space (Mah-space)	A rather variable unit of measurement: the distance from which a cock-crow or a bell could be heard
Magh da Chèo (Mah dah KEE-oh)	The Otherworld of the anamacha—literally, Plain of Mists

Menach (MEHN-Ock)	Title for a cleric of Elia
Menhir (men-ear)	A standing stone
R. Meadham (MEER-ahn)	For pronunciation, the consonant "dh" sounds like a rolled "r" that is almost a guttural "g." The River Meadham is the central river of the island, roughly dividing the more mountainous north (Albann Bràghad) from the more gently rolling southern landscape (Albann Deas).
Moon-time	Menstrual period. The herbs rue and shepherd's purse are used to ease the cramping and bleeding.
Mundoa (Muhn-DOH-ah)	The Empire of the southern mainland or the people thereof
Mundoci (Muhn-DOH-kee)	The capital city of the empire
Muras (Murh-ahs)	A town on the River Meadham where the river is bridged
Neart (Nyart)	Strength
Onglse (ON-gul-see)	The island fastness of the draoi
One-God, the	The official deity of the Mundoan Empire; the emperor is the one-god's representative in this world
	Also known as the First Maker.
Pale Ones	The minor deities who serve the One-God (and thus the emperor) and do His bidding in the world
Pamukkale	The Mundoan mythological hell

Pencraig (PENN-craygh)	The town where Voada and Meir lived
Piuthar-màthar (Pie-you-ther Mah-her)	Aunt
Pléasc (PLAY-usk)	Shatter or burst
Rumeli (Roo-MELL-ee)	The continent; the land of the Mundoa, where they have established their empire
Sarik (SAW-rik)	A turban worn by the emperor and other dignitaries in the Mundoan Empire
Savur	Capital of Albann Deas on the east coast at the mouth of the River Iska, from where the Great-Voice rules
Sea of Serpents	The sea to the east of Albann—it extends well west until it meets the main continent again.
Seanmhair (SHUNN-eh-vah)	Grandmother
Sihirki (Suh-HERE-kee)	The Mundoan term for those who are able to use magic
Siran (SEER-ehn)	A town in Albann Deas. The final battle between the Mundoan forces and those of Ceanndraoi Voada, the Mad Draoi, took place near there in Year 22 of Pashtuk's rule.
R. Slaodach (SLAHL-dack)	A river that flows into Gediz Bay
Storm Sea	The ocean to the west of Albann—an endless ocean, as far as the Cateni or Mundoa know

Stormwind Road	The road from Gediz on the west coast to Pencraig in the east
Sun-path	The line described by the dawn of the summer solstice and the sunset of the winter solstice or the dawn of the winter solstice and the sunset of the summer solstice. It is believed that the Cateni dead must walk one of those two paths in order to ascend to the next plane of existence.
Taibhse (TOY-cha)	Cateni word for spirit or ghost (plural: taibhsean (TIE-chan))
Teine (TCHEE-na)	Fire
Tha! (Hah!)	An exclamation of approval. Yes!
Tirnanog (TIR-nah-nog)	The Otherworld of the Cateni—the land of the gods and the spirits
Trusa (TROO-SAH)	The former capital city of the Mundoa, razed by Voada and her forces, which is currently being rebuilt. Cateni name: Iskameath.
Uisge (OOSH-kah)	Water
Velimese (VELL-eh-mees)	A town in Albann Deas
Voice	The person representing the Emperor/Mundoan authorities in a town or city. His spouse is called the Voice-wife. The Voice is universally someone of Mundoan origin.
R. Yarrow (YAH-roh)	The river that runs past Pencraig. The River Yarrow's source is Loch

Yarrow, and it feeds into the greater River Meadham.

Var (VARH)

A town on the southern coast of Albann Deas

Zar atmak (Zahr AT-mack)

A Mundoan game of chance that uses six-sided die

Acknowledgments and Notes

Special thanks to . . .

- Denise Parsley Leigh, for being the only person upon whom I inflict my first drafts, for her insightful (and gently blunt) comments. Denise, you shape every story I write as you've also helped to shape my life. I love you.
- Sheila Gilbert, who brought me into the DAW family and whose editorship of my last several novels and kind friendship in general have been a true gift. Sheila (as I've said in the past, has relentlessly made certain that each of my books has been as good as I could possibly produce at the time, and for that she has my endless gratitude. Sheila is more than just an editor; she is a mentor, and best of all, a friend.

Notes:

- Though this is the second book in a two-book series, I've tried as much as possible to allow readers to enjoy *A Rising Moon* without having read the first book, *A Fading Sun*. Still, you'll understand more of the backstory if you read the first volume. I'd love to hear from you if you read this book without reading the first volume—let me know if I succeeded or not.

- This book is fiction. Not history. Those of you who read the preceding novel, *A Fading Sun,* already know that the first book was loosely based on Roman Britain of the first century C.E. and the rebellion of Boudica. However, the historical Boudica's story ends and we learn nothing in the surviving Roman texts of what happened to her two daughters after her death. So Orla's story is *entirely* fictional. As with the first book, the landscape is imaginary, the Mundoan culture is emphatically (and very deliberately) *not* Roman (it's more Turkish than Roman) and I've not allowed historical facts to stand in the way of how I've portrayed the Cateni/Celtic culture—not to mention that there's genuine magic in this world. *A Rising Moon* is, to some extent, the way I *wish* the historical Boudica's story might have ended.

Books read as research for this novel:

- Tacitus. *Annals* (Loeb Classical Library). Translated by John Jackson. New York: Harvard University Press, 1937. I was especially interested in Book XIV, Chapters 29–39 , which cover Boudica's revolt in Britain. In *A Fading Sun,* the speech that Voada gives to the Cateni just before the final battle is a paraphrase of the words that Tacitus puts in Boudica's mouth in *Annals, Book XIV, chapter 35,* but given that Tacitus wrote about *The Annals* half a century after the actual event, it's highly unlikely that Boudica actually said any of those words.
- Hingley, Richard and Christina Unwin. *Boudica: Iron Age Warrior Queen.* London: Bloomsbury, 2005. This is an interesting study of Boudica that examines the various ways she's been imagined, presented, and used symbolically from the time of the Romans through the present day. The concept is that Boudica has worn the masks of many agendas throughout history, not all of them complimentary and certainly few of them accurate. In these two

books, she wears a mask of my own making, and it was as false as any of the others.

- Robb, Graham. *The Discovery of Middle Earth: Mapping the Lost World of the Celts.* New York: W. W. Norton & Company, Inc., 2013. The author's contention is that the Celts deliberately and knowingly mapped out their kingdoms in now-lost, precise straight lines aligned to the solstices and to the compass points, and that important locations were often found at the intersections of those lines. Frankly, I felt Mr. Robb's arguments were hazy, tenuous, and ultimately unconvincing (take any sufficient collection of random dots on a page, and you'll be able to connect several dots with a straight line), but that didn't stop me from borrowing a few concepts . . .

- Curriculum Development Unit. *Celtic Way of Life.* Dublin: O'Brien Press, 2000. This slim volume concentrates (unsurprisingly, given the publisher) on Celtic tribes in Ireland. Rather scant on details or references to source material, but still a decent overview.

- As usual, I also prowled the Internet for articles and information on an *ad hoc* basis during the writing of this book, far too many sites and places to list or even to remember at this point. The Web is a wonderful resource and tool. I'm old enough to have written stories and novels before the answers to questions could be found with a quick googling, and am grateful that the Web is there for all writers.